USA TODAY BESTSELLING AUTHOR
ROXIE NOIR

AUTHOR'S NOTE

It was only a matter of time until I wrote a cowboy romance.

Mae and I are both small-town girls who left for the big city, but you know what they say: you can take the girl outta the country, but you can't take the country outta the girl. Just like her, I've got an accent that comes out when I'm back home and a weakness for cowboys.

For everything I got wrong about rodeo, I'm sorry, and I hope it's not too distracting.

Kettle, OK, Lawton, TX, Sawtooth, WY, and the Pioneer Days Rodeo are all made up. Las Vegas, NV and Brooklyn, NY, are real (but you knew that).

Hope you like reading this as much as I liked writing it.

Love,

Roxie

CHAPTER ONE

MAE

THE TODDLER STARES AT ME, his tiny face surly. I stare back, praying for the right moment.

"Smile!" calls his mother, standing off to the side.

She's probably wearing a thousand dollars worth of clothing right now, her hair, makeup, and nails all done to perfection.

He does *not* smile.

To my right, my co-worker Edwin shakes a teddy bear that jingles, grinning like an idiot.

"Hey, buddy!" he says in the high-pitched voice that he uses when he pretends he's the stuffed animals. "Can you smile for me?"

I'm watching through the viewfinder. No smile.

Throughout this ordeal, Santa has remained perfectly neutral, his cheery, red-cheeked smile precisely in place, his hat and beard and uniform *just* so.

"Xander, come *on*," Xander's mother says. "Can't you smile for Santa?"

I'd be cranky too, I think. If I were two years old and had to get dressed up, then got dragged to a fancy department store on the Upper East Side and was forced to sit on some stranger's lap.

Edwin shakes the bear again.

"Come on, Xander," he says, in his bear-voice.

Xander stares at Edwin like Edwin just casually suggested genocide.

Then, almost in slow motion, Xander's face crumples. His forehead scrunches. His mouth opens wide.

I know what's coming, and I brace myself for about the twentieth time that day.

There's a moment of silence before he *screams*, but it's a doozy. It takes everything I've got not to roll my eyes and cover my ears, but working in Santa's Fun Factory for two weeks has pretty much given me nerves of steel, and I don't even flinch.

Xander takes a deep breath between screams, and in that split second, Santa takes action. He bends down, puts his kindly face next to Xander's, and says something I can't hear.

He looks at Xander. Xander looks at him, like he's suddenly uncertain, his enormous eyes taking in this red-hatted, white-bearded stranger.

Santa says something else, and Xander closes his mouth. Now he's staring at Santa in *awe*, like he can't believe the amazing thing he just heard.

Still talking just to Xander, Santa points at the camera, and Xander looks at me. He's still not sure about this whole thing, but he seems at least willing to entertain the notion. His mom hands Santa a tissue, and Santa quickly wipes the tears from Xander's face, then nods at Edwin.

Santa smiles again, exactly the same way he did before.

"Hey, Xander!" Edwin says in bear-voice.

Xander *grins*. I hit the shutter several times in a row, just in case, and then Xander is bounding off of Santa's lap,

Melissa hands him a candy cane, and he and his mom are off.

"Thank God for Gary," Edwin whispers to me, as Gary — Santa — opens his arms and welcomes the next child in his perfectly jolly voice.

"He's magic," I whisper back.

"Of course he's magic. He's Santa," says Edwin as a small dark-haired child climbs onto Santa's lap.

"I'm a believer again," I say. "Maybe I should go ask for a real job for Christmas."

Edwin snorts, and then it's time for the kid to get her picture taken.

This happens roughly a hundred times a day, and it's only November third.

It's about to be a *very* long holiday season.

* * * * * ★ ★ ★ * * * * *

HOURS LATER, I open a locker and throw my hat in. The jingle bell on it sounds a single tinny, echoing ring as it hits the metal. I feel like everything hurts: my feet, from standing all day; my neck, from bending over a camera; even my eyes, from looking at that tiny screen for eight hours.

Edwin walks in again as I'm grabbing my street clothes out of the locker, a black t-shirt and jeans.

"If I hear 'Jingle Bells' one more time, I might commit homicide," he says.

"Have you heard the version with all barking dogs?" I ask. "It's even worse."

"That's not real," he says. "Is that real?"

"It's really real," I say.

He shakes his head, making his own jingle bell hat tinkle softly.

"Me and Melissa are gonna get a drink somewhere in a few," he says. "You want to join? You look like you could use one."

I sigh and lean against the lockers. Even though I don't really drink, I could go and hang out with them for a bit.

On the other hand, I've got a lot of work I need to do retouching the stills I took last week out on Coney Island, especially if I'm putting them in my portfolio. If I stay out too late, I won't get any of that done tonight.

If I never get *that* done, I'll be photographing kids on Santa's lap for the rest of my natural life.

"No thanks," I say. "I gotta do some work."

"You do too much work," he says, seriously. "Have some fun once in a while, Mae."

"I'll have fun when I'm dead," I say, laughing as I walk past him toward the bathroom.

"The phrase is *I'll sleep when I'm dead*, weirdo," he calls after me, teasing.

"That too," I say, and the bathroom door shuts behind me.

I get out of my red-and-green ensemble quickly, heaving a sigh of relief when I pull on my jeans, t-shirt, and comfy shoes. My hair goes back in a ponytail, and I finally feel *normal* again.

"Next," I say to Edwin when I step out of the bathroom, and he steps in.

I give my elf outfit a good, hard sniff, and decide I can wait one more day to wash it, stuffing it back into the locker. I put on my coat, grab my purse, and head out the break room door and back into Kensington's.

I pull out my phone as I walk past the makeup counters, nodding at the girls standing behind them, like we've all been to war together or something.

Then I frown, because I've got about a million notifications: voicemails, emails, texts. Usually I've got one or two, *maybe*, at the end of a day.

Before I can even look through them, my phone starts buzzing again.

JANICE PENN, the caller ID says, and my heart leaps.

Janice is my agent.

I clear my throat, hit the button, and answer.

"Hello?"

"You're from Texas, right?" she asks, skipping a greeting.

I blink at a rack of thousand-dollar designer coats.

"Yeah," I say.

"Perfect," she says. "I got you a gig. Shooting a rodeo for Sports Weekly. You fly out of La Guardia tomorrow morning at six."

I stop short, my brain swirling.

Sports Weekly?

"Did you say Sports Weekly?" I ask. I'm staring at a mannequin wearing a very sparkly dress, pretty certain that I misheard what she said, because *Sports Weekly* is a very, very big deal, and they're not about to hire me.

"I did," she says. "They're doing a big story about some hot young rodeo star who they think might turn the corner and be a real celebrity. Jackson Cody."

The name nudges at something in my brain, but I can't quite put my finger on it.

Did I go to high school with him?

I *did* go to high school with more than one guy who wound up on the rodeo circuit, though I'm sure if someone local had hit it big, I'd have heard about it from my parents.

Did my brothers know him somehow? Was he a friend of a friend or something?

I can tell it's going to drive me crazy.

"They hired someone else, but the poor bastard's appendix burst and they need someone *tomorrow*," Janice goes on. "I sent them your photos of Texas high school football, and *voila*. They're offering nine hundred a day."

"I'll do it," I say quickly. "Yes. Definitely. I'll definitely do it. Absolutely."

I press my lips together, forcing myself to stop telling her *yes*.

"Great," she says. "I'll email you the plane ticket and everything. Glad you could take the job."

"Me too," I say, but she's already hung up on her end.

New Yorkers, I think. Even after two years here, sometimes I still feel like an alien in this city.

Still standing in front of the sparkly mannequin, I look up Jackson Cody on my phone. Most of the pictures are of a guy on a bull, standard plaid-jeans-and-cowboy-hat ensemble, and I scroll through his Wikipedia page, wait for anything that might trigger my memory.

Born in Wyoming on a cattle ranch, graduated high school, started winning rodeos. Seems to party a lot and sleep around more, which isn't exactly a surprise.

I flick my thumb over my screen one more time, annoyed that I can't figure out *why* this guy's name sounds so familiar, and I finally get to a closeup.

I freeze like a deer in the headlights, my stomach twisting, Jackson Cody's ruggedly handsome face grinning at me from my phone.

You have to be kidding me, I think. *There's no way that's him.*

I look up at the mannequin, but she's no help at all. I close my eyes, like maybe if I give them a break I'll look back and there will be someone else's picture there.

I open them. Still the same guy.

Unbelievable.

I put my phone in my pocket, straighten my spine, and walk for the exit of Kensington's.

It's fine, I tell myself. *I'm sure he doesn't remember, and even if he does, it doesn't matter.*

You were kids. Now you're adults, and you can both act like it.

I swallow and head for the subway, but I'm feeling strangely unconvinced. Maybe because the last time I saw Jackson Cody, I acted like anything *but* an adult.

He's a big rodeo star who's notorious for drinking and sleeping around, I think. *He won't even remember you.*

I sure do remember him, though.

Jackson Cody is the reason I pretty much don't drink any more.

· · · ★ ★ ★ ★ ★ · · ·

LA GUARDIA at four in the morning isn't any more pleasant than La Guardia any other time of day, though it's at least a little quieter, since *everyone* is half asleep and too tired to kick up much of a fuss.

I check in, my heart lurching as the lady behind the desk heaves my camera equipment onto a conveyor belt. The huge, orange FRAGILE tag doesn't do a lot to ease my mind, but it's out of my hands.

You can't control everything, Mae, I remind myself.

The security line is short, and I hand my ID and boarding pass over to the officer at the podium.

He looks at my ID. He looks at my boarding pass.

He looks at my ID again. He looks at me, his brow knitting, *just* a little.

My stomach sinks, because I suddenly know *exactly* what happened.

"Can you step over here?" the officer asks, nodding his head to one side.

Crap.

"What's wrong?" I ask.

"Just wait right there," he says.

I haven't slept. I'm hungry. I haven't even had coffee yet, because I'm at this stupid airport at an *ungodly* hour.

I feel like a toddler on Santa's lap, and I wish I could just *scream.*

Instead, I wait politely, because momma didn't raise a fool.

After a while, another guy comes over and confers quietly with the first officer for a few moments, then looks at me.

"Your ID and boarding pass don't match, Miss Guthrie," he says.

"It was an oversight," I say, taking a deep breath. "I go by Mae Guthrie professionally, and the ticket was booked by a client who wasn't aware of my full legal name."

"What kind of client?" he asks.

"I'm heading to a job shooting for *Sports Weekly*," I say.

Did you seriously just say 'shooting' at a TSA checkpoint?

"Shooting photographs," I say quickly, the words practically tripping over themselves. "I'm a photographer, and I'm going to an assignment for some rodeo in Oklahoma. The whole thing was really last minute, I didn't sleep last night, and I just plain forgot to tell them to book me as Lula-Mae, not just Mae."

He's still just looking at me.

"I'll ask them to change it for the ticket back, but *please* let me get on this plane," I say.

I can feel myself starting to unravel, and for a moment, I'm afraid that I'm going to cry in this stupid security line, in front of all these *people*, all because my parents couldn't give me a normal name.

"You're fine," he finally says. "We just gotta double check all this stuff. Go ahead."

My face flushes with relief.

"Thanks," I say.

I get through the rest of security without a problem. By some miracle, the person checking the X-Ray machine has seen a camera before, so they don't have to dismantle my whole carefully packed case to make sure it's not a bomb.

Even though I get coffee, I'm asleep before the plane even takes off.

CHAPTER TWO

JACKSON

OUT OF NOWHERE, someone knocks so hard on my door that it just about falls off its hinges, and I jump about a foot out of bed.

"Hold your horses!" I shout.

I'm already awake. It's almost nine and I've been waking up with the sun since I was old enough to put on my own boots, so I sit up and toss the book I was reading onto the peeling nightstand of this cheap motel.

I guess I don't move fast enough, because the banging starts again, and this time the redhead in the bed next to me finally wakes up and squints at me.

"Lord have mercy," she whispers.

"I'm *coming*," I shout. I stand and look around for a towel or something, because I'm buck-ass naked and I don't open doors buck-ass naked.

Finally I spot the girl's cowboy hat on her nightstand and grab it. I grin at the quick memory: her, hat on, giving me a good hard ride after half a bottle of Jack last night.

The thought gives me a half-chub, but I clap the hat over it and crack the door open.

"Are you *tryin'* to knock this whole place down?" I ask.

Raylan gives me a quick once-over, thumbs tucked in his belt, and then grins.

"Cock-a-doodle-doo, sunshine," he says, a shit-eating grin on his face.

"I been up since six," I say, leaning against the door frame, hat still firmly over my dick. "I got nowhere to be until noon. My *itinerary* says so."

"Well, your *itinerary* is wrong, because you got a meeting with a reporter in thirty minutes," Raylan says.

"What reporter?"

"Sports Weekly," he says. "Wayne's all worked up about it and sent me to come find you and clear the bunnies outta your room."

Practically on cue, I can hear the girl roll over in bed and sigh.

"Tell Wayne I'll be out in two shakes," I say.

"Ten-four," Raylan says, and I close the door.

I toss the girl's hat onto the bed and head for the bathroom.

"You gonna be in Sports Weekly?" she asks.

"Guess so," I say, and close the door behind me.

I take a quick shower, hoping she'll just leave while I'm in here. We had a good enough time, but now I can't remember her name.

Did it start with an N? I wonder, soaping up quickly.
Nancy? Nicole?

I've got no idea. None of those sound even vaguely famil-iar, but I've always been bad with names.

They ought to just stick name tags to their tits, I think, and laugh to myself in the shower. *Maybe then I'd get some of them right.*

Show someone walking away and I can tell you exactly

who they are by their gait, the way they walk and move. *That's* what I'm good at.

Not names.

Nadine, maybe?

I rinse off, cut the water off, and wrap a towel around myself before stepping back into the room, hoping she's gone.

She's not. She's still naked except the hat, and now she's kneeling on the bed, hands on her knees, eyes a little blood-shot and ringed with last night's makeup.

"Hey cowboy," she says. "How about one more round?"

Then she bites her lip and looks at the bulge in the towel.

I shouldn't. I can't remember her name and I'm meeting a reporter in fifteen minutes, but I look down at her on the bed, a little worn-out looking but hot, naked, and *ready.*

My dick's *never* listened to my brain and it's not about to start now.

"I gotta go soon," I warn her.

She crawls forward on the bed toward me, eyes on my erection straining at the towel.

"I can be quick," she says, and yanks my towel off, her eyes on my quickly-hardening dick.

I don't think I'll ever get tired of the way women look at this thing.

Before we can do anything, there's another knock at my door.

"Shit," I mutter. She looks up at me uncertainly, and I hold one finger up to my lips.

Maybe if we're quiet, whoever it is will think we've left already.

The knock sounds again.

"Jackson, I know you're in there," a man's voice booms.

It's Wayne, the guy who organizes Oklahoma Pioneer

Days. He's ex-military, and while I'd never call him high-strung to his face, he wants things run a certain way.

Having a quickie with a buckle bunny fifteen minutes before you meet a reporter for a major magazine is exactly what Wayne *doesn't* want.

"Jackson," he booms again.

"You gotta get," I whisper to the girl, who makes a pouty face as I pull on my boxers and jeans.

"Comin'!" I shout, walking toward the door, still shirtless, hoping my pants hide my erection well enough.

I pull the door open to Wayne's unhappy face. He gives me a slow once-over, arms crossed in front of his chest.

"What in *tarnation* are you doing in there?" he asks.

"Gettin' ready to meet a reporter," I say. "I thought you'd want me wearing pants."

His eyes travel past me and land on something in the room, and his frown deepens. I resist for a moment, but then I turn and look.

It's an open, half-empty bottle of Jack Daniels.

"Don't you ruin this for us," he says, pointing a finger at me. "Oklahoma Pioneer Days is a *family* event, you hear me?"

"Absolutely, sir," I say.

It's times like this I'm glad I was raised right. I can at least *act* respectful when I need to.

"That don't mean *start* a family while you're here," he adds.

"No, sir," I say.

"Sookie's in five," he says, and holds up five fingers just in case I'm unclear on how many that is.

Then he walks away, hands balled in fists at his sides, his spine straight. Still moves like he's in the military.

The girl peeks her head out of the bathroom and looks at me, then winks.

"I can do five minutes," she says.

"He'll have my hide," I say, reaching into my suitcase for a shirt.

She pouts again.

"Sorry, darlin'," I say. "I had a real good time last night." *Natalie? Naomi?*

"Me too," she says. "Don't worry, I'll be around."

She gets dressed fast in her denim miniskirt and fringed shirt, and I shoo her out of my room. Then I screw the cap back on the liquor, pull on my boots, and get on down to Sookie's Diner with one minute to spare.

· · · · · ★ ★ ★ ★ · · · ·

SOOKIE'S DINER looks exactly like a place called Sookie's Diner should look. Red-checked tablecloths, thrift store knickknacks on the walls, and tons of those kinda-ugly wooden plaques with funny little sayings on them, like *Cowgirl up!* and *Save a horse, ride a Cowboy!*

I can get behind that last one.

Wayne and his wife Darlene are sitting at the table already, and Wayne looks meaningfully at the clock on the wall when I come in.

"You're two minutes late," he says.

"That clock's fast, and I'm earlier than they are," I say.

Darlene hasn't said anything yet, but she's giving me a good once-over, like she's making sure that I don't have a condom wrapper stuck on me anywhere and I don't reek of whiskey.

I don't *think* I do. No guarantees.

"Sports Weekly is doing a big feature on the Oklahoma

Pioneer Days rodeo," she finally says, lacing her fingers together in front of her.

She's got a perfect manicure, fancy earrings, and a face full of makeup. It would be easy to mistake Darlene for a glammed-up rodeo wife, but I've been riding at Pioneer Days for a couple years now. I know Darlene, and the woman can rope a steer in her own right, no matter how prim and proper she looks.

"Okay," I say. The waitress stops by with a cup of coffee for me, and I thank her.

Then I watch her walk away. She moves a little stiffly, but I'd be willing to loosen her up.

Darlene clears her throat, and I stop watching the waitress walk away.

"We could be at the center of a perfect storm that makes rodeo mainstream," Darlene goes on. "Play everything right, and bull riders could be as famous as basketball players."

I raise my eyebrows.

"And I'm the Michael Jordan of rodeo," I say.

"Not yet," Wayne says. "You still got a couple to win before you get there."

"Think I could have my very own line of cowboy boots?" I ask.

"Don't count your chickens before they're hatched," Darlene says. "You got a ways to go."

Wayne leans across the table, making his most serious face.

"You ought to take this seriously, Jackson," he rumbles. "We're talking rodeo championships being as big as the Super Bowl. We're talking sponsorships, contracts, gigs doing commentary on ESPN once you retire. Play this thing right, and you'd be the biggest rodeo star of all time, because you'd be the *first*."

I take another sip of my coffee. My name in lights sounds nice, but I don't even know what I'd do with a million dollars. Buy a ranch out in the country, I guess, and then what? Retire?

The concept feels totally foreign to me.

All I've ever wanted to do is *ride*, because there's nothing in the world like the rush of staying on a bull for those eight seconds.

A couple years ago, I got hurt pretty bad. When I woke up, I realized: this is what's gonna kill me, and that's if I'm lucky. I don't know a single rider over fifty who doesn't walk with a limp, and there's plenty worse off than that.

Commentating on ESPN? Doing cowboy boot commercials? That's for someone else. Someone who thinks he'll make it past thirty-five.

Wayne leans forward over the table.

"Just act with the *slightest* hint of decorum for five day," he says, his voice low.

I glance out the window, trying not to smile.

"That's not what they're here for," I say. "We both know they wouldn't be interested if I was straight-laced and squeaky clean."

"Jackson, just be *discreet*," Darlene says. Her eyes are like iron. "No loud intercourse in bar bathrooms. No showing your johnson to anyone who asks. No disappearing to Mexico for a day and showing up an hour before you're supposed to ride, like you did in San Antonio."

"I won San Antonio," I point out.

"See if you can win without nearly causing a catastrophe for once," Darlene says. "There's a difference between a good story and a scandal."

"Jackson, all we're saying is take it down a notch for

once," Wayne says. "Take a girl back to your motel room instead of the alley behind the bar."

I look from him to Darlene and back. I've known them for a couple years, and they're nice people, if firm. They just want Pioneer Days to hit the big time, and I know they've worked hard for it.

I don't really give a shit what people think about me, but for the two of them, I'll give it a shot.

No Mexico. Girls in the motel room only. Maybe in bar bathrooms if they can be quiet.

"Okay," I finally agree. "I'll try it."

They both nod and then look at the door of the diner, their expressions suddenly turning professional. I turn to look at the two people heading toward us.

In front is an older man, gray-haired and gray-bearded, wearing a button-down work shirt. He doesn't look like he's from around here, but he doesn't stick out.

Then he steps aside and I get an eyeful of the *other* person.

Lord above.

It's a girl carrying a camera over one shoulder, her blonde hair side swept, her eyes raking in the knickknacks on the wall. She walks toward us and I forget to breathe for a just a second, because all I can watch is the straight line of her shoulders over the way her hips roll as she moves.

I'm mesmerized. It's like watching the ebb and swell of the ocean, except the ocean's never gotten my dick hard.

I stare. She looks around the diner, completely casual, totally seemingly unaware that even in jeans and a black t-shirt, every movement she makes *screams* sex, at least to me. Her face has the barest hint of freckles, and even though her eyes have circles under them, they're a perfect sky blue.

She walks closer with those languid, sultry movements, and I realize something.

I know her.

I can't place her right away, but I'm total certain that I *do.* I start flipping back through the memories of all the women I've been with.

It's a lot, but this girl is *memorable.* I ought to be able to place her.

I can already tell it's gonna vex me.

"You're Wayne and Darlene Nelson?" the bearded man asks.

"We sure are," Wayne says, getting out of the booth and shaking his hand.

Not a rodeo type, I think, looking at her again.

Where have I even been that I'd meet a girl like her?

Then Wayne clears his throat, and I realize they're all staring at me.

I rise from the booth and Bruce shakes my hand.

"Jackson Cody," I say. I force myself to look at him and not the girl.

"Bruce McMurtry," he says. "I'm a reporter for Sports Weekly. This is our photographer."

"Mae Guthrie," the girl says. She holds out her hand and keeps her spine perfectly straight, like she's trying to look taller than she is.

The second I hear her voice, I know *exactly* who she is.

I can't help but grin.

"Miss Guthrie," I say, taking her hand in mine. "Welcome to the Pioneer Days Rodeo. I'm Jackson."

She's got a firm handshake and a steely, don't-take-no-shit look in her eyes.

"Thank you," she says, her voice stiff and a little formal. "But it's just Mae."

"Sure thing," I say. I hold onto her hand for another moment before I let it go.

I'd bet fifty bucks she remembers *me*. She's got her hackles up the way women do when they unexpectedly run into someone they're embarrassed about, like she's praying that I don't tell our entire breakfast table the story of our little tryst.

It's been years. That's why it took me a minute to remember who she was, but as soon as she spoke up I remembered that voice saying *Come on, Jackson* right into my ear in the bed of my pickup truck.

Hell, I *still* think about that night sometimes, and I've got plenty of other nights to choose from.

"Take a load off and sit down," Wayne says, and the three of us scoot in around the big circular booth.

Mae flicks her eyes nervously at the seat next to Wayne, but Bruce is already lowering himself into it with a sigh, like he's got bad knees, so I pat the cushion next to me.

"Come on, I don't bite," I say. "Not unless you ask real nice."

Darlene shoots me a glare before turning up the wattage on her smile.

"Sookie's has got the best flapjacks this side of Oklahoma City," she says brightly. "You two must be hungry after that long flight. How far *is* it from New York City?"

"It's about four hours," Bruce says. "We managed to get a direct flight, so it wasn't too bad."

They keep chatting, so I turn my head and look at Mae, who's studying the menu like there's gonna be a quiz.

"Where you from, Miss Guthrie?" I ask.

"Mae," she says, not taking her eyes off the menu.

"Well then, where you from, *Mae*?" I ask.

"I live in Brooklyn," she says, not exactly answering my question.

"You like New York City?" I ask, leaning back in the booth and letting my eyes run down her body for just a moment.

"I do sometimes," she says, her eyes still on the menu. "Other times it's cold, crowded, and the people are rude."

"Sounds like it's the second time right now," I say.

"You're not wrong," she says, and then sighs, leaning her head on her hand on the table. "Do you know the difference between a flapjack and a pancake?"

"I don't think there is one, and I'm nearly an expert on diners," I say.

"Nearly," she says, and her blue eyes get a glimmer to them. "What, are you one credit shy of your degree?"

"I never *was* much for school," I say.

"Not even if the class is on bacon?" she asks.

I laugh.

"I damn near failed out of kindergarten," I say. "That's nothing but ABC's and 1-2-3's. You know how hard that is to fail?"

"You seem like you've learned them now," she says, and the sentence has the slightest hint of a lilt to it, like she's keeping the lid tight on an accent that's clamoring to get out.

"By the skin of my teeth," I say, taking another sip of coffee. "I got myself a reputation for making teachers cry by the time I was eight years old."

"You made a grown woman cry when you were eight years old?" she asks.

Now she's leaning back in the booth, her blue eyes smiling at me, and I'd almost swear to God she's *flirting*.

"That was just the first time," I say, grinning at her. "Ain't you done your research? I'm a heartbreaker."

Just then, the waitress steps up to our table and sets down coffee in front of Mae and Bruce.

But for just a moment Mae keeps on looking at me, those sky-blue eyes unreadable, before she turns and orders flapjacks.

Somewhere, deep down inside me, I feel a twinge.

CHAPTER THREE

MAE

I DON'T THINK he remembers.

I can't quite tell, but I don't *think* so. He's not acting like someone who remembers... well, *that*. He's definitely flirting with me, but from what I've read, that's Jackson Cody's default setting.

But there's no hint of recognition, no *don't I know you from somewhere* look in his eyes, and even though I'm definitely relieved, I'm also the tiniest bit disappointed.

After all, I remembered him for *years*. I spent the drive from the airport to here psyching myself up for seeing him again.

Even so, the moment I saw him my heart hitched in my chest.

Jackson Cody looks almost *exactly* the same as he did when he was nineteen and I was eighteen. Same tall frame, same wide shoulders, muscles hard from a life of farm work.

Same dark brown hair that never quite lies down, same cocky grin, same square jawline, like he's a movie cowboy.

Same hazel eyes, somewhere between green and brown, the color of forested mountains on a rainy day.

Good thing I know better than to fall for it again.

As soon as the waitress walks away, the older man at the table — Dwayne? Wayne? I think it was Wayne — puts his beefy hands on top of the table and looks around at us.

"Well, y'all, I'm pleased as punch that *Sports Weekly* is covering our little rodeo," he says, his accent getting a little more folksy.

I raise my eyebrows a millimeter. Oklahoma Pioneer Days isn't *little*, but I recognize that characteristic down-home humbleness, that way that country people sometimes have of waving away their accomplishments.

"Darlene, have you got the schedules?" he asks.

Darlene pulls a file folder out of a bag and passes out glossy pamphlets to Bruce and me.

"Now, you can't attend everything," Wayne says. "But I thought you might like to go over this and we'll work out what you two ought to prioritize."

"Besides bull riding," Jackson says. "That's a given."

I want to roll my eyes at his cocky grin, but he's right. We *are* here because he's poised to become the greatest rodeo champion of all time, at least if he wins this and competes in the finals this December.

"Right," Wayne says, and then starts going over the whole schedule in excruciating detail with Bruce, who has a million questions.

I try to pay attention, but my brain feels like it keeps slipping out of gear. I've been up for thirty-six hours straight.

This job is huge. *Sports Weekly* is huge. If I do it well, I'll never be taking pictures of a mall Santa again — but first, I have to not screw this up.

The problem is Jackson Cody. Even though I promised myself we'd be strictly professional, it's been five minutes and we're already flirting.

It's five days, I tell myself. *Just keep it together for five days.*

How hard can it be?

· · · ★ ★ ★ ★ ★ · · ·

Six Years Earlier

"YOU *SURE* NOBODY'S gonna find us up here?" I ask, stumbling out of Christy's truck.

"It's Derrick's brother's boss's land, and he don't care if we use it," she answers, hopping out of the driver's side. "Come *on*, Lula-Mae. Be bad for once in your life."

I look at the near-empty bottle of peach-flavored Boone's Farm wine in my hand.

How did that get almost-gone?

My brain feels blurry, like there's a time delay between what's happening and when I figure it out.

"Lula, come *on*," Christy says, laughing and coming back toward me. "You ain't gonna get in trouble."

"Am I drunk?" I ask her, still standing there.

We're both wearing tank tops and cut-off shorts, and there's a raging bonfire in the clearing ahead of us, pickup trucks and thirty-packs of beer circled around it. It seems like half my high school graduating class is here, too, and for a moment, I wonder how long they've been congregating up here to get drunk.

I've definitely never been invited before.

Christy just laughs at me.

"If you've gotta ask, you're not drunk enough," she says. "Come on, I thought you liked that stuff."

"It's like alcohol *candy*," I say. "I *love* it."

I take another long swig, then follow her toward the bonfire.

It's a couple weeks after high school graduation, and suddenly, nothing I do has the same consequences that it used to. There's no more tests to fail, no more papers to write, no more teachers to please.

I've got a full ride to the University of Texas at Austin in the fall, but until then?

I'm *free*.

I take another drink of the peach wine. It tastes like sugar, alcohol, and freedom.

Christy's got a beer in her hand now and the two of us are walking around, me still clutching this wine bottle. I can hear people whispering *it's Lula-Mae*, but I'm way too drunk to care.

"Christy!" a man's voice shouts, and we turn toward him. Christy looks him up and down.

"Buck, I didn't know you were back in town," she says.

Even drunk in the firelight, I can tell Christy is blushing.

"Sure am," he says. "There's a rodeo over in Odessa this weekend so I figured I'd come by and see my folks."

Buck's a year older than us, and he quit school in the middle of his senior year to ride rodeo full-time. I thought he was a total idiot, but Christy disagreed.

He was never my type, but I've heard her sing his praises *endlessly*, like he was Jesus Christ himself come down to earth.

"It's great that you're still ridin'," she says, taking a long pull of her beer.

"I'll keep ridin' for as long as I can get on a bull," he says, and grins his cocky, swaggering grin at her.

Christy looks like she goes weak in the knees, and I roll my eyes, too drunk to be subtle.

Then someone else is behind him. The new guy claps Buck on the shoulder, leaning over the other man toward us.

"You ladies know Buck?" he asks, a grin on his face.

It's a *really* handsome face.

I clutch my wine bottle harder. I feel myself turn ten colors. My mouth goes dry and my guts pretty much turn themselves inside out, and for a second I have the crazy urge to just run away.

There aren't a lot of new people in Lawton, Texas. When there are, they're *never* hot men my age.

This guy is.

Not only is he hot, he's looking at me in a way that boys don't look at me. He's got this intense expression on his face, like he doesn't know that I'm Lula-Mae Guthrie, valedictorian, National Honor Society Member, captain of the debate team, and card-carrying Good Girl.

I feel weird. I feel like there's a spotlight on me.

Suddenly, I realize what feels like when someone undresses you with their eyes.

I look down at the ground and heat floods through me, pooling between my legs.

Oh gosh, I think. *Is this because I'm drunk?*

This has gotta be because I'm drunk.

"I'm Jackson," he says, holding out one hand, still staring me straight in the eyes.

My insides feel like spaghetti, but if spaghetti was alive and angry.

"I'm Lula-Mae," I say, my voice coming out breathless. "I'm here."

I meant to say something like *I go to the high school where Buck went,* but it didn't work. I snap my mouth shut.

Jackson just laughs.

"I'm here too," he says, his hazel eyes twinkling.

"Jackson's been traveling the circuit with me," Buck says. "I dragged him here for the weekend so my mom could feed him her biscuits and gravy."

"Ain't they good?" Christy asks.

I take the opportunity to drink more peach wine, trying to drown the angry spaghetti in my stomach. Christy talks to them for a minute, but mostly she talks to Buck, and then before I know it her hand's on his arm and she's giggling and then they're walking away, leaving me standing here with Buck's super-hot friend.

Jackson just whistles as they walk away.

"Never seen Buck be a ladies' man before," he says to me.

I roll my eyes, and everything swims.

"She's got it *bad* for him," I say. "Christy's my best friend but sometimes I think if I have to hear Buck's name one more time I might just smack her upside the head."

He just laughs.

"I've never heard him so much as say her name," he says, looking after them again.

Then he shrugs.

"Maybe don't tell her that," he says.

"My mouth is... locked?" I say, the wine preventing me from getting the saying right.

He laughs and lifts a beer to his mouth, taking a couple long swallows as I try to think of what to say next. I've probably got a couple seconds before he heads off to find someone else.

Guys like him don't talk to dorks like *me*. They want fun girls like Christy.

"So, you ride rodeo with Buck?" I finally say.

"Sure do," he says. "Little bit of everything, but bull riding is my main event."

I gasp involuntarily, like an old lady or a little kid.

"That's *dangerous*," I say. "Aren't you afraid you'll fall off or get gored or something?"

Any other time, I'd be less impressed, but this bottle of wine is almost gone and so is my better judgement.

Jackson grins and tucks his thumb into his belt.

"The danger's what makes it fun," he says.

I get a little warmer between the legs.

"Really?" I ask.

"Of course," he says. "Every second up there, it's just you versus this raw force of nature, you knowin' that at any second it could toss you off and crush you like a bug, and all you've got to do is make sure that don't happen."

He winks at me.

"It's a hell of a rush, Lula-Mae. Come by the rodeo this weekend and I'll give you a lesson."

I laugh.

"It'll be a cold day in hell first," I say.

Suddenly I realize two things: one, my wine bottle is empty, and two, he's gotten closer.

"I bet you'd make a pretty good rider," he says, grinning down at me.

I drop the wine bottle, and it makes a dull thunk on the ground.

"What makes you say that?" I ask.

"You move right," he says, and puts one hand on my hips.

Part of me wants to step away and resist what's happening. That's the part of me that's an honor student, the part that color-codes homework assignments in her planner.

A much bigger part of me wants me to stay right there, and that part is drunk for the first time and thinks that once, *just once*, maybe I should have some fun with a hot cowboy whose last name I don't even know.

"How do I move?" I ask. "Like I'm hard to shake off?"

"You walk real fluid," he says, and puts his other hand on my hips, then wiggles them a little bit.

Now I'm *aching* and looking up at him. I've had a boyfriend before and we did *stuff*, but it never made me feel like this.

"You gotta move easy and go with the flow to be a good rider," Jackson says, his hazel eyes smiling down at me. "Stay loose and keep your balance but be in control. It's all in the hips," he says.

He winks at me.

"How do you know what I walk like," I say. "I ain't moved since I came over here."

"I watched you walk in," he says. "I watched you and I thought to myself, that girl oughta *ride*."

I narrow my eyes. I can practically hear my mother saying *Lula-Mae, you know boys only want one thing, so keep your legs shut.*

Momma never covered what to do if I want the exact same thing.

"Do girls even ride bulls?" I ask.

"Not most girls," he says. "But I got the feeling you ain't most girls."

He bends down and kisses me, right there in front of the fire. My head swirls with the alcohol and for a moment I nearly lose my balance and fall over but then he's got his arm around me, keeping me upright, and my hands are on his chest.

Underneath his t-shirt he's pure muscle, and I run my hands down it as he opens his mouth against mine, the ache inside me deepening. He tastes like beer, but I couldn't care less.

When I finally surface, I glance around, but no one's looking at me. Half of them are making out and the other half are dead drunk.

"I got my pickup here," he says. "You wanna go sit down?"

I nod breathlessly and follow him. We stop by a twenty-four pack and he cracks a beer and hands it to me. I can feel my classmates watching as I follow him back to his truck.

They're probably wondering what on earth *he* is doing with *Lula-Mae*, of all people.

Let them wonder.

He's got a blanket and a few cushions in the bed of his truck, and we climb in and lean against the cab, the glass cool against my back in the hot night.

"You just graduated, right?" he asks.

His hand is on my bare leg.

"Right," I say. "Don't worry, I'm eighteen."

He laughs.

"That ain't what I was asking, but thanks," he says.

"What *were* you asking, then?" I say, taking a sip of beer.

I don't even like beer, but I'm so drunk I can barely taste it.

"Just making polite conversation," he says, a chuckle in his voice. "What's next?"

"UT Austin," I say.

"College girl," he says. "Fancy."

I snort and take another sip.

"My front yard's as full of busted cars as everyone else's," I say. "I got a full ride because I want to get the hell out of Lawton."

"Well, I'm glad you're slumming it with us this summer," he teases. "Remember the little people when you're on top."

I take another long gulp of beer, my eyes flicking up to the skies. Then I put the near-empty can down.

Now I'm sure I'm drunk, so drunk my face is nearly numb and talking is a little hard.

"Jackson," I say, his hand still on my thigh. "Did you bring me here to the back of your pickup to talk about my future, or did you bring me here for some *other* reason?"

He opens his mouth, eyes dancing, but instead of listening I get on my knees and then swing one leg over him until I'm straddling him and we're face to face.

I have *no* idea what's gotten into me.

Wait, yes I do.

An entire bottle of cheap wine and a shitty beer.

Jackson puts both his hands on my butt and squeezes. I giggle, biting my lip, suddenly not quite sure where to go from here.

"Told you you'd be a good rider," he says, moving my ass up and down in his hands.

"You ain't quite as dangerous as a bull," I say, and kiss him hard before he can answer me.

I'm sloppy drunk, but I shove my tongue into his mouth and he pushes back with his own. He grabs my hips and grinds me against the thick, hard rod in his pants.

I frown.

"The hell is in your pocket," I mutter.

He laughs and grinds me against it again, and it feels *good* rubbing up against me like that, whatever it is.

"You like it?" he asks.

"Kinda," I say, breathless. I'm moving my hips against it on my own now.

"Ain't got nothing in my pockets," he says. "That is one hundred percent All-American *cock*."

I gasp and cover my mouth, and he *grins* like he's won the lottery.

"Come on, you liked it before," he says. "Just give it a chance."

I do. I think I've lost control now, because as shocked as I am that someone *said* that to me, I still *like* this.

Jackson kisses me again as he moves his hands under my tank top, me still writhing against him, his fingers pinching my nipples through my bra.

"You like that?" he whispers.

I reach behind myself and unhook my bra, then take it off through the arm hole of my tank top and toss it behind me.

Jackson pushes my top to just above my nipples and then bends his head down, biting and licking at one and then the other, and it feels amazing, like my insides are turning to boiling liquid. I want him to do this forever, it feels so good.

Almost on their own, my hands find the buckle of his belt, and before I know it I'm unzipping his jeans and he's pushing my tank top back down over my breasts.

Then I stare at his boxers in slight confusion, frowning. I was expecting a dick, and I'm not quite sure how to get it out now.

Technically, I've never done this before, but Jackson finds the opening in his boxers and suddenly it's there, thick and long and straight and very, *very* hard. After another moment of uncertainty I grab it by the base and squeeze, and Jackson makes a noise like I'm doing it right.

Then he's unbuttoning my shorts and reaching in and it feels strange to have someone else's hand there, but it feels *good*.

Once he finds my clit it feels *really* good as his rough fingers circle it, making me gasp, my own hand still awkwardly on his erection, not quite sure what to do with it because I've only ever touched a penis through clothing before.

His hand moves deeper and then I can feel it on my lips, his fingers gently nudging between them.

"Damn, Lula-Mae, you ain't faking," he says.

"Faking what?" I ask, trying to move my hips against his hand.

I desperately want *something* from him, and to be honest, I barely even know what.

I want this, but *more*. A bunch more.

He puts his hand over mine on his cock and slides it up and down, from the root to the tip and back, and he leans his head against the cab of his truck and groans.

Oh, I think. *I guess that's what I'm supposed to do.*

I do it again, then again, and he slowly slides one finger inside me, the feeling strange and *wonderful*, his palm still pressing against my clit.

"Jackson," I whisper.

"Yes, Lula-Mae?" he murmurs.

"Let's *do* it," I say.

I've totally forgotten that there are other people around, or that the back of this truck in the middle of a field isn't exactly private.

I just want to *do sex stuff* with him.

"I didn't bring a rubber," he says.

For a moment I have no idea what he's talking about or why it's relevant, and *then* it dawns on me.

But every cell in my body is pounding with drunken desire, and I don't give a shit about a condom.

"It's fine," I say. "Don't you want to?"

"Hell yes," he growls, his eyes sliding down my body, right in front of him, but there's still something hesitant about the way he says it.

I squeeze his dick again and slide my hand up and down

and he looks up at me, in a way no one's ever looked at me before.

I have no idea what I'm doing, but I lean forward, steadying myself against his chest with my other hand as everything wobbles in front of me, and put my lips practically against his ear.

"Come on, Jackson," I whisper.

He chuckles.

"You get what you want, don't you, Lula-Mae?" he asks, grinning, his fingers circling my clit again.

Then: sirens. I look over my shoulder and there are blue lights flashing across the field.

My heart seizes in my chest and everything *spins*.

I yelp, try to stand and fall sideways, the metal of his truck bed booming beneath me.

"You all right?" I hear Jackson ask, but I'm panicking.

I've never had a run-in with the police before, and I'm positive it's going to ruin my life. First I'll get arrested, then the university won't let me in any more, then I'll be stuck in Lawton forever. I'll be working at the McDonald's for the rest of my life.

"Lula-Mae, calm down," Jackson says, his hand on my shoulder. "It's gonna be fine, but you gotta button your pants."

I zip and button quickly, my hands shaking, and Jackson tucks his dick back in.

"Everyone please remain calm," a voice crackles through a megaphone.

I can feel the tears rising in my eyes, my hands shaking.

Jackson actually *grins* at me.

"You never been at a party that got busted up before?" he asks.

I shake my head *no*. I feel like I can barely breathe, my chest tight with panic as everything just spins and spins.

He jumps over the side of his truck, then offers me his hand. It's slightly sticky and I blush, but I take it.

"They're just gonna tell us not to be here," he says. "It's fine."

I jump over the side of the truck and we walk a few steps before there's a spotlight on us.

It pauses and I squint, trying to see who's behind it.

Then a voice says, "Lula-Mae Guthrie?"

Everything lurches. My chest tightens.

I'm going to be flipping burgers forever.

"I'm sorry!" I say, bordering on hysterical.

"God almighty, what are *you* doing here?" the voice asks, and I recognize Phil Warren, a family friend.

I'm trembling like a leaf, and this is where I break. I cover my face with my hands and start *sobbing*.

"I'm sorry!" I get out between sobs, gasping for air. "Please don't tell my parents. Please, god, don't tell my parents."

"Lula-Mae, are you all right?"

He sounds worried, not mad, but my face is hot and covered in tears and snot and I just sniffle and nod, an absolute mess.

"You been drinking?" he asks, but it's obvious he knows the answer.

"A little," I whisper.

Phil sighs.

"All right, come on," he says.

I walk toward him, leaving Jackson standing there in the field. I'm too embarrassed to even look back at him.

Phil lets me sober up at the station for a while and then takes me home. By some miracle, he promises never to tell my parents as long as he doesn't catch me partying like that again.

He doesn't, because that's the last time it happens. In August I leave for college and only ever visit Lawton again, and I never go to another bonfire party.

I major in photography and have a 3.9 GPA, almost perfect. I lose my virginity to a nice guy from Louisiana. Whenever I'm not studying I'm working, and by the end of four years, I've got enough saved to move to New York City and leave Texas behind forever.

I get an apartment in Brooklyn and I hustle my tail off, stringing together enough freelance jobs to pay the rent.

Through it all, I almost manage to forget the time I got wasted and *almost* had unprotected sex with Jackson Cody.

CHAPTER FOUR

JACKSON

Present Day

AFTER BREAKFAST we walk back into the gravel parking lot that connects Sookie's Diner to the Prairie Motel. Across the street is the Oklahoma fairgrounds, where we're gonna be for the next seven days. All I can see from here is the front ticket office, done up Old West style, and over it the arc of the Ferris wheel.

In the distance, to the right, is the arena. My belly tightens in excitement.

That's *my* stomping ground.

"Y'all let us know if you need anything," Wayne says. "You doing anything before the opening ceremonies tonight?"

"I'm going to walk around and get a feel for the place," Bruce says, glancing over at the fairgrounds. "Start talking to some people, that kind of thing."

Wayne looks at Mae.

"I need to set up my equipment and make sure everything made it here in one piece," she says. "And I think I need a nap if I want to stay awake tonight."

Wayne and Darlene both nod politely.

We all shake hands. Bruce, Wayne, and Darlene start to drift off, but Mae and I stand there for another moment. She's looking across the street at the fairgrounds, and I'm just looking at her. Thinking of her voice saying *Come on, Jackson*, and getting a half-chub just from that.

"Need any company during that nap?" I ask, and paste on my most charming grin.

Hell, it worked last time.

Mae's gaze flicks to me and holds mine steady for a moment. Then she laughs.

"I nap alone," she says, and she says it almost like I was joking.

"You know the saying," I tell her.

She raises her eyebrows just a little.

"Save a horse, ride a cowboy?"

Mae bursts out laughing.

"Wow," she says. "You really do live up to your reputation."

"I had to work pretty hard to get it," I say.

"Does that work?" she asks. "The 'save a horse' thing?"

"You have no idea," I say.

Usually, I don't even have to try that hard.

"You want to know the secret?" I ask.

I take a step closer to her, my thumbs tucked into my belt. She doesn't back away.

"Is the secret rodeo groupies?" she asks.

"If you're gonna be here, you should learn the lingo, darlin'," I say. "The buckle bunnies line up for me because women talk, and word's gotten around about me."

She frowns slightly.

"Buckle what?" she asks, ignoring the important part of the sentence.

"Buckle bunnies," I say.

She shrugs.

"That's what you call rodeo groupies?" she asks, and I nod.

"Rodeo winners get buckles, and bunnies get what's underneath. It's debatable which prize is better."

She lifts her eyebrows again, and her eyes crinkle a little like she's trying not to smile.

"I should write that down. It's colorful," she says.

She's acting like I'm not hitting on her at all, completely ignoring my advances.

It's driving me *crazy*.

"I'll take a raincheck for that nap, then," I say.

Mae glances behind me at something, and suddenly I have a bad feeling.

"Jackson," says Darlene's voice. "A word?"

"Nice meeting you," Mae says, and nods at Darlene. "See you around."

She walks toward the motel, that same look of amusement in her eyes. I watch her walk for a moment, then take a deep breath and turn toward Darlene.

Even though I'm a good eight inches taller than her, I've got the sense to keep my mouth shut.

"How stupid *are* you?" she hisses.

Not stupid enough to answer *that* question.

"It's bad enough that your bed might as well be a revolving door of hussies," she says. "But, hand to God, Jackson, you *will not* ruin this article for Pioneer Days."

I smile and spread my hands.

"Come on, Darlene—"

She puts up a hand to stop me.

"Don't you *come on, Darlene* me, Jackson. I'm old enough to be your mother and it don't work on me. But you keep trying to get into that girl's pants, *that* is what this story is gonna be about. It ain't gonna be about rodeo, or bull riding, or the long proud western traditions of this great country. It's gonna be about a pervert in a cowboy hat botherin' a nice young woman, you mark my words."

"I was just having a little fun," I say.

"Don't," Darlene says. "You want to be a big star, Jackson Cody? You want your name in lights and a line of cowboy boots? Then don't let them write a story about how you hounded a photographer to sleep with you from the moment you met her."

"She ain't even the writer," I say, but I know it's a losing battle.

"You think he won't find out?" Darlene says. "That man finds stories for a living, and I guarantee a rodeo star sniffing at that girl's panties like a hound dog on the scent is a story."

She looks at me, iron in her eyes, and I know she's goddamn right.

I watch the news, I read the paper and the glossies sometimes. There's nothing they like better than tearing someone down. If I keep hitting on Mae, *that's* the headline.

I glance at her form, almost to the motel.

She turned me down anyway, I think.

"That's not the story that Pioneer Days needs written about it," Darlene says.

Right. It's not just about me.

"All right," I say. "I'll try to behave."

I sneak another glance after Mae, just as she turns the corner.

Behaving ain't gonna be easy.

"Bed the bunnies and ride the bulls, Jackson," she says,

squeezing my shoulder in an almost-motherly fashion, though my mother would never say *that*. "And you leave Mae Guthrie *alone*."

I nod once, and Darlene turns around and marches off, probably to order someone else around.

I hate it when she's right.

Still, I think about the way Mae's hips move and roll, the sweep of her neck as she looks around. For a moment I think about her hips in my hands, peach wine on her breath as she straddled me that summer night.

She looked a little different back then. She was younger, not so self-assured, and drunk as all get out, but I'll be damned if I don't still think about it. Hell, I went back to Buck's house with the worst case of blue balls I've ever had, and I *still* jerk off thinking about it sometimes.

And now, Lula-Mae Guthrie is practically next door and I can't have her.

It's gonna be a rough couple days.

CHAPTER FIVE

MAE

GOOD LORD, he's charming.

I don't look back even once as I cross the parking lot, but I'd swear I can feel his eyes on me as I walk. They're like a hot breeze slipping through my clothes and caressing me, even though it's downright chilly in Oklahoma in November. I'm starting to understand what all the buckle bunnies see in him.

I smile as I unlock my motel room door, because *buckle bunnies* is a pretty good phrase.

I don't even turn the lights on in the room, just flop face-down on the bed in the dark and inhale the scent of cheap laundry detergent.

At least it smells like detergent and not something else, I think. *I wouldn't want to take a black light to this room.*

I wrinkle my nose and roll over on the bed, so at least my face isn't pressed into the probably-gross comforter, and I try to make a mental list of everything I need to do before tonight.

Instead I think about Jackson, offering to keep me company during my nap. I don't think I've ever been propositioned that boldly by someone who wasn't wild-eyed and shouting on the subway, and I've definitely never wanted to take someone up on it before.

There's something magnetic about Jackson, and I can't even put my finger on it. He's unbelievably good looking, sure, but I've met good-looking men before. Is it the way that he's beyond confident, like he knows you're going to wind up in bed with him, it's just a matter of when?

Is it the way that *somehow*, he talks to me like I'm the only other person in the world?

Whatever it is, it's working, because instead of doing my job, I'm lying on this bed thinking about Jackson. At least there's good news: he definitely doesn't remember me. Otherwise, why not bring it up when we were alone?

You're not eighteen anymore, I remind myself. *You're not a drunk virgin just out of high school, even if he kind of makes you feel that way.*

For one thing, you've touched several penises since then. Including poor Andrew's.

Andrew was a guy on my freshman hall, and even now, when I think about him I feel guilty. We hooked up about a month into my freshman year of college.

He was the first guy I got with after my disaster night with Jackson, and I'll just say that when I first saw him naked I was... expecting *more*.

Turns out Andrew was a little above average, actually. Not that I got to see him naked again after that night. Guys don't like it when you look at their erections, make a face, and say *oh* in a disappointed voice.

I still can't believe I did that. God, I was such a jerk, and I didn't even mean to be. It's been five years and I still feel awful, though I'm sure Andrew is doing fine.

I take a deep breath and put one arm over my face,

willing myself not to fall asleep before I can at least check my equipment and take a shower.

Just don't sleep with him, I think. *That's all there is to it.*

By tonight, I'm sure there will be crowds of buckle bunnies eager to take him to bed, at least if what I've been reading about Jackson is even half-true. I probably won't even talk to him one-on-one again.

He was probably just hitting on you out of habit, I think. *He sees a woman alone and tries to get her into bed.*

Like when you get tapped on the knee and kick. It's just a reflex.

The thought is mostly comforting, if a little disappointing.

I yawn and kick my shoes off, pulling my feet onto the bed and rolling onto my side. Just resting for five more minutes.

· · · · ★ ★ ★ ★ · · · ·

I WAKE up to my phone ringing in my pocket, and I jerk upright with no idea where I am or what's going on. The afternoon light is slicing through the small gap in the curtains, and I'm so disoriented I almost don't know which way is up.

But I pull out my phone anyway. It's Bruce.

"Afternoon, Mae," he says. "Sorry if I woke you."

I clear my throat, rub my eyes with one hand, and try to get a grip. I hardly ever take naps, because whenever I do, I'm just *out* of it for the rest of the day.

"It's fine," I say. "Did you want to talk about tonight?"

"I'd like to convene in my motel room in about thirty minutes, if that works for you," he says.

A panic hammer hits me right in the chest, and I scan the room for a clock, because I don't have a clue what time it is.

"Thirty minutes sounds great," I lie.

"Excellent," he says. "I made some good contacts today, and I'm looking forward to working on this assignment with you."

"Same," I say.

Well, except instead of doing something, I fell asleep by accident for several hours. But otherwise, same.

We hang up. I leap off the bed, hit the lights, and race into the shower.

· · · · ★ ★ ★ ★ · · · ·

THIRTY-FIVE MINUTES later I'm dressed in a different black t-shirt, jeans, and a jacket. My hair is dried, and I've got a camera and lens suitable to medium-distance action shots.

Sure, my motel room looks like a tornado hit it and I nearly pulled out a chunk of hair trying to blow it dry as fast as possible, but nobody needs to know about that part. They just need to know that Mae Guthrie, consummate professional photographer, is on the job.

Bruce's door is slightly open, and he leaves it that way after I come inside. I'm confused for a moment, but then I realize: he's a middle-aged man and I'm a young woman. The open door means that anyone can walk by at any time and see that all we're doing is talking.

It's smart. It makes me relax a little, and it makes me appreciate Bruce.

"So the trick of this assignment," he says, sitting in an ugly wooden chair opposite me, "is that it needs to combine a couple of things. It needs to be a story about the sport of rodeo, of course, but it's also a snapshot of rodeo culture as it exists right now, as well as a biographical piece on Jackson Cody."

"Piece of cake," I say dryly. It gets a smile from Bruce.

"After Larry's appendix burst, I actually went through the portfolios of several photographers," Bruce says. "You had the shortest resume but the best photos."

"Thank you," I say, sitting up a little straighter.

On the inside, I'm jumping up and down and pumping my fists.

"In particular, you had a series of photos of high school football players in your hometown, and there was one that stuck with me. It's in the locker room, and the quarterback and a few other players are standing there, after a game, pads still on. They'd just won, and they're laughing. There's one locker open in the background, and inside it there's a Whataburger uniform, because one of the players had rushed to the game from his shift."

I just nod. Bruce McMurtry is a well-known sports journalist, and he's telling me why I got picked for the assignment that could change my life.

"That picture is what I'm looking for from this," he says. "That juxtaposition of life at the rodeo for these people, especially for Jackson, and life outside the rodeo. People come here for a reason, for fun or escape or just diversion, and I want your photos to make it exactly clear to the reader what it offers them."

I almost ask him if he'd also like me to lasso the moon while I'm at it, but I don't. I just nod again.

"I grew up around this kind of thing," I say. "I've got a pretty good idea of what I'm looking for. Tonight's all about the spectacle of rodeo. Rhinestones, glitter, big American flags, all that. It's also about figuring out lenses and shutter speeds."

"Perfect," he says, and stands. "I think this is going to turn out beautifully."

We walk to the arena, chatting about our plans in bursts and snippets.

But inside, I think I'm about ready to explode with a combination of pride and nervousness.

This is my big break, my one shot, and I'm going to *nail* it.

CHAPTER SIX

JACKSON

RAYLAN HANDS me the flask back, and I swish it from side to side, frowning at him.

"You're gonna drink me out of house and home," I tell him, tilting the flask up. I take the last swallow of whiskey and let it settle in my belly before I put the flask back in my pocket.

"What, out of that trailer in your momma's back yard?" he asks.

"Don't knock it," I say.

Raylan and I have been traveling from rodeo to rodeo together for a couple years now, ever since Buck left. He probably knows more about me than anyone alive except maybe my mother. Hell, we even slept in the same bed more often than not for a while since it was all we could afford.

"When you're a big star you ought to buy your own double-wide," he says, still grinning. "Maybe get a house that don't feel like it's gonna fall over in a high wind."

We're leaning up against the barrier, and in the arena in front of us is a whole team of eight-year-olds, riding small horses around, fully decked out in their cowboy best as the announcer tells us all their names. Apparently these kids have won some kind of civic award from school, and their reward is riding a horse around in front of all these cheering people.

There's a country song playing loud, there's horses and cowboys and even a couple cowgirls, and out of the blue it *gets* me, just like it does every time.

It's the feeling that I'm home now. That I'm exactly where I'm supposed to be, doing what I'm supposed to do.

The music is cheesy and the announcer isn't really funny, but I remember the first time I rode in a rodeo. I was even younger than these kids, sheep riding at the Converse County Fair back home in Wyoming.

I barely remember my first kiss, but that first ride is crystal clear, even now. Clutching the wool on the back of some old, cranky ewe. The gate opening and the sheep jogging out, me clinging to its back for all I was worth. The sheep never got above a trot, and I only lasted four seconds before I fell off anyway, but even at that tender age I was hooked.

Rodeo's all I've ever wanted to do since. There just ain't nothin' else like it.

The kids on horses exit. The announcer talks for a minute about one of the sponsors, Ford trucks, and then the rodeo queen comes out, a smiling blond eighteen-year-old in full cowgirl regalia, rhinestone hat included.

She takes a circuit, followed by all the girls who wanted to be queen but lost, sitting proud on their big horses.

It goes on like that, people entering and exiting, girl scouts and boy scouts and the high school rodeo team, all that small-town America stuff that I grew up with and still love.

I'm a country boy at heart. I like horses and big trucks and pretty girls and the smell of dirt. I can't help it.

Speaking of pretty girls, I've been scanning for Mae but I haven't seen her yet. I thought she'd be here somewhere, but maybe she decided to skip this and get a good night's sleep. There's no real sports happening right now, just the showy stuff.

Then Raylan nudges me and cocks his head at the announcer's platform, on metal legs about fifteen feet above the ground, over the bucking chutes. On it is a blond woman wearing jeans and a black t-shirt, a camera up to her face.

"That the photographer?" he asks, looking up at her.

She takes the camera away from her face, looks at the back, and adjusts something very carefully, a look of total concentration on her face.

"Yeah, that's Mae," I say.

"You failed to mention that she was a pretty young thing," he says, and gives me a joking look. "From the way you talked about her, I thought she was practically an ogre."

Something tightens in my chest, something unpleasant and ugly. I brush it away and shrug.

"You know now," I say. "Besides, she's working. Good luck."

Raylan just laughs, like he's not fooled at all.

"She turn you down?" he teases. "You're sore about *something.*"

"Not in so many words," I say. "I got a talking to from Darlene about her."

"When has that ever stopped you?"

I look at Mae again. Now she's standing on the platform. It's got a railing around it, but the platform's not too big and the railing doesn't look that sturdy.

"Darlene made a good point about sleeping with the

person whose article is gonna introduce you to bankers in Connecticut," I admit.

"You're not half as dumb as you act, you know," Raylan says.

"I'm here, ain't I?" I ask, grinning. "I'm plenty dumb. If I had any sense I'd have become a firefighter or a coal miner or some other safe occupation. I can pass one girl up. It ain't like I'm hurting for pussy."

He stops looking at Mae and sweeps his eyes around the grandstand, grinning.

"That's God's own truth," he says. "Ain't none of us hurting for pussy."

Mae's standing next to a guy in a suit and bolo tie, showing him something on her camera. As I watch, she slips the strap from around her neck, moving the camera so he can see it better as she points to something on the back of it.

In the arena, some teenagers are doing a cattle-roping exhibition, lassoing cows, knocking them over and tying their legs together. They're not quite skilled enough to make it look effortless, but they're pretty good.

They let the cow back into the chute. The next one opens.

Just as the steer bolts out, there's a commotion on the platform above, arms waving.

Something falls into the sand about thirty feet from where we're standing, something black and a little boxy. Raylan and I both watch it for a moment, frowning. Then I realize what it is.

It's Mae's camera.

Up above, she's got both her hands over her mouth, as the steer and the cowboys chasing him tear around the arena, not paying her or it any mind at all.

The steer corners and then doubles back. A lasso falls

into the sand behind it, and now the steer is bearing down on Mae's camera.

I vault over the barrier and run for it.

CHAPTER SEVEN
MAE

THIS PLATFORM ISN'T big enough for all the people up here, and it sways a little bit every time anyone new walks on or off. It's unnerving, so I just try to keep my feet as I show the marketing guy from Ford the pictures I've been taking, removing the strap from around my neck so he can see a little better.

"That's a good shot," he says, looking at a photo of a kid flying off the back of a sheep.

"Thanks," I say. "The trick is to get it right when they're falling off."

He laughs.

The platform sways again, and almost in slow motion, the marketing guy sways too. Then he stumbles, throwing his arms out to catch himself, but instead he knocks into me.

My camera flies out of my hands and goes off the plat-form, and I think time stops as it falls. My heart collapses in on itself.

Even through the noise of the rodeo, I swear I hear a soul-crushing *crunch* as it hits the ground.

I hit the platform floor on my knees, gripping the edge,

and watch the cattle chute gate swing open. A steer busts out of it and gallops around the arena, followed by two cowboys, my camera just sitting there, ready to get trampled.

I feel nauseous, my head spinning. The guy who bumped me is saying something, but the blood is roaring through my ears because I just dropped five thousand dollars' worth of equipment and it's about to get smashed into smithereens.

Just rope it over there, I think. *Just stay on that side, and then I can go down there and get it back, please, God, please...*

The steer makes a sudden turn. A lasso misses, and now he's headed back toward us from the opposite side of the arena. I can't even breathe. I can't believe how *stupid* I am.

There's a quick flash of motion down below.

Someone vaults over the barrier, lands on his feet, stumbles, and then runs hell-for-leather for my camera, his hat covering his face.

My fingertips go cold.

What is he doing, I think.

"Don't!" I shout uselessly. "Get out of there!"

Not that anyone can hear me.

Please, God, don't let this idiot die to get my camera back, I think.

I feel lightheaded.

The steer's bearing down. It's going straight for my camera *and* this moron trying to grab it, galloping and snorting. I'm gripping the railing around the platform so hard my hands are white, holding my breath.

I don't want to watch someone get trampled, but my eyes won't shut. He's feet away, the steer still coming on, and then in one quick motion he bends down, his hat falls off, he grabs the camera by the strap, and then he keeps going, a split second before the steer tramples that exact spot.

Then he leaps onto the gate of the bucking chute right

below us. The steer blows past, the two cowboys chasing after it, both of them hollering at the top of their lungs. The guy who saved my camera waves at them and looks up at me.

It's Jackson.

He's grinning like he just won the lottery. People start cheering, and he gives the grandstands a wave too.

He's insane, I think. *Jackson Cody is an actual lunatic with a death wish.*

The adrenaline is still rattling through my veins, and I feel shaky as I stand up, getting dizzy for a moment. My heart's pounding in my chest, and I barely hear the guy behind me apologizing as I head for the aluminum steps down to ground level, everyone watching me.

When I get there Jackson's standing just this side of the bucking chutes, blowing sand off my camera like it's a seashell he found at the beach. Even the way he *stands* has this cocksure swagger to it, like he's absolutely confident of everything he does, like the world revolves around him.

A knot tightens in my stomach, because I can feel people looking at me, looking at *us*. Maybe he's not *famous* famous, but everyone in this arena right now knows who he is, and he just risked his life to save some idiot's camera.

I walk over, still shaking, my heart beating wildly. He looks up at me and grins, the camera in his hands.

"You drop something?" he asks.

"What were you *doing*?" I say. "That thing almost trampled you to death!"

Jackson laughs.

"You're welcome," he says.

"You can't just *do* that," I say, suddenly angry. "What if you'd gotten run over? Then it's *my* fault you're dead, because I dropped my camera."

"Nobody's gonna put you on trial, darlin'," he says. "I'm not known for doing things I don't want to."

"Are you known for being a complete and utter idiot?" I ask, my voice pitching a little higher.

I'm not being very nice, but the last thing I want is Jackson Cody's blood on my hands. People are still looking at us. If I caused his death somehow I'd probably get lynched.

"I'm a professional bull rider," he says, his voice teasing. "Being a complete and utter idiot is *all* I'm known for."

He steps closer to me and holds the camera out. I feel eighteen again. There's some deep, primal part of me that still likes this: the swagger, cockiness, the sheer *enthusiasm* for danger.

He just risked his life for a camera. *My* camera. It's stupid and reckless and macho in the very worst way, but God help me, it's still making my insides flutter and I hate myself for it.

"I'm not known for causing needless deaths," I say. "Would you mind if we kept it that way?"

I take the camera and our hands touch, but he doesn't let it go.

"You got a good grip on it?" he asks, teasing, those hazel eyes looking down at me like we're alone in this arena of a thousand.

"I can handle it," I say.

He slides his fingers over mine as he lets go, and they're rough and calloused, hands used to farm work and heavy labor.

I slip the strap back over my neck and look down at the camera, praying it's not *too* broken from the fall, but Jackson doesn't leave, he just stands there in front of me.

"How busted is it?" he asks.

I hit the power button and hold my breath. The screen comes on, though the picture is blurry.

I exhale.

"Not as busted as it could be," I say.

Something's broken for sure, but the camera's in one piece, not a thousand.

Still, I can't believe what an *idiot* I am.

"Can you fix it?" he asks, crossing his arms in front of himself and looking down at it like he's examining a truck engine.

"I don't know," I say. "Probably not, but I've got a backup camera. This one's better, but I'm not totally screwed."

"Good," he says. "I was afraid my pretty mug might not make Sports Weekly."

"So that's why you risked your own hide to get this thing back?" I say.

"My hide?" he says, and laughs. "You've been around cowboys too much already, darlin'."

Crap.

I've mostly shed the West Texas twang I grew up with. Back in New York, when I tell people where I'm from, they're usually surprised.

But here, where *everyone* talks like this? I can practically feel my accent elbowing its way back into my speech.

"Please don't call me *darlin'*," I say, still looking down at the camera.

"It's just a nickname," he says.

"I've got a real name," I say, and finally look up at him, into his laughing eyes. "It's Mae."

"You sure Mae's not a nickname?" he asks. "It's awful short is all."

My stomach twists and I narrow my eyes.

Does he remember?

"Nope," I say. "Mae's what's on my birth certificate."

Technically, it's true.

"All right, *Mae*," he says, and then someone calls his name.

We both look at another guy waving Jackson's hat in the air. One side of it's a little crushed, but it could be in worse shape.

Jackson nods, then looks back at me.

"We're gettin' drinks at Betty's Lounge when this is over," he says. "You should come by. There ought to be some good photo opportunities. And if we ask real nice, they'll turn on the karaoke machine."

"Maybe," I say.

"Have some fun for once, darlin'," he says, and winks at me.

Then he walks away before I can even open my mouth to protest, and I watch him go.

Heads turn after him — male, female, it doesn't matter. He nods at two girls, both dressed up in their rodeo finest, and says something. They both burst into giggles once he passes, and I feel a pang of solidarity with them. No matter how prickly I am to Jackson on the outside, deep down, I turn to *jello* when he looks at me.

I wish my camera weren't broken, because this could be a good shot: a cowboy walks away, heads turn after him.

Then he turns a corner and I feel invisible again, like I fade into the background, and I take a deep breath of relief.

This is how I prefer things. I'm *behind* the camera, after all.

* * * ★ ★ ★ ★ * * *

WHEN THE RODEO'S over for the night, Bruce and I hold a quick conference on the way back to the motel. I don't want to talk about dropping my camera, but he saw the whole thing, of course. Thankfully he's nice enough not to lecture me.

"You brought a backup, right?" Bruce asks.

"Of course," I say.

He nods, and we move on.

We go over the plan for the next day — a parade, barrel racing, a bunch of roping events — and then we're at the motel.

"I think I'll turn in," he says. "I'm bushed. You?"

I hesitate.

"I heard all the cowboys are going to a bar to celebrate," I say.

Bruce raises his eyebrows a fraction of an inch.

"I might go down and document a little," I say. "Get some flavor for the article."

"If you're not too tired, it's a good idea," he says. "Oh, to be young again and able to stay up all night. Have a good time."

· · · · · ★ ★ ★ ★ · · · ·

I PARALLEL park our small white rental car right in front of Betty's Lounge, amazed at the sheer amount of street parking that's available here.

I could park *anywhere*, in front of *whatever* store I want. I don't even own a car in New York, but I'm familiar with the nightmare of trying to find a parking spot. In Kettle, Oklahoma, I've got my pick.

Bettty's is a pretty standard bar, and everything about it screams *regular America*: the neon beer signs in the window, the men wearing jeans and baseball caps at the bar, the news on the TV over the bar. As soon as I walk in I hear a shout go up and look over to the right, where a group of cowboys are sitting around on some couches around tables and doing shots.

Jackson's in the middle, and he puts the shot glass down on the table, shakes his head from side to side, and shouts, "Yeah!"

There's already a girl next to him, wearing tiny cutoff shorts and a plaid shirt even in November, smiling up at him and laughing.

You're here for flavor, I think. *This is flavor.*

I get a good grip on my camera and walk toward them.

CHAPTER EIGHT

JACKSON

I'VE ONLY HAD three shots of tequila but I'm starting to get buzzed. They keep showing up and so I keep doing them, and I'll probably keep going until they stop coming or I can't do another one.

There's a cute blonde on my left and a cute girl with golden-brown hair on my right, and every time I say something they both laugh, so that's good. Betty's is filling up, even though it's still only nine-thirty.

I don't think Mae's gonna show up, and the disappointment chafes at me like a stiff tag in a new shirt, even though I try to ignore it. I shouldn't have even invited her in the first place, so it serves me right.

Betty herself comes over. She's in her forties, her hair just going gray, and she brings a pitcher of beer and a slew of pint glasses.

"On the house," she says, setting it all on a table. "Y'all are good for business, you know."

Raylan laughs.

"I'll drink to that," he says.

"I know you will," Betty says, wiping her hands on her apron. "You'll drink plenty to that."

"Cheers," Raylan says. He pours himself a beer, clinks it against the pitcher, and then drinks half of it.

"You ladies want some?" I ask the girls on my left and right.

"Sure!" says Left.

"I'd love some," says Right.

I'm a gentleman, so I pour their drinks before I pour my own. Someone's shouting something a couple feet away, and I hear the clink of shot glasses again. People hoot. Another girl comes and sits next to Raylan.

"All right," I say loudly, holding up my glass. A few people stop talking and look at me, then hold up their own glasses. "Here's to Oklahoma!"

It's the first thing I thought of, but everyone cheers. We clink glasses and drink beers.

More shots show up. We drink to more things. The girl on my right gets replaced with another girl, or at least, I think she does. The new girl is a little more handsy, always touching me on the arm and shit.

Raylan gets Betty to put out the karaoke machine, and him and Clay go over and work on figuring it out until they've found the power switch, and then they argue over which Johnny Cash song they should sing first.

I head to the bathroom. When I come back, my seat's still there, and I realize that Betty's is wall-to-wall plaid and cowboy boots. It makes me smile, and I sit back down and drink what's in front of me.

A while later, I see a flash go off behind Raylan's head. I don't think anything of it for a moment, until I realize that also behind Raylan is a blond head.

Then I sit up and lean forward, elbows on knees.

"What," says Raylan. He's got an arm around a girl, both of them pretty drunk.

I'm getting there, too.

"Is that Mae behind you?" I ask.

He twists his head and looks, then turns back to me, both eyebrows raised.

"I thought you had a restraining order," he says, a wide smile plastered onto his face.

The girl on my left looks up at me. There's no girl on my right. I guess she's found something else to do.

"It ain't an order, it's a suggestion," I say. "I'm gonna go be civil."

I walk up behind Mae, but she's taking a picture of two ropers, both of them grinning, thumbs tucked into belts. I'm a good head taller than her, so I just watch what she's doing from over her as she snaps a few shots, changes something, takes a few more.

"Those ain't really candid," I say.

She jumps. The two cowboys laugh, and she turns to me with an exasperated look on her face.

"Don't just sneak up on people, Jackson," she says.

"Sorry, darlin'," I say.

"Please don't call me that," she says, looking at the camera. The two other cowboys drift off to go drink something else.

"Sorry, *Mae*," I say. "Let me buy you a drink to make it up to you."

"No thanks," she says. "I'm working, you know."

"Just one," I say. "It'll loosen you up."

"What good is that gonna do for taking pictures?" she asks, but there's laughter in her voice.

I shrug.

"I don't know," I say. "Maybe invite the muse in or some artistic shit."

"My muse is a teetotaler," Mae says, looking around the bar.

"Your muse is no fun," I say. "Aren't they supposed to get a little wild so you can make great stuff?"

She laughs.

"Is that how it works?" she asks. "The muse comes, gets buck wild, and then you make art?"

"That's how mine works," I say. "She's a cowgirl, though. Drinks like a fish. Swears like a sailor. Tons of fun. But all she ever tells me to do is ride animals that try to throw me off."

I take a long swig of beer, and try to ignore the voice telling me to put a hand on Mae's shoulder while we talk. I don't think it's a muse, though.

"Maybe I ought to audition new ones," I say. "I bet I'd make a great cowboy poet."

Her flash goes off, and she looks down at the screen.

"Whoops, sorry," she says.

"You afraid I was going to start writing poetry right now?"

The flash goes off again, and this time Mae grins.

"I can take a hint," I say, humoring her. "No drinks, no poems, no fun. Come on, I'll introduce you around to the people whose pictures you're taking."

Mae shakes a good twenty or thirty hands: cowboys, wanna-be cowboys, buckle bunnies, the guys who handle the animals, even the veterinarian on call for the rodeo. The girl who was sitting next to me before is sitting next to Raylan now, but I don't really care. It's not like I knew her name.

Soon enough, a synthesizer starts up over the speakers and then Raylan's doing a drunk Johnny Cash impression, singing *Ring of Fire* and getting almost all the words wrong, even though he knows this song cold.

"Don't quit your day job!" someone shouts during a break in the song.

"I want my money back!" someone else shouts.

Raylan grins and flips them both off, and then Clay, another cowboy, jumps onto the stage and throws one arm around Raylan.

"We got this, y'all," he says into the microphone they're now sharing.

They don't got it. The singing gets worse, but the crowd loves it. Mae's sitting on one couch where Raylan was, laughing along and snapping photos. There's yet another girl sitting next to me, right across from Mae, and she's got her hand on my shoulder, her body up against mine.

All I can think about is a voice that whispered *Come on, Jackson*, into my ear six years ago.

I get hard instantly. The girl who's on me curls her body against mine just a little harder. *Fuck.* She thinks it's for her.

If I have a couple more drinks it could be.

I keep my eyes on the karaoke — they've moved onto Brooks & Dunn — and try not to think about Lula-Mae.

That song ends. Another one starts, and I get pulled onto the stage. Now there's six of us up here and we sing *Friends in Low Places*, and I'm shouting at the top of my voice, not even bothering to attempt the tune.

Midway through a girl comes bounding onto the stage and throws a fuzzy pink boa around my neck, and everyone laughs as I look at the thing, puzzled. Out in the bar, someone whistles loudly.

"Give us a dance, cowboy!" someone else shouts, so I pull it over my shoulders and shake back and forth for a moment.

Everyone goes nuts, and the girl who threw it comes back

on stage. She grabs either end of the boa and I let her pull me off with it, right past Mae.

Mae's snapping away, looking at the camera and not at me. Someone hands me a shot and I sniff it. Jack Daniels. I shoot it, and the girl pulling on the boa around my neck laughs drunkenly.

"Looks like I lassoed me a cowboy!" she shouts, still tugging.

"Ain't no lasso," someone says.

The girl rolls her eyes, but I'm already taking the boa off myself.

"You want to lasso you a cowboy," I say. "You got to have the right equipment first. Namely, a lasso."

I tie a lasso knot in the boa, looping it in on itself. It's the worst rope I've ever had the pleasure of using, but I manage, and then I try to work the thing.

Everyone laughs. A feather boa doesn't make for a very useful lasso. Someone grabs it from me, someone a little better at roping than me, and after a couple of tries he manages to land the lasso around an empty beer pitcher.

I sneak another glance at Mae, who's laughing along, still watching through the camera. The world's starting to feel a little unsteady, and then I realize I've been looking at her a little too long. I'm still looking, too drunk to drag my eyes away when my brain tells me to.

Finally she looks at me, her eyes so bright they almost glow in the dark, and as she holds my gaze something changes in her face, like she's thinking of a secret that the two of us have, alone, even in the middle of this crowd of people.

Come on, Jackson.

I guess we do have a secret.

The cowboy with the boa lasso manages to rope someone else's head. Another boa appears, and I'm wondering if there's a box somewhere in this bar full of weird costume props. Now Mae is standing and people are on the couch, two girls and a cowboy, all posing like they're in a photo booth.

Mae's being very obliging. I wonder if the pictures will turn out the way they think, and then a girl pulls me down onto the couch and I'm way, way too drunk to resist.

She grabs my hat from where it was sitting, puts it on herself, and then sits on my lap, a boa around my neck. Mae snaps the picture and the camera's in the way of her face, so I can't see it.

The girl kisses my cheek. *Snap.* She pulls my hand onto her ass and I squeeze, out of habit. *Snap.*

She takes off my hat and holds it in front of our faces.

"I bet these pictures are going to be so hot," she whispers.

"Yeah," I say, because I'm pretty sure I have to say something.

"You going home alone tonight, cowboy?" she asks me, her tequila breath hot on my ear.

It's getting a little stuffy here, behind my hat, but I'm on autopilot. I've got one hand on her ass and one on her thigh.

"You tell me," I say.

The girl kisses me on the mouth. Her lips are soft but almost flaccid, she's at a weird angle, and she's drunk. Her mouth is only half on mine when she pushes her tongue past my lips and giggles, the cowboy hat still covering our faces.

I try to kiss her back, but it's all teeth and tongue and tequila, so after a second I give up and turn my head away.

I push the hat down, but Mae's turned away, snapping photos of the other couch.

The girl over there's taken her shirt off and is just holding a cowboy hat in front of her tits and giggling. Mae just keeps taking pictures, a look of total concentration on her face. In a minute the girl is on her knees on the couch and Raylan's behind her, and she's making a face at the camera that I think she thinks is sexy.

"You wanna get out of here?" the girl on my lap purrs into my ear.

"It's still early," I say. "Give it some time."

She pouts, but my eyes slide past her and to Mae, who's perfectly sober, quietly snapping away.

I bet Mae's the only one who's going to remember most of this tomorrow, I think.

CHAPTER NINE

MAE

THIS WASN'T REALLY how it was supposed to go, but I'm rolling with it. Instead of quietly taking pictures from the background, somehow the pictures have become the main attraction.

Right now, there's a half-naked lady on a couch holding a cowboy hat over her chest. She's alternating between looking at the camera flirtatiously and trying to get her bra back from Raylan, who's holding it just out of her reach.

She's not trying that hard. Neither of them are, but it's a good diversion from Jackson, who's got a girl on his lap right now and keeps sloppily making out with her.

I don't mind. There's no version of reality in which I have a claim on him, and it's not like I didn't know what I was getting into by coming here.

That doesn't mean I have to *watch*.

"Ray*lan!*" the half-naked girl squeals, and lunges across his lap for her bra, her ass sticking into the air.

Raylan looks at the camera and grins, and I snap it.

"Okay, everybody," says a woman's voice behind me, and I turn. Everyone turns, and the crowd quiets a little.

It's a middle-aged woman, streaks of gray in her brown hair, stern face.

"This ain't a nudie establishment," she says, picking up two empty pitchers. "Ladies, please keep your clothes *on*, you got that?"

She stares hard at the half-naked girl. The half-naked girl actually blushes. I'd love to get a picture of them both, a wide-angle shot, but I'm not in a good spot for it. Crap.

"Sorry, Betty," the girl says, and everyone else mutters an apology too.

Betty grabs a few more empties and leaves. Amazingly, most of the cowboys there look slightly chastened, and I raise my eyebrows.

The half-naked girl takes her shirt and bra and slinks off to the bathroom. I take the chance to fade into the background again, lean against a wall, and just watch.

Karaoke kicks up again. The girl finally gets off of Jackson's lap and walks off somewhere else, and he stands and joins another karaoke group. None of them can carry a tune in a bucket, but everyone is so wasted that they hardly notice, or if they notice, they don't care.

I'm trying some shots with a slightly longer exposure, the camera kept still on a table, when one of the cowboys who isn't singing walks over to me. I think his name is... Clay, or Wyatt, or Trevor, or something else typical.

"You takin' pictures?" he asks, coming up behind me. His voice is slurred, and it makes his accent sound particularly thick.

"Actually, I'm a minion of Satan and I've been sent here with this soul-capturing device," I say. "If I can capture a hundred souls in one day, he'll give me a bonus. I'm saving up to buy a house in the nice part of Hell."

I click the shutter and hold my breath, giving the exposure an extra moment. Then I look over at Clay-Wyatt-Trevor, and he just blinks at me.

"What?" he says, his face a mask of confusion.

"Yes, I'm taking pictures," I say.

He frowns.

"You said something about Satan," he says.

"You must be hearing things," I say. "I'm a photographer for *Sports Weekly*, covering the rodeo."

I know I shouldn't mess with drunk people, but it's so tempting sometimes, especially when I'm the only sober one around.

"Right," he says, and gives his head a little shake, like he can knock his confusion out through an ear. "You like it?"

I turn away from the camera for a moment and look at him. He's young, probably college-aged, though I don't know if he's ever been to a college course.

Most of these guys haven't. Rodeo riders are young, because the younger they are, the more reckless, and the faster broken bones and punctured lungs heal.

Bull riding breaks people, and it breaks them fast. Most of the guys here are my age or younger, and it can be easy to forget.

"I like—" I start, but someone else swoops in and snatches my camera off the table, laughing wildly and running away.

"Hey!" I shout, and go after him, my heart squeezing in my chest.

He turns and looks at me. It's Jackson's friend Raylan, and he rushes off to a knot of young men.

"Cover me, y'all!" he says, and pushes between them.

I grind my teeth together, but I know better than to get outwardly upset. I know Raylan's type. I grew up with Raylan's type, and he never got much beyond pulling cute girls' pigtails just to get a reaction.

He's just gotten away with it for about ten years longer than he should have.

"I hope you got four thousand dollars if you break that," I call.

I force myself to walk, not run, to where he is. He's standing behind a couple other guys, his back turned.

The other guys look a little alarmed when I say *four thousand dollars*. It's not hard to push my way past them, and then I stand there, arms crossed.

"Give it back, Raylan," I say.

I just watched him play keep away with another girl's bra, and I'm not about to fall into the trap of looking like I'm enjoying this or flirting with him.

"Come get it," he says, and turns around.

I have a bad feeling that I know what he just did with my camera. Black flames of rage kindle in my chest, but I don't do anything. I know better than to seem upset.

Instead, I hold out one hand.

"This is my job," I say. "You break that one, I'm out on the street."

Now the other cowboys look *really* nervous. Raylan considers this, the humor draining from his face.

The karaoke song ends, and suddenly everyone's looking at our standoff.

"It's right here," he says, wiggling it a little.

My stomach lurches. If he drops the camera, I'm *screwed*. I'll probably have to go into Oklahoma City to get another one and put *that* on my credit card, and God only knows when I'll be able to pay it off — not to mention I'll lose a day of shooting.

From the corner of my eye, I see Jackson walk over. For a moment, I'm afraid that Raylan is going to toss the camera to him or something, and then Jackson's going to run somewhere with it.

It's like I'm on a playground. With children, except these children ought to know better by now.

The flames of anger grow.

"Give me the camera," I say, keeping my voice low and soft.

Raylan looks around at the other people, but they all look uneasy, and I think he realizes he's the only one still playing the game.

He hands it back, and I take it with both hands, holding it as tight as I can.

Then he smirks.

"Let me know if you see anything you like," he says.

Now I'm *certain* I know what he did with my camera. I turn it on, and after a second, the viewfinder screen lights up.

I scroll back one picture and I'm not thrilled to see I was right: there's a blurry, grainy photo of a flesh-toned tube sticking out of a pair of jeans.

Raylan's grinning, and I'm so mad I'm shaking.

They would never do this if I were a man, I think. I wouldn't have to play these stupid games. I wouldn't get hit on by the people I'm trying to photograph.

I could just do my job.

I know better than to show them how angry I really am, because that's just want these cocky, idiotic, amped-up manchildren want. Instead I cock my head slightly and frown, like I'm trying to figure out what it's a picture of.

"Is that your finger?" I finally say.

The other guys chuckle. Raylan's grin broadens, like he's trying to cover something.

"Ain't no finger," he says.

I squint.

"You sure?" I ask, and then extend one pinky, trying to match the angle of the penis in the picture.

The other guys laugh more, and Raylan starts to frown.

"You can just admit you like it, you know," he says. I think he's trying to sound cocky, but he just sounds sulky.

Now I laugh.

"It's not even that cold in here," I say, and now everyone's on my side here, and we're all laughing at Raylan, who's flustered and trying not to act it.

"That wasn't all the way out," he says, but no one's listening anymore.

I hit the delete button. I'm still nearly shaking with fury, but I feel like I've got a handle on the situation. I feel like I've won.

"Raylan, if I wanted pictures of small peckers, I'd photograph birds," I say. "Leave my camera alone from now on."

I turn and walk away, pretending that I've got something else pressing to do. Out of the corner of my eye, I can see Jackson go up to Raylan, but I step away before I can hear anything.

I pretend to take more pictures, but I'm barely paying attention. I'm still mad and slowly getting madder: mad that I have to put up with this bullshit, mad that I have to insult someone's penis in order to get my job done, mad that no one else seems to *mind*.

After about fifteen minutes, I give up. I grab my jacket and slip out of Betty's quietly, hoping that no one's noticed me leave. It's only eleven, but the whole rodeo crowd is beyond drunk, so I don't think anyone's paying attention.

I haven't even crossed the street before I hear someone shout my name. It sounds like Jackson, so I take a deep breath before I turn around, forcing my anger back down.

"Yes?" I say, all my muscles going stiff.

"You okay?" he asks.

He smells like beer and whiskey, and his eyes are a little loose in his head.

"Just tired," I say. I keep one hand firmly on my camera.

He jerks one thumb over his shoulder.

"Listen," he says. "I'm real sorry about Raylan, he's like this when he gets drunk but he don't mean anything by it. He was just having some fun with you, but I think you put an end to that."

I snort.

"Don't worry, I'm learning that apparently harassment is just part and parcel of this gig," I say, sarcasm slicing through my words.

Jackson looks drunkenly taken aback.

"Harassment?" he asks.

"Yeah, that's the word for when someone shows you their dick against your will," I say. "You need me to spell it?"

I take a deep breath, because I don't want to get into a fight with the guy I'm here to photograph. I know full well that he'll never think there's anything wrong with what Raylan did, just like he didn't think there's anything wrong with propositioning me for sex an hour after we met.

"Jackson, I just want to do my job," I say. "Not look at bad pictures of Raylan's junk. Not spend my time turning down your advances. Just my job."

We look at each other for a long moment, and for a second, I think I might be getting through to him.

Then he tucks his thumb into his belt and grins that swaggering, sexy grin that he has. For once, it doesn't work on me.

"So don't turn 'em down," he says.

I turn and walk across the street without even waiting for the light to change.

"Mae!" he shouts. "Mae, come on."

I get into the car without even looking back, drive back to the motel, and pretty much fall into bed. Of course Jackson completely missed the point, but what was I expecting? He spends all his time in a world where men are macho caricatures and women are buckle bunnies.

You could just leave and go back to New York, I think. Stop dealing with these immature jerks. Invent an emergency or something.

It's tempting, but there's no way I'll give up the best chance I've got at really *making* it.

Totally unbidden, I think of Jackson clinging to the gate of the bucking chute today, grinning up at me, rescued camera in his hand. I know full well that he was just showing off, but I can't help thinking he was showing off for *me*, and he risked his neck to do it.

As sleep pulls me under, I think: *I'd really like to stop wanting to have sex with Jackson Cody.*

CHAPTER TEN

JACKSON

THE NEXT DAY'S got a rough start. I wake up the minute the sunlight hits the cheap green curtains, just like always, even though it feels like a pair of gorillas are slugging it out in my head. I take a deep breath, sigh, and then look to the other side of the bed.

Empty.

I look at it for a long moment, even though my eyes feel like someone's taken a high-pressure fire hose to them, and I wait for the night before to piece itself together. We were at Betty's. There were shots and karaoke, and I know there was a girl sitting in my lap, asking me if I was going to take her home.

I close my eyes again and scoot over in the double bed, the cool sheets briefly making me feel better, and more comes back.

Mae taking photos. Some girl with her shirt off, Betty coming over and putting a stop to that. More karaoke, and then Mae giving Raylan a dressing-down for some dumbass thing he did.

The sidewalk. Mae telling me she just wants to do her

job, her leaving, me going back inside where I did another shot of Jack.

I pull a pillow over my face, remembering what happened next: getting in Raylan's face, both of us drunk as hell. I think I shouted something about dick harassment and he shouted something about a bitch who couldn't take a joke, and then we got pulled apart.

There's flashes of me making out with some girl in the bathroom, then flashes of getting a ride back to the motel from the rodeo veterinarian, who kept asking if I was gonna puke in his car.

I didn't. I think.

I came home alone and crashed, and now I'm here, paying for it.

"Goddamn," I mutter, and push myself out of bed.

· · · * ★ ★ ★ ★ ★ · · ·

EVERYONE'S HURTING TODAY. Everyone except Mae, who didn't drink a thing, and seems refreshed and spry as a spring chicken.

I pull myself together with about ten cups of coffee and a pound of bacon, then grab one more cup and stand around the arena, watching the ropers practice on each other. The rodeo proper doesn't start until two in the afternoon, so until then there's nothing to do besides wander around, breathing in the tense air.

Bull riding doesn't start tonight. It starts tomorrow night and goes for three nights. By the end of the third, someone's the champion.

My pulse pounds, just thinking about it. The head rush, the pure force of nature, the feeling when you leap off after eight seconds and the crowd roars.

There ain't nothing like it in the whole world.

After about an hour, I see Bruce and Mae making their way around the arena. There's still thirty minutes before the rodeo opens again, so people are trickling into the stands but most are still hanging around the fair, riding the Ferris wheel or buying knickknacks in the old west town they've got set up.

I realize that the two of them are walking over to me, so I stand up a little straighter, try not to look so hungover. I'm sure Mae can see right through it, but maybe Bruce won't know.

"Jackson," Bruce says.

"Howdy," I say.

"Do you have a minute to walk through the stable and talk bulls?" he asks. "I wanted to get your take on them."

"I could talk bulls all day," I say, and smile at the two of them.

Bruce just nods and writes something down, but Mae looks at me with an undecipherable look on her face. Like she's made of iron. But for once, she's not taking my picture, and I'm grateful because my hungover mug doesn't need a place in Sports Weekly.

The stables aren't far, and as we walk I ramble on about the bulls: where each of these guys are from, who their sires are, who they've bucked off so far this year. Bruce takes notes and Mae just follows along, not saying anything.

I talk more so I don't look at her too much.

Inside the stables, I ramble more. I walk them down the center aisle and name each bull to them: Screaming Heat, Twist and Shout, Muscle Grunt, Bank Robbery, Hopalong, Mr. Torque, and Crash Junction.

"Screaming Heat's a kitten," I say, looking at the big, ugly white bull. He snorts. "Twist and Shout ain't bad, but when I rode him in Laredo I really had to spur him to get much enthusiasm. Muscle Grunt and Hopalong I ain't rode, but I've heard they're about average. Good days, bad days."

"Which one are you hoping for in the draw?" Bruce asks.

I nod my head down the barn and they follow me to stand in front of a stall. Inside's a big, ugly, brown bull with bloodshot eyes. He glares out at us, and I take a step forward.

Bruce and Mae don't, though I hear her snap a picture.

"This is Train Robbery, my second choice," I say. "He's scored the highest average for all the rodeos he's been in. Kicks like a motherfucker, goes buck wild right out the gate. Unseats most riders, but earns good scores for the ones who stay on."

Train Robbery barely moves, just blinks at Bruce and Mae. They both look back.

"He don't look like much now, but just wait until he's in the arena," I say, gazing at the big, placid animal. "He's gentle as a lamb in the chute, but the second that gate opens? Watch out."

Mae takes a picture, then frowns at her camera. Bruce makes a note.

"That makes Crash Junction your top choice?" he asks.

I can't help but grin.

"Yessir, it does," I say.

I cross the aisle to another stall, this one with a big white bull in it. The bull glares at me, and I wink at him, just for fun.

"This here is Crash Junction," I say. "And he's zero for, what is it now, fifty?"

"Fifty-two," Bruce says.

Mae raises her eyebrows.

"Nobody's stayed on the full eight seconds?" she asks.

"No ma'am," I say, but she's looking at Crash Junction

again. "He's got a front end drop like a freight train, a tight spin, and he switches directions on a dime."

Crash Junction snorts again.

"Riders just fly right off of him," I say. "Most riders, anyway. Ain't that right, buddy?"

I hear the camera click again, and Crash Junction swings his head around to look me dead in the eyes. Bulls aren't very smart, but I'd swear that this one knows what we're saying about him, and he wants me to try riding him just as bad as I do.

Riding Crash Junction is dicey as hell. No one's ever stayed on him for the full eight seconds, which means no one's ever scored many points from riding him.

After that eight-second mark, there's a total of one hundred points for the taking: fifty based on how well the rider rides, and fifty based on how hard the bull makes the ride. The tougher the bull, the higher the score.

Anyone who can stay on Crash Junction for the full eight seconds and doesn't fuck up his other rides is practically guaranteed to win Pioneer Days.

I want it to be me so bad I can taste it.

"And you think you can ride him?" Bruce asks.

"I *know* I can ride him," I say. "The second I get on him, he's met his match. Nobody bucks like Crash here, but nobody rides like me."

It's not bragging if it's true.

"What's your strategy?" Bruce asks.

"Stay on," I say.

He raises his eyebrows, but I just shrug.

"It's all practice," I say. "Ride until the body knows exactly what it's doing, because out there, with the clock going and the crowd shouting, you can't think of a single thing besides *stay on.*"

I glance at Mae, and she's staring at me instead of the camera for once. We lock eyes, and after a moment, she lowers her gaze and my heartbeat speeds up a little.

"Which one of these was sired by Kill Switch?" Bruce asks, and I point down the stables to Hopalong, who isn't quite as good as his daddy was.

The three of us drift that way. Bruce asks a couple more questions, and we chat for a bit until he looks at his watch.

"Rodeo starts in ten minutes, and I've got a few things I'd like to ask the veterinarian," he says, and holds out his hand. I shake it.

"See you back out there," I say.

"I'm going to take a few more shots," Mae says. "The light in here is tricky."

Bruce walks away. We both watch him go and then look at each other. I feel like her sky blue eyes are piercing right through my skull and into my brain, wreaking havoc.

Being around Mae makes something deep and primal come alive inside me. When she's around, I feel like a caveman. I want to pick up giant rocks and throw them just so she can see. I want to wrestle saber tooth tigers to keep her safe, and then I want to take her home and make her *mine*.

I want to hear her shout my name.

Fuck, just the thought is getting me hard again.

"Last night—" I start.

"Don't," Mae says, holding up one hand.

We're silent for a moment, the bulls and horses making faint noises all around us.

Mae points back where we were.

"Stand back where you were, by Crash, and look at him."

I do as she says.

"Tilt your hat back so I can see your face," she says.

I make a clicking noise at Crash Junction and he swings his head my way again, his eyes on me.

No one says anything for a long time, until I finally speak up.

"I was going to apologize," I say, still looking at the bull.

She doesn't answer right away.

"You were?" Mae asks, her voice a little flat.

I push forward.

"Yeah. For trying to get into your pants," I say.

No response. The shutter clicks.

"And for interfering with your work," I say. "I'd be bothered as hell if some asshole kept dogging me."

Click. Click. Click.

"If you get closer, is he gonna hurt you?" she asks.

I look at Crash. He might try.

I step forward so we're almost face-to-face, his horns on either side of my head.

"You don't have to get that close," Mae says, moving to one side and snapping away furiously.

"He's good right now," I say. "Besides, what kind of cowboy would I be if I were afraid of some bull in the stable?"

I reach out and grab his horn with my right hand, looking right into his eyes. Between Mae right there and this animal in front of me, my veins are buzzing with electricity. I feel like I might jump out of my skin at any second, but I stand still while Mae gets her shot.

At last, she lowers her camera.

"Okay, you're making me nervous," she says.

I take a step away from Crash Junction. The stables are empty except for the two of us, our voices swallowed by wood and hay and the soft snorting of the animals.

"Thanks for the apology," she finally says. "Raylan won't

even look at me. Is that just because I told everyone he's got a small penis, or did something else happen?"

"I talked to him after you left," I say.

"You talked," she says.

"We exchanged words," I say. "You handled him better than I did."

"I've known plenty of country-fried assholes just like him," she says, then looks at me. "Sorry."

I laugh.

"Sounds like a menu item at Golden Corral," I say. "I didn't know you cursed, Miss Guthrie."

She lets that one pass.

"I curse when it's called for," she says, putting the lens cap on her camera and slinging it back over her shoulder. "Don't worry, I know all the bad words."

"You never did tell me where you're from," I say, still pretending I don't know.

"Brooklyn," she says.

"Not where you live now," I say. "Where you're *from*. Where you grew up. You didn't get that twang in Brooklyn."

Mae makes a face, scrunching her nose and looking away, and it's so cute I smile at her.

"You can hear it?" she asks.

"Sure can."

She sighs.

"I grew up in West Texas," she says. "The accent is gone most of the time, but get me around a bunch of cowboys and it comes back full force. Next thing I know I sound like I'm driving a rusted-out pickup truck with a shotgun in my lap and a dog in the back."

I whistle.

"That's pretty serious," I say. "You're not so bad as all that just yet. Just the pickup."

"I'll have the gun and the dog by the time the rodeo's over," she says.

We look at each other for a long moment, alone with the animals. I have to fight the urge to grab her and kiss her, to run my hands down her body.

"We should get," she says after a minute. Then she turns and walks out.

We walk back out of the stables and meet Bruce, then head to the arena and they split off. I spend the afternoon pretending to watch cowboys rope steers, but really, I'm watching Mae at the edge of the arena no matter how hard I try to stop.

I should stay away. I know it, but I can't. We're working together, for one thing. I'm going to be seeing plenty of her for the next three days at least, so we might as well be cordial.

Across the arena, a cowboy comes up to her and says something. I think it's Clay. She listens for a moment, then smiles politely and nods, and he walks off. I wish I knew what he'd said, but it's probably none of my business.

When it's over, I walk to the motel aimlessly, wanting to watch TV or something to get my mind off everything. The longer I'm around her, the more I can't help but remember those few minutes in the back of my truck, Mae straddling me, her hips moving—

Fuck, I'm hard again. It's getting to be a permanent condition these days, an itch that nothing else is gonna scratch.

There's your problem, I think. You've got to be forthright. Tell her you remember.

Start over from the beginning.

It's an idea, but I don't know if it's a good one. Maybe Mae doesn't want to remember and I should just pretend that we met yesterday.

I don't know how much longer I can pussyfoot around this, though.

Take the bull by the horns, Jackson.

Ain't that what you do?

I pull out my truck keys. Then I drive to the nearest liquor store to see if I can't find some peach-flavored Boone's Farm.

CHAPTER ELEVEN

MAE

OPERATION *STOP WANTING to sleep with Jackson* is not going well.

When I woke up this morning, between finally getting enough sleep and giving myself a pep talk, I thought I was almost there. Just because he's hot and has *that* smile doesn't mean I have to actually want to sleep with him.

I started my day with a new goal: appreciate Jackson Cody from afar. Yes, he's very pleasing to look at, so why ruin it by torturing myself with something I can't have?

It lasted about two hours. Then he apologized and took the bull by the horns — literally — and I failed miserably at appreciating from afar, because there's something raw and primitive about a man who's *that* confident, that unafraid of a challenge.

The worst part of all might be that I broke my vibrator a month ago, and I still don't have a new one.

After the stables, he stands across the arena and watches the ropers while I shoot them, and then after the rodeo he disappears.

That's a good thing, I tell myself. *He's probably off*

drinking with his buddies again, getting some buckle bunny tail.

I force myself to remember the night before, that girl on his lap, making out with him sloppily.

See? I think. *Ew.*

Bruce and I have dinner, and then I head back to my room and load the day's pictures onto my laptop and dive in.

Just as I get to the series of Jackson and the bull, shot in the low light of the stables, there's a knock on my door, even though it's almost nine at night. Probably Bruce. I rub my eyes, getting sore from a whole day of looking at things, and walk to my door.

Jackson Cody is standing there, smiling down at me. My heart bangs against my ribcage, because no man has a right to look this good in just a work shirt, jeans, and boots.

"Evenin'," he says, and holds up a bottle of wine wrapped in a paper bag, the two flimsy plastic cups from his own motel room balanced upside-down on top of it.

"I don't even drink," I say, looking at the bottle. It's the first thing I think of.

As much as that deep, needy part of me wants to invite him in, I can't. Nobody can see Jackson Cody going into my motel room. It's *extraordinarily* bad form to sleep with the people you're hired to shoot, especially when the whole article is focused on them.

He looks down at the bottle.

"Whoops," he says, and pulls the bag off, crumpling it in his other hand.

It's a bottle of peach-flavored Boone's Farm Wine Drink. They changed the packaging, but as soon as I read it, my heart lurches.

I look from the bottle to Jackson, then back at the bottle.

"What the hell?" I finally ask, my voice a whisper.

"I want to start over," he says.

I cross my arms and glare.

"Not like that," he says. "I just want to talk. Clear the air, get both of us on the same page."

I'm just staring at the bottle of wine.

"When did you remember?" I ask, my voice low.

"The moment you opened your mouth," he says.

"You remembered this *whole time?*" I hiss.

A car pulls into the parking lot behind him, its headlights washing over us for a quick moment.

"Lula-Mae, I just want to talk. I swear," he says.

"You can't come in," I say. "Everyone will know, and then they'll talk. And don't call me that."

"Can we talk somewhere else?" he asks.

I take a deep breath. He's probably right. We'll just get everything out in the open, and then I can go back to pretending I don't want to sleep with him.

"Okay," I say.

"You know the west gate to the arena?" he asks.

I nod.

"Meet me there in five minutes," he says. "Give me a head start."

He walks away and I close the door to my motel room, and then I just stand there for a minute, reevaluating everything that's happened in the last two days.

When he shook my hand at the breakfast table, he knew who I was. When he hit on me afterward, when he rescued my camera, when he invited me out drinking.

He remembered me, drunk and horny in the back of his pickup, the *whole* time.

I put on shoes and grab a jacket. I close my laptop and put my camera in its case, even though it feels weird not to take it with me.

After exactly five minutes, I walk toward the arena. I try to look like I'm on official photography business, but I don't know if anyone cares or not. Probably not. It's dark out there except for the occasional street light. The sky is full of stars even though the carnival is in the lot next door.

I round a corner and see a shape standing up against the gate. The shape's holding a bottle of wine.

"Ready to break some rules?" Jackson asks, a smile in his voice.

I open my mouth, but he cuts me off.

"If we get caught, I'll say it was my idea to show you some good angles of the arena," he says. "I'll take all the blame."

I exhale and shrug, suddenly nervous. Jackson walks to the right and disappears behind the bleachers, walking to a gate locked with a combination lock. He enters three numbers and the lock clicks open.

"They don't change the locks too often," he says, and opens the gate, letting me through first.

I'm still on high alert, and I'm a thousand percent aware that I shouldn't be here, doing this, *alone* with Jackson Cody. But I'm also not about to back out now.

Just don't get caught, I think. *That's all.*

It's dark under the bleachers, and I follow his silhouette out, around the grandstands. We climb to the very top of the metal bleachers, in front of the press box, and then sit down and lean against the structure. Jackson sets the plastic cups on the metal bench in front of it and twists the top off the wine drink.

"You want any?" he asks, pouring himself a few fingers.

I sigh.

Why the hell not? You're already here.

"Just a sip," I say.

He pours me half an inch, and we raise our glasses, touch them together, and I take a drink.

It tastes like a Jolly Rancher, but worse and alcoholic.

"Oh *god*," I say, covering my mouth with one hand. "Wow."

Jackson's also making a face and shaking his head.

"Lord have mercy, this is bad," he says.

"How did I ever drink a whole bottle of that stuff?" I ask, scrutinizing the tiny bit in my glass. "It's awful."

"You're not the first eighteen year old to get tanked on this," he says. "That's more or less what they make it for."

I laugh, even as my chest tightens. I take a deep breath and steady myself.

"So six years ago I got really drunk at a party and we... met," I say.

"That's a fair summary," he says. "We were teenagers then and we're older and wiser now."

"We snuck into the grandstands and we're drinking *this*," I say. "I think we're just older."

I turn the plastic cup in my fingers, nervous about what I'm going to ask next.

"Did you tell anyone?" I ask quietly. I can't look at him, only at the sandy arena below.

"Not anybody here," he says. "I bragged some back then. But I didn't think you wanted anyone here knowing that about you."

"I didn't," I say, and I sigh with relief. "Thanks."

There's a moment of silence.

"I didn't tell anyone either, for the record," I say.

"I wouldn't have minded," Jackson says. He's leaning back against the wooden press box, and he turns his head toward me. "It'd make everyone else jealous as hell if they knew I'd gotten with the hot photographer."

I blush, glad he can't see it in the dark.

"It's not like any of you are wanting for company," I say.

"Men like a challenge," he says. "After a little while, girls who fall into your lap are a little too easy. Most of the time. Present company excepted."

I laugh.

"I was really drunk," I say. The scent of the wine is making me feel like I'm back there again, breathless and horny and completely inexperienced.

"I did notice that," he says.

"I'd just graduated high school," I say, and I lean back against the press box, feet on the metal bench in front of me as I look down the dark stands into the even darker arena.

"Would you believe that was the first real party I went to?"

"I would absolutely believe that," he says, keeping his face straight.

"Oh, come on," I say. "Was it that obvious?"

"You didn't seem like you'd had a lot of experience," he says, a little more tactfully this time. "You got a little excited when the police showed up."

I cover my face with my hands, mortified.

"I'd forgotten that part in my embarrassment about all the rest," I say, my voice slightly muffled. "God, I was not very cool about that."

"Nope," Jackson says.

I take my hands off my face and lean forward, my plastic cup on the bench next to me. I look past the arena and out to the parking lot, cars shining in the mercury vapor lights.

"I really thought I'd almost ruined my life," I say, my voice low.

"Because you were at a party that got busted?"

I shake my head.

"Because I lost control," I say. "I got plastered and nearly had unprotected sex with someone I didn't even know."

I swallow. Jackson's quiet.

"You remember the girl I was there with? Christy?"

"She went off with Buck?" he asks.

I nod.

"She's my age. Twenty-four. And she's got three kids with three different dads. She works at Wal-Mart and lives with her parents."

I take a deep breath.

"And there's nothing *wrong* with all that. She loves her kids, but it's not what I want. It's never been what I wanted, but after that night, I realized how easy it could be to wind up like that and never get out of Lawton."

Tears are pricking behind my eyeballs. I've never said this out loud to anyone before, because there's no one else who knows what happened, or what almost happened.

Jackson leans forward, his elbows on his knees, and he looks at me as I desperately fight my tears.

"Lula-Mae, there's not a person in this world who hasn't screwed up a couple of times," he says.

"I know," I say, my voice nearly a whisper. "I just hate how I could have ruined everything."

"You turned out just fine," he says.

"Thanks," I say.

He's quiet for a long time as we both look forward, down the stands.

"If it helps, I probably wasn't gonna let you ride bare-back," he says.

I flush bright red.

"Probably?" I ask.

"You made a pretty convincing case," he says.

"I did?" I ask. I don't remember making a case at all.

"Sure," he says, then looks at me and grins. "You were hot and ready to go and I was nineteen and prone to bad decisions."

"Oh," I say.

He shrugs.

"But you seemed like a good girl who got a little crazy for one night. Hell, you'd never given a hand job before. I had the feeling you wouldn't want to swipe your v-card on some guy in the back of a pickup truck."

I squeeze my eyes shut.

"Can I tell you something?" I ask.

"Of course," he says.

"That was the first time I saw a dick in person," I say.

Jackson laughs, and after a moment, I do too.

"I had some suspicions," he says.

"I made out with some guys in high school, but that was it," I say. "I had no idea what I was doing."

"Enthusiasm counts for a lot," he says. "Especially with nineteen year olds."

I pick up the peach wine and take the last swallow, then grimace.

"This is *really* bad," I say.

"So you're not getting drunk again?" he teases.

"I've had about two tablespoons and I think I might puke," I say.

"Try to make it down to ground level first," he says. "Don't want anyone knowing we were up here."

A thrill runs through me, as I'm reminded: *I'm sneaking around with Jackson.*

We're already here. If we get caught, whoever catches us will already assume the worst.

He's right next to me, and we're both leaning against the

press box at the top of the stands, the whole arena spread before us. My pulse is pounding through my veins, and somehow, we've closed the distance between us from a foot to an inch, and we're sitting here laughing about the past like old friends.

"I come up here the night before my first ride every year," Jackson says.

"With girls?" I ask. Then I bite my tongue.

"Alone," he says. "It helps me get my nerves under control if I can see the place empty and quiet. It seems smaller now than it does when there's people in it. That way, when I get on that bull tomorrow inside the chute, in the second before he goes, I imagine it's empty, just me and him, and I don't have to worry about anything else."

"You still get nervous?" I ask.

"Every single time," he says. "I get nervous, and then I get on that bull, and I just ride."

Even here, talking quietly in the stands, there's a soft swagger in his voice, a cockiness that *does* something to me.

"I could never do it," I say.

"I did offer to teach you," he says.

"You were just hitting on me," I say, teasing him. "Telling some wide-eyed girl that she ought to try rodeo."

He pauses.

"I was kinda hoping you'd show up that weekend," he says. "I didn't think you would, but I kept on picking out blond heads in the crowd."

"I think I stayed home and organized my report cards by letter grade," I say.

"I won it, you know," he says, and then he turns his head toward me.

My heartbeat speeds up, and I can feel the warmth rolling off of his body. I stare rigidly straight ahead, eyes locked on the arena below. My self-control is hanging on by a thread.

"You win a lot," I say.

"I just pictured you in the stands," he says.

My palms get sweaty.

"Lula-Mae," he says.

I take a deep breath and turn to look up at him, his hazel eyes glimmering in the dark, serious and searching me.

"My first ride is tomorrow," he says.

"I'll be in the stands this time," I say, my voice barely above a whisper.

He takes my chin in his hand.

"I know I promised," he says. "But just give me one kiss for good luck, Lula-Mae."

"One," I say, even though I know it's a lie, and I'm about to embark on something reckless and stupid.

He locks eyes with me for a moment. I hold my breath and think *this is my last chance to leave*, but I know there's no way I'm leaving. I'm sunk. I'm finished.

Then Jackson presses his lips to mine. They're warm and a little rough, and a shower of sparks washes over me, a shiver running down my spine.

His hand moves from my chin to my shoulder and then to my back, and I press myself into him, my fingers in his hair.

Jackson pulls back a little, just enough to look at me as we're both breathing hard.

"That was one," he whispers.

"Feeling lucky enough yet?" I ask.

"Not quite," he says, and draws me back to him.

CHAPTER TWELVE

JACKSON

I PRESS my lips to Mae's again and her fingers curl in my hair, like she's trying to pull me in against her. My heart's going like a jackhammer and I have the wild urge to push her back and lay her down on this cold metal bench, but I force myself to slow down, to savor every second of this.

Slowly, I open my mouth against hers and slide my tongue against her bottom lip. She hesitates for a moment and then deepens the kiss, her tongue against mine as her body presses into me.

I've got one hand on her hip, clutching it through her jeans, the other on her back and I can feel her muscles work as she leans into me hungrily, her mouth against mine. She pulls back and bites my lower lip, and it sends a shock of desire through me, though I'm already rock hard.

Mae looks at me with those blue eyes, dark with lust, and she finds the top button on my shirt with one finger, hooking it over the top. She's breathing hard and she locks her gaze onto mine. It takes every ounce of self-control I've got not to pick her up and push her against the wall of the press box.

I want to taste her and make her moan. I want to hear her say my name while I'm buried in her.

"This is a bad idea, Jackson," she whispers.

"Then stop," I whisper back.

I bend and kiss her neck, her heartbeat racing beneath my lips, and she sighs. The first button of my shirt pops open, and I grab her hand in mine, squeezing it.

"I thought this was a bad idea," I murmur into her collarbone.

Suddenly, the lights go on in the arena below, and we both freeze. She's half on my lap and my head is in the curve between her neck and shoulder as she pants for breath.

It's still dark in the stands, but two men walk into the sandy ring below. Quietly, slowly, Mae slides off of me, her eyes wide in the darkness. She runs one hand through her hair, and then she stands.

I grab her hand.

"Wait," I whisper. "They can't see into the stands when the lights are on, but if you leave, they'll see you."

Mae just nods, and I give her a long look.

She's got more riding on this than me. If I get caught, Darlene gets mad, and *Sports Weekly* calls me some names. I'll live. As long as I can keep riding, I'll live.

Mae, on the other hand, has everything to lose. If *Sports Weekly* thinks she's sleeping with me, they could pull her from the assignment. They'd never hire her again, and every other magazine would know why.

"I'll get them outta here," I whisper to her. "Sneak back out the way we came once we're gone."

I squeeze her hand and then rush down the stands before she can protest. Both men look up. I recognize one as Wayne, and the other as Travis, one of the other organizers.

Wayne frowns.

"Jackson, what are you doing here? This is closed off."

I smile and saunter down the last few steps, even though my pulse is racing.

"Sorry," I say. "I come here sometimes to get away from everything and think."

Travis looks me over head to toe, then shrugs. Wayne looks annoyed, but not like he's all that upset.

"We were just checking that the barriers are all up to code," he says. "You remember that incident in Tulsa a few years ago. Better safe than sorry."

A barrier failed when a bull knocked into it, and a kid on the other side broke his leg. His parents sued the Tulsa Fair and won a lot of money.

"They looked pretty solid today," I say.

They both nod, but Wayne still looks worried. I realize again how seriously he takes this, and how badly he wants Pioneer Days Rodeo to make the leap to the big time. How much he wants ESPN and SportsCenter to care about rodeo.

If he found out I was just canoodling with the photographer and making his chances at all that worse, he might kill me.

"I'll help you two check," I say.

We split off the arena into thirds, and I walk my third, shaking and kicking and rattling the barrier the best I can. I'm not worried about that. I know that under his Good Old Country Boy demeanor, Wayne's ferociously driven and detail-oriented, not the kind of guy who'd let something like this slip.

Every thirty seconds, I glance up at the stands. I can't see a thing, but I can't get my mind off of her, up there, watching me. It feels like tiny sparks are skipping along my nerves, and I'm all keyed up. I want to get out of there so Mae can leave, because if I'm nervous, she must be dying.

Finally we meet in the middle of the arena.

"I do believe we're good," Travis says, his hands on his hips, his belly just sticking out past his belt buckle.

Wayne nods.

"Thanks for indulging me," he says. Then he looks at me. "You too, Jackson."

"I've got a vested interest in not plowing through a barrier," I say.

"You feeling good about tomorrow?" he asks.

My eyes flick up to the stands, where I know Mae's watching us.

"Yessir," I say.

"When's the bull drawing?" asks Travis.

"Twelve-fifteen tomorrow," Wayne answers before I can.

Each rider gets assigned a bull by lottery, so I can only hope for the roughest bulls. If I get a cupcake like Screaming Heat, it's harder to win.

"You hoping for Crash?" Travis asks.

"You know it," I say. "Go big or go home."

Travis just shakes his head. He used to ride — most of the organizers did — so he knows what I'm hoping to get myself into.

"Good luck, son," he says. "You're gonna need it."

We leave the arena, and I go out last. Just before I leave, I look at the stands one more time, give Mae a thumbs up, then hit the light switch. The arena goes dark again.

· · · · · · ★ ★ ★ ★ · · · · ·

PIONEER DAYS HAS a couple attractions besides the rodeo. One is the carnival, which runs all day and into the night. It's got all the usual rides, games, and attractions: you can eat funnel cake and then spin around on the Scrambler until you puke, then try to toss rings onto a bottle and win a giant stuffed bear.

It's got a fair, with prize-winning pies, tomatoes, chickens. All that 4H stuff.

And it's got Wild West Town. I don't know where they get this stuff, but it's about two blocks of fake wooden storefronts, hitching posts, saloon doors, and all. Every day at noon they act out a gunfight. People eat it up.

The bull riding lottery is right after the gunfight. I guess they did it that way to get a crowd, but it just means that I have to stand around in a crowd of tourists while two actors point fake guns at each other.

I keep looking through the crowd for Mae, because this seems like the kind of thing she'd photograph, but maybe not. I just want to know she snuck out okay and didn't get caught.

That's the worst reason for her not to be here: Bruce found out she'd snuck off with me, told her bosses, and they pulled her from the job. I tell myself that can't possibly have happened.

There's some plot to the gunfight — someone's the Sheriff, someone's the outlaw, there's a twist in the middle when a woman comes in and hollers at them to stop — but I'm not paying attention until it's over and someone's lying in the street, pretending to be dead.

"All right!" an announcer says, his deep voice booming over the PA. "If y'all could just step into the Gold Strike Amphitheater over here, we'll be doing the bull selection right now."

I head over, trying to look casual. Before I know it, Raylan's fallen in next to me, and he nods. I nod back.

"Who you hoping for?" he asks.

"You know who," I say.

Raylan laughs.

"Of course you are," he says. "I'm going light. Got my fingers crossed for Train Robbery. If I can get above a seventy average, I make the finals."

I don't *need* to ride Crash Junction to make the finals, but I *want* to. He's the biggest and the baddest, and I want to conquer him. It's that simple.

"I think you got this in the bag," I tell Raylan. "Me and you are gonna be sipping whiskey in the high-stakes poker room this time next month."

He laughs.

"So I can lose all my money the minute I make it?" he asks. "You know what my father always said? 'Son, the best way to double your money is to fold it in half and put it in your back pocket.'"

"Smart man," I say.

It's like the other night never happened. That's how our friendship goes: sometimes we have to rough each other up a little, but it's the nature of the beast. Can't be around someone too long without wanting to do that.

"I ought to listen to him sometimes," Raylan says, and then Wayne's on the wooden stage, getting everyone's attention.

Raylan and I are standing in the back. Up front, they bring out a bulletin board on wheels and a folding tables three boxes with holes cut in the top. The bulletin has the bull riders' names in a line down the left, with three slots to the right of each.

Pioneer Days isn't exactly a high-tech enterprise.

"Ladies and gentlemen, now begins the bull selection for Pioneer Days bull riding!" Wayne says, trying to stir up as much enthusiasm as he can. He gets polite applause.

"Well, what do you say we get this started?" he asks rhetorically.

Across the amphitheater, I see Bruce walk in. Mae follows a second later, and my heart does a flip in my chest.

At the very least, she got back to the motel without getting caught. Her eyes rake the crowd, and when they find me, we look at each other for a long moment before she looks away.

"Day one," Wayne says. "First cowboy is Trevor Anderson, and he'll be riding..."

Wayne reaches into the cardboard box and swishes his hand around.

"...Muscle Grunt!"

He pins a piece of paper that says MUSCLE GRUNT onto the board next to Trevor's name and moves on to the next one. I'm a ways down the list, but I pay attention anyway. Someone else gets Crash Junction, but then Wayne calls out my name.

"Jackson Cody," he says, dramatically swishing his hand in the box again. "...Train Robbery!"

I nod, but on the inside I'm pumped. Train Robbery's good, and besides, I don't want to ride Crash Junction first and get all tuckered out for the next two days. I'd rather save the best for last.

On day two, I get Mr. Torque, who's okay but nothing special. I might have to lean into him some with the spurs to really get his blood up, but that's okay.

I'm being optimistic, of course. The very best riders get thrown more often than not, and I know it's more than likely that either Train Robbery or Mr. Torque is gonna get the best of me. I just get up and get back on the next day.

The bull selection for day three feels like it takes about a year. Time crawls at a snail's pace, and with every name they call, I'm afraid that Crash Junction's gonna go to someone else and I won't get my chance.

That is, right up until Wayne calls my name. He reaches into the box and looks at the slip of paper for a moment before looking up and right at me.

"...Crash Junction!" he says.

I let out a whoop, and next to me, Raylan laughs.

"Never seen someone so excited to get his ass handed to him," he says.

"Just you wait," I say, grinning as Wayne pins Crash Junction next to my name on the board for day three.

On the other side of the small amphitheater, I see a camera move. As she lowers it, Mae smiles at me for half a second, and then looks away.

I crack my knuckles, the adrenaline already spiking through me the way it always does. There's five hours until the rodeo starts and I ride Train Robbery, Mae watching.

Bring it the fuck *on*. I got this.

· · · ★ ★ ★ ★ ★ · · ·

THE HOURS CRAWL BY, then fly, then crawl again. It feels like a high schooler sings the National Anthem for two hours, but the first block of bull riding is over in thirty seconds. I watch as much of it as I can, hanging over the barriers, looking at how each bull moves and kicks and spins, judging how each rider handles them. It's good practice to always watch the competition.

Across the arena in a gated-off press area are Mae and Bruce. She's snapping away, talking to him, and he's taking notes. I keep thinking that she's looking over at me, but it could be my imagination. Even as I'm watching, I can't get that kiss out of my mind. Her hands in my hair. The feel of her heartbeat underneath my lips when I kissed her neck.

Then there's just a couple of rides until it's my turn, so I jump down to get ready. I put on the protective vest that keeps me from getting gored. I've got my glove and my chaps and my hat, and then I'm just hanging around the bull pens, jumping out of my skin from nerves.

I watch another cowboy get on his bull, wrap the rope around his hand. He nods and the gate man swings the gate outward and the bull launches himself out of it, kicking and bucking and spinning. The cowboy's off in six seconds and he lands in the dirt and rolls.

The rodeo clowns come in and chase the bull toward the exit chute. Once the rider's off, the bulls are more easygoing, and this one trots to the exit chute without causing any trouble.

The cowboy stands up, grabs a gate, and climbs over, and then it's my turn.

I've done this a thousand times, but it's impossible not to feel like my whole body's on fire with anticipation and nerves. Eight seconds isn't long, but it's long enough.

I jump onto Train Robbery's back, and even in the confined space of the bucking chute, he's not happy about it. The handlers hold him steady for a moment while I get situated, wrap the bull rope around my gloved hand, and take a deep breath.

In that last moment, I find the blond head above the camera, and I smile at Mae.

Then I nod at the gate man. He opens the chute, and Train Robbery flies out.

CHAPTER THIRTEEN

MAE

WHEN I WATCH BULL RIDING, I feel like I'm watching a horror movie. Roping events aren't that bad: some men ride horses, tie up cows, and then let them go. That I can handle, no problem.

But bull riding? I want to watch through my fingers. Every time someone falls off, I gasp despite myself.

Even when a rider can stay on for the full eight seconds, there's no graceful dismount from a bull. It's not like the bull stops and someone comes up to it with a stepladder.

The rider still has to jump off a bucking bull and land in the sand. Every time someone gets up, I take a deep breath of relief, because right now all I want is to not watch someone die today.

Of course, I'm the one person in this arena who can't close her eyes. I photograph rider after rider, cringing every single time. Even the rides that go *well* look painful.

Then the announcer calls Jackson's name, and I start to sweat. Next to me, Bruce leans forward onto the barrier, and I look down into the viewfinder of my tripod-mounted camera.

Jackson jumps onto the bull he drew — Train Robbery — and even in the chute, the bull's not happy about it. My heart thumps in my chest and my mouth goes dry.

He'll be fine, I think. *This is what he does.*

I watch him situate himself as the crowd cheers. There's a knot of women down in the front of the stands holding up signs and screaming for him, and I grit my teeth and ignore them, but the sound of cheering and screaming and people stomping in the metal stands is almost deafening.

Nobody got this excited about the last cowboy.

At the last second, Jackson looks over at me, and I think he smiles. My heart clenches and I break out into a cold sweat.

Please, God, I think, and then he nods at the gate man and the bull bursts out of the gate.

Train Robbery leaps forward, kicking his back legs into the air, and Jackson lurches forward over the bull's shoulders but keeps his seat, arm waving in the air. My heart is in my stomach and I can't watch, so I look through the viewfinder. Anything to make this seem less *real.*

I don't think I breathe. I keep hitting the shutter, but I have no idea what I'm capturing. My eyes are just on the clock at the other end of the arena, counting up to eight as Train Robbery bucks and twists and spins and somehow, miraculously, Jackson stays on and in control.

A buzzer sounds. Train Robbery doesn't stop bucking, but after another second, Jackson flies off, like he's half jumping and half thrown. He lands hard on his side and I tighten my fists against my palms, but then he rolls over and runs a couple of steps.

The rodeo clowns are already shooing Train Robbery to the exit chute, and the big bull is lumbering along. He doesn't look worse than annoyed.

The crowd goes crazy, cheering and stomping and screaming, and I finally take a deep breath, unclenching my fists.

"A qualified ride from Jackson Cody!" the announcer shouts. There's more screaming, more stomping.

Jackson picks his hat up from where it fell and puts it back on his head.

He turns toward me, breathing hard.

Our eyes lock. Even halfway across the arena, I feel like his gaze is burning into me, scorching me from inside out. I swallow hard.

He touches the brim of his hat, just barely tipping it, our eyes locked the whole time. I think I actually go weak in the knees. It ignites something inside me the size of a bonfire, and I want him *right* now, so bad it hurts.

Then he turns and pulls himself over the gate, disappearing into the pens. The next rider's announced.

I grit my teeth and look into the camera again, hoping I got some good shots. I force myself to breathe normally, to pay attention, and to act like one look from Jackson Cody didn't just liquefy my insides.

· · · · · ★ ★ ★ ★ · · · ·

I SPEND the rest of the rodeo agitated. I can't get that *look* out of my head, and to make matters worse, after a few minutes he pops up on the opposite side of the arena to watch the rest of it.

Except every time I look over, he's looking at me.

When it ends, everything is a flurry. Jackson is answering reporter questions from Bruce as well as the local TV station, the paper, and a couple rodeo magazines. Every time he takes a step, there's a flock of women asking for his autograph, and he signs every single one with a smile on his face while I take pictures and stand around and act like I don't care where he is or what he's doing.

After a while, Bruce and I decide we're finished, and we leave Jackson standing in the arena, still smiling away and signing autographs for cowgirls wearing a whole pile of sequins.

I wish I could stop thinking about that *look*, and I wish thinking about it didn't make me feel like a pile of jello. I wish I wanted to sleep with *anyone* else, even Bruce, but I don't. Just Jackson.

I try to watch TV in my motel room, but I'm too worked up. I can't sit there and half hope that Jackson knocks on my door and half hope that he doesn't, so I grab my jacket and camera and head for the fair. At least I can get some shots of kids eating ice cream and those big, spinning rides throwing neon light into the Oklahoma night sky.

I don't make it to the fair. As I walk through the gates to the fairgrounds, waving at the guy in the booth, I see Jackson walking toward me.

For a second I panic and tell myself to just keep walking, because I'm certain that if anyone sees us talking, they'll *know*. Not that there's much to know. Not yet.

He walks up to me and stops.

"Hey there, Mae," he says.

"Hey there, Jackson," I say. I try to sound flippant, even as my stomach feels like a balloon filled with bats.

"I was just coming to see you," he says.

I raise my eyebrows and try to look casual, even as I look around. There are people swirling and streaming around us, but I don't know any of them.

That's not the question, though. The question is whether any of them know *him*.

"What for?" I ask. "Haven't you gotten your picture taken enough?"

"I wanted to make sure you got my good side today," he says, and he grins that cocky grin he has. "So I can know which side to show you tomorrow."

"That assumes you've got a good side," I tease. "Could be it doesn't matter which side you show me."

"So they're both good sides," he says. "Good to know."

I laugh, and Jackson looks behind me. I turn. There are two young women standing there, both in tight jeans and tank tops, cowboy boots, cowboy hats.

"You're Jackson Cody, right?" one of them asks, standing nervously.

"Sure am," he says. "How can I help you?"

"Will you sign this?" the other one asks, thrusting a rodeo program at him.

He takes it, then searches his pockets for a pen. I grab the pen I use for taking notes and hand it over, and he signs a messy *Jackson Cody* on two programs.

"Thanks," one of the girls says, sounding a little breathless. "You rode real good today."

"Thank you," he says. "I just got lucky."

I almost snort. I *know* he doesn't think that.

"Good luck tomorrow!" the girls say, and then walk off, whispering to each other, and Jackson turns to me, pen still in hand. He steps closer, a little too close for being in public.

"What'd you think, Lula-Mae?" he asks.

"Mae," I say, stubbornly.

"All right, *Mae*, what'd you think?"

His hazel eyes are dancing, and he looks so full of himself I can't help it. I shrug.

"It was okay," I say.

He raises his eyebrows.

"Just okay?" he says. "And here I thought I did pretty good, not getting thrown off or crushed."

"All right, fine," I say. I can't look him in the eyes for a moment. "It's terrifying. I thought my heart was gonna stop every time someone got on a bull, and I spent the whole time forcing myself not to cover my eyes."

He chuckles.

"I'm not cut out for this," I say, shaking my head.

"Nah, you're tough as hell," he says. "Even if you think you're not."

"I don't want to watch someone die," I say.

"That hardly ever happens," he says. "Besides, I've got luck on my side."

"How do you know it's luck?" I ask.

"It's a feeling I got," he says. "The problem with that is I think the luck I got last night might have run out."

"You say that like it's my problem," I tease.

He bends down, gets even closer. Sparks fly up my spine, but I don't move, even though I feel like everyone who passes by is staring at us.

"I'll kiss you right here if I have to, Lula-Mae," he says, low enough that only I can hear it.

"What am I, the Blarney Stone?" I ask.

I can almost feel the heat rolling off of his body, he's so close. Way, *way* too close for public.

"I'd kiss you again even if it got me thrown the rest of this tournament," he says.

A middle-aged woman glances at us, and I think she frowns, though maybe I'm inventing things.

"It can be right here," he says, leaning down even further. "There's a mirror maze over that way. There's a haunted house. There's an empty field the other side of that fence.

There's your motel room in ten minutes. Just tell me when and where, Lula-Mae."

My insides are a quivering mass of nerves and jello, but I stand up straight and look him in the eye.

"How scary is the haunted house?"

"You've got eight seconds until I kiss you," he says. He waits a beat. "Seven."

"Right here? Seriously?" I ask.

I don't know why I'm playing with fire, but I am.

"Six."

I look to the side and bite my lip, my entire brain shouting *no* and my whole body shouting *hell yes*.

"Five."

I know for a fact that I could tell him no and he'd leave.

"Four."

Say it, I think. *Tell him no.*

"Three."

I open my mouth to say *no, nothing's going to happen.*

"Promise me you won't get caught," is what comes out.

Oops.

"I promise I won't get caught," he says, a smile pulling up the corners of his lips.

"I'm serious," I say.

"So am I, Lula-Mae," he says. "Does that mean your motel room?"

Heat breaks across my whole body. I think I'm sweating again, because this is dumb and reckless and there's also no way I'm going back on it *now*.

I just nod.

"I'll knock on your door in ten minutes," he says. "Without getting caught."

"Okay," I say. "See you soon."

I look at him for another moment, resisting the urge to

hold out a hand for a handshake, like we've just completed a business transaction. *Anything* to make it seem like we didn't just agree to have sex in my room, because unless I'm really misunderstanding something, we did.

I walk back to the motel, praying I don't look the mess I feel like. In the room, I turn off some of the lights so that everything looks *kind* of sexy. I throw my dirty clothes into a bag and shove it into a drawer.

Ten minutes pass. Fifteen.

I wonder if I should slip into something *more comfortable*, even though the only thing I've got is an over-sized UT Austin shirt that I sleep in.

Seventeen minutes.

What if he's not coming, I think. Maybe he got distracted by doing shots or buckle bunnies or —

There's a knock, and I leap for the door, jerking it open.

Jackson's standing there, leaning against the frame. He touches the brim of his hat with one hand.

"Evening, Miss Guthrie," he says.

"Get in here," I hiss, then shut the door as softly as I can behind him.

He tosses his hat onto the table and then grabs me by the hips. He pushes me against the door and crushes his mouth to mine, hot and needy as he kisses me hard and slow, like he can barely hold himself back.

"Did anyone see you?" I whisper when we pull apart.

"Course not," he says. He kisses me below the ear, and then his lips slide down my neck. "I promised I wouldn't get caught."

We kiss again, and I slide my hands around his head, holding his lips hard against mine. I can already feel his erec-tion through his jeans and mine, and he slowly runs his hands down my body, then hoists me.

I wrap my legs around his waist and he holds me up against the wall.

"Still persuasive," he says.

My body feels like a river of fire. I'm breathing hard.

I hook one finger under the top button of his shirt and unbutton it, then unbutton the next two. He's watching me with a grin on his face.

Then he picks me up and then drops me on the bed, and he's on top of me, my legs wrapped around his hard, muscular waist, his clothed erection rubbing up against me.

"Ain't you got anything to say?" he asks, his lips against my neck.

I laugh.

"Like what? You want me to say *we shouldn't be doing this* again?"

His hands are under my shirt now, sliding up, and I arch my back and take my shirt off.

"I was looking for, 'Let's do it, Jackson.'"

"I'm not eighteen or drunk," I say.

"So you can say better than 'do it,'" he says, reaching under me and getting my bra off.

He takes one nipple between his fingers and rolls it softly, holding himself up on one elbow as I moan softly, his eyes intent on me, drinking this in.

"I jerked off thinking about that night for years," he says, his voice low, almost a growl.

"Romantic," I say, and he smiles.

"I didn't say it was," he says, pressing his lips to the hollow of my throat. "When I thought about it, I wasn't thinking about taking you to dinner and a movie."

He closes his lips over my nipple and swirls his tongue around it fast, and I move my hips against his, his clothed cock sliding against me with delicious friction.

"What did you think about, then?" I ask.

He takes his mouth off me.

"Doin' it with you," he says, and kisses the spot between my breasts.

"That's my line," I say.

He kisses the spot above my belly button and looks up at me, smiling, his hazel eyes practically glowing with lust.

"Well, sometimes I thought about getting those shorts off of you and eating you out until you came so hard you screamed," he says.

Even though I'm half naked, my nipples hard as diamonds, I blush.

"Sometimes I thought about what your mouth might have felt like on my cock," he says, kissing the spot below my bellybutton.

He unbuttons and unzips my jeans, then hooks his fingers under the waist. My body is raging with pure desire, and I arch my hips up so he can get my jeans and panties off.

"And sometimes I thought about taking you up on your offer and barebacking you right there in my truck," he says.

Jackson pushes my thighs apart and slides his thumb over my slit.

"Still wet as hell," he says.

Then he flicks his tongue over my clit, and my whole body jerks.

"Oh!" I say, then clap a hand over my mouth.

Jackson laughs, but he doesn't stop. He swirls his tongue around my clit over and over, lapping at it with such perfect precision that in no time at all I'm curling my toes and grabbing fistfuls of the comforter, forcing myself not to grab his head.

Jesus it feels good, almost mind-blowing. I've still got one hand over my mouth and I'm doing my best not to make funny strangled noises, but with every flick of his tongue I feel like another bolt of pleasure shoots through me, sending me sky-high. I moan through my hand, gasping, my back arching.

Jackson chuckles, his breath hot against me, and then his tongue slows.

"You can't shout if we're gonna keep this a secret," he murmurs, his lips just barely grazing me as he speaks.

"Don't stop," I command.

"Don't shout," he says, and runs a finger along my slit. "Think you can handle that?"

No.

I open my eyes, look around desperately, and grab a pillow. Jackson laughs, and I push it down over my face with both hands just as he pushes two fingers inside of me and crooks them.

"Oh *God*," I shout into the pillow, just as he starts flicking his tongue across my clit again, drawing circles and shapes. Lazy then hurried, slow and then fast until my whole body is shaking like a dam about to burst.

His fingers move against that spot inside of me in time with his tongue, and every single time I moan out loud, the sound muffled. I want to look down and watch him, but there's no way I'm taking this pillow off my face.

"*Yes*," I moan, right on the brink of coming. I press the pillow into my face harder.

He's got one hand wrapped around my hip and it tightens now, his tongue flicking faster and faster, and then finally I go over the edge like I've been hit by a lightning bolt.

I shout into the pillow. My toes curl and my body goes rigid, but Jackson just keeps going until my whole body jolts with every lick and I reach down to push him off.

I'm still breathing hard, but I shove the pillow off my face and then he's on top of me again. I can smell myself on his face and then taste myself as he kisses me slow and hard, and it's actually kind of sexy. He presses himself to me, his cock right between my legs, and I'm still aching.

"I didn't imagine you'd be so noisy," he murmurs between kisses.

I'm not, usually, I think.

"I didn't imagine we'd be doing it in a motel with paper-thin walls," I say back, winding my legs around him again.

"What *did* you imagine?" he asks.

I blush.

"I imagined you'd take your clothes off, for starters," I say.

He laughs and pushes himself up, kneeling on the bed, and tears off his shirt revealing a taut, muscled torso, abs for *days*, a thick scar right over his breastbone, and a horseshoe tattoo that says *lucky* inside it. Seconds later he's got his pants off, he's naked, and there's something in his hand as he's on top of me again.

I reach down and grab his cock, but when I touch it I raise my eyebrows just a hair. For years I'd assumed I mis-remembered how big it was.

I didn't.

Jackson laughs and the laugh turns into a groan as I tighten my fist around him.

"Don't look so worried, Lula-Mae," he says.

"I'm not worried," I say.

I'm a little worried.

"I'll make sure you've gotta scream into a pillow again," he whispers. "That was sexy as hell. I could eat you out all day."

His cock hardens in my fist, and I can feel my own body respond, aching, almost *desperate*, my legs locked around him.

"Or we could move on," I say, my voice barely a whisper. I *want* to say something sexy, but I have no idea what and I feel incapable of forming new thoughts.

"To what?" he asks.

"Sex?" I say, still blushing.

He laughs.

"You're saying you want my cock inside you," he says against my neck.

My face is burning, and I just nod.

"And you want me to fuck you until you come so hard you've gotta scream into a pillow," he says.

"Yes," I whisper.

One of his hands drifts down between my legs and strokes me there, making my back arch. A whimper escapes my throat.

"And you're also saying," he goes on in his low, rumbling twang, "that you're so wet for me you can barely stand it anymore."

"Right," I gasp.

"Good," he says. "Glad we cleared that up, because I wanna feel what it's like when you come with me inside you."

This is way, *way* dirtier than anyone's ever talked to me, but *god* it's hot.

He unwraps the condom in his hand and unrolls it over himself. Then he's on top of me, kissing me hard, his tongue in my mouth, and the tip of his cock eases into my entrance.

I make a noise, and Jackson bites my lip and chuckles.

"Tell me if you need that pillow," he says, but his eyes have gone half-closed and his breathing speeds up.

He slides out and pushes in, a little further, and this time I bite my lip but I moan anyway and his fingers dig into my side so hard it almost hurts. He does it again and again, easing inside me by degrees, like I'm delicate and he's afraid of hurting me.

"You feel *good*, Lula-Mae," he whispers, just before he slides out and thrusts one more time until he's all the way inside me.

"Oh *hell*," I whisper. I think I'm trembling, because this feels good in a way I had no idea something could feel, and Jackson is biting my ear and I think he might be laughing, just a little.

"Your dirty talk could use some work," he says, as he thrusts again, slow and hard.

This time I just grunt and bite my lip, trying my best to keep quiet even if it's not working very well. He keeps going and I sink my nails into his shoulders, totally lost to pleasure when suddenly he pulls out. I raise my head but he's already off the bed, standing and pulling me toward him by the legs as I yelp.

"What are you—" I start, but as soon as I'm at the edge of the bed he sinks himself into me again and I just moan out loud.

Jackson leans over, grinning, and slings one of my knees over his shoulder, pushing himself deeper. I gasp.

"You have *got* to be quiet," he says.

"I'm trying," I whisper.

He thrusts again and then again and I clench my jaw and squeeze my eyes shut, determined not to make any noise, but he's pressing every pleasure button I've got and my mind's not in control anymore. Jackson speeds up and thrusts harder and I arch my back and inhale sharply, then bite my lip.

"Let me see you come," he growls.

I'm unraveling and he keeps speeding up, the edges of my vision going white even as I reach for him, his torso barely in reach of my fingertips.

"Jackson, I'm gonna come," I say in a strangled whisper.

"Good," he says. "Because I can't hold out much longer."

Then he reaches down and pinches my clit lightly between two fingers and I *explode*. Jackson claps his rough hand over my mouth as every muscle in my body jerks at once, the dam inside me breaking in long, shuddering wave after wave. Jackson's still inside me and he's still hard and then his forehead's on my collarbone and he's growling through his teeth, his cock pulsing inside me.

I grab him by the back of his head and push his face against my chest even as I fight not to scream, my whole body shaking. Gradually, it's over and we're both gasping for air.

He takes his hand off my mouth and I release his head. He's still inside me as he turns his face to the side and starts laughing, his voice low and husky. After a second I join in, even though I have no idea why we're laughing.

After a minute he stands and pulls out. He tosses the condom into the bathroom trash and then comes back and flops on his back on my bed, and the force of it makes every spring squeak.

"Hush," I say.

"You do *not* get to tell me to hush," he says without even opening his eyes. "God*damn*, Lula-Mae."

CHAPTER FOURTEEN
JACKSON

SHE SCOOTS up beside me on the bed, her head on my arm as she curls up a little on her side, facing me. I bend my elbow and stroke her shoulder with my fingertips, feeling lazy and warm and sated.

"You can't stay," she says, her voice quiet again.

"Are you kicking me out of your bed?" I ask, drawing circles on her with my fingers.

"Not yet," she says. "But don't fall asleep."

I knew all along I couldn't sleep with her, but I feel an odd twinge of disappointment as she says it. I usually fall asleep in whatever bed I'm in and it's fine, but I think I *want* to sleep here, next to her.

"You've gotta learn to relax, Lula-Mae," I say.

"Don't get into the habit of calling me that, either," she says. She slides one hand over my chest, her fingers warm and slightly ticklish. "People might start asking questions."

I put my hand over hers and turn to face her.

"You sure do have a lot of requirements for a girl who just woke up the whole state of Oklahoma with her screaming," I tease.

She blushes hard, her fair skin going pink.

"Sorry," she said.

"*I* didn't mind," I say. "I took it as a compliment."

She gets redder, and I laugh.

"Don't worry," I say. "I'll sneak out before anyone catches on."

If they haven't already, I think, and my heart skips a beat. With every passing minute, I care less and less what Wayne and Darlene think, but I know Mae is serious, so for her I'll keep my mouth shut.

Her fingers are moving on my chest, and I can feel them trace the shape of the scar. Well, one of the scars. The big one.

"You can ask about it if you want," I say.

Pretty much every girl I sleep with either asks about the scar or already knows what happened. I've worked out the perfect two-sentence explanation: angry bull threw me, then gored me. Protective vest saved my life when he only shattered my breastbone instead of skewering me straight through.

She taps it.

"Do I want to know?" she asks.

I almost say *most women do* but swallow the words.

"I bet you can guess," I say.

"How many bones have you broken?" she asks.

I curl my fingers around her shoulder, suddenly cautious. This isn't how this conversation usually goes. Usually the girl says *how'd you get that scar* and I tell her and she goes *ooooh* and her eyes light up, but Mae seems worried, almost concerned.

"That depends on how you define a bone," I say.

She looks at me, then narrows her eyes.

"You didn't break your dick," she says with certainty, and I laugh out loud.

"I've never broken a *boner*," I say as she giggles. "Thank God."

"How many?" she asks again.

I exhale, staring at the ceiling.

"No idea," I say. "But I've got enough pins in me to set off every metal detector in a five-mile radius."

She grimaces. I raise my left arm and show her a long scar that runs almost the length of my forearm.

"Compound fracture," I say. "That's when the bone sticks through the skin. Now it's got a metal plate."

I think she turns green.

"You got that riding?" she says, like she already knows the answer.

"Yeah," I say. "I only broke one bone not riding. My elbow when I was twelve and jumped off the roof of the barn."

I expect her to gasp, but instead she laughs.

"I broke my wrist jumping off the chicken coop when I was eight," she says. "My older brother convinced me that if I ate enough dandelion seeds I could fly."

"I don't remember what I thought," I say. "Just that I regretted it afterward."

She taps the scar on my chest with her fingers, looking thoughtful for a moment.

"I won't tell you if you don't want to know," I say.

She narrows her eyes, thinking. Then she swallows.

"No, tell me," she says.

"A couple years ago, I was in Reno, at their Gold Rush festival," I say. "I drew this bull named Daffodil, and he was the meanest motherfucker I've ever been on."

"Daffodil?" she asks.

"Hand to god," I say. "He wasn't all that difficult to ride, but the second you were off he'd come *after* you. Asshole wanted vengeance. Old Testament style."

I think she's holding her breath.

"He threw me, and I landed okay, but I was in a rush to get out of there. I moved a little too fast, stumbled, and he got me right here."

I tap her hand against the scar.

"I was wearing a vest, so he only shattered my breastbone and tore me open, didn't kill me," I say.

I've told this story a thousand times, relived it a thousand times. Hell, I've watched the footage of it over and over again, and after a certain point, I just think *that poor bastard.*

"At the hospital, they told me a quarter of an inch left or right and I'd be a goner," I say. "I punctured a lung, my diaphragm, broke pretty much all my ribs. It was real dicey for a couple days there."

"Jesus," she whispers.

I shrug.

"I don't remember it all that well," I say. "I was under, and then they gave me plenty of morphine, so by the time I really knew what had happened I was okay. My parents took it pretty hard, though."

"I can imagine," she says.

"I got the tattoo after," I say. "Felt like I should commemorate it somehow, since I got lucky."

Mae's quiet for a long time, and I almost wonder if she's fallen asleep.

"But you're still doing it," she says. "Even though it almost killed you."

"Because there's days like today," I say. "When I ride real good and there's a pretty girl watching me."

"I think you like the bad days too," she says, ignoring my *pretty girl* comment.

"I like everything but the worst days," I say. "There ain't nothing like it in the world."

She doesn't answer me, and we both just lay there, half-tangled together. I don't fall asleep but Mae drifts off and my arm goes numb. I don't move it.

I stare at the popcorn ceiling and think about how I'm going to get out of her room. I think about my ride tomorrow. I think about whether we're going to do this again, even though I know that every time I even *speak* to her the ice we're skating on gets thinner.

Suddenly she jerks awake and sits up halfway, blinking at me.

"It's not morning," I say, flexing my hand to wake it up.

She runs a hand through her hair, her legs under her, still buck naked and gorgeous as hell, and I stop looking at her and sit up before I get an erection.

"I should go," I say, so she can't say it first.

Mae nods.

We stand and pull our clothes back on. I'm careful to tuck my shirt in and smooth my hair down so it doesn't look like I've been up to no good, and Mae goes to the window and looks out at the parking lot through a crack in the curtains. I hit the lights in the room so the open door won't attract attention.

"Coast clear?" I say, putting my hat back on.

"Looks like you got a straight shot," she says, and turns to me. She puts one finger under my belt and pulls me closer, her eyes big in the dark. It's enough to get me hard again, but I try to ignore it.

"Anything else?" I ask, my hand on her waist.

"Try not to break anything," she says.

"Especially my dick?" I murmur.

She laughs, her finger tightening under my belt.

"Anything," she says again. "And good luck, in case I don't see you before you ride."

I kiss her again, slow and lazy like we've got all the time in the world. I let my lips explore hers until her mouth opens against mine, our tongues entwining, her body pressed against mine. I'm rock hard again, and I want to pick her up, throw her on the bed and take her at exactly this speed, so slow and sensual I think I might pop.

Instead the kiss ends, and I know I have to leave while I've got the chance. I tip my hat at her.

"Goodnight, Miss Guthrie," I say.

She rolls her eyes but smiles.

"Good night, Jackson," she says.

I step out into the dark parking lot and walk for my truck, then pretend I'm searching the cab for something. After a while, I pretend to give up and head back into my own room, nerves still jangling.

CHAPTER FIFTEEN

MAE

I WATCH Jackson walk away through the crack in the curtains. No other doors open, no one seems to be looking out. No cars come into the parking lot.

Besides, I tell myself, *no one has memorized who's in which room.*

He walks to his truck, opens the cab, and starts looking for something inside it. Another car swings into the parking lot and its headlights flash across Jackson, but now he's just a guy getting something out of his car.

I give myself another few seconds and then close the crack in the drapes and turn on the TV a little louder than I should. I flip on a bedside lamp and wonder why I bothered getting dressed again, because now I'm just going to shower and go to bed.

In the bathroom, I wind about a mile of toilet paper around the condom wrapper before I throw it away. I know it's silly, because whoever cleans my motel room isn't going to care if I had sex or not, but it makes me feel better to make *certain* no one knows.

All the while, I pray that whoever's next door takes sleeping pills and uses industrial-strength ear plugs.

Maybe tomorrow we should do this in his motel room, I think. And I should wear a muzzle, apparently.

Then I think: *tomorrow? So we're doing this again?*

I rake conditioner through my hair, rinse, cut off the water and step out of the shower.

Stop it, Mae, I tell myself firmly. *You will drive yourself crazy. Even if you sleep with him again, after that you're going home to Brooklyn, so just have some fun while this lasts.*

For once in your life.

I dry off, put on my sleep shirt, turn the TV off, and crawl between the covers.

I wish Jackson could have stayed, I think before I fall asleep.

· · * ★ ★ ★ ★ * · ·

I DRIVE MYSELF A LITTLE CRAZY. Relaxing and going with the flow have never quite been in my nature, and normally I like that about myself — it got me out of Lawton, after all — but now, I keep seeing glimpses of Jackson from a hundred feet away. I think my stomach is trying to strangle my lungs.

I shoot the talent competition portion of Miss Pioneer Days and see Jackson walk by the tent. A middle-aged woman comes up to him, he signs something, and then she kisses his cheek. He smiles. I look away.

I stand by the rodeo gates, chatting with Darlene, showing her some of my shots from that day. She's telling me about how she was Miss Pioneer Days once upon a time.

"My mother made my evening gown," she says, laughing.

"She did?" I ask.

Darlene nods.

"She knew how to do everything like that," Darlene says. "She grew up on a ranch, then married a rancher herself and had six kids while running the place half the time. Just as good at helping birth foals as she was at making biscuits."

"I can't do either of those things," I admit. "Last week I sewed a button onto my coat after it fell off and I was really, really proud of myself."

She laughs.

"On the other hand, my mother doesn't own a computer and can barely use a cell phone," she says. "But my kids all have matching Easter outfits that she made."

"What did your evening gown look like?" I ask.

I make a mental note: *Tell Bruce to ask Darlene about all this.*

"First, it was the late eighties in rural Oklahoma," Darlene says. "So keep that in mind."

I nod.

"It was bright pink," she goes on. "Bubblegum pink, almost Pepto-Bismol pink. Have you seen *Steel Magnolias?*"

Now it's my turn to laugh.

"Of course I have," I say.

"The color pink Julia Roberts loves in that movie," she said. "It was off-the-shoulder, and then had puffy sleeves down to my elbows."

I raise my eyebrows.

"The skirt had a peplum, and then it was tight all the way down with a slit just past my knee, which is the furthest up the rules would allow. It was almost impossible to walk in that thing, but let me tell you, I was hot stuff," she says, laughing.

I believe her. She's in her late forties and still looks fantastic, with the confidence age gives some people.

"She was the *hottest* stuff," a voice behind me says.

I turn, and Wayne is walking up. Darlene's still laughing.

Jackson is with him, and right away, my heartbeat goes erratic. I'm instantly certain that everyone can read our secret on my face, even as I nod politely to the two men and barely make eye contact with Jackson.

They're here because they know, I think. *Oh god, everyone's found out, and my editors are going to find out and then I'm screwed forever and ever. Oh no.*

"You're sweet," Darlene says.

"It's true," Wayne says.

I sneak another glance at Jackson, but his face is politely blank. I immediately feel a different kind of anxiety.

What if that was just a casual thing and he doesn't want to do it again?

I take a deep breath.

Lula-Mae, you have got to stop this nonsense, I tell myself sternly. *You are being insane.*

"Wayne says you're thinking of changing which vendor you get the arena sand from next year," Jackson says to Darlene.

"Yes," Darlene says. "Do you have a minute? I could use some opinions."

"I'm all yours," Jackson says to her.

"Sorry, Mae," she says. "The glamorous side of rodeo is calling my name."

Jackson nods at me once, and then he and Darlene walk away together. I'm relieved, or disappointed, or some combination of those two things. Relievappointed.

"You getting everything you need?" asks Wayne.

"Absolutely," I say. "I think I'll have about a thousand more pictures than I can possibly use."

He nods, arms folded across his chest.

"Well, you seem to be handling things quite well," he says, a little cryptically.

Immediately, I flip through everything he could possibly mean: is he talking about Jackson and I, or about Raylan taking a picture of his dick, or just about soldiering on after I broke a camera?

"Thanks," I say. "I'm having a good time being at a rodeo again."

He claps me on the shoulder, his meaty hand hitting me with a little more force than he probably intended.

"We'll just stay outta your way, then," he says. "You need anything, you holler."

I need a new personality that comes with the ability to relax, I think, but I just smile.

"Will do," I say, and Wayne walks off to go organize something else.

· · · ★ ★ ★ ★ ★ · · ·

WHEN THE RODEO starts that afternoon, I'm actually relieved. I'm not looking forward to men possibly getting trampled by livestock any more than I was yesterday, but at least I have a place where I have to be and a job I have to be doing.

If I'm standing here, taking pictures, it's totally *normal* for me to be looking at cowboys. Even at Jackson, who's taken up residence across the arena from me. Every time I glance over at him, he's looking at me. I think he's half-smiling, though he's far away and it's hard to tell.

Finally, I glance at him and he's gone. My chest tightens. That means he's riding soon, those eight long seconds. Eight seconds if he's lucky.

Which he ought to be, if last night was any indication.

The gate opens and a different cowboy blasts out, the bull bucking and leaping and writhing. He doesn't make it four seconds before he's flung off, looking like a rag doll as he flies through the air and then falls a little funny on his shoulder.

I grit my teeth together but he rolls and gets up, the rodeo clowns shooing the bull to the exit.

As they do, I realize: it's Train Robbery, the bull Jackson rode yesterday. This guy didn't last even half as long as Jackson did.

A tiny bubble of pride swells in my chest, as if I had anything at all to do with it. As if Jackson is *mine*, someone I can be proud of.

I adjust my camera so it's looking at the gate again and wait for the announcer, heart thumping. I know Jackson is soon. I think of the thick, ugly scar on his chest, weird and smooth under my fingertips. I think of the long scar on his forearm and shudder, but I force myself to look through the camera.

"Up next, Jackson Cody riding Mr. Torque!" the announcer says.

The crowd cheers. They cheer harder and louder for him than for anyone else. The women in the front of the stands are there, and their signs are even bigger today: JACKSON IS SEXY and GO JACKSON GO!

I swallow and look at the camera, because that's my job.

Jackson leaps onto the bull. Mr. Torque doesn't try to buck him off right away like Train Robbery did. The bull doesn't seem happy, but he's not *enraged*.

He'll be fine, I tell myself. *He does this all the time. He'll be fine.*

Jackson's head comes up. He looks at the crowd, scanning

the stands from right to left until finally his deep hazel gaze settles on me.

I nod once, just barely. He nods back, the brim of his hat dipping slightly. I think he's smiling.

The gate's pulled open and Mr. Torque runs out, leaping in the air, twisting and bucking. He kicks his back legs up and dives and for one second, Jackson flies in the air and I'm certain he's flying off, but then he regains his seat, one hand still in the air.

I watch through the viewfinder. I have to. I snap away, following the bull with my camera, even as cold chills rock through my body as the timer counts up.

Leap, kick, twist, spin, and I can't believe it hasn't been eight seconds, the longest eight seconds in the world.

At last the buzzer goes off and Jackson finally flies off, landing in the dirt and rolling away as the other men in the arena turn Mr. Torque and head him off.

I take a deep breath and unclench my hands. I pray I don't look half as rattled as I feel, because I feel like anyone who so much as glances my way will *know*.

The crowd's going nuts again. The women with signs are jumping up and down. Some of them are waving *pom poms*, and Jackson grins at them and waves with one hand.

"Another qualified ride from Cody," booms the announcer. "Ladies and gentlemen, he is having one *heck* of a showing here at Pioneer Days, first on Train Robbery and now on Mr. Torque..."

Still grinning and breathing hard, Jackson turns toward me and we lock eyes one more time.

Don't do anything, I think. *Please, not in front of all these people.*

He winks.

It takes a split second, but he *winks* at me and then

jumps up and pulls himself over the gate effortlessly, disappearing behind the barriers. My insides feel like a whirlpool, like quicksand, like I could be sucked down into something dangerous if I'm not careful.

Because when he does that? When he risks his life like it's nothing, when a stadium full of people are screaming his name and he looks over at *me?*

It does something to me, expands some deep, needy, *hungry* part of me that I didn't know I had until now. For a second I think about abandoning my camera and running backstage. Finding Jackson and leaping into his arms, covering his stupid handsome face with kisses.

I adjust my camera so it's pointing at the gate. I breathe deep and hope I'm not acting weird.

Another cowboy mounts a bull, nods, and rides out. I take pictures. Five seconds and he's been tossed off into the sand and scampers off.

Slowly, my heart stops feeling like it might explode.

* * * ★ ★ ★ ★ ★ * * * *

AFTER THE RIDING IS OVER, I finally head behind the scenes. I need pictures of this, of handlers leading bulls out of their pens, of the madness and exhilaration and bandages that happen at a rodeo.

I'm there for a long time and I don't see Jackson. For once, I'm relieved, because I'm so keyed up by his stupid wink that I'm a little afraid of what I'm going to do. Instead, I shoot a cowboy getting his ribs taped up. I shoot a twelve-year-old kid leading a bull out like it's no big deal. I shoot two cowboys drinking out of a paper bag and sitting on the curb and laughing.

As I watch, one of the other cowboys start arguing with

someone who seems to either be his wife or his girlfriend. She's got a pink cowboy hat on, cowboy boots, cutoff shorts, but she's giving him hell about something I can't quite understand. I feel a little sleazy standing there and snapping their photo, but I do my best to fade into a wall as they yell at each other.

It's part of the rodeo, after all. I'm supposed to be getting this from all sides.

"Are you snooping, Miss Guthrie?" a voice says, and my finger slips awkwardly off the shutter. The picture's blurry.

"Don't give me away, for God's sake," I murmur without even looking at Jackson.

"Last night, she caught him drunk with a girl on his lap, and today he didn't make it three seconds before he fell off," Jackson says, keeping his voice low. "That's why he's in a pile of trouble."

A few people walk by and block our view of the fighting couple for a moment.

"Would it be different if he'd stayed on the bull?" I ask.

Jackson shrugs.

"Probably," he says. "Women feel different about winners."

I don't look at him. I'm afraid he might wink at me again, or tip his hat, or just *look* at me and I'll just dissolve right here.

"You'd know," I say.

"I don't claim to know a thing about women," he says, and I swear I can hear that cocky grin in his voice. "Just about winning."

I roll my eyes. A family passes us: cowboy dad, regular-looking mom. Toddler perched on the dad's shoulders. It's slowly emptying out back here, enough that there's no one really around us right now.

"When am I coming over?" he asks. He's still leaning against a post a few feet away, looking casual as all get out, but his voice changes. Now it's low and intense, something barely restrained about it.

My stomach twists. My heart leaps. Every muscle in my body tenses, and I force myself to act normal.

"Presumptuous," I tease, even as fire pools between my legs.

"You even use ten-cent words to tell me off?" he asks, still laughing.

"It means—"

"I know what *presumptuous* means, Lula-Mae," Jackson says. "And I was *presuming* that making you come twice last night might get me invited back to your bed."

I widen my eyes and shoot him a very clear *don't say that in public* glare, but he's not looking around. He's just looking at me, his hazel eyes burning, and I feel like flames are unfurling through my whole body. Spreading like wildfire.

I force myself to look back at the camera and take another picture. I still need to wait until this area clears out completely, and then I need to fuss with the lighting so I can shoot this maze of chutes and cages and bars properly. Give it the treatment it really deserves.

I'm tempted to take Jackson back to my room right now and then return to the arena later, but I've got the feeling I'm not going to be in the mood *afterwards*.

"I've got a while before I finish up here," I say, taking a deep breath and gathering every ounce of self-control I've got. "I want to get a few shots of everything when it's empty, you know, *the arena after everyone's gone home* kind of thing."

He looks like he's about to say something, but then he stops. He nods.

"Gotcha," he says, then stands up straight. "I'll get outta your hair."

"Sorry," I say. "I just need to finish this now, so..."

He waves a hand and grins.

"I'll live for a couple hours," he says. "Just don't you be *too* long, Miss Guthrie."

Two kids walk by, followed by a middle-aged man.

"Sounds good," I say, too loudly. "Nice working with you!"

Jackson chuckles, then leans in for a moment.

"Jesus, Lula-Mae, you trying to tell everyone about our torrid affair?" he asks, his voice low and soft and dangerous. It sends a shiver down my back.

Then he winks and walks off.

Apparently this is *an affair* and it's *torrid*. My palms are sweaty.

I wipe them on my jeans and try like hell to focus.

CHAPTER SIXTEEN
JACKSON

I DON'T WANT to walk away. I *want* to grab her and push her up against the bars of a bull pen, her mouth under mine. I want to pull her into the bucking chute and push her clothes off, taste her again, take her on the sandy floor of the arena until she shouts loud enough that they hear it down in Texas.

But that's no good. She's at work. I pull anything like that and she's out of a job, maybe forever.

I go eat a late dinner. A group of sixteen-year-old boys comes up to me and tells me I rode real good, and it turns out some of them ride so we get to talking. I know that it'll take a year before most of them are back on their parents' farms, because rodeo doesn't work out for most people, but I don't tell them that.

I tell them it's the best goddamn thing there is, because it's true. Their eyes light up even as they try to act cool.

I walk through the motel parking lot. Mae's light isn't on yet. I watch fifteen minutes of TV and glance out my window again. Her light still isn't on.

This ain't you, I think. *You ought to be out drinking at Betty's, two bunnies on your lap.*

I check again. Her light's still not on. I cut off the TV and take a walk over to the fairgrounds, where I buy a funnel cake because I can. The girl who sells it to me blushes as I order, and I tip my hat at her as I leave, because I'm a gentleman.

Sometimes.

I walk past the arena on the way back to the motel. I glance over at Mae's room. The light *still* isn't on.

Fuck it, I think.

The gate to the arena's still open, and I walk through it, then behind the barrier to the staging area, all the bull pens where they keep the animals until it's time to ride. It's quiet back here and lit only in spots, the bare bulbs throwing odd shadows all over the place. Smells like livestock, but it's the kind of smell you get used to in a minute.

If I didn't know it so well, I might be jumpy. Instead I walk through the shadowy pens and eat funnel cake, leaving a trail of powdered sugar behind me, looking for Mae.

Finally I come around a bend and there she is, camera facing down a long row of pens on one side and chutes on the other, pointed at me. Mae pops her head over the camera.

"That impatient?" she says, a smile creasing her eyes.

"It's been two and a half hours," I say. I crunch another tube of the funnel cake, walking down the long hallway toward Mae.

I hear her click the shutter.

"I don't remember agreeing to have my picture taken," I tease her.

"I'm sure you signed a release," she says.

"I've got an image to maintain, Miss Guthrie," I say. "And eating funnel cake while I'm waiting on the photographer to finish so I can have my way with her ain't it."

"Funnel cake's not so bad," she says. "You've barely got any powdered sugar around your mouth."

She doesn't even look around. I raise my eyebrows.

"You alone in here?" I ask.

"Not anymore," she says.

I walk up to her and she grabs a piece of funnel cake. She chews it and then licks the powdered sugar off her fingers. When she's finished, she looks up at me, her blue eyes half-lit in the weird darkness.

"What?" she says, and then smiles. "It's fried sugar. It's delicious."

She takes another piece and eats it.

"You done here or what?" I growl.

She licks her fingers again. God *almighty* I'm hard, and I'm certain she can tell.

"I'm done," she says. "Let me pack this up and—"

I kiss her. It takes her by surprise and her teeth scrape against my lip, but I don't let her go. I slide my hand around the back of Mae's neck and I hold her to me as she kisses back fiercely. We both taste a little like funnel cake as she opens her mouth and lets me in, swirling her tongue around mine.

When we pull apart she bites my lip just hard enough and then laughs.

"That's for winking at me," she says.

"If that's what a wink gets me tomorrow I ought to blow you a kiss," I say.

I kiss the side of her neck, the skin there soft and warm, her hair tickling at my nose. It takes everything I've got not to rip her clothes off right this minute.

"Jackson, don't you *dare*," she says.

"If I can ride a bull I can blow you a kiss," I say.

"Come on," she says, her eyes suddenly serious.

I grab her hips and slide my thumbs up under her shirt. She sucks in a breath, but her face doesn't change, and slowly, I walk her back against a wall.

"I won't," I say, my voice barely above a low whisper. I kiss her neck again, the cords in it standing out, and I run my hands up her torso to the sensitive skin just under her bra. "I know I'm your dirty secret."

"You don't have to say it like *that*," she protests, but her eyes slide shut, and that breathy tone comes into her voice.

"Say it like what?" I go on. "Which part isn't true?"

Under her shirt, I unhook her bra. She makes a sound in her throat and closes her hands around my belt, pulling me in closer.

"This is a secret," I say.

I push her bra up and run the pads of my thumbs over her nipples. She flexes her jaw and turns her head to one side, like she's trying hard not to make noise.

I lean in, my mouth next to her ear.

"And I am *dirty*, Lula-Mae," I whisper.

She slides one hand over my clothed erection slowly, from root to tip, and a shudder runs through me, a million tiny explosions on my skin, all at once.

"Found something you want?" I say. I run my hands over her breasts, my rough callouses against her sensitive skin, and she gasps and arches her back, squeezing my cock again.

"I think it found me," she says, and squeezes it again.

I swear my toes tingle, but she pulls on my belt again and my mouth is on hers, my hands up her shirt. I pinch her nipples hard this time and she moans into my mouth, the vibrations running the length of my body. I growl back at her, pushing my rock-hard cock against her.

"We're not gonna make it to my room, are we?" she asks.

"Nope," I say.

She looks at me for a moment, then slides out of my embrace and grabs the front of my shirt, grinning. Mae pulls me into the deep shadow of the bucking chute.

The walls are about six feet high and aluminum except for the gate that looks out onto the dark arena. I can just barely see over the top, but Mae pushes me against the aluminum wall with a bang, and I let her.

"For all the noise you make I'd swear you wanted us to get caught," I say.

She's furiously unbuttoning my shirt and she nips at my collarbone before she slides her hands along my sides. Her touch is almost electric, and for the moment, I let her be in control as she pulls me against her.

Mae drags her lips along my chest, softly kissing the scar. Her hands undo my belt and unbutton my pants, and I think all the blood left in my body surges to my cock as she grabs it, shoving my pants down just enough to get it out.

I groan.

"Who's loud now?" she asks, her lips in the hollow above my bellybutton. I'm rigid, because I think I know what's coming and I can barely breathe with anticipation.

Now she's kneeling, her hand slowly stroking my cock right in front of her face. She's looking up at me, her eyes absolutely devilish in the dark.

"You looking for the go-ahead?" I say. I'm trying to tease her, but I'm *desperate* for her to put her mouth on me, as hard as I've ever been in my life.

"I don't need permission," she says. "I can't take a minute and appreciate?"

I laugh, but it turns into a groan, and I press myself into the cold metal of the bucking chute, glad that there's some-thing behind me.

"Appreciate all you like, Lula-Mae," I said. "You get me so fucking hard that you can do whatever you want. I'd crawl through a meat grinder if I thought your lips might touch my cock."

Her hand strokes again, and she laughs.

"Gross," she says.

"It's true," I say.

"Jackson, shut up," she says.

Before I can respond her mouth is hot and wet on the head of my cock, and I hear myself groan. I reach up behind myself and grab the top of the chute wall, because I feel like I need *something* to hang onto right now.

Mae pulls her head back slowly, sucking hard, and at the end she swirls her tongue around the head once before sliding her lips down again, this time just past the head, her tongue rigid against the underside. She pulls back again, sucking hard, her tongue swirling.

With every stroke she goes a little further until I can feel the tip of my cock against the back of her mouth, tight and wet and warm.

"Fucking hell, Lula-Mae," I whisper.

She keeps going, but she goes slow, driving me absolutely crazy. My toes are curling and there's a tightness in my lower belly that feels like it might never let go, not if she keeps *this* up.

I look down just as she takes me in her mouth again. She looks up at me as she pulls back, then keeps the head of my cock in her mouth an extra second, swirling her tongue around it. I swear to God she's smiling at me, and it's one of the hottest things I've ever seen.

"I'm gonna come if you don't stop," I say, but she engulfs me again, and I fight like *hell* to keep control until she pulls back and looks up at me.

"And?" she asks.

"And I'd rather come fucking you," I say.

Mae blushes and opens her mouth to say something, but I

reach into my pocket and pull out the condom I grabbed from my room earlier.

She laughs, but I think her eyes light up.

"Do you just carry those everywhere with you?" she asks. Her hand's still on my cock, and it's a little hard to concentrate.

"Just when I'm gonna be around a hot girl who's too responsible to bareback," I tease.

She snatches it from my hand and tears it open, and then she's rolling it down my cock with firm, hard strokes. I pull her up so she's standing, her mostly clothed and me mostly undone. I can taste myself on her lips as she kisses me voraciously, and it's sexy.

Everything she does is sexy.

I undo her jeans and slide my hand into the warmth between her legs. My fingers get slick with her juices instantly and she makes a noise into my mouth.

"Did sucking my cock get you this wet?" I murmur. I draw a circle around her clit with two fingers, and I can feel all her muscles tense.

Mae scrunches her nose a little when I say that, and I chuckle even though I'm breathing hard.

I take my hand out and spin her around. I push her against the gate that leads to the arena, and she closes her hands around the bars. I reach between her legs again, my head on her shoulder, my body pressed hard against her back.

"Sorry, Miss Guthrie," I growl. "I meant to say, did performing fellatio on my erect penis cause you to be so aroused? I know you like those ten-cent words."

She turns her head toward me and shoots me a look, even though she's breathing hard.

"Shut up, Jackson," she says, but she's smiling.

"I can't talk dirty to you even if I say it fancy?" I ask.

"Especially not then," she says.

I push her jeans down with my other hand and move those fingers along her slit, and she arches her back, pressing herself against me. It's an obvious plea, and there's nothing I want to do more than take her up on it and slide inside her perfect, tight channel.

"That's fine," I say. "Seems like *I thought all day about fucking you* works just fine."

I slide my cock between her thighs, already slippery with her juices. Mae gasps as I rub the head against her clit.

"I know you won't say it, but I think you did too," I say. "I think that's why I can't wink at you anymore, because the next time you might just tear your clothes off and come running."

She laughs, her voice throaty.

"I've got more self-control than that," she says, even as she presses herself against me, sliding my cock against her.

"Do you?" I ask.

"Not much more," she says.

I bend and kiss the nape of her neck, fine blond hairs sticking to my lips. Mae looks over her shoulder at me, her lips curving up into the wickedest smile.

"Come on, Jackson," she says. "Don't tease me."

Suddenly, my dick feels like it might pop. I *need* to be inside her, a need stronger than anything I've ever felt. I slide the head of my cock until it's against her opening and take a deep breath. I force myself to slide inside her slowly, since I'm still a little afraid of hurting her.

But the moment the head of my cock is in her, Mae arches her back and pushes her hips toward me. In one motion, I'm buried up to the hilt.

My vision goes white. She moans, and I'm left breathless.

She pulls forward slowly and I can feel her pulsing

around me, and there's a moment when I'm afraid I'm just going to lose control completely, right here on the first thrust. Her pussy feels like a fist gripping my cock, except this is ten times better than the world's best handjob.

Mae pushes her hips back again and engulfs me. I'm standing still, just watching my cock disappear into her as she groans, because it's so unbelievably hot that I don't want to ruin it.

"Maybe I should stand still and let you do the work," I murmur.

I've got both hands on her hips, just letting her fuck me. She buries me inside her again and I can feel her muscles twitch.

"That feels good," she whispers.

Good isn't the right word. It feels amazing, perfect, beyond *good.*

I rock inside her, thrusting almost microscopically over and over again, and Mae groans.

"You like that too?" I whisper.

"Yes," she says.

I take a deep breath and pull out more before I rock back against her, over and over again. I want to fuck her slow so I can watch her writhe and moan for a long time. I want her in ecstasy for as long as possible, because when I watch her come it turns on a part of me I've never felt before.

"This?" I ask.

I thrust deeper, longer.

Now Mae's just moaning, her forehead against her upper arm. Her hips are moving in time with my thrusts like she's hungry, desperate for as much of me as there is.

I keep going. I try to take it slow, but God it's hard. I'm fighting not to lose control as Mae moans and writhes in front of me. I swear I'm afraid that I'm going to wake up from a dream any second now, because this feels almost impossibly good.

Suddenly she takes one hand off the gate and reaches backward, twisting her torso around. She puts her hand on my arm and then kisses it softly. I sink myself inside her as far as I can, watching her eyes fill up with pleasure.

"Jackson," she says, pushing back against me.

She blinks, like she's not quite sure what to say, and she bites her lip for a second. I bite her shoulder, because even now, totally inside her, I have the urge to mark her as *mine*.

"Yes, Lula-Mae?" I growl. It feels like the world is dissolving.

She pauses, then half-laughs. Like she's *embarrassed* about what she's about to say.

"Harder," she finally whispers, and blushes.

My balls tense up. The knot inside me tightens, and I feel her squeeze around me.

"You want me to fuck you harder?" I ask, my lips brushing against her ear.

She swallows and nods, looking at the ground.

"Lula-Mae, I am balls-deep inside you right now," I whisper. "You're moaning like there's no tomorrow, and in a minute, you're gonna be shouting down this whole building, if last night is any indication."

I bite her earlobe, and then thrust into her once, *hard*, and she groans.

"You don't have to be embarrassed if you want me to fuck you harder," I say, and I curl my fingers into her hips and thrust again, driving hard and deep.

"Oh!" Mae shouts.

I keep going, each stroke fueling the fire inside me hotter and hotter.

"Oh *god*, Jackson," she whispers.

I think her knees buckle, because the next thing I know, we're unstable, leaning against the gate, and then moments later we're both on our knees in the sand. I feel almost like an animal, like this is the purest, rawest expression of lust I've ever felt.

Right now I don't care if someone comes in and we get caught. I don't think the National Guard could stop me from finishing, from making the most beautiful girl I've ever seen lose her mind and come so hard she *screams*.

She's hanging onto the gate and I'm hanging onto the gate, and it's banging back and forth on its latch.

"Slow down," she gasps.

"Make up your mind, Lula-Mae," I growl, but I do what she says. I'm squeezing one of her hips in one hand, and I feel like I'm holding on by a thread but I keep going. At the end of every stroke she pushes back against me and moans, louder and louder.

"Jackson," she gasps. "I'm gonna come."

"Say my name again," I tell her. "I like the way you say it when I'm fucking you."

"Jackson," she says, and this time her voice has a raw, desperate edge to it. "God, Jackson. I'm so close. This feels so *good*."

My cock twitches, and I know I'm not gonna last for much longer. Not if she talks like *this*, fucks me this enthusiastically.

Mae whimpers, and now her muscles are tightening around me. She's panting for breath.

"Let me feel you come," I say. "Lula-Mae, I *need* to feel you come."

"Oh god," she says, and then her muscles clamp down around my cock. My vision gets blurry.

"*Jesus*, Jackson," she says, louder this time. "Jackson, god*damn!*"

Now she's nearly shouting, but it's just sounds. Her muscles are contracting around me and I get swept under, still desperately thrusting into Mae. I come so hard I think my ears pop but I can't even tell because Mae's biting her hand and shouting anyway, her eyes squeezed shut.

I feel like I come forever, like she's draining me. I'm still moving a little, long after I've finished and gone soft, my lips against her shoulder, my arm around her waist.

We're still on our knees. Mae leans her forehead against the metal gates and takes a long, ragged breath.

"Lula-Mae Guthrie, you are gonna be the death of me," I murmur.

She exhales, her belly tightening under my arm.

"We shouldn't have done that," she whispers.

"*Now* you're whispering?" I whisper back.

"Better late than never?" she asks.

CHAPTER SEVENTEEN

MAE

JACKSON KISSES MY SHOULDER AGAIN, through my shirt, and then pulls out. Even that sends a tiny shock through me, and I stay still for another moment, forehead against the cool metal.

I think I'm shaking. I'm not sure I can stand. I know for a fact that I've got a half-ton of rodeo sand in my pants right now, since they're around my ankles.

I hear the snap as Jackson pulls the condom off, then zips his pants.

"Be right back," he says, his voice low, and then he walks out of the chute.

I grab the next bar on the gate and stand slowly, half pulling myself. I take a deep breath, run my hands through my hair, and then shake the sand out of my jeans as well as I can, considering I'm still wearing them.

When Jackson comes back in, I'm re-fastening my bra, and he watches as I reach through the neck of my shirt and re-arrange my boobs.

"What?" I ask, but I'm laughing.

"Nothing," he says, tucking his shirt back in.

After a second, we survey each other, and I nod at him.

"Like you just took a walk," I say.

"You look like you've been taking pictures for three hours," he says.

"Good," I say.

This was *unbelievably* dumb, but I can't think about that right now. I still feel like I'm floating away on clouds, like I just want to curl up next to Jackson and feel his body next to mine.

Not in the cards.

He steps closer to me and slides a hand down my back. I tilt my face up and then he's kissing me again, slowly and gently. Almost *thoughtfully*, like he's considering my lips carefully.

When we finally pull apart he kisses my forehead.

"Maybe tomorrow we ought to get a fleabag motel some-where else," he says. "You can wake up those neighbors all you want."

I laugh and feel myself blush.

"Sorry," I say.

He just chuckles.

"I don't mind at *all*, Lula-Mae," he says. "It's the rest of creation who you're waking up."

I have *no* idea where this is coming from. I've had boyfriends. I've had casual hookups. I've had good sex before, but I've never been a screamer.

Until now, I guess. Apparently Jackson's dick turns off the part of my brain responsible for keeping the volume down.

We stand there for a long moment in each other's arms. I turn my head and look out the gate toward the sandy arena, and I think: *tomorrow's the last night.*

I go home the morning after, and Jackson goes... somewhere else, and that's it. This is a casual sex relationship with a clear end-by date.

"You get enough pictures?" he asks, his voice rumbling through his chest.

"Yeah," I say. "There's only so many you can take of an empty place."

Then I look from him, to the dark arena, and back. The whole pavilion has a roof but the sides are open, and the moonlight is just starting to slice in from one side, cutting across the sand.

"Wait," I tell him. "Stay there."

I detach myself and walk to my camera, still mounted on the tripod. I set it by the entrance to the bucking chute. Jackson watches me with his hands in his pockets as I mess with the settings and switch from one lens to another.

I take a test snap. It's Jackson, just watching me, and the second I see it I know I can never, ever show it to anyone else.

He's not looking at a photographer. He's looking at his lover, and it couldn't be more obvious.

Technically true, just not fit for print.

"Did you always want to take pictures?" he asks.

"No," I say, still fiddling. "Not until college, actually."

"What did you want to do before that?"

"I was gonna be a lawyer," I say.

"Why a lawyer?" he asks.

He tilts his head and I take another shot, trying to get the balance right between the moonlit sand, the gate, and Jackson in the shadow.

"Lawyers make a lot of money and people respect them," I say. "It was that or a doctor, and I'm a little too squeamish to be a doctor."

"You're covering a rodeo and you're squeamish?"

"Not *that* squeamish," I say. I hit the shutter again. "But I don't think I'd like reaching into peoples' guts all day."

I adjust the lens.

"What about you?" I ask.

"It was always rodeo," he says. He turns his head and looks toward the arena, a really good shot. "Been hooked ever since I was a kid. It's all I ever wanted to do."

"I never really *wanted* to be a lawyer," I say. "I just wanted… I don't know. I wanted more than Lawton had to offer."

Jackson nods.

"When I'm not traveling I live in a trailer on my parents' ranch," he says. "It rattles like hell in the wind and freezes in the winter and leaks in the rain."

"Haven't you won enough to get something better?" I ask.

"Sure," he says. "Most of my friends from home have settled down. They all married their high school sweethearts and now they've got two kids and a dog and a mortgage in Sawtooth."

Sawtooth is his hometown, in the middle of nowhere, Wyoming.

"But you wanted more?" I ask.

He runs a hand through his hair. I shoot it.

"I don't know if I wanted more, exactly," he says. "Just different. Now I wonder if I'm stuck in the exact same kind of holding pattern that got them."

"Jackson, you're about to become the biggest star the rodeo world's ever seen," I say.

"Maybe," he says.

"Maybe," I say. "But a week and a half from now, your face is gonna be on newsstands from California to New York City. Is that different enough for you?"

"I think so," he says, and then leans against the wall of the chute, crossing his arms in front of himself. "But the closer I get, the more I wonder if I should have just married Cassie, settled down, gotten work on a ranch. Have a steady, quiet life."

"Who's Cassie?" I ask.

"High school sweetheart," he says. "She's married now, two kids and one on the way. At least, that's what my mom says. Mom gives me lots of Cassie updates."

"She think you should have married Cassie?"

I adjust the exposure and snap two more, holding my breath. My stomach squirms, and I ignore the twinge of jealousy.

"She thinks I should have done anything that wasn't riding bulls," Jackson says.

"Understandable," I say.

There's a moment of silence. Jackson's looking at the arena and I'm looking at him, trying to be objective, but between the light, the way he *moves*, and his perfect handsome face, I'm also just staring.

"I feel that too," I admit. "I go home and my friends are getting married, having kids, and I see them and think, what does that feel like? To be satisfied with what you've got and not always be reaching for the next thing?"

Jackson looks over at me, face serious, arms crossed.

"Are you asking me?" he says.

"No," I say. "I don't think you know either."

He just smiles and ducks his head.

"You got me," he says.

"I don't think you'd be happier with two kids, a wife, and a job," I say softly. "I think you'd be wondering what would have happened if you'd given this a shot."

Far away, the gate creaks open. We stare at each other, wide-eyed.

"Go," he says, his voice low. "I'll cover for you."

My heart skips a beat, but then it thunders back. I shake my head.

"Face the arena and grab the gate," I say. "We're having a photoshoot."

He does it. I snap away blindly, and then a few moments later, I see another man rounding the corner.

"You're still here?" Wayne's voice says.

"Jackson came by, so I decided to get a few shots before tomorrow," I say.

"Jackson's here?" Wayne asks.

I point into the bucking chute.

"Hey Wayne," Jackson calls out. "I think I ought to hire her for my nudie calendar."

Wayne rolls his eyes.

"I'm sorry," he says to me. "He swore he'd behave."

I can barely keep the smile off my face.

"He's all bark and no bite," I tell Wayne. Wayne peeks into the chute and Jackson waves.

"Watch yourself," Wayne tells him.

"On it," Jackson says, grinning.

Wayne nods at me again.

"Have a good night," he says.

He walks off, around the arena, out of sight. I snap a few more photos.

"We should go," I tell Jackson once Wayne's out of earshot, and start putting my equipment away.

Jackson saunters out of the chute.

"No bite?" he says. His hazel eyes are flashing, and I laugh.

"I can show you *bite*," he says, his voice lowering to a dangerous register.

I lift my camera bag to my shoulder, glance after Wayne, and then give Jackson a quick but hard kiss.

"I know," I say.

· · · · ★ ★ ★ ★ ★ · · · ·

THE NEXT DAY goes by in a rush. It's the last day of the festival and so everything feels like it's amped up to eleven. There's a sold-out, stuffed-to-the-gills crowd, and they're tipsy and loud. After the rodeo there's going to be fireworks, a concert, the whole shebang.

I'm just hoping it'll be enough distraction for Jackson and I to sneak off somewhere. I'm forcing myself not to think about the fact that it's going to be the last time, because this is *not* a relationship, this is *casual sex*, our worlds can never meet, he lives in a trailer in Wyoming and I live in Brooklyn. Et cetera, et cetera.

Hell, I almost forgot that this is his big night.

He's riding Crash Junction, the only undefeated bull left in the country. Already this week, Crash threw one cowboy in three seconds and one in two. He's notorious, and the crowd's amped up.

Jackson doesn't even *need* to ride him. Unless everyone else stays on their bulls and gets super-high scores, he's headed for the Rodeo World Finals next month. If he does half-decently tonight, he's probably going to finish Pioneer Days in first place.

I also try not to think about the buckle bunnies who'll be lining up for him.

As we're waiting for the bull riding to start, Bruce and I are standing in the press area. It's more crowded than usual tonight — there's a news crew, a couple papers, and even a rodeo blogger — but it's still a welcome relief from the press of the crowd.

"Are you missing any shots?" Bruce asks.

I shake my head.

"I don't think so," I say. "I went through everything last night, so I think I'm good."

He nods.

"I hate this part," he confesses. "It's like packing, when you think you've got everything you need, and then you show up on vacation and you've forgotten to pack any socks, except you can't just go to the drugstore and buy a really good quote."

I laugh.

"You can at least sort of make those up," I say. "I get the perfect moment, but someone moves? Forget it. Gone forever."

"That's why I stick to writing," Bruce says, and smiles. "It's a little less dependent on outside conditions."

After three days of being together most of the time, I think we might be having a personal conversation.

"Alriiiiiiight ladies and gentlemen!" booms the announcer, his voice thundering over the arena speakers.

Everyone in the stands cheers.

"Are you all ready for the final night of Oklahoma Pioneer Days?" he asks.

They are. Loudly, they are.

"I said, *are you ready?*" the announcer asks, and everyone screams, claps, cheers, stomps.

It goes on like that until the bull riding finally starts. The first cowboy's bull runs out of the gate and throws him right away. Poor guy doesn't even make it a second, and Bruce shakes his head next to me.

"The last night's always rough," he says. "They're tired out and sore."

Somehow, that hadn't occurred to me. I'm starting to

wonder at the luck of Jackson pulling the hardest bull tonight.

More cowboys ride. The knot in my stomach clenches as most of them get thrown, and fast. I watch man after man limp off, and now more than ever, I'm realizing how much this sport breaks the people who love it. I'm certain they all have stories like Jackson's: compound fractures, shattered bones, pins and plates everywhere.

The crowd can't get enough, though. The more men get thrown, the more they cheer.

Finally, Jackson's next. When the announcer says his name, everyone in the stands screams. My heart pounds. My palms get sweaty.

I want him to stay safe and unhurt, of course. But more than that I want him to *win*, to ride this bull that no one else has, because I get it. I get *wanting* something.

By my side, hidden from Bruce, I cross my fingers. Even that feels wild and daring.

"This ought to be good," Bruce says, leaning against the barrier.

Crash Junction is in the chute, and with a flush of embarrassment I realize it's the one where we were last night.

No one knows, I tell myself. *Calm down.*

I think of Jackson saying *you're gonna be the death of me*, his lips against my neck. His voice gentle and teasing. I force myself not to smile, even as a bolt of heat flows through me.

Crash is already jumpy and angry, butting his head at the gate. Jackson's on top of the wall, and for a moment, he straddles it and looks at Crash, like he's taking the full measure of the animal.

Then he jumps on. Crash Junction lurches, and Jackson *laughs* as he tightens his rope. He pats Crash on his shoulders and says something to the animal, and the cowboys standing just outside the chute laugh.

I feel like there's a boulder on my chest, pressing down. I think of Jackson's scars. Of his *lucky* tattoo. I realize I never wished him good luck for this match.

Good luck, I think. I bite my lip so I don't say it out loud.

At the last second Jackson looks over at me, a smile around his eyes. I wish I could jump up and down and scream for him, but I can't so I just stand there.

The gate opens.

For a moment, Crash Junction doesn't move.

Then he barrels out, suddenly going top speed before he lurches to a stop, shaking his back from side to side. He leaps in the air, kicking his hind legs and plunging his forelegs to the ground and he hasn't any sooner landed then he's leaping again, twisting, spinning.

I hardly know the first thing about rodeo bulls, and even *I* can tell why Crash Junction is notorious. It doesn't take an expert to know that this bull is dangerous, way more difficult than any I've seen yet.

I've got my thumb on the shutter and I'm just taking snap after snap mechanically. I'm barely looking at the viewfinder, just watching Jackson fight to stay on this animal.

The clock is counting up the seconds but it's slower than molasses in winter, like its batteries have wound down.

Crash bucks and spins and twists. Three seconds. Four seconds, longer than anyone's held onto Crash so far at Pioneer Days.

Five seconds. Jackson almost goes over Crash's head but rights himself, his face a mask of concentration.

Six.

"He's off center," Bruce says.

He's right. Jackson's slid a little to one side, and I can tell that he's starting to go, hanging on desperately to his rope.

Seven seconds, and the crowd is crescendoing, cheering and stomping in the metal stands. I'm holding my breath, frozen in place.

Crash shakes again and Jackson flies off. I yelp, then clap my hand over my mouth. It takes a fraction of a second, but he lands on his shoulder and rolls and springs to his feet but Crash has already stopped going crazy.

The rodeo clowns in the ring get Crash out of there. The crowd in the stands sighs in disappointment like they've got one massive set of lungs, and I feel like my fingers and toes are buzzing with excitement and relief.

Jackson jogs back to the gate without looking at me, grabs it and pulls himself up.

Please look at me, I think. *Come on.*

As he goes over the top, he finally glances my way.

His eyes are burning, but in a different way than usual. This isn't his cocky *how do you like that* gaze, the one that makes me weak in the knees. This is a *it's not over* glance, an *I'll get that bastard or die trying* glance.

It's still sexy. I still want to run backstage and wrap my legs around him, but I feel like I suddenly saw a different side of Jackson.

For the first time, it occurs to me that he wins because he's *worked* for it.

Jackson's score flashes on the screen, and I adjust my camera to the gate again. Bruce looks up at it and nods.

"Still gonna be real hard to beat," he says. "That was a hell of a ride, even if it didn't qualify."

"For first?" I ask.

"Yup," he says.

· · · · ★ ★ ★ ★ · · · ·

JACKSON WINS.

As they announce it, they bring him back out to huge applause and he stands in the middle of the arena, grinning and holding up a huge, tacky belt buckle.

Women scream. Men scream. Everyone is half-drunk on Coors and the thrill of watching rodeo.

In the middle of it, I stand quietly. I take pictures of him and the two runners up. Jackson looks happy, he looks relaxed and pleased, but I can tell that there's something off.

It doesn't take a genius to figure out that it's Crash Junction. Jackson's Everest.

Always reaching for the next thing.

After the fireworks, when the crowd has gone on to the free concert, the media finally gets to go down into the arena and talk to the winning cowboys. The TV crews ask the usual questions, "Are you disappointed you didn't qualify on Crash Junction?" and "Are you excited to be heading to the finals next month in Las Vegas?"

The answers are yes and yes, obviously. Jackson plays up his folksy twang a little, does his best *just a country boy* thing. I stand in front and take pictures, and despite the noise and hubbub and cameras everywhere, I can feel him looking at *me*.

I can't wait. I want him *now*, not in secret in a couple of hours.

As the knot of reporters and cameras disperses, Jackson comes over to Bruce and me.

"You need anything else?" he asks.

Yes, I think.

Bruce flips through his notes, and I pull out my own notes, pretending to go through them.

"If there is, I can't think of it now," Bruce finally says.

"You've got my phone number," Jackson says. "Feel free to call if you think of anything."

"Same," I say, even though my heart's beating so fast it's practically vibrating in my chest.

"You want my number too?" Jackson asks.

His voice is perfectly casual, but for a moment I freeze and look at him, not exactly sure what he's suggesting.

"Take it," Bruce says. "Just in case."

I get Jackson's number, then call him so he has mine. As he puts his phone back in his pocket, I'm pretty sure his eyes *sparkle* as he looks at me.

"Well, folks," he says, thumbs tucked in his belt. "It's been a pleasure working with you. You're heading out early tomorrow, right?"

"Practically the crack of dawn," Bruce says. "It's been a good time watching you ride. See you in Vegas."

They shake hands.

"It's been great shooting rodeo again," I say. I shake hands with Jackson and try not to think about where else on my body his hands have been.

"Glad you could fill in at the last minute," he says. "Maybe I'll see you in Vegas too."

"Maybe," I echo, because I have no idea whether I'll be asked back.

Then he turns and walks away. Bruce and I mosey out of the arena and toward the motel, and Bruce is oddly quiet for a moment.

"You ever heard of Amber Simon?" he asks.

I shake my head.

"Doesn't sound familiar," I say.

"She's a photographer," he says, slowly. "I worked with her about ten years ago, when I was covering basketball."

"Is she good?" I ask.

Is he going to put me in touch with her for networking? I wonder.

He nods.

"She was, at least. I haven't seen any of her work since then."

He pauses, and I frown. This isn't going the way I thought it was.

"While we were covering the playoffs, it came out that she was having an affair with Lamar Bryson, the Lakers' star player," he says.

My entire body flashes cold.

"She was?" I manage to say, even though I feel like I'm not breathing.

Bruce nods.

"It was probably harmless, just unprofessional," he says. "Her photos were still very good, but a gossip magazine got a photo of the two of them making out and ran it. *Sports Weekly* fired her on the spot, and word got around pretty fast that she'd been sleeping with one of the people she was photographing. After that, no one else wanted to hire her."

"Oh," I say. I can't think of anything else.

"I ended up having to report on it a little," Bruce says. "I'd have preferred not to, but when those photos were everywhere, it forced my hand. It became a story."

"What's she doing now?" I ask. I clench my hand into a fist to keep it from shaking.

"I'm not sure," he says. "I think she moved back to South Carolina and became a wedding photographer."

I understand exactly what he's telling me. It's a warning, loud and clear, and it's ringing through my ears.

This could be you, he's saying. *I know what's going on, and here's what could happen.*

"I see," I say.

If Bruce knows, who else knows? Does everyone know?

My head is whirling. I feel like I'm walking through mud, but I keep going, one foot in front of the other.

But maybe we could still...

No. It's over, finished, the end. I'm not risking my entire career for one more night with Jackson. It doesn't matter *how* good it is. This is my life, and I'd be an idiot to pick sex over my career.

I'm leaving tomorrow morning, anyway. It's not like I'm giving up the love of my life or something. Even if he's rakish and charming. Even if he's easier to talk to than anyone else I've ever met.

Even if we're kindred spirits, even if we're more alike than I thought. Even if I really feel like he *gets* me.

"See you tomorrow at 6:30?" Bruce says, and I realize we're standing in the motel parking lot.

"Bright and early," I say.

As I walk back into my room, my phone goes off. It's Jackson.

MEET **me at 9:30 around the side of the motel.**

CRAP.

CHAPTER EIGHTEEN
JACKSON

AT 9:15 I drive my truck around the back of the motel. Then I hop out, lean against the back, and wait.

I should be out drinking and celebrating with everyone else. They're all getting drunk at Betty's again, and I'm sure there's a whole pile of women there too. In an hour, they'll all be arm-in-arm, singing old country ballads off-key.

And here I am, waiting for a girl to meet me in secret. And I'm *excited*. I'd rather be here than drunk with two girls on my lap.

She never texted back, but my phone says she's read it.

At 9:35, a figure comes into the shadow behind the motel, looks around for a moment, and then walks toward me.

"Hope that's you and not a psycho killer," I tease.

"It's me," she says, but her voice is oddly stiff. She stops a couple of feet in front of me, just out of arm's reach.

The pit of my belly goes cold.

"The Lamplighter Motel's got a room with our name on it," I say.

I take a step forward and she takes a step back.

"Bruce knows," she says.

In the dark I can see she's looking at the ground, not at me.

"What do you mean?" I ask.

"I mean *Bruce knows*," she hisses. "What else does that mean?"

"It means, is he going to write about this?" I ask. "Are we news now?"

"I don't think so," she whispers.

"Did he tell anyone else?"

"I don't *know*, Jackson," she says, her voice choking up. "I'm not fired yet. That's all I've got."

I put a hand on her shoulder but she pulls back.

"I knew this was dumb from the second you showed up with wine at my door," she mutters. "I can't believe I did this."

"So we're not going anywhere tonight?" I ask. My voice sounds hollow, even to my ears.

Mae just shakes her head.

"I've nearly ruined my life because of you enough times," she says, and suddenly anger flares through me.

"I'm not the one who got drunk and practically hopped on my dick six years ago," I say.

She shoots me a glare.

"You could have stopped this any time, Lula-Mae," I go on. "And you didn't."

"I am now," she says. She still won't look at me.

"You don't think it's too little, too late?" I ask.

"I think every second we spend together is dangerous," she says. Now she's leaning against the truck, still just out of reach, arms crossed defensively in front of her.

"Because we might get caught?" I ask. "Or because you know you're the reason we got caught?"

"I'm the reason?" she says. She finally looks at me, her blue eyes blazing, even in the dark. "I'm not the one who tracked me down in the arena last night, practically in public."

"You're the one who screams loud enough to wake the dead," I say.

She blushes and glares. She opens her mouth but closes it without saying anything and looks away again.

"I'm not about to apologize for *that*," I say.

"Of course you're not," she mutters. "You win rodeos and sleep with lots of women and everyone loses their shit over you because you're the golden boy. I'm sure you don't *apologize*."

Anger seethes through me, and I take a step toward her. I feel like everything that's happened the past couple of days is bubbling up in a black boil right now: Raylan being a dick, Darlene giving me talking-to after talking-to, sneaking around with Mae, falling off Crash Junction.

Knowing the whole time that Pioneer Days is gonna end and we're gonna go our separate ways.

Mae telling me that I can't even have her this one last time.

"Okay," I say. I try to keep my voice steady, but there's a hard, rough edge biting into it. "I'm sorry we slept together and we had such a good time that everyone found out. I'm sorry you wanted it as bad as I did."

Mae snorts.

"Nice apology," she says.

I take a step forward and now I'm right next to her, our bodies almost touching.

"But most of all, Lula-Mae, I'm sorry that if you changed your mind this minute, I'd still take you up on it in a heartbeat."

"I'm not going to change my mind," she whispers. Her glare shimmers with tears.

"Your loss," I say.

"I'm leaving tomorrow morning anyway," she says. "One more time doesn't matter."

"So why not do it?" I say. "If it doesn't matter."

"You know why," she snaps. "Because I'm not giving up my career over some fling."

I'm not stupid. I always knew there was a timestamp on this, but hearing her say that hurts more than I thought it would.

"You're right. Some casual fuck sure isn't worth it," I say, the words coming out more bitter than I mean.

Now she has the nerve to look at me like she's wounded, though she doesn't say anything.

"I gotta go," she says, and stands up straight.

I don't stop leaning on the truck.

"Good luck, Lula-Mae," I say, even as something deep inside me twists.

"You too, Jackson," she says, her voice cool and quiet.

Maybe I'm seeing things in the dark, but I'm almost certain a single tear tracks down her face.

"Go on," I say.

She turns and leaves, and I watch her walk back around the motel. Her hips still move and roll in the sexiest way I've ever seen, and angry as I am, I get hard just watching her leave.

Goddammit, I think.

I kick one of the tires on my truck, fists clenched into balls.

Goddamn fucking Lula-Mae. Goddamn Bruce and goddamn Wayne and Darlene and goddamn Crash Junction.

I kick the tires a couple more times. I pace a loop around

the truck, feeling like I might crawl out of my own skin with anger and horniness, with my frustration over falling off Crash Junction but also the thrill of winning.

I take a deep breath. I get into my truck and crank the engine.

Fuck it, I think. *I'm getting drunk at Betty's and forgetting all about this.*

· · · ★ ★ ★ ★ ★ · · ·

IN NO TIME AT ALL, I've downed six shots of whiskey and I'm watching three guys sing *She Thinks My Tractor's Sexy* very, very badly. Two girls are on stage with them, not even singing, just dancing drunkenly.

It's obvious that they're trying to dance sexy. In another couple shots I'll probably agree with them. Someone shows up with a tray of whiskey, and I take one.

"That's a sipping whiskey," says Betty's voice.

I look up. There she is.

"Try to make it last at least four sips," she says.

I take a sip and look up at her.

"There's one," I say.

Betty moves on. I take another sip, and she's replaced by a pretty brunette in a pink cowboy hat who spills into the seat next to me.

"Hi Jackson," she says. "I'm Anna."

"Hey there," I say.

"I loved watching you ride," she says, batting her eyelashes at me.

I take another sip.

"Even though I fell off?" I ask.

She laughs, then bites her lip. I think it's supposed to be sexy, but she looks a little like a rabbit.

"Everyone falls off," she says.

I keep drinking. Anna keeps drinking. The guys keep singing.

Before I know it, Anna's on my lap, leaning against me, laughing and biting her lip. My hand's on her ass, and I think I'm squeezing it. It's a nice ass.

"You must be tired after doing all that riding," she says, curling her fingers through my hair.

"Ain't that tired," I manage to say. "I could still manage a couple more rides."

She laughs, the sound a little too nasal.

"A couple rides," she says. "Damn, Jackson, I guess what they say is true."

"Course it is," I say. "No false advertising here."

My dick's at half-mast, and I move my hips so it moves against her.

She bites her lip again, then slides her finger around the shell of my ear. I'm too drunk for it to feel like much.

Then she leans in and kisses me. Her lips feel weirdly droopy, and her mouth is wet as she pushes her tongue into me, not that I can complain. I'm sure I'm too drunk to be any good at this either, so I just squeeze her ass and try to pull her against me.

We make out for a while, right there in the middle of the bar. To be honest, I'm barely paying attention. I'm just on autopilot. *Anything* to forget about how I don't get to do this with Mae ever again.

"Want to get out of here?" she asks, breathily.

My vision is sliding left and right. My dick's finally two-thirds hard, and I think I'm good for the last third by the time we get there.

"Sure," I say.

She gets off me, then leads me out the front door. We walk twenty feet down the sidewalk.

On the opposite side of the street, I see a blond head. My heart leaps for a moment, but it's not Mae, and now I'm drunk and frustrated and angry at myself for getting so excited.

I grab Anna and push her up against the plate glass of a closed shop.

"Oooh," she says, and I kiss her hard. I run my hand up her legs and push my finger under the hem of her shorts while we kiss sloppily.

I force myself to pay attention to *this,* to the hot girl I'm actually going to fuck tonight. The one who's present.

I hear a low whistle, and I break the kiss with Anna and look toward the bar entrance.

It's Raylan, Clay, Trevor, and a couple other guys, walking toward us.

"Don't let us bother you," Clay says, grinning.

"We're going for smokes," Trevor says. "You need anything?"

Raylan looks the two of us up and down.

"I'm good," I say.

"What happened?" Raylan says. "The photographer turn you down again?"

My whole body goes rigid.

"What?" I say.

Raylan's swimming in my vision, but he smirks.

"What's her name. Mae? She have a change of heart?"

Clay and Trevor snicker.

I step away from Anna, who's frowning.

"What are you talking about?" I ask, moving toward Raylan.

"I ain't stupid," he says. "I got the room next to hers. I

didn't think she'd put out, but I guess when you're Jackson Cody and you plow your way through—"

I grab him by the front of the shirt and shove him up against the wall. Everything lurches and swims, but how *dare* he talk about Mae like this, in public.

"You better keep your damn mouth *shut,* you son—"

He punches me in the stomach and plain flashes through me as my bruised ribs scream. I stumble backward, nearly falling over.

"What's your fucking *problem,* Jackson?" Raylan shouts.

I swing at him. It's a terrible punch, but it still lands on the side of his face and his head snaps around though it doesn't connect quite right.

He shouts again and now I'm off balance, but so is he because we're both drunk. Raylan grabs for me and misses, and we both fall to the sidewalk.

I've been in plenty of fights and I scramble to my feet and nearly fall over him, then grab him from behind in a headlock.

"Say you won't tell nobody," I shout, right in his ear.

"You ain't my boss!" Raylan shouts, both hands tugging at my arm around his neck.

I nearly fall over but I hold on. There's one thought pounding through my head, and that thought is *fucking Raylan needs to keep his mouth shut.*

That's what Mae wants, and maybe I can give her this one thing.

"Say you won't tell!" I shout again, but then Clay finally grabs me from behind and pulls me back by the elbows, locking my arms behind me. He gets me off balance at first, and then Raylan is scrambling up and Trevor's holding him back.

"Let me go!" I shout.

"Get off!" Raylan shouts.

"Hell no," says Clay.

I could probably get free, but my shirt is ripped and I'm breathing hard and God Almighty that punch hurt.

"Fuck you, Jackson," Raylan spits out.

"Keep your damn mouth shut," I say, and spit on the sidewalk. "Just keep it shut."

Raylan spits on the sidewalk too, and we glare at each other for a moment.

"You gonna start again if we let you go?" Trevor asks.

I shake my head. Raylan shakes his.

They release us. I shake out my arms, glaring at Raylan. He glares back.

Anna comes up to me and puts one hand on my arm, but I move it away and look at her.

"Sorry, darlin'," I say. "Not tonight."

Raylan snorts, but for once he doesn't say anything.

· · · · ★ ★ ★ ★ ★ · · · ·

I WAKE up the moment the sun rises. My stomach's rolling and my head feels like someone's mining my skull from the inside. I barely make it to the toilet before I puke my guts out, then sit on the edge of the tub, my head in my hands.

I don't remember what happened after the fight. I think I went back into the bar, did another shot, and someone sober took me back here. I'm just glad that I'm alone this morning, and that I didn't do something impossibly stupid.

It doesn't matter, I think. *She's leaving, remember?*

I throw up again. Then I get into the bathtub and sit there, naked except my boxers. The porcelain feels good against my skin.

She ain't dead, I think, staring up at the shower head. *Just in New York. It's not even a different country.*

I cover my eyes with my hands, because it's bright in here. I wish I could reach the bathroom light switch from the tub, but I can't.

She's not even working for Sports Weekly once that issue comes out, I think.

Too bad that's not your only problem, Jackson.

You were a dick to her when she turned you down last night.

Goddammit.

After a couple more minutes I drag myself out of the bathtub and drink a couple little plastic cups of tap water. My stomach doesn't like it, but sooner or later, I've gotta keep something down.

Outside, I hear a man's voice. Then a woman's.

Mae's.

I don't move. A trunk slams. A door shuts. An engine starts.

I have the urge to rush to the window, to watch her drive away with Bruce in the rental car. Like some sort of pathetic puppy.

Instead, I get back into bed and listen to the car drive away. Then I lay there, trying to go back to sleep.

An hour later, there's a knock on the door. I pull my pants on, stomach lurching, and I open it.

It's Raylan, wearing sunglasses. There's a bruise purpling on one cheekbone, and he looks like hell. He holds out a huge bottle of blue Gatorade.

"Thought you might be feeling it this morning," he says.

I open the door wider.

"Come on in," I say, and take the Gatorade. "Thanks."

I fall into one crappy chair, take a drink, then wipe my mouth. He falls into the other.

"Sorry about last night," I say.

Raylan shakes his head.

"It's all right," he says. "Been a while since we got into a drunken fight on the sidewalk."

"Six months at least," I say.

"Was the last one Topeka?" he asks.

"Either that or Santa Fe," I say.

"I forgot about Santa Fe," he says.

"I skinned my elbow on the sidewalk in Santa Fe," I say. "Took a month to heal."

We both take long swigs of the blue drink. I'm slowly starting to feel less nauseous.

"We good?" I finally say.

Raylan nods.

Then he looks around.

"You alone in here?" he asks, sounding puzzled.

"Unless there's someone under the bed," I say.

He gives me a weird look.

"You won and went home alone?" he asks.

"Apparently so," I say.

"Shit, Jackson," he says. "I still got one asleep in my bed."

I lean forward. My head pounds.

"Raylan," I say. "I don't know what you know about me and Mae, but you have got to keep it to yourself."

"You made that point last night," he says, and points to the bruise on his face.

"I said I was sorry."

He finally smiles.

"Shit, I was just kidding until you punched me," he said. Goddammit.

"She'll get fired," I say, my head in my hand. "I don't give a shit about me."

"I ain't gonna tell nobody," Raylan says. "So long as she don't make me look bad."

I look at him. He laughs, then rubs his temples.

I stand and grab a bottle of Advil from my suitcase and set it on the table between us. Raylan takes about five, and I do too.

By the time we leave four hours later, the hangover's almost gone.

· · · · · ★ ★ ★ · · · · ·

THERE'S three weeks between the end of Pioneer Days and the start of the Rodeo World Championships in Las Vegas. Raylan and I drive home from Oklahoma. I drop him off at his house in Eastern Colorado and then drive alone to my parents' ranch eight more hours north in Sawtooth, Wyoming. I listen to country western radio the whole time.

It's bright and clear and cold, though it hasn't snowed yet. The sky stretches from horizon to horizon in a nonstop blue dome, and there's nothing but waving yellow-green grass for nearly as far as I can see. It's empty and wild, but this is where I'm from so I guess it's home.

My parents welcome me home, and my mom even babies me for a full day before she puts me to work again. I don't mind. I like baling hay and feeding animals and fixing fences and staring into ancient tractor engines with my dad, debating over which part is busted this time.

If I'm doing something, I'm not thinking about Mae. I'm not replaying our last conversation in my head, trying to figure out what I should have said instead.

I miss her. I miss her, and I want her, and I think I *like* her, and I hate it.

Sadie, my sister, even visits for a few days with her kids. Her husband can't come, but my three nephews tear around the house and raise hell.

"Tyler's almost old enough to ride a sheep," I tease her.

Sadie gives me a stern look.

"Heck no," she says. "These boys are *not* doing rodeo."

"I'm offended," I tease her.

"I never should have let your father put you on a bull," my mother sighs.

I shrug.

"I'm pretty good at it," I say.

"You scare the life outta me every time you get on one of those animals," my mother says.

We all go silent for a moment, looking at each other. Tyler bangs a dump truck against the floor next to a dog. The dog doesn't wake up.

"Cassie had her baby," my mom volunteers. "Another boy. Cute as a button."

"Yeah?" I say, as noncommittally as possible.

"That's three now," my mother points out.

"Mhm," I say.

* * * * * ★ ★ ★ * * * ·

THE NIGHT before my issue of *Sports Weekly* hits the stands, my parents suddenly insist on going out to dinner. The nearest town, Sawtooth, is forty-five minutes away, but we pack up the six of us — my parents, me, Sadie, and her kids — and head to Luigi's House of Spaghetti.

Everyone's strangely quiet but nervous. I start to think that something might be up.

When we get there, the windows are dark.

"I think it's closed," I say.

"Oh, no," my mom says. "They're just using those new environmentally friendly lightbulbs."

That doesn't make any sense, but I go with it.

They make me go first, and the moment I push the door open, the lights fly on.

"SURPRISE!" a room full of people shouts.

I stop in my tracks and look around, and then I start laughing.

"It's your release party!" Sadie says.

On a table is a big stack of *Sports Weekly*.

"I thought it came out tomorrow," I say.

"We know people," my mom says, and winks. "Stores got it in yesterday and I pulled some strings."

Of course she did. Sawtooth has a population of three thousand. She knows everyone.

Sadie hands me a copy, and I look at it.

I'm on the cover. It's weird as hell to see myself there: smiling at the camera, looking kind of cocky. Arms folded. I'm leaning against the side of the arena, hat on.

I don't even remember Mae taking this picture, but she took a lot of them.

In big letters across the bottom, it says

MEET JACKSON CODY
Rodeo's Newest Rockstar

I let out a whistle.

"Rockstar," I say, because I don't know what else to say. Even though I knew I was going to be on the cover, it feels surreal.

"Open it!" my mom says.

I start flipping through, but she shoves an open copy into my hands, so I take that.

Spread across two pages is one of the shots Mae took in the stable. I'm facing Crash Junction.We're staring at each other. I've got him by one horn. There's sunlight peeking through the windows and we're both half-lit and golden.

It nearly leaps off the page with energy, with potential. Staring at it, I've got the feeling that something is just *about* to happen, something powerful and raw, and this photo captures the last quiet second before everything explodes.

Hell, it takes my breath away, and I was *there*.

"It's a great article, honey," my mom says, and kisses my cheek.

· · · ★ ★ ★ ★ ★ ★ · ·

LATE THAT NIGHT, in my trailer, I finally get to read the whole thing: story by Bruce McMurtry, photos by Mae Guthrie.

It's good. It's exciting. Reading it, even I get keyed up about my final round, riding Crash Junction. I'm disappointed when I fall off.

The photos are mostly action shots, though there's one from the night we all went to Betty's, five of us holding up shots. Raylan's saying something.

On the last page is one she took of me on our last night together. I'm standing in the bucking chute, face half-lit, moonlight on the sand past the gate. I'm looking toward it.

When Mae took it, I could practically still feel her on my skin.

CHAPTER NINETEEN
MAE

THE PHOTOS ARE due to my editors three days after I get back to New York, so all I do for those three days is edit. I pick the best hundred from thousands and then go over them in detail. I fix lighting levels, I sharpen textures, I compare two pictures that are almost exactly the same until it feels like my eyes might bleed.

After a while, I can even manage to ignore that they're all pictures of Jackson.

At the end, I send them off and fall into bed for twelve hours.

· · · · · ★ ★ ★ ★ · · · ·

I STAY BUSY, because it keeps my mind off things. I go back and forth with the people at Sports Weekly, and I string together a couple more freelance jobs. The rodeo finally paid enough to give me a slight cushion, something to fall back on if work ever gets really slow, but I don't want to get lazy and rely on that.

Maybe when it comes out I'll suddenly be in demand,

but that hasn't happened yet. I do a low-level fashion shoot and take pictures for a private high school's marketing brochure.

I go out with my friends and my roommates, Sasha and Dani. I show them pictures of the sexy cowboy and they're all smitten instantly. They try to get his number, and I laugh and tell them no.

I don't tell them that we got a lot more than professional.

Then it's release day. I steel myself as I walk to the news stand. I've never actually bought *Sports Weekly* before, but it's right up front, next to The Economist and the New Yorker.

Jackson's on the cover. Grinning at me. I stare back at him.

It's a great picture, but he's so good-looking it takes me a little by surprise. Not that I didn't know, but I think I started to take it for granted after looking at his face for seventy-two hours straight.

I wonder how many women have walked by here only to pick up a copy and suddenly develop a new crush. I buy a copy and then stand on the sidewalk, going over every single photo.

I can remember where I was when I took each of them, and I remember what was happening for most of them.

The centerfold photo, with Jackson's hand on Crash's horn? He was about to apologize for being an asshole.

The picture of the group doing shots? A minute later he was on stage, singing *Friends in Low Places*.

The last photo, the one of him in the bucking chute? We'd just finished having sex, and he was talking quietly, staring out into the arena. Wondering if he'd be happier if he'd settled down and had kids.

That quiet, introspective Jackson isn't in the article. In it he lives up to his reputation as cocky charmer who can never quite follow the rules, who drinks too much, parties hard, goes through women like a hot knife through butter, and wins rodeo after rodeo.

I wonder which one is the real Jackson. It's probably both.

· · · · · ★ ★ ★ · · · ·

IT'S NEARLY ten that night when Jackson calls. I almost don't answer, because I have no idea what to say — sorry for being a jerk, but we're still probably never going to see each other again?

"You see my cover story, Lula-Mae?" he asks. He even *sounds* far away.

"Of course," I say. "I bought myself a copy."

"They didn't give you one?" he asks.

"I got impatient," I say. "It's good. Bruce is a good writer."

"It's the photos that make it," he says.

I laugh.

"I thought so too," I say. "Did I get your good side?"

"They're all good sides," he says.

I hear a bang on the other end.

"What was that?" I ask.

"Shut a cabinet too hard," Jackson says. "I'm at my house."

"You mean your trailer on your parents' ranch."

"It's a house," he says. "It's got walls, a roof, and I'm hooked up to the electric and water."

"That also applies to a lot of barns," I say.

"Miss Guthrie, are you implying that I'm an animal?" he says, and I can hear the smile in his voice.

"Well," I say. "If it walks like a duck and talks like a duck…"

"If I have to be an animal, you can do better than a duck," he says.

"A goose?" I tease. "A swan?"

"If I have to be a bird, an eagle at least," he says. "Something with a little majesty."

I laugh, and the line goes silent for a moment. I think again about the last time we talked, how we left things angry and uncomfortable. I hate that it's hanging over my head.

"I'm sorry for being such a bitch," I say, my words all coming out in a rush. "I could have been a lot nicer."

"I was an asshole," Jackson says. "I had no right to get mad at you for not wanting to sleep with me again."

It wasn't that I didn't want to, I think, but I don't say it out loud.

"Thanks," I say, and flop backwards onto my bed.

"Did Bruce ever say anything else?" he asks.

"Not a peep. To me, anyway, and I don't think he'd tell anyone else."

Jackson sighs into the phone.

"Raylan knew," he says.

I tense up.

"Kinda because I told him. We were real drunk and he made a crack and things got a little out of hand," he says.

"Out of hand?" I ask.

"I took a swing at him," Jackson says, sounding resigned. "I mean, we get into it a couple times a year because we spend so much time together we gotta let off some steam. But he was kidding until I put him in a headlock and made him swear not to tell."

I don't know if I'm embarrassed or impressed by this. Maybe both.

"We're good now," Jackson says. "Besides, it doesn't matter any more. The magazine's out."

"We're free to be pen pals," I say, trying to make a joke. "I always wanted one as a kid."

"Did you know that Wyoming has this thing called the internet?" Jackson says.

"Shut up," I laugh.

"It's true," he goes on. "It's not just for fancy big city folks anymore."

"You're putting words in my mouth."

"It's faster than the pony express, even," he goes on.

"Okay, I get it," I say, still laughing. "You don't want to be pen pals. Fine."

Pals is not the word for what I want from him.

"I'm just saying, we could video chat instead of writing letters," he says.

I look down at myself quickly: oversized t-shirt, ugly old boxer shorts, hair in a bun because I haven't washed it in three days.

"Maybe later," I say. "I'm already in my pajamas."

"I wasn't even going to ask what you were wearing," he says.

"You weren't?" I say.

There's a pause. I bite my lip and squeeze my eyes shut, because now I'm wondering what *he's* wearing, whether he's also lying on his bed, thinking about me.

"That doesn't mean I didn't wonder," he says, slowly. His voice drops in a way that sends a shiver through my whole body, and I turn bright red.

"Do you want to know?" I say.

In the kitchen of my apartment, one of my roommates starts doing the dishes, and I wonder if she can hear me talking on the phone. I get off my bed, turn some music on, and flop back on my bed.

"I feel like a bad cliché," Jackson says. "I swear I just called to say hello."

There's a low ache starting inside me. It's torture. I don't want to want him but I still do, even when it's just his voice.

"An oversized college t-shirt and an old pair of boxers," I say.

Immediately, I wish I'd lied.

"Are you in bed?" he asks.

"I'm on my bed," I say. "Where are you?"

"I'm sitting at my kitchen table," he says. "I've got the lights off and I'm looking out the window at the stars."

I look at the tiny window in my bedroom. The curtains are closed, but I know what's behind it.

"I'm looking out the window at a brick wall, and I can hear my roommate doing the dishes," I say.

Jackson laughs.

"Can your roommate hear you?" he asks.

"I hope not," I say.

There's a pause, and I hear something creak on his end. Something about this feels dangerous, in a completely different way than being with him in person did. It feels like somehow, this makes it *real*.

"If you hung up now and pretended this never happened I wouldn't blame you," he says.

My heart seizes.

"Do you want me to hang up?" I ask.

"No," he says.

I swallow. Then I take a deep breath, close my eyes, and steel myself for the sentence I'm about to say.

"Jackson, I'm so wet right now," I whisper.

He exhales, and I can't say why, but it sounds like he's smiling.

"From talking to me?" he asks. His voice is low and growly again.

"Yes," I say. My face is on fire, and I'm certain that I'm bright red.

I have *no* idea how to have phone sex, but here goes nothing.

"Take your clothes off," he says. "I want to imagine you naked."

I do it and flop back on the bed.

"My nipples are hard, too," I say.

Do I just describe the things that are happening?

"Touch them," he says. "I like how you moan when I rub them between my fingers."

I pinch one nipple and then rub it between my fingers. I squeeze my legs together but it doesn't even quell the throbbing there. I hear myself sigh into the phone.

"Shit, Lula-Mae, I'm hard as a rock," he says.

"Tell me more about that," I say.

Not sexy.

Jackson chuckles into the phone.

"I'm sitting at my kitchen table, staring at the sky and thinking about you touching yourself halfway across the country," he says. "You're driving me wild and I can't even see you."

"This feels better when you do it," I say.

Jackson groans.

"Take your cock out and stroke it slow," I say. My eyes are still shut, my legs still clamped together against the constant, hollow throb as I imagine Jackson next to a window, big cock in one hand, eyes closed as he leans his head against the wall.

"I'd rather have you here," he says. "Thinking about you and jerking off gets old, you know."

"It's only been a week and a half," I say.

He just chuckles. I bite my lip.

"I wish I was there too," I say. "Even if I was just watching you touch yourself."

"Really?" he says.

I slide my hand down my belly, over my hips.

"Really," I whisper. "You're sexy."

"Tell me what you're doing now," he says.

I slide one finger over my clit. I'm so turned on that it feels swollen, sensitive to the touch.

"Rubbing my clit," I say.

In the kitchen, the water goes off, and I pray my roommates can't hear me.

"I wish I was eating you out," he says, half-groaning. "I wish I had my tongue on your clit and my fingers in your pussy, and I could watch you come undone."

I gasp, my fingers sliding along myself.

"I want my face between your thighs as you come and come," he says. "I want to lick you until you think you can't come again, and you're shaking."

He swallows, breathing hard. My fingers are circling my clit faster and faster.

"I want your cock," I blurt out, and he groans. "Inside me."

"Say it again," he says.

"I want your cock inside me," I say.

My toes curl. I gasp again, trying not to make much noise. I imagine Jackson, cock out at the table, and I imagine getting on top of him and riding it.

"Fuck, Lula-Mae, I can't hold on when you talk like that," Jackson says.

"Make me come," I say. My fingers are slippery and working my clit fast as I think about the last time we had sex, when I came so hard I thought I couldn't move afterward.

"If I was there I'd fuck you so hard you screamed when you came," he says. "Just for how good your pussy feels when you come—"

On the other end there's a small crash and a faraway groan.

I grit my teeth together and let my orgasm burst through me, my fingers working like mad. A single noise works its way out of my throat but the waves are already wracking through me as I roll onto my side, my ear on top of the phone as I squeeze my legs together, trying not to make any noise.

I'm breathing hard, shockwaves still going through me. I can feel my pussy twitching.

I keep my eyes closed, listening to Jackson come, imagining how he looks, with one hand around his thick cock.

"Shit, Lula-Mae," he finally says, his voice still far away. Then there's another noise, and suddenly his voice is closer.

"Sorry," he says.

"Did you drop the phone?" I ask.

"Yeah," he says, and he's laughing.

"What happened?" I ask. I start to giggle along with him.

"Nothing," he says quickly.

"Jackson," I say.

"I need to clean off my kitchen table is all," he says.

I dissolve into giggles, one hand still between my legs.

"Gross," I say.

"Your fault," he says.

"I didn't say *come on your kitchen table*," I say.

"Yeah, but you said the stuff that made it happen," he says. "I kinda got taken by surprise."

"You've never masturbated before?" I tease, blushing a little.

I don't know why I'm blushing. I'm pretty sure I just said some pretty filthy things, and that was fine.

There's a pause.

"I came pretty hard," he finally says. "You should talk dirty more often."

"I've never had phone sex before," I admit.

"Well, you did great for a phone sex virgin," he says, his voice low and slow. "As my kitchen table can attest."

"Ew," I say again.

"Once we got past *tell me more about that*, anyway," he teases.

We talk for another hour. He tells me about his parents, about his sister and his nephews, about the magazine release surprise party. I tell him about Sasha and Dani, my roommates, about how I found the perfect pair of mittens, and how I saw a rat glaring out at me from a frozen, old jack-o-lantern.

When we hang up it's past midnight, but I lay awake in my bed for a while.

I don't know what's happening. I don't think there's any possible way it can work out, and I have no idea how to take a first step.

But I'm happy.

· · · · · ★ ★ ★ ★ ★ · · · · ·

WE START TEXTING EACH OTHER. I wake up the next morning to see he's already sent a picture of the sunrise over a long, flat horizon. I text him back a picture of a cup of coffee.

Jackson: Not a morning person?
Me: Ugh.

It keeps up all day the next two days, these light, flirty, fun texts. He sends me pictures of his nephews, his tractor, and his favorite goat, Flossie. I send my subway stop, my roommates, and the window from my apartment.

After a day or two, I realize: this is how we're sharing each other's lives. I can't meet Flossie in person, but he can show me. When I say *getting on the subway*, now he knows where I am.

Two days after the phone sex, I get package and a post-card. The postcard has a picture of huge, stark, rugged mountains and says YELLOWSTONE NATIONAL PARK on it.

The back says:

We can be pen pals, too.
- Jackson

P.S. I live clear across the state from Yellowstone, but the gas station had this in stock anyway.

As I'm standing there reading it, Sasha comes out into our tiny living room and looks from the postcard to the box and back.

"That's the hot cowboy," she says.

"Nosy," I say.

"You're pen pals?" she says. "Do you know about Skype?"

"It's a dumb joke," I say.

"So he's sending you postcards and you're texting him all day," she says.

Dani comes out of her room too.

"What's this about the hot cowboy?" she asks, grinning.

"*Now* you're ganging up on me," I say, laughing.

"Got any naked pictures of him?" Sasha asks, getting out a box of cereal.

"*No*," I say.

I wish I did, but I really don't.

I put the postcard on the table and grab my keys to tear open the cardboard box. It's from Amazon, and I open the outer box to reveal a smaller, smooth white box inside.

Dani looks at it and just starts laughing. I frown, because I thought it was a new camera strap.

On the side of the stark white box is a very tasteful picture of a large purple vibrator.

Dani and Sasha are both staring at me, giggling, but I'm just confused. I look at the address on the outside of the box, wondering if I just awkwardly opened a package that was for a neighbor, but it's to me.

"Why do you look so confused?" Sasha finally asks, pouring milk over her cereal and trying not to giggle.

"Because I didn't order a fancy vibrator," I say.

Dani leans forward and snags the packing slip out of the box.

Then she read it and grins.

"What," I say. I reach out and try to snatch it from her, but she waves it away. She hands it to Sasha, and Sasha starts grinning.

I suddenly have the feeling I know who the vibrator is from.

It's from someone who *goddamn knows* that I have roommates, because I sent him a picture of my roommates *yesterday*.

I turn ten shades of red and probably every other color too.

"It's from Jackson?" I manage to ask.

"There's a message, too," Sasha says.

"Please no," I say.

She laughs.

"It just says, enjoy, wink emoji, talk to you soon, Jackson."

Thank *god*.

"Okay," I say, trying to figure out how to keep this situation cool. "Well, okay, neat, I'll just put this in my room, I guess."

"Mae," says Sasha. "That model's gonna take a couple hours to charge."

I raise my eyebrows.

"What? I know stuff," she says. "Anyway, you've got time to come back and tell us the truth about you and the sexy cowboy."

"With details," says Dani.

I plug the vibrator in, come back, and tell them. I skip a lot of the details.

· · · · · ★ ★ ★ · · · ·

THE NEXT DAY, my agent Janice calls. She wants me to shoot stills for a TV show that's filming in New York, and it's grueling. It's four eighteen-hour days in a row, but the pay is good and I like working, so I take it. I text Jackson behind-the-scenes photos and loopy selfies at dawn. He texts back about getting ready for the World Championships in Vegas.

I'm kind of nervous about them. At least in Wyoming, there's no other women around, sitting on his lap and feeding him shots and making out with him. It's all wholesome farm stuff and a small town.

I finish the last day of shooting at nine in the morning.

While I'm on the subway with no signal, I get a phone call from Janice.

Sports Weekly wants to send me to Vegas to shoot the Rodeo World Championship. I sprint aboveground and call her back.

"Hi, this is—"

"Yes!" I shout.

CHAPTER TWENTY

JACKSON

I HAVEN'T TALKED to Mae in four days. She's texted me and I've texted back, and I know she's busy working crazy eighteen-hour days, but it's weird how I *miss* her.

It snows, just a dusting, and I send her a picture of my trailer. I send her a picture of my mom's apple pie.

I get a postcard of a trash barge that says *New York City* on it. The back says:

This is the realest post card I could find, pen pal.
- Mae

I stick it to my mini fridge like a dork.

I look at house listings in Wyoming. For real houses that aren't on my parents' ranch, because I've finally got the urge to have something real and not temporary.

Besides, if Mae ever visits, she can't visit me *here*. This trailer is barely fit for me, a bachelor who's on the road most of the year. This is not a trailer fit for female eyes.

I'm tinkering with an old tractor when Mae calls. It's

weird that she's calling me in the middle of the morning, so I get a little nervous.

"Hey," I say.

"I'm so tired I think I might be psychotic, but I'm coming to the rodeo thing in Vegas," she says.

I stand up with surprise.

"You are?" I say.

"I am," she says. "*Sports Weekly* asked me to shoot it."

"So you're working it," I say.

"Yeah," she says.

I can hear traffic behind her. She must be outside. I wonder what that means, exactly, but I also can't stop grinning. I get to see her again. In one week.

"Congrats," I say. "They hired you back, they must have liked your work."

And not found out about us, I think.

"They said they did," she says. She sounds happy but dead tired. "Look, I have to go to sleep or I think I might pass out in the street, but I wanted to let you know I'm gonna be there."

I hear her unlocking her door, and then the noise of the street fades.

"I'm really excited to see you again," she says, softly.

"Not as excited as I am," I say.

We hang up so she can sleep, and I just stand in our tractor shed and stare out the door at the patchy white on the ground outside.

One week. In a week, I get to see her.

I abandon the tractor and go make some plans.

· · · · · ★ ★ ★ ★ · · · ·

SHE CALLS ME THAT NIGHT. I'm lying in my bed reading a book, but I keep having to read the same paragraph over and over again. I practically throw it across the trailer when my phone goes off with a video chat.

I grin. I *like* our video chats.

She's sitting at her desk, using her laptop, wearing an oversized t-shirt. I hold mine over my head.

"Hey," she says.

"You awake now?" I ask.

"Finally, yeah," she says. "Sorry I was out of it this morning."

"You're coming to Vegas, though," I say.

"For work," she says. Her blue eyes look steadily into the camera on her phone. She swallows. "I think we should figure something out."

"Like getting a suite at the Mandalay Bay?" I ask, grinning up at my phone.

She frowns.

"*Sports Weekly* put us at the Wynn," she says.

"Most of the cowboys are staying by the convention center," I say. "Mandalay Bay is clear at the opposite end of the strip."

Comprehension breaks over her face slowly, and then she laughs.

"So we're not gonna run into anyone," she says, her eyes sparkling.

"No one at all," I say. "I can even go full incognito and ditch the hat and the boots if I have to."

"What a sacrifice," she teases.

"I'll barely know who I am anymore," I say.

"Do you even own regular shoes?" she asks.

"Yes," I say.

I think I do. If I don't, I'll get some.

"With no boots, no hats, and a plaid shirt you'll just look like some hipster," Mae teases. "You're a dime a dozen in Brooklyn."

"I *know* that's not true," I say.

"Maybe I shouldn't even bother going to Vegas," she says, leaning forward in her chair.

"I *promise* to make it worth your while," I say. "The suite's got a view of the strip. I splurged."

"That's what you got a suite for?" she asks.

Now she's grinning wickedly and I'm getting hard, fast. She's been working so much that I haven't even spoken with her in four days and we haven't had phone sex for longer than that.

"The view of the city is a bonus," I say. "It's mostly so you can scream as loud as you want."

I stand up and move to my kitchen table. No, it's not the ideal spot for jerking off, but it's got the best video chat setup. I already *said* this trailer wasn't fit for women.

"I only scream as loud as you make me," she says.

Mae leans back and I can see her nipples poking at her t-shirt.

"Then you're gonna be screaming a *lot*," I say.

Her eyes slide to one side, and she pulls one leg onto her chair.

"I know I said thanks for the gift," she says slyly. "But I haven't thanked you *properly*."

"What gift is that?" I ask.

"The postcard," she says. "So here goes: thank you for the postcard."

"Tease," I say.

"It's a very nice postcard," she says.

Then she leans forward.

"My roommates went out tonight," she says.

"So you're alone there?" I ask.

She nods, then blushes.

"They kind of found out that we're... having a thing, actually," she says.

"You told them?" I ask.

"Well, we text each other fifty times a day," Mae says. "Oh, and you *mailed me a vibrator without telling me*, and I opened it in front of them."

That honestly hadn't occurred to me.

"Sorry," I say.

"Well, now they know why I won't give them the hot cowboy's phone number," she says.

"Am I the hot cowboy?" I ask.

She laughs.

"Of course," she says, laughing. "I had to listen to my friends talk about how hard they'd bang you when your article came out."

I raise my eyebrows.

"The consensus was 'pretty hard,'" she says.

"They can get in line," I say. I lean back against the wall of my gross trailer. "You like the present?"

"I haven't tried it yet," she says. "It seemed impolite to send it on its maiden voyage by myself."

"I think maiden is the wrong term," I say, and Mae giggles.

She holds it up in front of the camera. It's silicone, long and thick, phallic but not exactly shaped like a dick. Toward the base it's got a branch that sticks out at an angle.

The branch is for the clit. The reviews assured me it was *very* effective.

"This is stupid," I say. "But I'm a little jealous of that thing right now."

She lifts her eyebrows. The picture on the camera shakes

a little, and then the view is her bed. In another second she's on it, sideways, naked.

"It gets to make you come tonight and I don't," I say.

She rolls onto her side.

"I don't get wet riding the subway and thinking about the things I want to do to the vibrator," she says, her voice low and confessional.

I grin.

"What do you think about when you ride the subway?" I ask.

"Partly about work," she says. "And partly about how much I miss wrapping my legs around you."

"I miss you wrapping your legs around me too," I say. "And the noise you make when I kiss your neck."

"Take your shirt off," she murmurs. "You're sexy and I want to look at you."

I do it, and she smiles.

"Do you want to know a secret?" she asks.

"Yes," I say.

"I had a dream about giving you a blowjob, and when I woke up I was so turned on I had to masturbate before I could go back to sleep," she says.

My cock strains at my pants, and for a moment I'm worried about the zipper. I slide my palm against my erection, breathing deep, trying to control myself.

"I also had a dream about the next time I see you," she says. "When I know I won't be able to control myself for long, so I wear a skirt with no panties."

"And?" I ask.

I undo my pants, breathing hard. I can see her look at it, and she rolls onto her back and takes her nipples in both hands.

"And the second we're alone, I get on top of you and ride

your cock," she says. "Wait, no. That's not a dream, that's a fantasy."

I grab the base of my cock and pull it out, then adjust the camera to make sure she can see it. I'm rock hard, practically on the verge of exploding. It doesn't seem to matter how much I jerk off these days. I'm so frustrated that thirty minutes later, I'm hard again.

Mae looks at it and smiles, and I give it one slow, hard stroke. Her eyes light up.

"Do it again," she says, and she slides a hand down her belly, over her hips, to her mound, her eyes still on me.

God, I love how much she likes watching me.

I stroke my cock again and groan. Her hand moves further down and starts moving. She sighs, tilting her head back and closing her eyes.

It's insanely sexy, and it's almost physically painful that I'm not there. More than anything, I want her body beneath mine, writhing. Saying my name.

She opens her eyes and looks at me.

"I wish you were here," she says, her fingers still circling her clit.

"I wish I was there too," I say. "You feel a whole lot better than my hand."

She moves and then the vibrator is in her hand. She turns it on and flicks her eyes to the screen, then moves it down her body touches it to one nipple.

Mae squeals and then starts giggling.

"Sorry," she says. "That actually just tickles."

Then she moves it between her legs. She holds her breath and bites her lip, and touches it very carefully to herself. After a few seconds, she exhales, half-moaning as she circles her clit with the tip of the vibrator.

"I haven't had one of these in a while," she says. "I forgot how fun they are."

"Now I *am* jealous," I say.

"Maybe you should be," she says, rolling her hips again. "You don't vibrate."

She bends one knee and tilts her body so she's facing the camera just a little more, and then she looks at me through half-closed eyes.

"What now?" she asks. "Your present, your show."

I take a deep breath and take my hand off my cock as my balls clench. I'm within seconds of firing.

"Oh, come on," Mae says, her voice low and breathy. "You're getting to watch something good."

God*damn*.

"Turn the vibration off," I say.

"You're no fun."

"I thought it was my show," I tell her.

I grab the side of my kitchen table so I don't put my hand back on my cock. Mae clicks the vibration off, but keeps sliding it along her clit in a circle.

"Still feels good," she says. Then she smiles and looks at me confessionally. "Jackson, I'm so horny everything feels good."

"Put it against your pussy and turn it on low," I say. "Don't touch your clit."

She does. I watch her toes curl as she moans, her hips rolling.

"Don't put it in," I say.

"Are you torturing me?" she asks.

"Just a little," I say.

I'm leaking pre-cum like a faucet, and I just watch her, breathing hard as she rubs herself.

"Do I ever get to put it in?" she finally asks.

"Turn it off first," I say. "And go slow."

She turns it off but plunges it halfway inside her with a long, loud moan.

"I said *slow*," I say.

"I tried," she gasps, as she pulls it out. "I can't have you, I can't have your vibrator..."

This time she takes the whole thing, and as she does she arches her back again and *groans*, a long, low animal sound from somewhere deep in her throat.

I put my hand on my cock again and swallow, hard, watching as she fucks herself. Her face is flushed bright red and her eyes are half-closed and watching me, on the screen.

It takes a second before I realize she's matching her rhythm to mine.

"You're pretending I'm fucking you," I say.

"What else am I gonna do with this?" she murmurs. "Of course I'm pretending it's you. I'm pretending you're here and you've got my knees over your shoulders like you did that first night."

"The night my cock made you nervous?"

She laughs.

"I got over *that*," she says.

She's still fucking herself with the vibrator in the same rhythm I'm stroking my dick, and it's a terrible substitute for actually getting to fuck her but it's probably the second best thing.

"Turn it on," I say.

She does.

Her back arches and she squeezes her eyes shut, her other hand grabbing the bedspread in a fist.

"Oh *shit*," she gasps. "God, Jackson, I'm gonna come."

Now I'm matching my strokes to hers instead of the other way around as she works the vibrator, her whole body a vision of ecstasy. She's moaning loud enough to wake up her neighbors for sure.

"Jackson," she gasps.

I'm right on the brink, my entire cock pulsing as I watch her fuck herself. Thinking I'd give *anything* to be that vibrator right now.

"I wish it was you inside me," she whispers.

I reach for the box of tissues on the table but it's too late because I *explode*, every muscle contracting so hard I get jizz on the ceiling, and it just keeps coming.

On my phone, Mae shouts, "God yes!" and then I can *see* the orgasm wracking through her body as her eyes slide shut. She arches her back and turns onto her side, her hand disappearing between her legs as she writhes, turning her face into her bedspread.

"Oh my God, Jackson," I hear her moan. Her whole body tenses one more time, and even though I'm finished I just watch her, enrapt.

She finally turns to look at the camera, and I think she's about to say something when she comes *again*, bringing her knees to her chest and then arching her back.

It's hot beyond words. I want to keep watching her come forever.

Finally she's on her side, panting for breath, and she takes the vibrator out, turns it off, and tosses it to the other side of her bed.

I try to subtly clean up with a tissue. I feel like I'm thirteen again, because that's the last time I made this big of a mess. I'm twenty-five, and I should *probably* be able to control myself.

"I think I like the gift," she says. She's still lying on her side, legs half-curled in front of her, and now she's pulled a pillow under her head.

I walk across the trailer back to my bed, tucking myself back into my pants as I go.

"I'm glad *you* like it," I tease. "You're not the one who's got a complex now about being inferior to something with batteries."

"You're impossible," she says. "You made me come from two thousand miles away and you're upset about it."

I flop onto my bed, turn onto my side, and grin.

"I'm less upset now," I say.

I like talking to her like this, curled in our beds. In some tiny, stupid way it feels like we're together, having pillow talk. For a few moments, we just lay there quietly, together, thousands of miles apart.

"There's something I didn't tell you," she says, suddenly.

Anxiety wraps around my chest.

She has a boyfriend. She's married. She's got cancer and has six months to live.

"What is it?" I say, trying to sound as calm as possible.

She reaches her hand out and taps a finger on her bedspread a few times before she finally speaks again.

"I've been on the pill this whole time," she says.

Mae drops her eyes to her finger. It's kind of adorable how awkward she is talking about sex except for when she's talking dirty to me.

I grin. Of course she's been on the pill, because Mae's nothing if not cautious.

"You *still* want to ride me bareback," I tease. I'm glad I just came, because otherwise I'd be rock-hard already.

"I just wanted to discuss the possibility," she says, her face slightly pink. "See how you felt about it, and talk about... logistics."

"I feel like I'd love to fuck you skin-to-skin," I say. "And

Lula-Mae, of all people, when you say you're on the pill, I believe you."

"So you *don't* think I'm trying to ensnare you with a secret baby so I can get your rodeo money," she teases.

"I don't think you need a baby to snare me," I say.

Her fingers stop tapping. She looks at the camera, and suddenly my heart's pounding in my chest.

We text all day, we talk half the night, we send each other stupid postcards, and I want her so bad I can taste it, but I've never actually *said* anything to her. For starters, I have no idea what to say.

There's a long pause.

"Good, because I don't think that works all that well anyway," she says.

"You'd also be disappointed with rodeo money," I tease.

"Yeah, if I'm gonna have a baby to get someone's money, I think I want a hockey player at least," she says. "Or maybe soccer?"

"We don't have to talk about whose baby you're going to have," I offer.

I try to sound light, but the thought of Mae with anyone else, even someone who doesn't even exist, is unbearable.

She laughs, and I frown.

"First you're jealous of a sex toy, and now you're jealous of a hypothetical situation that's not gonna happen," she says.

"I am not," I say.

"You're making your jealous face," she says.

I have a jealous face?

"Why would I be jealous?" I ask. "You didn't just ask any of *them* if they'd bareback you."

"Well, technically, the vibrator already—"

"I'm throwing that thing out a window," I mock-growl.

Mae laughs again.

"If I get to see you in person I'm okay with that," she says. "But look, there's one more thing."

"You want me to get tested," I say.

"I think we should both get tested," Mae says.

I raise my eyebrows.

"This isn't my first rodeo," she says. Then she grins. "Pun intended."

"I should demand to wear condoms just for that," I say. "Puns are contagious."

She sticks out her tongue at me, and I laugh.

"I'll get tested, Lula-Mae," I say. "They can stick a hundred needles in my dick if that's what it takes."

"You're sweet, but I don't think that's gonna be necessary," she says.

CHAPTER TWENTY-ONE

MAE

THE WEEK before going to Las Vegas is brutal. No matter how busy I try to stay, each day crawls by slower than the one before it.

Jackson goes a couple days early so he can get a feel for everything, practice a little, all that. The night before he drives down, we establish some basic rules for public behavior.

Well, I suggest them and Jackson agrees.

No texting, in case someone else can see our phones.

He must change my name in his phone to "Mae Sports Weekly Photographer," like he needs help remembering who I am. We are to call only for professional reasons.

Handshakes only.

No staring.

No *winking*.

No flirting.

No calling me Lula-Mae, or Miss Guthrie, or darlin', or anything that suggests our relationship might be anything other than purely professional.

The night before I leave, as I'm packing, Sasha comes into my room and holds up a pair of cowboy boots.

"You want to borrow these?" she asks.

"Where did you *get* those?" I ask. "And when?"

She laughs.

"I'm actually not sure," she says. "I *think* I borrowed them from someone for Halloween one year, but when I went to give them back they told me to keep them."

I take them from her. They're well broken-in and soft.

"When in Rome," Sasha says.

"Now all I need is a pair of cutoff jean shorts that show half my butt and a rhinestone cowboy hat," I say.

"Tell me what you *really* think about rodeo groupies," she teases.

I scrunch my nose, and she grins.

· · · ★ ★ ★ ★ ★ · · ·

THE FLIGHT to Vegas is totally uneventful, except for the fact that I want to kill everyone in both airports for walking at a snail's pace. I find Bruce, and we share a taxi to the Wynn, where Sports Weekly is putting us up. I left New York at 5 a.m., so with the change in time zones, it's still only mid-morning by the time we're heading to the arena for the bull drawing.

This is way, *way* bigger than Pioneer Days. I'd expected that, but as soon as we're within a couple blocks of the sports arena, it's wall-to-wall hats and buckles. Inside, the place is stuffed with people selling belt buckles and wall plaques with funny sayings and hats, and we make our way through the crowd to the press room, where they're drawing bulls again.

The list of cowboys is about a hundred long, and Jackson

is near the end. This time, they've got the names projected on a screen, and instead of drawing slips of paper one by one, someone hits a button and a bull's name pops up next to a cowboy's name.

I know Jackson's in the room somewhere, but from where I'm standing in the back I can't find him in the sea of seated people. I feel like the air is vibrating, or maybe it's just me feeling like a thirteen-year-old with a crazy crush on the cute boy in her gym class.

This rodeo has the same basic structure as Pioneer Days, just way bigger: they ride three days in a row and the winner has the highest average score. So each cowboy gets three bulls picked, one on each night of the rodeo. I don't recognize the first two bulls that Jackson gets assigned, but someone *else* gets Crash Junction.

The announcer starts going down the list for the third day. He names cowboy after cowboy, and nobody pulls Crash Junction. Jackson's only three from the end of the list, and as they close in on his name, I cross my fingers.

It makes me nervous as hell to think of Jackson riding Crash again. Crash *still* hasn't been ridden. He's the only undefeated bull to ever make it this far in a season.

But I remember Jackson's face after Crash threw him. That determined, driven, *fierce* look in his eyes. There's no doubt what Jackson wants.

The announcer calls the cowboy in the list ahead of Jackson. He doesn't get Crash Junction. I hold my breath: there are only four names left. That's a twenty-five percent chance.

I cross my fingers.

"Jackson Cody," the announcer says.

Someone hits the button, and a moment later, a bull's name pops up next to his

CRASH JUNCTION, it says.

A corner of the room erupts in loud cheers, whistles, stomping, and the general carrying-on that only cowboys are capable of. I press my lips together so I don't smile, even as my heart twists in my chest.

The minute that the draw ends, everyone stands. Bruce and I push our way through the throng toward where Jackson was sitting. When we get there, he's surrounded by a ring of people with notebooks and cameras. There's even someone with a video camera and a woman asking him questions.

It's more than I expected. As much as I thought about this, I didn't realize how in-demand he was going to be, or how much media was going to be here.

Maybe this is all a bad idea, I think. *Maybe I should just stay away from him in Vegas, if he's going to be under this much scrutiny.*

I know it'll never happen. I've got lots of self-control, but not *that* much.

We hang back. Other people are asking Jackson questions and he's answering them, laughing, grinning, looking perfectly cocky and in control and relaxed. I watch him voraciously and try to act normal, but I think my bones are turning to lava just being this close to him.

I want to shout. I want to scream *I'm right here*, but I don't. Bruce writes things down in his notebook. I snap a few pictures and try to breathe normally, just watching him. I feel like a teenage girl at a rock concert or something. I don't know what to do with my hands, or how to stand, or where to look.

Jackson scans the knot of reporters again, and it's obvious he's barely listening to what they're asking him, smiling and nodding.

Finally, he looks at me. We lock eyes, and I squeeze my

hand into a fist, forcing myself not to laugh with the giddiness that's bubbling up through me.

Slowly, Jackson grins.

Stop it, I think, but I don't want him to stop. For that second, we're the only two people in this room, and nothing else matters. Not the group of reporters, not all the other cowboys, not the rules we set up. Just us.

Then someone else gets his attention and the moment's broken. I look down at my camera, trying desperately not to smile, but there's something warm and fuzzy and completely ecstatic in the pit of my stomach, and it won't quit jumping up and down.

· · · · · ★ ★ ★ ★ · · · ·

IT TAKES A LONG TIME, but the crowd around Jackson finally thins, and that's when we walk up to him.

"Bruce," Bruce says, holding out his hand. "*Sports Weekly*."

"Good to see you again," Jackson says, shaking his hand.

"Mae," I say, holding out my hand as well.

He takes it. We shake, and then he holds on just a beat longer than necessary, his hazel eyes sparking. I feel like his hand is electric. I don't want to let go, but I do.

"I remember," he says.

I almost laugh.

"Good to see you two again," he says.

The three of us chat for a few minutes, about Crash Junction, about maybe winning three rodeo world championships in a row, about how rodeo is suddenly turning a corner into mainstream.

Finally, Bruce glances across the room.

"Excuse me for a moment," he says. "I need to ask him something."

He walks away, and suddenly Jackson and I are alone together. Other people are milling around, but they're not within earshot.

"I *hope* you remember my name," I tease.

He crosses his arms in front of himself and grins.

"No breaking rules," he says.

"Which rule am I breaking?"

"No flirting," he says. His eyes sparkle dangerously.

"That rule is clearly open to interpretation," I say. "I just meant I hope you remember my name because I took a lot of photos of you."

"Sure," he says. "Not because I've been—"

"Someone's behind you," I mutter.

He stops and glances over his shoulder casually. Two middle-aged men are sauntering by.

"This is harder than I thought," I say, watching the two men.

"That's not the only thing," Jackson says.

I just shoot him a look.

"Sorry," he says.

His cocky, charming grin clearly says *I'm not sorry.*

Across the room, Bruce shakes someone's hand and starts to walk back.

"I've got something for you," Jackson says.

I give him an exasperated look.

"Not *that,*" he says, keeping his voice low. "Not right now, anyway."

He clears his throat and pulls something out of his pocket.

"You should have my business card," he says a little too loudly, and hands me a small white rectangle that says

Jackson Cody, Professional Bull Rider.

As I take it, I realize there's something underneath it, a hard plastic card that says *Mandalay Bay* on one side.

"Room twenty-oh-eight," he says.

"Tonight?" I ask, sliding it into my pocket. My heart is racing like my blood is high-octane fuel, every nerve surging.

"I'd say right now if I thought we could get away with it," he says.

"I wish we could," I say.

It's taking everything I've got not to jump on him right here, but I don't. A moment later Bruce is next to us again and even though on the inside I'm shaking and on fire and also experiencing some kind of sexual tornado-earthquake, Bruce and I make professional chitchat for another moment.

Then we shake Jackson's hand again and leave.

· · · ★ ★ ★ ★ ★ · · ·

THE RODEO ITSELF FEELS ENDLESS. I hate that Jackson's so close to the end, because the entire time I'm keyed up and nervous for him.

Finally he's up. This is slowly becoming a pattern: he jumps on the bull, situates himself, looks over at me. The chute opens and he rides, and I think my heart stops for the full eight seconds but he makes it and jumps off.

The crowd is *deafening*, and for a moment, Jackson stands there, grinning. He waves at the stands, then picks up his hat and puts it on his head. I get a great shot of him, facing me, people holding up signs and screaming their lungs out on the bleachers behind him.

Then he looks right at me and touches the brim of his hat, and I can practically feel his eyes burn right through me.

I don't know how I'm going to survive the hours between now and tonight, but I don't think there's any alternative.

Jackson pulls himself back over the gate and he's gone. The crowd takes a while to die down, and then they announce the next cowboy.

As he's getting onto his bull, Bruce looks over at me. I look back. Neither of us says anything.

· · · · ★ ★ ★ ★ ★ · · ·

I GET DINNER WITH BRUCE, along with a few other reporters and photographers. There's even someone from *National Geographic*, and I'm briefly star struck.

"You did that photo essay on nightclub culture in Siberia," I say. "I really liked it!"

That's the best you can think of?

"Thank you," she says. She's got shoulder-length brown hair, streaked with gray, and down-to-earth manner that seems almost alien in Las Vegas. "I really enjoyed your *Sports Weekly* spread."

I fumble my way through the conversation. By the end, I've exchanged information with most of the people there. As Bruce and I are heading back to our hotel, I realize: I just *networked*.

"Got any plans for tonight?" he asks while we're on the elevator.

"I'm bushed, so I'm just gonna turn in," I say.

Did you just say bushed? I think. Come on, Lula-Mae.

He nods.

"These early flights are killer," he says. "See you tomorrow."

I'm not actually *bushed*. I don't turn in. Instead, I wait around for another twenty minutes and then sneak down the back stairs. I walk two blocks and get a taxi at a different hotel and take it to the Mandalay Bay. I check that I've got Jackson's key about twenty times, and by the time I'm walking through the lobby I'm practically a warm puddle.

When I walk up to twenty-oh-eight, I'm strangely nervous. He could have another reporter in there, or some of his friends, or worst of all, another girl. Deep down I know he wouldn't — he gave me his room key, for crying out loud — but we've never actually talked about whether we're exclusive or not, and sometimes my stupid brain won't quit.

I knock. No answer. I knock louder, but there's still nothing. It's almost nine, so he's probably just not back yet.

I unlock the door and enter. The suite is totally dark as I step inside. After a moment, my eyes adjust and I can see pretty well. It's not huge, just a living room and a bedroom with a massive bed, but it's nice. The windows look out over the strip, and from here I can see the light at the top of the Luxor and the Eiffel Tower at Paris.

I turn on a few lights and walk through. The bed is made, but Jackson's got his stuff lightly strewn around: jeans draped over a chair, shirt balled up on the seat, his protective vest on the desk, a hat on the table. I feel a little nosy being there with his stuff and not him, but I'm also curious. For all the time we've sort of spent together, I've never been in a place where he lived, or even where he was staying.

It's strangely *nice* to be near his stuff, kind of warm and oddly comforting. Like a giant weirdo, I pick up his shirt and smell it.

It smells like the last time I kissed him, outside the bucking chute at Pioneer Days. I toss it back onto the chair and walk into the other room. My panties are probably soaked through already with pure anticipation, and I try to calm myself down as I flop into an overstuffed leather chair.

Then I look down at myself and get an idea.

Why not? I think.

I strip down to my cowboy boots and thong. Almost naked, I go back into the bedroom, grab the hat off the table, and put it on. I turn out most of the lights, get back in the chair, and hope Jackson hurries up.

· · · · ★ ★ ★ ★ ★ · · · ·

I'M THERE for another twenty minutes. Just when I'm wondering if I should put my shirt back on or something, I hear the sound of the door being unlocked.

I hold my breath. The stupid, anxious part of my brain says *what if you're coming on too strong*, but I swat it down.

The door closes.

"Hello?" Jackson says.

My toes curl inside my boots, and nerves tighten my chest.

"In here," I call.

"The dinner went late," he says. "I kept trying to leave, but — holy fucking shit, Lula-Mae."

He stops in the doorway and stares. I kick my feet up.

"Howdy," I say, suddenly not nervous anymore.

Jackson grins slowly and tosses his jacket onto the couch. He's just looking at me like he's memorizing my body, his eyes slowly raking over me. There's already a bulge in his pants, and I am *throbbing* with excitement.

"I found your room," I say.

"You made yourself right at home," he says, stopping five feet away from where I'm practically writhing in this chair.

"I had a key," I tease. "I thought I'd get comfortable."

He's still just staring, a deeply hungry look in his eyes.

"Are you gonna come over here or what?" I ask, leaning my head against the arm rest.

"I'm just appreciating," he says.

"Appreciate closer," I say. "You've done enough *looking* lately."

"But now I get to look while you're here," he says. "Did you know you're even sexier when you're naked in my hotel room?"

I move a little, arching my back and stretching my legs. I feel like I'm in a pinup shoot or something, but my brain is not in control right now. I just want him to come over here, for the love of god.

"I *need* you to come touch me," I say.

Jackson's eyes flash dangerously and his grin falters.

"Say it again," he says, his voice dropping.

"Get over here and *touch* me, Jackson," I whisper. That's all it takes.

He closes the distance, and then he's leaning over me, his body against mine. He crushes his mouth against mine, insistent with need, and I wrap my legs around him and arch my back.

Jackson groans and I bite his lip as he pulls back. His hand tightens around my hip, his fingers digging into me, and he laughs.

"I missed that," he says.

"Getting bitten?" I ask.

"I missed getting bitten," he says, and kisses me again, hard, the bulge in his pants pressing deliciously against me. "I missed the noises you make. I missed your body under mine."

I don't know what to say, so I kiss him again. I've got one hand in his hair, pressing his face to mine and I slide the other down his chest and find the hard length in his jeans, my body running on pure desire. I get a growl from deep in his chest so I squeeze.

"I missed *that*," he growls.

Then his lips are on my neck, on my collarbone and then he's biting one nipple just hard enough to make me shout. Jackson slides off the chair as my hands find the buttons on his shirt and fumble with them.

Now he's on his knees and I'm half off the chair, his mouth on one nipple as he pulls his own shirt off. I watch, panting for breath, and run one hand over his hard, muscled chest, his abs, his scar and his *lucky* tattoo.

He pulls my panties off with one yank and reaches down, sliding two fingers around my clit so tightly it makes my toes curl, and I fall off the chair a little more.

"Oh my god," I gasp. He teases my nipple with his tongue and moves his fingers down, nudging at my entrance as I arch my back.

"I love how wet you are," he says. "You were just in here, thinking about fucking me, weren't you?"

"What else was I going to think about?" I say.

His fingers move over my clit again and my whole body jerks with the sheer, impossible pleasure of it.

"This is all I've thought about for a week," I say.

"Just a week?" he says.

Now I'm on the floor too, Jackson kneeling between my legs. I grab his belt and pull, and he takes the hint and gets his pants off, kicking them halfway across the room, his cock springing out at full mast. I grab it and he groans as I stroke him.

"Better than your hand?" I ask.

He slides his hands under my ass and squeezes. Then he lifts me, the muscles in his arms bulging. I wrap my legs around his waist, my back against the seat of the chair.

"Do you know how hard it was today to see you and do nothing?" I murmur. "You can't look at me like that in public, Jackson."

"Like what?" he teases.

"You can't eye-fuck me while everyone's staring at you in the arena," I say. "I was dangerously close to jumping in and tearing your clothes off."

"Sounds okay to me," he says.

"Your other fans might stone me to death."

"They'd have to get through me first," he says.

I move my hips and the tip of his cock nudges against my clit, pleasure quaking through me. Jackson puts his lips against my ear.

"I got tested," he says. "I'm clean, but I brought the paperwork if you want to see it."

"You think I'm gonna stop this to look at paperwork?" I ask.

"Well, I was hoping not," he says. He takes a deep breath and runs his lips along my jaw.

I think I might explode with desire and anticipation.

"I meant to make this romantic," he says. "I was gonna put on some Barry White and undress you real slow and seduce you right for once."

I lean our foreheads together, then move my hips against him, pushing the head of his cock into my entrance.

"Seduce me later," I whisper. "Right now I need you inside me."

Jackson thrusts and sinks himself inside me, pushing my back against the chair as we both moan.

"Oh *fuck*, Lula-Mae," Jackson says, his head against my shoulder. "This feels better than I remembered."

I wrap my arms tight around his shoulders as he moves inside me.

"It's because I finally talked you into barebacking," I murmur into his ear.

He goes slow at first, and I can feel him holding back, trying to be gentle. His cock hits every single sensitive spot inside me again and again, and I feel like my entire body is lit like a string of Christmas lights, burning hot and bright.

I turn my head and nip at Jackson's ear, and he growls, thrusting harder.

"I missed *this*," I whisper.

Harder.

I make a noise that's half-moan, half-whimper, and Jackson puts his forehead against mine again, our faces together.

"You missed my cock?" he says.

He slams into me and white-hot pleasure bolts through me, from the crown of my head to my toes. I nearly shout.

"I definitely missed your cock," I gasp, and Jackson chuckles. He's going impossibly deep with every thrust, and I know I'm close to the brink, ready to go over any second.

"I'll never get tired of hearing you say that," he murmurs.

"Of me saying I like fucking you?" I ask.

Now I've got both my hands on his face, a fireball gathering inside me that's going to explode any moment.

"Can I come inside you?" he asks.

"Please," I whisper. "Let me feel you come."

He thrusts one more time and there I am at the edge. I grip Jackson's shoulders as tight as I can, our faces pressed together.

"Oh god, Jackson," I whisper, and then I come.

I come so hard that everything goes white and silent for a moment, and then someone is shouting "Jackson!" and I'm nearly knocked breathless as my whole body contracts with wave after wave of pleasure. I think I'm saying, "Oh god,

Jackson," over and over, and then he's squeezing my hips so hard it hurts.

"I fucking love watching you come, Lula-Mae," he growls, and then he's deep inside me and I can feel his cock throb and then explode. I squeeze him as hard as I can between my legs and we rock together until he's totally spent, sweat trickling down the back of his neck.

We're both breathing hard, our faces still touching, and he kisses me again. This time it's slow and sensual and we explore each other lazily until we finally pull away.

We untangle ourselves from each other and just sit on the floor, leaning against the chair. Jackson puts his arm around me, and I relax into him. He kisses the top of my head.

"You kiss your mother with that filthy mouth?" he asks.

I laugh.

"You're one to talk, Jackson," I say.

"Have I been a bad influence?" he says. "You haven't asked me to *do it* with you since that first time."

"Are you ever gonna let me live that down?" I tease.

"I don't intend to, no," he says.

I sigh dramatically, curled against him, warm and happy and tingly all over.

And for once, not worried about getting caught.

CHAPTER TWENTY-TWO

JACKSON

AFTER A COUPLE MINUTES on the floor we get up, because the floor isn't actually very comfortable. Mae yawns and stretches as she stands, then pads barefoot to the bathroom. I don't even remember getting her boots off, but I guess we did.

"It's like a Turkish bath in there," she says when she comes out.

"What do you know about Turkish baths?" I ask.

"I'm very sophisticated," she says, and walks past me.

The bathroom is nice, full of marble and mirrors though I've never been to a Turkish bath so I couldn't say how much it's like one. When I come out, Mae's standing by the big window, looking out. I turn the lights in the room off so we can see better, walk over to her, and put my arms around her.

"This *is* a good view," she says.

"You ever been to Vegas before?" I ask.

"Nope," she says.

"I thought it was mandatory for every family in the west to drive through at least once," I say. "We never stayed, but I went to a few of the cheap buffets on the outskirts when I was a kid."

"Where were you going?" she asks.

"I don't even remember," I say. "Grand Canyon? California?"

Her skin is soft and warm against me, and her hair tickles my chin just a little. She's leaning back into me and I feel almost like we're melting together, perfectly relaxed and comfortable.

Right here, right now, nothing else matters.

"I've never been to California," she says. "Which is weird, right? It's not that far."

"We could get in a car right now and go," I say. "The state line is an hour away. Probably less. We'd make the ocean before sunrise."

Mae laughs softly and leans her head back against my chest.

"Then what?" she asks.

"That depends on who's in charge," I say. "If it were me, I'd get a cooler of beer and we'd stay there all day, just the two of us. If it was you, I think we'd stick a foot in the water and then drive like hell to get back here so you could finish your job."

"So you'd forfeit the last two days of the World Championships to hang out on the beach," she says.

She turns her head and looks up at me, her deep blue eyes sparkling with mischief.

"Sure," I say.

"Liar," Mae teases. "You didn't come all this way not to ride Crash Junction again."

I laugh.

"You got me," I say. "We're gonna have to put off our fantasy beach vacation until after I win."

I let myself think for a moment that we'll go. I know we can't, because Mae's job isn't over until the photos are with her editors, and if I'm lucky, I'll have days of press conferences and meetings and awards ceremonies.

Still. The two of us, waves lapping at our feet, clinking beers together on the sand. It's a good thought. We stare out the window together, my arms around her.

"We could go to Paris and Venice without leaving the Strip," I say.

"I always thought the clanging of slot machines was so romantic," she murmurs.

"Well, if you aren't gonna let me whisk you off to the ocean, it's the next best thing," I tease.

"There's nothing between casinos and running away together at midnight?" she asks, laughing.

"The Venetian has canals," I say. "Though you can't go in them. Trust me on that."

She raises her eyebrows and looks up at me expectantly.

"I was drunk," I say.

"Sounds unusual," she teases.

"I was drunk and Clay dared me to jump in and swim to the other side," I say. "But those things are about two feet deep, so instead I just pulled him in and he pulled in Raylan and before I knew it, the canal had twenty people in it and we were all getting escorted out."

"Most of the twenty people being girls," Mae says.

"Right," I say. "I'm barred from the Venetian for life, but it's not like they've got my face posted at the doors."

"Maybe instead of going to California tonight I should just get the full Jackson Cody Debauchery Tour of Vegas," she teases. "You know how to party, after all."

She sounds perfectly lighthearted, but something small and heavy starts gathering in the pit of my stomach. I haven't exactly been an angel, after all. I haven't even been one halfway.

"That's a long tour," I say.

"What, you don't want me to see it?"

"I think you probably need to tie one on if you're gonna dance on a table," I say. "Otherwise, it ain't really the debauchery tour."

"So I can't just watch some other girl dance on a table while I sip club soda?" she asks.

"I'd much rather watch you dance on a table," I say.

"The tour's for me, not you," she teases. "I'm the one getting drunk, dancing with girls, and jumping into fountains. You're just my guide."

I swallow. My stomach squirms, thinking about all the other women, because there have been a *lot*. I think Mae knows, but I'm beginning to realize I'm not sure she really does.

If she did, would she have ever slept with me in the first place?

She deserves somebody better, I think. *Somebody who at least knows the names of all the girls he's slept with.*

"You okay?" she asks.

I blink.

"You're the only one," I blurt out.

She half-laughs.

"I kind of assumed that when you gave me your room key," she says, but her voice has gone a little stiff. "It would be pretty awkward if I walked in on you and someone else."

"I mean since we met," I say, and I swallow hard. "The second time, not the first."

She wraps her arms around herself, and I can see goosebumps rising on her arms.

"Can we get in the bed? I'm freezing," Mae says.

I grin at her.

"You don't have to ask to get into my bed," I say.

She walks past me and I swat her lightly on the ass. A moment later we're under the covers, my arms around her.

"It's not like I swore off men after that," she says. "Just alcohol and breaking the rules. And, to be honest, I'm glad my first time wasn't in the back of a pickup truck, in the middle of a party, while I was hammered."

"I really did jerk off to that for years, though," I say.

Mae laughs.

"In a romantic kinda way," I say.

"So you jerked off into a bouquet of roses?" she asks.

I snort.

"Who's disgusting *now*?" I ask. "For a nice girl, you're real filthy."

"You'd know," she says, snaking one hand over my side and pulling me a little closer.

My dick stiffens, just a little. I take a deep breath, trying to control it, because I still haven't said what I'm trying to say and I want to do it before Li'l Jackson takes over.

"Wait," I say, and she pauses, her blue eyes flicking to my face.

"What is it?" she asks.

"There have been a *whole* lot of women," I say. "I lost count after a while."

She puts one hand on my chest and bites her lip for a moment, looking down. Then her eyes meet mine again.

"Jackson," she says softly. "I know how to use the internet."

"Okay," I say, not really sure where this is going.

"So I looked you up," she says. "You know you've got a four-point-seven rating on Rate a Rodeo Stud dot com with seventy one votes cast, right?"

I have no idea what the hell she's talking about, and I just stare at her for a long moment.

"What is that, and a four-point-seven outta how many?" I finally hear myself ask.

"Are you serious?" she asks.

I just nod.

"It's a website where women — buckle bunnies, I guess — rate the sexual performance of the cowboys they've slept with," Mae says. "Last time I checked, you'd been rated seventy-one times, so I assume you've slept with way, way more girls than that."

She watches my face, and I think she's having a hard time not laughing.

"Some of them got pretty detailed," she says. "The rating's out of five, so four-point-seven isn't bad."

"You knew this whole time," I say.

"I googled you when I got the assignment for Pioneer Days," she says, like it's the most obvious thing in the world.

"And *that* came up?" I ask.

"Do you not google yourself?" she asks. "I *know* Wyoming's got the internet."

I have no idea what to do or what to say. I can't believe that this whole time, Mae's not just known numbers, but *details*.

"I'm sorry," I finally say.

"I can't believe you didn't know about it," she says. "Though it explains why you didn't brag about your four-point-seven."

She swallows.

"I only read a few of the reviews, to be honest," she said. "It felt kind of weird to read that about someone I was gonna have to work with."

"Were they detailed?"

Mae rolls onto her back, and now my head's on her shoulder, my arm slung across her as I stroke her hip.

She's still here, I remind myself. *She knew all this and she's still here.*

"One was pretty detailed, but the writer didn't use any punctuation or capital letters so it was basically impossible to read," she says. "One just said 'Cute guy, good sex, five stars,' and one thought you did sloppy work because you were drunk."

"Shit," I say, her skin smooth under my hand. "I'm sorry."

"It's okay," she says slowly. "I'm not thrilled, but I'll live."

I've gotta get myself off that stupid site, I think.

"It's just you now," I say. "I promise."

There are a million things on the tip of my tongue, like *because you're the only one I want* or *it's only you forever* or just *I love you,* but I don't say any of them.

"You too," she says, wrapping an arm around my back. "Promise."

I lie there for another moment, just thinking all this over. There's one very, very important question I still haven't asked.

"How does a four-point-seven stack up overall?" I ask. "Is that good, or bad, or about average?"

"It's pretty high," Mae says. "You got good ratings on dick, charm, and technique, but your follow-up score was low."

I can't help but laugh.

"That's pretty accurate," I say.

"Of *course* you think that," Mae teases.

"Okay, Miss Guthrie," I say. "Let's hear your review."

Mae laughs and blushes.

"I *should* give you a terrible review so no one else wants

to sleep with you," she says. "'Fell asleep before I achieved orgasm. Smelled bad. Snored. Zero stars.' Think that would work?"

"So you'd tank my rating out of jealousy," I say.

"Hell yes," Mae says.

Then she looks past me and thinks for a minute, narrowing her eyes. "Or I'd give you a really good rating, since I'm not sure I want my boyfriend to be famously bad at sex."

She's never called me her boyfriend before. It sounds good.

"Well, I'm not sure a single rating would have much effect on your boyfriend's score one way or the other," I say.

I scoot closer to her, my face in the crook of her neck, so I nip at the soft skin there. I'm getting hard again, fast, and I know she can tell.

"Okay," she finally says. "How about, 'Charming, enthusiastic, and very good at sex. Sometimes talks too much during the act.'"

"I do not," I say, and gently bite the shell of her ear.

Mae gasps.

"'His cock might have an inexhaustible power source, but it's pretty nice, so I don't mind,'" she continues her review. "'Drives me wild enough to do things like talk dirty by pretending to review his sexual performance.'"

Now I'm halfway under her, my chest against her back. She takes my cock in one hand and squeezes it. I groan into her ear, the pressure of her hand sending pleasure flooding through my body.

"Is that the whole review?" I ask.

I slide my hand up to her breasts and squeeze one, pinching her nipple between my fingers.

Mae moans and arches her back.

"I need a good ending," she says, her voice getting ragged. "Something punchy, you know?"

"Well, you already used 'very good at sex,'" I tease.

She strokes my cock again, her chest rising and falling under my hand.

"You just want me to talk dirty to you," she says. Her voice is getting breathy like it does when she's starting to lose control.

"Guilty as charged," I say.

"How's this, then," Mae says, and swallows. "'Jackson Cody turns me on so much it should be illegal. I spent weeks watching him jerk off on camera, and I thought it was one of the sexiest things I'd ever seen, but sometimes he talks too much when I just want him inside me already.'"

"Impatient," I say into her ear.

"Four-point-six stars," Mae finishes.

"Point *six*?" I say.

"I'm willing to revise for a good performance," she says.

Now we're both on our sides, and she arches her back so the tip of my cock is resting against her entrance. My dick throbs, somehow going even harder, and I try to savor this tiny moment just before all my senses get obliterated by the sheer overwhelming pleasure of Mae.

Then I give up and sink myself inside her tight channel and both of us groan together. She's beyond wet and so turned on that she feels swollen, her pussy clenched around me like a fist as I'm all the way inside her.

Mae pushes back and moans, and I grab her hip and move myself inside her.

"*God* that feels good," she whispers.

"I'm always afraid I'm gonna come the second I'm inside

you," I whisper into her ear. "I swear to god you fit me perfect, Lula-Mae."

I pull back and then slide inside her again, listening to her moan. It might be the sexiest sound I've ever heard, at least aside from all the other noises she makes.

I want to go slow this time. I want to savor this, because it feels so *good* that I don't want it to be over right away.

We move together in a rhythm that's almost lazy, her body against mine. I feel almost lost as her muscles start to tighten around my cock. Mae starts pushing back into me, trying to move faster and faster.

I put my hand on her hip and squeeze, holding her still. She turns her head and looks back at me, panting for breath, so I thrust inside her slow but hard and watch her eyes slide shut, her hips moving back as if she can take more of me in.

"Come on," she whispers, trying to move faster.

"No," I growl. "Let me fuck you slow for once."

She sighs. I lock my fingers around her hip and hold her still for a minute, buried to the hilt. I can feel her throb around me, and it's perfect and delicious.

"Lula-Mae, I'm not gonna give you what you want," I murmur.

I pull out and slide into her again. Her toes curl and an explosive, breathy moan comes out of her mouth.

"I'm gonna give you what you *need*," I whisper.

She just nods. I wrap my arm around her waist and keep moving as slow as I can make myself, filling her with every stroke until she moans. It's driving me wild and I feel like I'm hanging on by a thread, about to swing over the edge and into the abyss, but I keep going.

"Jackson," Mae murmurs.

I fuck her deep and she moves her hips again. Her pussy

is pulsing around me, almost throbbing, and I can tell she's gonna come soon.

"I'll never get enough of you saying my name," I say. "Especially like *that*."

"Like you're about to make me come?" she asks, her voice low and breathy.

"Exactly," I say.

I keep going, slow and deep and hard, and it's almost torture, but Mae is moaning and gasping for breath, coming undone before my eyes. I can't get enough. The most beautiful girl I've ever seen is here, and she's mine, and *I'm* doing this to her.

"Don't stop," she gasps. "Please don't stop, Jackson, *please*."

"Not for the world, Lula-Mae," I growl in her ear.

"I love that you're bare inside me," she whispers. "I — oh, *fuck*, Jackson — "

I can't hold out any longer. I slide my hand between her legs and circle her clit.

Almost instantly, her muscles clench around me and she throws her head back. I think she's gonna shout but she hardly makes any noise at all, just a quiet, barely-there moan, but I can *feel* how hard she's coming as her pussy tightens around me like a vise.

"Oh fuck, Jackson," she whispers. "Jesus fucking *Christ*, Jackson."

I go over. I can't feel her come and hear her whisper my name and do anything *but* come so hard I just about forget my own name. I murmur her name into her hair over and over again as we move in perfect rhythm, both totally lost to ecstasy.

After a long time, we both go still but I've still got my arm around her, holding her as close against me as I can. She puts her hand over mine and laces our fingers together, then kisses my knuckles softly.

I don't say anything, because I can't think of a single thing to say that encapsulates this sensation, this perfect feeling that for once I'm exactly where I want to be. I'm not thinking about bull riding or championships or Mae getting on a plane. I'm not thinking *anything*, because my brain is just a happiness fog.

It's a long time before I realize my arm has pins and needles in it, and slowly, we both roll onto our backs. Mae puts her arm over me and her head on my chest and kisses the left side of the horseshoe.

"You were right," she says, her voice low and lazy.

"About what?"

"I did need that."

"Any interest in revising your review?" I ask.

Mae laughs.

"That four-point-six really got to you, huh?" she teases.

"Well, you keep coming back for more," I say. "I can't be that bad."

"If it's a five-point scale, then two-point-five is average," she says. "And four-point-six is pretty good."

"You like this better than *pretty good*, though," I say.

She rolls onto me a little more and rests her chin on my chest, her eyes dancing.

"Okay, fine," she says. "Four-point-seven."

I lean my head against my pillow and sigh dramatically, and she rests her cheek on my chest again, laughing. She traces one finger over the scar over my breastbone, then slowly, her fingers drift to other scars: one down my arm from the time I climbed over a barbed wire fence and fell off, one on my stomach from the time I fell off a bull funny and my belt buckle broke and cut into me.

I have the urge to tell her the story behind each one, or at least the stories I can remember. I want Mae to be able to read me like a book, to be totally laid open for her.

After a long time, she sighs.

"I should go," she says. "It's late and I barely got any sleep last night."

"You could stay," I say.

"I wish," she says softly. "I can't get caught, Jackson."

After another moment she sits up and swings her feet off the bed. She looks out the window for a moment and I look at her profile, and then she stands and walks to the other room.

I get up too, and together we hunt down our clothes. She gets dressed and I put my boxers on.

"There," she says. "Do I look decent?"

"You look better than decent," I say, and kiss her on the forehead. "You sure you can't stay?"

I know I should stop asking, but the thought of getting back into that bed without her is almost physically painful. I want to wake up with her next to me, just once.

"Come on, Jackson," she says.

I kiss her, and it's slow and lazy and full of longing.

"Good luck tomorrow," she says.

"And no eye-fucking?" I ask, sliding an arm around her waist.

"Maybe a little," she concedes. "I think I won't be quite as wound up after tonight."

"I don't know if that's good or bad," I say.

She bites her lip, then looks up at me.

"I know it's useless to tell you to be careful out there," she says. "But..."

She trails off, touching the scar in the middle of my chest.

"Try not to get another one of these, okay?" she says.

"You worry too much," I say, grinning at her. "I know my business, Miss Guthrie."

Mae makes a face, but I kiss her again.

"I'll see you tomorrow," I say, hating this moment. "Try to act normal, okay?"

She just laughs.

CHAPTER TWENTY-THREE
MAE

I RIDE THE ELEVATOR DOWN, leaning my head back against the cool metal. I can still feel his arms around me, his lips on mine. I can still see his face in the dark, lit only by the Vegas strip glowing outside the window, and it's making me crazy.

I just breathe. I'd rather be in Jackson's bed, snuggled under the covers and laughing, but instead the elevator doors open onto the casino floor. It seems even brighter and louder at nearly one in the morning than it did earlier, like I've walked into some special, clanging hell.

At least it's safe to go home this late in Vegas, I think.

In the cab, I start driving myself crazy. I've never been great with uncertainty, and I have no idea what we're doing.

He said there was no one else, but does that just mean now? For the future? Are we exclusive? Are we *dating*?

What does he even do in the off-season? I wonder. *Am I just his girlfriend when I'm around, but when he goes to other rodeos there's other girls?*

I think this is real, but does he? Or are we just having fun?

Is this a friends with benefits scenario?

I know I'm being an idiot. I know all signs point to *this is a real thing*, and they also point to *just talk to him about it already*, but sometimes once I get going on this train of thought it can be hard to hit the brakes.

I pinch the bridge of my nose and look out the window at the scorchingly bright strip as it rolls by, and make myself take a deep breath.

You worry too much, I tell myself. *Way too much.*

It doesn't help that I'm dead tired and worried about us getting found out. Not to mention worried about Jackson doing an insanely dangerous thing every day.

Everything is combining into one giant puddle of anxiety, each little thing tumbling into the next and the next. It's not like I've ever been particularly chill in the first place.

The taxi drops me off one casino away from the Wynn. I pay the driver and start walking, the sidewalk still jammed with people. I force myself to count my steps and not think about anything else.

· · · ★ ★ ★ ★ ★ · · · ·

ON THE UPSIDE, I'm so busy at work that I barely have time to think about any of this. I'm at the arena, which is way off the strip at the University of Las Vegas, by seven in the morning. Bruce interviews a whole batch of rodeo front-runners and I take their pictures as they pose with their belt buckles and chaps and hats.

I've got fifteen minutes for lunch before steer roping starts, so I run through the arena building and toward a sandwich shop in the student union, because I'm *starving*.

I walk in, out of breath, and the door chimes. The guy ordering at the counter looks over his shoulder.

It's Jackson. Of course it is. The *one* person I shouldn't be speaking to in public.

He nods. I nod back and try to read the menu, but I have no idea what I wind up ordering. The guy behind the counter gives me a number, and I wander out of line to go wait.

Jackson's also waiting. The sandwich shop isn't that big, but it's pretty full of rodeo people. Mostly I think they're spectators, but I recognize a couple of cowboys.

"It's Mae, right?" Jackson asks as I stand near him and pretend like I haven't noticed him there.

"Right," I say, trying to smile politely. "Hi again."

"What kind of sandwich did you get?" he asks. His arms are crossed and he's standing a few feet away, but I can feel him looking at me like I'm naked.

I swallow and look at my receipt.

"Roast beef and horseradish," I say. "You?"

"Chicken salad," he says.

The shop calls a number and another guy steps forward, grabs his sandwich, and leaves. Jackson turns and looks at the counter.

"My dinner tonight got canceled last minute," he says, keeping his voice low and normal-sounding, like he's talking about potato chips.

"So you're available early?" I ask.

My heart thumps, and something warm and liquid begins to snake through me, just like always.

"Let me take you to dinner," he says.

He picks up a bag of chips and shows them to me.

"Pickle chips?" I ask, and wrinkle my nose.

"I heard they're good," he says, but he puts them back.

Someone else walks in. We're quiet until she starts ordering, and then Jackson steps next to me again, so we're facing the same way, talking quietly without looking at each other.

"We can't," I say, pretending to be incredibly interested in reading the labels on the soda fountain.

"Far away, off the strip," he says quickly. "Vegas is big."

At least he didn't call me Lula-Mae in public, I think.

"I don't know," I say.

"Please?"

I take a deep breath. I want to say yes, to go out in public with Jackson like we're normal people and not people having some secret torrid rodeo affair.

I cannot believe I just thought the phrase *torrid rodeo affair*.

"It has to be low-key," I say.

"Is that a yes?" he asks.

"I'm serious," I say. "This is stupid, Jackson."

"Chicken salad sandwich for Jack?" a woman behind the counter calls. Jackson steps forward and takes it, and I stand alone in the middle of the sandwich shop, heart racing. He grabs some napkins and packets of mustard, then nods at me again.

"I'll pick you up," he says quietly. "Text me where."

I just nod.

"Good to see you again," he says, louder now, and smiles at me.

"You too," I manage to say.

Jackson leaves, and I wait for my sandwich, feeling like a pile of sweat and nerves and stupidity.

· · · · ★ ★ ★ ★ · · · ·

I'M ALMOST USED to watching him ride. Even I have to admit it's impressive, because bull riding is hard, dangerous work, and Jackson's *good* at it.

Hell, he's the best. My heart might stop every time I think about it, but I also get a thrill every time the crowd cheers for him. There's a flash of fierce pride every time someone screams his name, and God knows I could watch his cocky swagger all day long.

Today he's riding a bull named Screaming Heat. The bull doesn't sound like anything special, but Jackson got a good score yesterday, so he's neck-and-neck with another cowboy. He *needs* this ride to qualify if he's going to win this thing, so the closer we get to his name, the tighter the knots in my stomach get.

Tomorrow he rides Crash Junction, but I'm trying to take things eight seconds at a time.

"Up next is Jackson Cody on Screaming Heat!" the announcer finally says.

The crowd loses their minds.

I thought yesterday was nuts, but today they're twice as loud, easily. People are jumping up and down and waving signs. In the media area, everyone pushes forward, all eyes on him.

I force myself not to smile. *This is just another ride,* I tell myself.

I steady the camera on his form jumping into the bucking chute. Screaming Heat snorts and shakes.

Jackson tightens the rope, and just like always, he looks at me for a moment.

Please please please please please please is all I can think, a heart-pounding prayer that he'll be okay.

The gate opens. Screaming Heat bolts out and the clock starts, the seconds ticking up slowly. My palms are sweaty with anxiety but Jackson's *got* this, riding the bull with confidence and *panache*, totally in control the whole time.

It's impressive. Also kind of sexy.

The clock ends, and Jackson jumps free and rolls once. There's a horrifying moment where I think the bull's after him, but then it trots off toward the exit.

Everyone screams. The whole arena echoes with the sound of it. There are even more signs today than there were yesterday, and people are waving them like mad, along with pom-poms and cowboy hats.

Jackson grins and waves at the crowd, turning in a quick circle. Just before he heads for the gate, he finds me again.

In what's becoming some kind of ritual, he looks at me for a little too long. Then he nods and touches the brim of his hat. He's breathing hard and looking at me like he *knows* that I practically dissolve when he looks at me like this.

I swallow hard, scrunching up my toes in my shoes, because as much as I hate how dangerous bull riding is, *this* moment?

It *does* something to me, something deep and dangerous. It makes me feel like I'm nothing but raw lust and libido, and I want to jump onto the sand and run to Jackson and kiss him, right there, in front of everyone. I want him so much it takes my breath away, and I think he knows it.

I hit the shutter and get it on camera. I'm never going to send it into Sports Weekly, but I want it for myself.

Then it's over. Jackson pulls himself over the gate. The cheering eventually dies down and the rodeo goes on.

· · · · · ★ ★ ★ · · · · ·

WE FINALLY WRAP up hours later. Bruce interviews half the bull riders, I think, and I spend a while photographing the after-rodeo scene: cowboys sneaking drinks out of flasks, bulls and cows and horses being led away.

Cowboys signing autographs for fans, talking to them, joking around. Jackson especially. A group of female fans asks me if I'll use their phone to take a picture, and eight of them crowd around him, smiling at me.

I do it, but I'm a little jealous. There are no pictures of the two of us.

I get a text when the arena's finally emptying out. I look around to make sure no one's looking at me, and I spot Jackson across the room, phone in hand.

He looks at me. I look at him.

Jackson: ?

I look toward the doors and think for a moment about the place I'm least likely to get caught.

Jackson: Come on, Lula-Mae.
Me: Okay, there's a Super 8 on the road behind the Wynn. I think it's a block north. Pick me up outside that.

We look at each other across the room, and at the same time, we both smile.

Jackson: In an hour?
Me: Yeah.
Jackson: :-D

I don't look at him again as I leave, because I'm afraid I'm just going to start laughing with sheer giddiness.

. . . ★ ★ ★ ★ ★ ★ . . .

VEGAS IS STRANGE. The moment you're more than a block off the strip, it doesn't feel like you're in Vegas anymore. It feels like you're anywhere in the western United States, with one-story houses and apartments, Starbucks, and McDonalds.

Jackson wouldn't tell me where we're going, but I'm glad Sasha and Dani talked me into taking a dress with me. It's not fancy, just a sleeveless little black dress, but it's better for whatever we're doing than jeans.

I think, anyway. He said dinner, but for all I know, he could mean indoor skydiving and *then* dinner.

A cab pulls up. I swallow. The window rolls down and Jackson waves at me. I get in.

The moment my door closes, he pulls me across the seat and kisses me. I resist for a moment, but it's only a moment, and then I've got my hand on his face, my knee across his, and my tongue's in his mouth.

When I finally pull back, I realize Jackson dressed up too.

"You own a blazer?" I ask.

"Come on," he says, grinning.

"It's not even denim," I tease. "No boots, no hat, no giant belt buckle? Who are you and what have you done with Jackson?"

"I think *you* look pretty as a peach," he says, and puts his arm around me.

"You do clean up nice," I say.

"Thank you," he says, and kisses the top of my head. There's something sweet and protective about it, and for just a moment, I close my eyes and enjoy this.

"Where are we going?" I ask.

"A little French place I found," he says.

"What's it called?"

"It's got a French name."

I look up at him, waiting.

"Are you gonna make me try to pronounce French?" he asks.

I just nod.

Jackson sighs.

"Lee fro-mayge do-ray," he says. "Happy?"

I just laugh.

In a few minutes, we're in another part of Vegas entirely. It's not as massive as the Strip, but as we get out, I realize that it's just as flashy. The street has been closed to cars, and it's lined with older casinos, neon signs, and some kind of lit-up ceiling.

"Downtown Vegas," Jackson says. He puts his hand on my lower back as we both stand there, looking up, gawking like a couple of tourists.

"I didn't know there was a downtown," I say.

"Hopefully, neither does anyone else," he says, and winks at me. "Come on."

· · · · · ★ ★ ★ ★ · · · ·

LE FROMAGE DORÉ is one of the fanciest places I've ever been inside. I'm sure there's nicer places in New York, but *I've* never been there. The tables have long white tablecloths, multiple forks, and candles. It's dark. There's a live piano player in one corner.

Everyone is dressed *way* more nicely than the two of us.

When Jackson gives his name, the hostess *almost* smiles at him, even as she eyes our clothes, clearly unimpressed.

"Just one moment," she says, and then walks away.

Jackson and I exchange glances. The hostess goes to one of the servers and whispers something in his ear. He looks over at us, and he's not impressed either. Each table setting has two wine glasses and a lot of forks, and that much stuff always makes me nervous.

"How much do you really like French food?" I murmur to Jackson.

He looks around the restaurant.

"I have no idea," he finally admits. "I thought it sounded fancy."

The hostess finally starts walking back toward us. She's still not smiling.

"I can't believe they've started allowing people to wear *street clothes*," says a voice behind us.

I turn and look. It's a middle-aged woman who's pretending to talk quietly enough that we can't hear.

Screw this, I think.

"We passed a brewpub on the way here," I whisper to Jackson. "Last chance to change your mind."

"This used to be a *destination*," the woman behind me says.

"Let's go," Jackson says.

I pull on his hand just as the hostess walks up to us, and I push back through the exit. Some nicely-dressed people look offended, but then we're outside on the sidewalk, and I pull Jackson around the corner like I think someone's gonna come after us.

"I don't think we need to hide from a snooty French waitress," he teases me.

"Shh, they'll hear us," I say, fighting back a laugh.

"I can't take you *anywhere*," he says.

"You couldn't even pronounce the name of that place," I tease back.

"Why do you think I chose it?" he asks. "That means it *must* be good."

We walk to the brewpub, holding hands. It feels weird but *good* to be together in public, even though I'm scanning every face to make sure I don't recognize someone. It's a nice night, even though it's December, cool but not cold.

The brewpub is crowded, but somehow we get a small corner booth. As we push our way through the crowd, Jackson keeps his hand on my lower back. It's sweet and a little protective and it makes me want to shout *he's mine, everybody!*

I mean, I think he's mine. Pretty sure. It's on my mental docket for discussion.

The menu has five appetizers, three burgers, three sides, and two desserts. The rest is beer. The booth is one circular seat and we sit together in the middle, Jackson's arm around me.

I'm pretty sure a couple of women look over as we sit down and give Jackson the up-and-down. I fight the slightly insane urge to sit on his lap, make out with him, and flip them off.

"You still don't drink, right?" he asks.

"Why, is Boone's Farm on the menu?" I say.

Jackson laughs and I look at a chalkboard on the wall that lists dozens of beers. Jackson drags his fingers in little circles over my upper arm, unconsciously, and it sends tingles up my spine.

This happened anyway, I think. *You still had sex with Jackson, whether you drank and did everything right or not, and it turned out okay.*

Better than okay.

"Fuck it," I say out loud. "I'm getting a drink."

"Who in tarnation are you and where's Mae?" Jackson says.

"Sometimes I have beers and drop f-bombs," I say defiantly.

"What a rebel," he teases.

"At least I don't say *tarnation*," I say.

"At least I don't say f-bomb," he counters, grinning.

"I thought you liked it when I cursed," I say.

"I like it when you talk dirty," he says. "I'm just surprised you know all those bad words."

"I know way more than bad *words*," I say.

"Maybe we shouldn't have gone out in public," Jackson says, leaning toward my ear. His voice is going low and dangerous and it sends a spike of warmth straight through me.

"Am I embarrassing you?" I murmur.

"I might embarrass myself," he says, his lips barely tickling my ear.

A woman clears her throat, and we both look straight ahead. Heat rushes to my face.

"Hi welcome to the Fremont Brewpub my name is Mandy can I get you two anything to drink?" she says, looking completely bored.

We get the ten-beer sampler and an order of fries.

"I don't know what I was thinking," Jackson says. "I have to control myself all day."

"You were thinking that it might be nice to see the parts of Vegas that weren't your hotel room or the rodeo arena," I say.

"My hotel room is awful nice, though," he says. "Particularly after hours."

He's driving me crazy. Up until we sat in this booth, I was doing okay, but now that he's whispering things in my ear with his arm around me, I feel like someone's taken a match to a pile of dry kindling inside me.

"You're the one who insisted on a dinner date," I say. "I was just going to sneak over later tonight, like anyone having a torrid affair."

"Torrid?" he asks, grinning. "I haven't ripped even one bodice, Miss Guthrie."

"Only for a lack of bodices," I say. "Don't tell me all my foundation garments would be in proper order if I had any."

"Foundation garments? I'm outta my element," he says.

"If I had a bodice I'd let you rip it off," I say.

The beers arrive. They're all in little glasses, arranged from light to dark. I pick up the lightest one and Jackson grabs a beer from somewhere in the middle. We clink them together.

"To our torrid affair," he says, and we both take a drink.

Turns out I like beer a lot better than I remembered. It doesn't take more than a few sips of each before I'm starting to get tipsy, even though Jackson is stone cold sober.

The brewpub keeps getting louder and louder as everyone gets drunker. It's Friday night, after all, and sitting in this booth, I feel borderline invisible.

Mandy the waitress comes back and we order burgers. Jackson orders another sampler of ten different beers.

I narrow my eyes at him.

"Are you trying to get me drunk?" I ask.

He just laughs.

"I haven't tried at all," he says, eating a french fry. "This was all your idea, Lula-Mae. I just wanted to try a couple beers."

"Public," I say, wrinkling my nose.

He slides his hand around my hip.

"Not that public," he says.

"Just don't let me talk you into doing something we shouldn't," I say. "You know my track record with drinking when you're around."

I've got one hand on his upper thigh and I can feel the hard muscles beneath the dark denim. It's driving me more than a little wild.

"I'm not sure I can be trusted with that kind of responsibility," he says, grinning. "I don't think you've got any idea how persuasive you can be."

"Oh, you can turn down a drunk girl," I tease.

"I can turn down *most* drunk girls," he corrects me.

I take another sip of some delicious beer.

"You could turn me down," I say. "Want to practice?"

"No," he says.

I slide my hand up his leg anyway, but before I get to the zipper of his jeans he puts his own hand over mine and looks down at me.

"You're the one who doesn't want to get caught," he murmurs, our eyes locked.

My spine liquefies.

"I thought you didn't want to get caught either," I whisper.

"I don't want you to get fired," he says. "I don't care who knows about us otherwise. That was just in Oklahoma."

I swallow. All this sneaking around, all these rules and secrecy and hotel rooms across the city are just for *my* benefit.

"Oh," I say. "Thanks."

I don't know what else to say.

"It's kinda fun playing Romeo and Juliet," he says. "Sneaking around and shit, not getting caught."

"They died at the end," I point out.

"Then pick a happy story about secret lovers," he says.

I bite my lip and think. Jackson frowns.

"*Madame Bovary?*" he asks.

"I think she dies," I say. "You've read *Madame Bovary?*"

"I got hidden depths, Lula-Mae," he says. "It can't all be bulls, bourbon, and bunnies."

"What else don't I know?" I ask.

"I make an amazing pineapple upside-down cake," he says. "I memorized my grandma's biscuit recipe."

"What else?"

"I think it's your turn now," he says, grinning. "I've got a reputation to uphold and my baking secrets can't be getting out."

"My older brother used to buy my friends booze when I was in college and underage," I say.

"You're a badass," he says, totally straight-faced.

"I usually didn't pay him back, even when I said I would," I admit. "I once wrote a paper for someone else for a hundred bucks."

"I'm gonna call the cops," he teases me.

"I streaked once," I say.

Jackson grins.

"Go on," he says.

"It was past a couple dorms," I say. "I think I had one drink and someone said she thought I was boring, and I took the bait. It was just the once."

The new beers come. We drink up. I've probably had the equivalent of two drinks, but it's the most I've had to drink since I was eighteen, so I'm pretty drunk.

That's probably why I grab his hand and put it on my knee, then slide it under the hem of my dress. He doesn't move it up, but he doesn't take it off, either.

"Nobody's looking," I say.

"I'm starting to think maybe you shouldn't drink," he says, a slow smile spreading across his face.

"I'm starting to think maybe I should drink all the time," I say.

"Am I still supposed to keep you from doing something you shouldn't?" he asks. "Because that ain't fair, Lula-Mae."

"Public," I whisper.

"You put my hand up your dress," he whispers back. "I'll call you what I want, Lula-Mae."

I can't help myself. I slide my hand up his thigh toward the bulge in his pants, and he strokes the inside of my thigh with the pad of his thumb.

Just as my fingers are about to touch his cock, he takes his hand off my thigh and locks his fingers around my wrist, stopping my hand.

I try to move my hand up again, but he's got his fingers locked around my wrist and I can't move it. I try again. No matter how hard I try, he's in control.

Holy *hell*, it's hot. I feel like something just *explodes* into flames inside me.

I look at my hand and then up at Jackson.

"Let me go," I say, even though there's nothing I want less.

"Can you behave yourself?" he asks.

"Can I ever?"

I think I forget to breathe as I try to move my hand again and he still doesn't let me, his strong hand around my wrist. Our faces are inches apart.

"You're making it worse," I whisper, my voice throaty and raw.

"Don't try to talk me into doing something we shouldn't," he says.

"I wasn't talking."

"You're impossible," he says.

I kiss him. I press my lips to his gently and he presses back, hard and urgent. Then he pulls away.

"This is gonna end with you bent over a bathroom sink if you don't stop," he says.

"Promise?" I whisper.

I pull at my hand again but his grip is like a vise around my wrist.

"That's a guarantee," he growls.

I lean forward and bite his earlobe. I don't give a shit that we're in public. It's not like anyone here recognizes us. We're just some drunk people making out.

"That better not be an empty threat," I say.

"When have I ever promised you a good fucking and not followed through?" he rumbles. It sends a shiver down my spine.

I swallow hard and squeeze my thighs together, like that will somehow make me less desperate to have him *right now*.

"Jackson," I say. "Don't be gentle."

His hand tightens on my wrist. My breathing quickens.

"Right," I say. "Like that."

"Walk to the women's room and don't look back," he says, and releases my wrist.

I take another swallow of beer for courage and then leave the table. I barely notice all the other people in the pub as I push past them, because all that matters is the pure, hot ache that's filling my entire body.

The women's room is empty, and by some miracle, it's just a toilet and a sink, no stall doors. I don't know what to do, so I grab a handful of paper towels and wipe the sink off, my heart beating so hard I'm shaking.

I throw them in the trash can. The door swings open and Jackson steps in, locking the door behind him. He's got his blazer off, his sleeves rolled up, and an enormous bulge in his jeans.

We lock eyes in the mirror.

"I told you I couldn't control myself," he says, a smile around his eyes as he locks the door.

"Sorry," I say, but he's already behind me, his mouth on the back of my neck as he pushes my skirt over my hips and grabs me. I watch his fingers sink into my flesh in the mirror as he pulls me back against his erection, my hands still on the sink.

I make a noise and arch my back, trying to rub myself along his erection, even clothed. He runs his thumb along the thin fabric strip between my legs and I gasp, biting my lip to keep from making too much noise.

Jackson grabs the side of my thong and pulls *hard*, the muscles in his forearm bulging. After a moment it gives way and tears off and he spins me around, sits me on the counter. The marble is cool against me but before I can say anything Jackson's head is buried between my legs and he's sucking at my clit, flicking his tongue back and forth across it.

I lean against the mirror and put one hand on his head, stroking his hair as he eats me out, every swipe of his tongue sending a jolt of pleasure through my whole body.

"I love it when you eat me out," I say. I close my eyes and lean my head back. "*Jesus* that feels good."

He keeps going, sliding his tongue from my clit to my slit and back as I moan, edging closer and closer to climax as Jackson licks me.

"I'm close," I whisper. "Fuck, Jackson."

His tongue slows, and I hold my breath until he's just tracing a slow circle around my clit, not even touching it any more. I hear myself whimper, but then he's standing and pulling me off the sink.

Jackson crushes his mouth to mine and I can taste myself on him, even though I'm still feeling shaky and high from almost coming.

"I can't see you without wanting to taste you," he growls. "Every single time. You should know that, Lula-Mae. Every time we talk I think about putting my face between your thighs and licking you until you scream."

He kisses me again, deep, and I can still taste myself.

"You're a goddamn distraction," he says. "You should be illegal."

"Do you ever stop talking?" I ask.

I tug on his belt but he grabs my wrists in his hands and spins me around so I'm facing the mirror. My pussy throbs, hot and wet. I watch Jackson unbutton his pants and take his cock out in the mirror.

He strokes it once, slowly, and I watch him. There's just something *about* a nice hand on a nice cock.

"Are you taunting me?" I ask.

"I thought you liked watching," he says. He puts one hand on my lower back and leans into me, his lips against my ear.

"I can watch you jerk off from New York," I say. "But I'm right here *now*."

He slides his hand through my hair and then grabs a handful, *just* hard enough to pull my head back a little.

"Tell me what you need," he says into my ear.

"I need you to fuck me already," I say. "I've been waiting for this since last night."

He pushes inside me with one hard, smooth thrust, crushing my hips against the hard marble. My eyes slide shut and long, low *groan* comes out of my chest.

"Holy fucking *Jesus*," I hear myself say. He's still holding my head by my hair, making me arch my back as hard as I can.

Usually we start off slow but not this time, because Jackson is already fucking me hard and fast and deep. I'm up against the sink and he's completely in control. It's all I can do to hold on.

"Is this what you wanted?" he asks.

"Yes," I gasp.

"Balls-deep and bare in a bar bathroom?" Jackson says.

"Balls-deep and bare anywhere," I gasp.

The heat is already gathering in my core, and it's not going to be long before I just *explode*.

"You're dirty as hell and I love it," he says.

We lock eyes in the mirror, his head behind mine. He's *pounding* me, anything but gentle, and it feels so good that I think I might be splintering apart around the edges.

"Fuck me harder and make me come," I whisper.

Somehow, he does, and I just moan as he thrusts impossibly deep.

"That hard enough?" he asks.

I just nod.

"Open your eyes and look at me while you come," he commands.

I do. I lock my gaze onto him as he hits those perfect spots deep inside me, over and over again. I have to fight to keep my eyes open, but I do.

"Jackson," I whisper, and he pulls my hair a little harder.

I come. I keep my eyes open but I feel like I'm exploding apart from the edges, my whole body just *shattering* at once.

"*Fuck*, Jackson," I say again, because that's all I can think of, jolts of pleasure wracking my whole body as I come so hard my vision goes white for a moment. "*Fuck*."

I'm just barely aware that he lets my hair go and grabs my

shoulders, because then he's coming inside me in hard, urgent jolts, still looking at me in the mirror.

It takes a while before I realize he's just muttering *goddamn, Lula-Mae* over and over again until we finally stop moving, his forehead resting against the back of my head. The sound of our breathing fills the little bathroom.

Jackson leans forward and wraps his arms around me, and I can feel his heart pounding, his chest rising and falling. Even though we're in a bathroom and just fucked against a sink, I feel like everything in the world has suddenly gone quiet and still, like there's just us in this moment.

I take one of his hands in mine and put it on top of mine, then lace our fingers together from below. One by one, I kiss his knuckles, pressing my lips to his skin over and over as our breathing slows, as my heartbeat slows. I feel strangely desperate to do *something* that will keep this moment from slipping away, but this is all I can think of.

He watches me like he's about to say something, but he doesn't.

CHAPTER TWENTY-FOUR

JACKSON

MAE KISSES MY KNUCKLES. They're scarred and fucked up and she's doing it slowly but hungrily, like she *needs* to memorize every inch of my hands with her lips.

I have the strange, wild urge to tell her I love her, but I don't, because we're drunk and we just fucked in a bar bathroom and it's probably not the best time. So I stand there and let her kiss me and hold her close, drinking in this moment in the hope I can remember it forever.

After a moment, she stops kissing my hands and laces our fingers together, then just looks at me with her perfect blue eyes. I've got my head against hers and I turn and kiss her on the temple, because even though we just had not-gentle sex in this bathroom right now I feel oddly protective toward her, like she's delicate and fragile even though I know she's not.

"Jackson," she finally says. "What are we doing?"

Before I can answer, there's a knock on the door.

"Shit," I mutter, but Mae just starts giggling as she pulls her dress down.

"Just a minute!" she calls out.

A second later, we're both nearly decent. Mae finds her broken thong, throws it in the trash, and swipes between her legs with some toilet paper. I look away as she does it, as if it's not my fault in the first place.

Then I unlock the door and we leave. I nod at the annoyed-looking woman outside the door, and Mae tries to hide behind me, grabbing my arm and ducking her head. When we get back to the table, she's still giggling, her face bright red. Our burgers still aren't there.

"I think we got away with it," she murmurs, reaching for another beer.

I just shrug.

"At worst, they'll kick us out," I say, and wink at her. "Drink up fast."

We clink glasses again. I put my arm around her, and we both lean back into the booth.

"To not getting caught," I say, and we both drink.

There's a million things I want to say to her. I want to tell her that I started looking for a real house. I want to tell her that I'm dreading the day after tomorrow. I want to tell her that even though she's here I've missed texting her stupid little things all day long.

I want to tell her how much I wish we could just be like this all the time, a normal couple doing normal things and also having sex in the bathroom. I wish I could tell the world that she's *mine*, and I can't. Not now. Not yet.

Mandy the Waitress comes with our burgers and we both chow down. We talk about the rodeo, about our days, like normal people having a normal relationship.

After dinner we walk around downtown Las Vegas holding hands. When we reach the end of the street, we stop. Mae puts her head against my chest and for a long time, we stand there and I just hold her.

"Jackson," she says. "This is a real thing, right?"

I look where she's looking, at the lights and neon and glitz, at the showgirls walking around and smiling wide at everyone.

"It's as real as anything in Vegas," I say.

She looks up at me and frowns, and suddenly I'm not sure I know what we're talking about.

"I meant us," she says, and looks back at the street, my arms still around her.

"You're asking if we're a real thing?" I say. "I think so."

I have no idea what *real thing* means, but I'm pretty sure the right answer is yes. She doesn't say anything.

"I thought we were dating," I say, as something tightens around my heart. "I told my parents you were my girlfriend."

"Oh," she says.

Oh?

"What did you think was happening?" I ask.

She's quiet a moment.

"I didn't know," she says. "You said you're not seeing anyone else right now."

"Just you, Lula-Mae," I say. I squeeze her tighter and force myself not to think of her with someone else.

"Are you?" I finally ask.

Mae just laughs.

"No," she says.

"I don't know what I'm doing," I tell her. "I haven't had a girlfriend since high school."

"But you got seventy-one rankings on Ride A Rodeo Stud?"

"How long until I live that down?" I ask.

"Sorry," she says. "It's just... I don't know. It's a big number and it feels hard to live up to."

I kiss the top of her head.

"I had a lot of options and picked right," I say. "No one else has ever gotten a picture of Flossie."

Mae pauses.

"The goat?" she finally says.

"My favorite goat," I say.

"Is that how cowboys tell girls they're serious?" she asks, slowly. "They text them pictures of their favorite goats?"

"It's one of the ways," I say. "That or they take them on a tractor ride."

"That sounds like a sex move you do outdoors," she says, and I laugh.

"Come to Wyoming and I'll take you on a tractor ride," I tease.

"Will I have to stay in your jizz-covered trailer?"

"It's just the kitchen table that's covered," I say. "I cleaned it off. Though I—"

I stop short.

"Tell me," she says. "I want to know what I'm getting into."

"It got on the ceiling," I confess. "The first time you used the vibrator."

Mae turns her head and leans her forehead against me, and I can feel her shaking with laughter.

"You're disgusting," she says, and I grin.

"Your fault," I say.

We go quiet for a moment. Lights flash, and we can just barely hear the clang of machines from inside the casinos.

"I don't want to leave and go back to Wyoming," I say.

"We can't stay in Vegas," Mae murmurs.

"I could move to New York," I say.

"That's a terrible idea," Mae says. "I don't even like it that much, and it's got zero rodeos."

I exhale.

"I started looking at real houses that aren't a trailer on my parents' ranch," I say.

"Where?" she asks.

"Wyoming, but I only just started," I say. "I can look anywhere."

She doesn't say anything.

"Photography is mostly in New York, right?" I ask.

Mae just nods.

"And rodeo is all out west," she says, as if I didn't know, and then laughs. "We've known each other for a month, we're probably getting ahead of ourselves."

"But it's been a real good month," I say.

"Yeah," Mae agrees. She huddles closer to me. "You ready to head back to your room? It's freezing out here."

I put my jacket over her as we walk to the taxi stand, and she tries to give it back, but I just laugh.

"Let me be a gentleman for once," I say into her ear.

"As long as it's only once," she says.

I slip my hand under my jacket and over her hip, then suddenly remember she's not wearing underwear and grin. We get into a cab, and in the dark backseat I pull her toward me and grab her ass through her dress, then slowly pull the hem up.

"I almost forgot you didn't have panties on," I murmur.

"I didn't," she says, then smiles slowly. "Now I don't have to take anything off."

The taxi driver turns his radio up. Mae turns her eyes forward and slides her hand along my jeans, and this time I let her grab my erection and squeeze, the gold windows of the Mandalay Bay getting ever closer as my cock strains against denim for the millionth time that day.

"Do you have any idea what you do to me?" I ask.

"I've got a pretty good handle on it right now," Mae says. Her eyes are sparkling, even in the dark.

I kiss her slowly, trying to control myself. She squeezes me again and I force myself not to groan.

"Dirty," I whisper into her ear.

"I'm a nice girl," she whispers back.

"I've never heard anything further from the truth," I say. I push my hand between her thighs, even as she squeezes them together.

"I'm usually a much nicer girl," she says. "No one's ever ripped my underwear off in a bar bathroom before to eat me out."

I kiss her again.

"Why do I have the feeling it's not the last time?" I murmur.

"Because it was so much fun?" she says.

"Mandalay Bay!" the driver shouts, glaring in the rearview mirror.

I tip well.

We walk across the lobby and get into the elevator without saying anything to each other, then ride up with a family. The mom looks at the bulge in my jeans and glares at me, but Mae takes my hand and glares back possessively until they get off a few floors before us. Then she puts her arms around me, and I grab her ass.

"Next time, just pee on my leg," I tease.

She wrinkles her nose and looks at me like I'm crazy.

"To mark your territory," I say, and Mae laughs.

"Sorry," she says.

"Don't be," I say, and slide my hands under the bottom of her dress. "I wish everyone knew I was yours."

The elevator doors open and we walk into the hall.

I look both ways, then pick up Mae and toss her over my shoulder in a fireman's carry. She squeals and kicks a little, but gives up too fast to actually be upset. From here I can smell her arousal, and I try to open my hotel room with a credit card instead of the key, it's so distracting.

Inside I toss her on the bed and she laughs, and then she's sitting up, grabbing me by the belt and pulling me toward her, standing between her legs as she sits on the bed.

"Get your shirt off," she says, unbuttoning the bottom buttons.

"Bossy," I say, but then my shirt is off and she's pulling me by the belt again, her lips hot and urgent on my stomach.

"You make me crazy," she says, her voice buzzing against my skin.

"Why?" I ask.

She undoes my belt and then unbuttons my jeans, then runs her tongue slowly along the indentation of my hip. It makes my cock twitch with anticipation, straining against the zipper.

"Because you're fucking sexy," she says. "You make me feel like I'm a bottomless pit."

She kisses me again, and I think she *growls*.

"I feel like I have an itch that won't stay scratched, and it's your fault," she goes on.

She pulls down my boxers and jeans all at once, then stands and pushes me backwards until I'm sitting on the couch and she's kneeling on the floor in front of me. My cock's at full mast, swollen and throbbing as if we didn't *just* fuck in a bathroom two hours ago.

Mae doesn't tease me this time, just slides her mouth down my shaft until I groan, her tongue flat against the underside. She doesn't go slow but she doesn't go fast, and she makes these half-moan noises that feel like they're vibrating up my spine.

Her hair falls over her face and I push it away, the strands flowing through my fingers. She pulls back and looks at me, her lips just over the head of my cock, tongue swirling, and it's so sexy that I have to hold my breath for a moment as her mouth slides back down, almost to the base of my cock.

I think I might come. I almost tell her to stop, I'd rather fuck her, but it's impossible to get the words out when it feels so damn *good*. All I can do is groan and watch her.

At the last second, she stops and leans her head against the inside of one knee. Her hand curls possessively over the top, and she takes a moment to just look at me.

Then she stands, her hands on my knees, and bends over me.

"Tell me what you—"

I grab the back of her head and lean forward and kiss her hard. Her mouth tastes musky, but it's *hot* in a dirty kind of way. I push my tongue into her mouth and taste her deeper.

"Ride my cock," I growl, my hand on the back of her neck.

She kneels over me and I kiss her again. I run two fingers over her slit, and her juices practically run down my hand. Mae moans into my mouth when I push them inside her, then take them out and slide them past her clit.

Her dress is around her waist. I take her by one hip and hold the base of my cock with the other. She slides down in one long stroke, utterly enveloping me as I groan into her shoulder.

"God, you feel so good," she whispers.

I unzip her dress behind her and push it over her head. She tosses it somewhere else and her bra follows. I kiss her neck and pinch both her nipples at once, and she moans as her pussy contracts around me.

"You like that," I say.

"I like everything you do to me," she whispers.

Mae starts moving her hips and riding me, and I lean my head back against the couch and exhale. Her tits bounce a little as she moves, and I can just see my cock disappearing inside her, again and again.

There's no better view in the world.

"You're beautiful," I say.

"Especially when I'm riding your cock?" she asks.

"Fuck yes," I say. "I could watch you do this all day."

"I could do this all day," she says, her voice low.

She leans forward and kisses me, her hips still moving.

"That good?" I ask, leaning forward and grinning.

I hold her hips down, burying myself inside her until she groans.

"Yes," she whispers. "Jesus, Jackson."

Her pussy contracts around me again, her breathing ragged.

"Go slow or I'm gonna come already," she whispers.

"What's wrong with that?" I ask.

"It feels too good to have you inside me," she says, a slow smile spreading across her face. "I waited weeks for this and I want it to last."

"I promise not to come yet," I growl.

I have no idea if I can keep that promise. I still think I'm going to come every time I enter her, for fuck's sake.

"Just let me make you come again," I say. "I love watching you."

Mae bites her lip, but she starts moving again, fucking me gently, her hands on my shoulders.

"Fuck me as hard as you want, Lula-Mae," I whisper. "I ain't gonna break."

I pull her onto me a little roughly.

"Oh *fuck*," she says, steadying herself with one hand against the back of the couch and one hand on my chest. I grin at her.

Mae rides me harder and harder. I've got my hands on her hips and I'm pulling her down onto my cock as hard as I can, the pure pleasure of being inside her shooting through my whole body.

"This feels so fucking good," she gasps.

"Come," I growl, leaning forward.

"Just fuck me," she whispers. "Please."

I push her hips onto my cock as hard as I can. I bite her collarbone and she moans explosively, her fingers digging into my shoulders.

"You make me come so hard," she whispers, and then she *explodes*. Her muscles tighten around me so hard I almost can't breathe. There's a moment when I have no idea whether I'm coming or not, as her nails rake across my back and I can feel every muscle in her body clench all at once.

"*Fuck*, Jackson," she says, nearly shouting.

I love how she says my name when she comes.

When she slows, I pull her face down to mine and kiss her. I'm still hard inside her, somehow. I move her hips against me and she gasps.

"I kept my promise," I murmur. "Even though you're an insatiable monster."

"I'm not a *monster*," she says.

"You're *my* monster," I say. "I bet you already can't wait for round two."

"What's round two?" she asks.

I don't answer her. Instead I lift her off of me, stand, and toss her over my shoulder again as she squeals.

"I can *walk*," she says.

I toss her on the bed and get on top of her. I'm so hard it feels like my dick might fall off, but I kiss her hard and she slides her hand down the shaft, already slick with her.

"What do you *think* round two is, Lula-Mae?" I growl in her ear. "Round two is we fuck again."

CHAPTER TWENTY-FIVE

MAE

I WAS PRETTY sure round two was *we fuck again*. I'm still shaky and high from round one, but now there's that light in Jackson's eyes. The primal, animal, caveman light.

He grabs me by one hip and rolls me over until I'm on my hands and knees facing the headboard, and he runs his fingers over my slit. I arch my back and look at him over my shoulder, because I feel like I'm in heat, and *all* that matters is fucking him again *right now*.

Then he slides in and I *groan*, my hands clenching the bedsheets. I push back against him until every inch is inside and I hear him growl. I already came once, so I'm even more sensitive than usual. His cock feels like it's completing a circuit in my body, every nerve suddenly electrified.

"Is this what you wanted?" he asks.

"Yes," I say, pushing back against him.

He grabs me by the shoulders and lifts me up to kneeling and then I'm bracing myself against the headboard on my elbows, bent over halfway as Jackson slides inside me again, a low rumble coming from deep in his chest.

"I can't do this for long, Lula-Mae," he says. "You make me feel like a teenager, like I might come just looking at you."

"Don't stop," I say. "I need this, Jackson."

"I know what you need," he growls. He pulls my hips against him, pushing himself *deep*, and I just shout.

"Fuck, yes, *please*," I gasp.

He does it again and again, slow and hard and deep. I think my brain has stopped responding to all other signals besides the complete, overwhelming force of the pleasure building inside me.

"I needed this too," he says, into my ear. "God, I needed this."

"I know," I murmur. "You think I don't know what you need?"

Slow, hard, deep.

"You *are* what I need," he says. "Here, outside, in a truck, against a sink. Drunk, sober. It doesn't fucking matter, Lula-Mae."

Again.

I can feel myself start coming apart, like I'm about to go to pieces.

"Lula-Mae, I'm gonna come," he whispers.

"Come inside me," I say.

I'm right at that edge, teetering on the brink, and Jackson thrusts slow and deep one more time.

"Yes," I whisper, and I just come unraveled. It feels so fucking *good* that nothing else exists for seconds on end, just the bursts of pleasure exploding through me.

Then Jackson growls and suddenly I feel him come inside me, his cock jerking deep inside me as he says, "Oh, fuck," into the back of my shoulder over and over again. Tremors are still rattling through my body, and I'm still propped up against the headboard by my forearms, panting for breath.

I turn my head and Jackson leans over me. He's still inside me as we kiss, hard and slow. I'm still moaning and panting, and he's urgent, like he *has* to do this right here, right now.

After a while, he stops. We slide into the bed, under the covers and fix the pillows that we fucked up. I'm half on his chest, one arm slung over him, our usual position.

We have a usual position, I think.

I don't realize that I'm tracing the scar on his chest until he puts his hand over mine and holds it still.

"Sorry," I say.

"For a girl who says she don't wanna know about my scars, you sure mess with them a lot," he says, half-teasing.

"I don't like knowing all the ways you could get hurt," I say. "It gives me too much imagination fuel."

"It's almost over," he says. "One more ride tomorrow and then I've got six weeks to recuperate. And I already rode Crash once."

"Yeah, he's a kitten," I say.

"He'll be curled up in a sunbeam and purring when I'm done with him," Jackson says, and kisses the top of my head. "I'll be fine. This ain't my first rodeo, you know."

"That's not even a pun," I say.

"I believe it's called a fact, Miss Guthrie," he says.

I sigh, and Jackson laughs. I roll onto him a little more, my chin on his chest.

"What happens if you win?" I ask.

"I get a really big belt buckle and eighty thousand dollars," he says. "Plus the everlasting glory of being the first three-time world champion, et cetera."

"You only get eighty thousand dollars?" I say, surprised.

"I think you mean I get eighty thousand *whole dollars,*" Jackson says.

I pause.

He shattered his sternum, and the one guy who wins everything only makes eighty grand?

"You ain't impressed?" Jackson says.

"It's just not a lot of money for a lot of danger," I say. I try to sound diplomatic, but I don't think I succeed.

"No one is here for the money," he says. "We're here because we love doing it."

"I know," I say. "There can't be enough money in the world to make rodeo worthwhile."

I want to ask *what happens to old riders* or *who pays your medical bills* or *what are you going to do after this,* but I don't.

He laughs.

"I live in a trailer on my parents' ranch and drive a twenty-five-year-old truck," he says. "My overhead is low."

"A jizz-covered trailer," I say.

"I *told* you, that's just the kitchen table," he says. "And it's your fault."

"I'm not sorry," I say.

We lie there for a moment, both of us curled into the same part of the massive king bed. Jackson starts messing with my hand, sliding his fingers through mine. Matching up our fingertips into tents. Folding my hand into his and then unfolding it.

"Do you need to go?" he finally asks.

"I should," I say without moving.

He flattens my hand onto his chest again and puts his over top of it. I can feel his heartbeat under my palm, and it's steady and reassuring, a slow *thump-thump.*

"I don't want to," I say, quietly. "I hate pretending."

"It's a couple more days," he says.

Thump-thump.

"I just wish it was different," I say.

"Stay," he says. "I'll be up early, but I'll set the alarm so you can get back in time."

I sit up, cross-legged, on the bed and look out the window, where Vegas is glowing. Jackson rests his hand on my knee, and I run my fingers over his knuckles. There's a thick scar across a couple of them.

"How'd you get that one?" I ask.

"Thought it was a good idea to rope a steer without gloves on," he says. "Rope burn."

I move my fingers down his arm to the long, thick one on his forearm.

"I told you about that one in Oklahoma," he says. "I got thrown. Compound fracture. I've got a metal rod."

My stomach does a flip, and I make a face. I turn his arm over and look at a thick white spot on his forearm.

"I was helping a buddy brand his cattle and walked into the brand," he says.

"You didn't notice it was there?" I ask.

"I might have been drunk," he says, and laces our fingers together again. "Most of the scars aren't from bull riding, most of them are from me being a dumbass," he says.

"Is that because you don't get hurt that much, or because riding mostly breaks bones?" I ask.

He half-smiles and looks away.

"I was trying to make you feel better," he says, and I laugh.

"Thanks," I say.

"Are you sitting up because you're leaving?" he asks.

"I'm just sitting up," I say.

He looks at me for a long moment.

"I could visit you in New York next month," he says.

"Plane tickets are cheaper in January, and I could stay with you."

I look out the window one more time.

Screw it, I think.

I lie back down and snuggle into Jackson.

"You're staying?" he asks.

"I shouldn't," I admit.

"Your favorite phrase," he says.

"Shut up," I tease.

I flatten my hand against his chest and feel his heartbeat.

"What do you want to see in New York?" I ask.

· · · · ★ ★ ★ ★ ★ · · · ·

IT'S two in the morning before we finally fall asleep, spooning in the middle of the massive bed. Jackson's got his arms around me and I'm warm and almost blissfully happy as I drift off to sleep.

It's fine, I think as darkness takes over my mind. *It's just logistics. We can work anything out.*

I wake up to a voice saying my name, and I feel like I'm surfacing from the bottom of a deep, deep lake.

"Mae," it says. "Lula-Maaaae, wake up."

"What do you *want*?" I ask.

I roll over, away from the voice.

He laughs.

"You weren't kidding," Jackson says.

I roll over again and look at him.

"Shut up," I say.

"Morning, sunshine," he says, and grins. Then he holds up a paper cup. "I brought you coffee."

I blink at it, then at him. I sit up, slowly, pushing my hair out of my eyes.

"It's five-forty-five," he says. "You should get going pretty soon if you want to keep fooling everyone."

He hands me the coffee and I take it. I look at him and take a sip, then another, longer sip.

Then I lean forward and smoosh my face against his shoulder.

"Why are you in a good mood?" I mutter.

"Sun's up, birds are singing, you're in my bed, I ride today," he says. "I got a whole list."

"Are you always like this?" I ask.

I lift the coffee to my mouth. The angle's not quite right, and I spill a couple of drops on my leg.

"Ow," I say, but don't move.

"Like what?" Jackson asks. "Awake before six?"

"And *happy* about it," I say. "We need some ground rules."

"Besides *let Mae sleep in as long as possible* and *bring her coffee in bed?*" he asks.

He has a point.

"We can talk about this later," I say, and take another long drink of the coffee. "Thank you."

I put my dress back on, and search for my underwear for a while before I remember what happened to it. I look at myself in the mirror and pray that I don't look too much like I'm taking a walk of shame.

I drain the coffee and toss it into the trash can. I still don't feel like a person, but Jackson comes over and gives me a long, slow kiss anyway.

"I think I have horrible coffee breath," I say when he pulls back.

"Yep," he says, and kisses me again. I'm still not really awake, but this feels wonderful and fuzzy, one of his hands on my lower back.

When we pull back this time, I put one hand on his chest where the scar is.

"Good luck," I say, and I mean both *go win this thing* and *please don't get hurt.*

He grins.

"You coming by the hotel suite of the three-time World Rodeo Champion tonight?" he asks.

"Don't count your chickens before they're hatched," I say. "And yes, obviously."

He kisses me one last time, and I leave. I buy another cup of coffee in the lobby and drink it in a taxi. Then I shower in my own hotel room, get dressed, go downstairs, and get two more cups of coffee.

· · · · ★ ★ ★ ★ · · · ·

EVEN THOUGH I work like crazy, I can only think one thing: *Jackson is coming to New York.*

It's not for another month. He's not moving there. I have no idea when I'll see him after that. But it's something, it's a little glimmer to hang my hopes on.

I feel like I spend the day surreptitiously watching Jackson interact with fans. Now that he's close to being a really, really big deal there's more of them than ever. He's smiling and polite and gracious to them, even when one lady kisses him on the cheek.

When the stands start filling up before the afternoon rodeo, there's even more signs. Most of them are the same WE LOVE YOU JACKSON or GET NUMBER THREE, though there's one that says KISS ME CODY, carried by a pair of forty-something women in tight jeans.

I watch them from the media area and try to burn holes

in the sign by glaring. It doesn't work. They sit in the front, so I get to look at the sign the whole time.

I don't even need a sign, I think grumpily. After all, it's thanks to Mr. Cody that I've gotten about seven hours of sleep in two nights, so really, this is his fault.

Not that I've got any intention of sleeping more tonight. The thought pools fire inside me, and I pretend to check some settings on my camera, even as I squirm. Tomorrow I have to leave, but I'm trying not to think about that.

The bull riding starts. I take pictures of it. The hours seem to drag on, even though it takes exactly the same amount of time every night.

Most cowboys get thrown before eight seconds, because that's how this is: hard and dangerous. The reporters in the media area with me are talking, and it's listening to them that I realize: Jackson isn't just *really good*, he's *phenomenally* good.

No one just wins rodeo after rodeo like he does. If he stays on Crash today, he'll have qualified in all three rides at the Finals, and that's *almost* as unprecedented as being champion three years running.

Oh, I think. Somehow, I didn't quite realize all that. My stomach feels like someone's trying to wring all the liquid out of it, twisting inside me, because I want him to win.

I really, really want him to win, because I know *he* wants this. I think of the night in the bucking chute when I shot him standing there, looking at the moonlit arena, when he told me he wondered if he should have settled down in Wyoming instead.

I'm glad you didn't, I think.

He's three rides away, then two. Then we're watching the guy before him ride, and he makes it to seven seconds only to get thrown. Honestly, it's a miracle I remember to take any pictures of him, because I'm just nervous about Jackson.

I think about what he said last night: *You're a distraction, Lula-Mae.*

I worry that I'm a distraction.

The previous cowboy climbs back over the gate. Crash Junction is already in the chute, and he's already unhappy about it.

"Next up, Jackson Cody of Sawtooth, Wyoming!" the announcer booms. Since it's the last night, he goes on about Jackson for a minute, but he's nearly drowned out by the crowd screaming and shouting and stomping.

Hell, I want to scream and shout and stomp too. I wish I had a giant sign that said GO JACKSON but instead I aim my camera and hold my breath.

He stands over Crash Junction and looks at the bull for a long time, like he's tracking the animal's movements, figuring out the patterns he'll use in the arena. I bite the skin on my lip and taste blood, but I don't stop.

Jackson jumps on. Crash lurches, but the chute keeps him contained. Jackson wraps the rope around his hand, and I take a couple shots of him, because he's smiling and confident and *sexy*, and I'll decide later whether I pass them on to *Sports Weekly*.

He looks up. He tips his hat to the crowd.

He looks at me and smiles, touching the brim of his hat again, and I smile back. In that moment, it doesn't occur to me to care if anyone sees.

Then the gate opens and Crash leaps out.

Please, God, I think, even though I haven't been to church since I was sixteen.

Please please please. Please. Please.

Two seconds are gone. Crash dives and whirls, leaping

and shaking and changing direction on a dime, but Jackson's still on. Three seconds. Four.

He goes a little off balance, I think, and a gasp goes through the crowd as Crash leaps off the ground and twists, all four feet in the air. Five seconds, and he leaps and drops again.

Six seconds. Jackson's hat falls off but he doesn't. Someone in the media box says, "He just *spurred* 'im!" and I have no idea what that means, but I think it's impressive.

The crowd is screaming at top volume. Everyone's on their feet.

Seven seconds. I can't breathe and my heart's stopped beating. The only thing I can do is aim my camera and keep shooting, but that's just muscle memory, purely mechanical. Even the other reporters in here are shouting, at the arena, at each other, pointing.

When the clock hits eight seconds, it's pandemonium. The announcer is hollering at the top of his lungs and the crowd is shouting and everyone is standing and just completely losing their shit.

I somehow get a shot of Jackson under the clock as it says 8.03, and I start laughing out of sheer joy.

He did it. He fucking *did* it.

Then he flies off Crash Junction.

At first I think he jumped, but no. Even in the air he's at a weird angle, off-kilter. I don't know how but I know something's *wrong*.

Jackson lands heavily on one side. His head snaps back, and the crowd suddenly hushes. I feel like an anvil's just landed on my chest.

No, I think. *Please no.*

Get up. Get up get up get up.

Crash turns and looks back at Jackson. Jackson's still on

the ground, trying to roll over, but it's not going well. Even from where I'm standing, clear across the arena, it's obvious he broke something bad.

Then Crash starts galloping toward Jackson.

I can't move. I can't breathe. I feel like it's happening in slow motion. The rodeo clowns in the ring are both sprinting toward Crash Junction, shouting and waving their arms, but they can't do anything. The media box is dead silent as Crash runs toward Jackson. I've got both hands over my mouth and I can hear myself saying *no no no no no no* over and over, but it doesn't help.

The bull runs straight over Jackson, and at the last second I cover my face. I can't watch. I think I might throw up and I feel like all the air's been sucked out of this arena. No one says a word, not even the announcer, not even the crowd.

It feels like a year that it's quiet. I'm pressing my hands against my eyes so hard lights are dancing in front of my eyeballs, but I can't look, I *can't*.

People start murmuring again.

"He moved," someone in the box says, and I force myself to look up. I've still got both hands in front of my mouth, as I watch people sprint toward Jackson. Seconds later, there's two people in uniforms with a stretcher. Jackson's foot moves.

There's no blood, but I know there doesn't need to be blood for something to be bad.

He's alive, I think.

It was just last night that Jackson told me he didn't have many scars from riding, because he mostly broke bones. Last night, when he said he wanted to go to the Statue of Liberty when he visited me.

My hands are shaking. My whole body is shaking. I feel like I'm watching something on TV, like everything in front of me is flat and two-dimensional and I'm totally removed, seeing it from somewhere else.

I watch the paramedics work, and they work fast, maybe too fast. Maybe too urgently, but I'm just standing here. I want to jump the barrier and run to him, help him *somehow*, but what the fuck am I going to do?

They carry him out of the arena, and I finally look around.

Everyone in the media box is staring at me. Finally Bruce reaches out one hand and touches me on the shoulder.

"Mae, are you all right?" he says.

I move my hands away from my mouth, and suddenly I realize my hands are wet. I'm crying. My whole face is wet, but I just stare at my hands like I don't understand what tears are.

"I don't think so," I tell him, and my voice sounds weirdly calm, even though my whole body is shaking.

The announcer says the next cowboy's name. There's another bull in the chute, and even though there's a hush over everything we're all carrying on.

I look around. Now everyone is pretending like they weren't just staring at me. Not that I give a shit.

"Where are they gonna take him?" I ask Bruce.

"Probably the university hospital, but I'm not sure," he says.

"I have to go," I say. I start backing away from my camera and bump into someone else. There's a hand on my shoulder to steady me, and now that I can breathe again I'm breathing too much, too fast, and getting lightheaded.

Everyone's staring at me again.

"Is this set up?" Bruce asks, pointing at the camera.

I nod.

"Just hit the button," I say. He nods once, then steps in front of it and looks through the viewfinder.

I look around at all the wide eyes, and then I turn and stumble out of the media box, and then I'm running. I shove through crowds of people and some of them shout at me, but I keep going.

At the entrance to the backstage area there's a big guy in a plaid shirt. He holds up one hand.

"Whoa," he says.

I try to duck around him but there's someone behind him, and I run full-tilt into *that* guy and have to stop.

"No media," he says.

"I'm not media," I gasp.

"You got a media pass," he says, looking at the lanyard around my neck.

I tear it off and throw it on the ground.

"There," I say. "I'm not here as fucking media, I swear."

I can hear my voice rising.

"You can't come back here," he says.

I try to dodge around him, but he blocks me.

"I ain't kidding, sweetheart," he says.

"I need to see him!" I shout. "Just fucking let me through!"

"You need to leave," he says. "You got three seconds before I escort you out."

"No," I say. "Look, I swear, I just need to—"

I try to duck past him again but he catches me by the upper arm.

"You vultures can't just come back here because you're pretty girls who can cry," he says. "Now *get out.*"

Just then, I see a familiar face.

"RAYLAN!" I shout.

Everyone in earshot looks over at me. The security guy lets my arm go, but he's still blocking me.

"Raylan, please!" I shout, trying to look over this guy's shoulder.

Raylan's pale, his face drawn, but he jogs over.

"Just let me in, please, I know Jackson, and I just need to get in," I'm babbling as Raylan comes up.

"She's all right, Dale," he says.

The guy crosses his arms.

"Come on, Mae," Raylan says.

I duck around Dale, and he doesn't stop me this time. Raylan's walking fast, and I just follow him.

"Thanks," I say.

Raylan just nods, walking faster. In a moment the ambulance comes into view. The lights are already on and they're loading a stretcher into it. Next to it is a knot of cowboys, faces serious, arms crossed.

I sprint to them, my eyes on the ambulance.

"Where are they taking him?" I shout.

One of the paramedics looks at me, her face somber and serious.

"University hospital," she says, then shuts the ambulance door. The sirens start blaring and the ambulance drives off.

I've never felt more helpless in my life. All I can do is stand there and watch until it turns a corner and drives out of sight, and then I look around at the men standing around. They're half looking at me and half looking at the ground.

"What happened?" I ask. I'm crying and breathing hard, and it comes out as a ragged whisper.

"Broken ribs, punctured lung, shattered leg at least," someone says. I think his name is Clay. "Could be a lot more."

"Is he..." I say, and let my voice trail off. I almost say *okay*, but it's the dumbest thing I could say right now. I just want someone to tell me that he's alive, that he's going to be okay. That this wasn't the last time I'm going to see Jackson.

Clay and Raylan shake their heads.

"How bad is this?" I whisper.

They look at each other.

"It's bad, Mae," Raylan finally says. "I don't know how bad, but it's bad."

I nod, swallowing hard. I'm doing my best not to have a total breakdown in front of these guys, but it's not really working.

All I can think of is us, in bed, my head on his chest. Him telling me he'd be fine.

Me being *such a bitch* this morning when all he did was bring me coffee.

"You want a ride to the hospital?" Raylan asks.

"Thanks," I say.

· · · ★ ★ ★ ★ ★ ★ · · ·

WE DON'T TALK on the drive, just stare out the windshield of Raylan's pickup truck. At the hospital, all the woman at the desk will tell us is that Jackson was admitted to the ER. She doesn't even know if he's stable.

Raylan and I sit there for an hour. Some other cowboys trickle in, and I just stare at the wall. I can't even concentrate well enough to read the tabloids scattered around the waiting area.

I think about Jackson showing up at my door with a bottle of Boone's Farm. I think about postcards, pictures of Flossie the goat, about how he told his parents I was his girlfriend.

I think about him saying *I don't want to leave here.*

I'm still sitting there, feeling catatonic, when Bruce walks in and over to us.

"What's going on?" he asks.

Raylan and I shake our heads.

"They don't know or they won't tell us," I say. I've finally stopped crying, but I think it's because my body's out of water for tears.

"I see," Bruce says. "Give me a minute."

He walks off. Raylan and I look at each other, and Raylan shrugs.

Fifteen minutes later, Bruce is back.

"Jackson's heading into surgery," he says, keeping his voice low. "He's got broken ribs, a punctured lung, and a lot of internal bleeding. It's gonna be a while."

"How long is a while?" I whisper.

Bruce shakes his head.

"Couple hours at least," he says. "Maybe longer."

This is good, right? I think. *That he's okay enough to have surgery?*

I have no fucking idea.

"Is he gonna..." I start. I swallow, then clear my throat. "I mean, will he—?"

I can't.

"It's looking better than it was," Bruce says.

"Did anyone call his parents?"

"They're heading down."

I look out the hospital window. It's dark outside, and I can see the glow of the strip far away. Raylan stands.

"How'd you find this out?" I suddenly ask Bruce.

"I've been a reporter since I was your age," he says. "I wouldn't be very good at it if I couldn't get information."

"I'm gonna head back to the hotel," Raylan says. "I may as well be useless in comfort."

I stand and give him a slightly awkward hug.

"Thanks for the ride," I say.

"I'm sorry about that picture," he says.

We detach and I cross my arms in front of myself.

"Thanks," I say.

Raylan leaves, and Bruce is still standing there.

"You too," he says.

"I'm not leaving," I say.

"I know you need to eat," he says. "You're no good to anyone here. You may as well have a meal, Mae. Jackson's gonna be under for a while."

I know he's right. I don't want to leave the hospital where Jackson is, but it's not like I can do anything while he's in surgery.

It's not like I can do anything, period.

"Okay," I say.

"You like sushi?" Bruce asks.

I nod.

CHAPTER TWENTY-SIX

MAE

THERE'S a fancy sushi restaurant next to the Wynn, and they seat Bruce and I at a table way off in the corner. I sip a tiny cup of green tea, and every time I put it back on the table, Bruce refills it from a ceramic teapot.

He orders. I'm barely listening.

I'm thinking of Jackson saying, *you're my monster.* Of him saying *I wish everyone knew I was yours.*

Finally, Bruce drinks his own tea and looks at me.

"Mae, I think you should tell me what's going on with you and Jackson Cody," he finally says.

I sigh and shove my fingers through my hair.

"We're dating," I say.

He looks like he doesn't quite believe me.

"Dating," he says. Bruce has been reporting on rodeo for a long time, so he knows as well as anyone that Jackson Cody doesn't *date.*

I take a deep breath.

"Yeah," I say. "We, uh..."

I don't know where to start. I don't know if I start with a

bottle of Boone's Farm in a pickup truck, or if I start at Pioneer Days, or if I start when he called me a week later.

"We started seeing each other in Oklahoma," I say, because that seems like as good an introduction as any. I go through the phone calls, the texting, mention that I've been visiting Jackson after-hours here in Vegas. I show him the pictures on my phone: Flossie, sunsets, tractors, fields. Jackson's cute nephews.

He believes me by the end.

"I know you warned me," I say.

"I tried," he says.

Sushi comes, and we start eating in silence. Incredibly, it makes me feel a little better.

"Am I fucked?" I ask Bruce.

More scenes flash through my mind: freaking out in the media area. Causing a scene backstage.

"I don't know," Bruce says. "I can only tell you what I think you should do."

I wait.

"Call your editor, Erica," he says. "The minute the offices open in New York, and tell her everything. It'll go better if she hears it from you first."

I chew on my thumb and nod.

"If you just went back to New York tomorrow morning, you could probably get away with it," Bruce says. "You and Jackson became friends at Pioneer Days, so it's natural that you had a reaction to him getting injured."

"I can't just go back," I whisper.

"I'm just laying out the options," he says. "I didn't think you would."

He pauses, chopsticks hovering over his plate, and looks at me.

"You're a good photographer, Mae," he says. "That

should be the first thing people think when they hear your name. Not something else."

Something else meaning *sleeps with the people she's photographing*, I assume.

"Thanks," I say.

· · · · · ★ ★ ★ · · · ·

AFTER DINNER, Bruce makes a phone call and somehow gets more information. Jackson's still in surgery. I go to my room and try to watch TV, but I can't. I end up taking a long walk down the strip, wandering through casino after casino. I'll take any loud, horrible, flashing distraction to get my mind off of what's happening.

I wonder if Jackson is waking up from surgery and no one's there, and then I just pray that he's waking up. At midnight, I find a number for the hospital and call, but I can't get anyone to answer my questions. I wander back to the hotel. I change my flight to one four days from now, because that seems like as good a time as any. It costs four hundred dollars and I put it on my credit card, praying that I get paid for this job before my rent is due on the first.

Then I make myself lay in my bed and shut my eyes.

Every time I drift off to sleep, I see it again: Jackson on the ground, Crash Junction galloping toward him. I wake up with a jolt. At five a.m., I give up. I call the hospital again, uselessly, so I shower and find their visiting hours. They start at eight.

I text Bruce a single question mark, because he seems to be the only person who can find anything out.

At 5:50, I sit at the table in my room and look out the window. I've got a view of the block behind the strip, facing east. There's not much to look at, just the horizon starting to turn pink and gray since the sun hasn't come up yet.

Call her and tell her, I think.

I don't want to. There's a tiny part of me that thinks, somehow, we can keep this a secret until I'm done with the job. That somehow I can see Jackson in the hospital and not have everyone know.

But Bruce was right, of course. My options are *go back to New York* or *fess up*.

At 5:59, I hold my breath. When the clock says 6:00 — 9:00 on the east coast — I pick it up and dial Erica. Her assistant picks up on the first ring, and when I tell her who it is, she puts me through right away.

"What's happening out there?" Erica says. "Any word?"

"Last I knew, Jackson was in surgery and it sounded pretty serious," I say. My throat's closing up. "I don't know what's happening right now. Also we've been dating for the past month."

There's a long pause.

"You and Jackson?" she says.

"Yes," I say, and then I spill the whole story. I start with Oklahoma but I end up going back to the bonfire party, then to Oklahoma, then to Vegas, then to the middle part, and it's a goddamn mess.

Through the whole thing, Erica just says, "I see," over and over, and I have no idea what *that* means.

I finish. There's a long pause.

"Thank you for telling me first," she says, but her voice is rigid. "Though I wish I'd known sooner."

"I apologize," I say, and hope my voice isn't shaking. "I'll still have the pictures to you by Tuesday."

"That would be excellent," she says. "I'll have to get back to you about everything else, Mae."

When we hang up the phone, Bruce has texted me back. **He's out.**

I grab pants, pull my hair into a ponytail, and leave.

· · · · ★ ★ ★ ★ ★ · · · ·

HIS ROOM IS in the ICU, which isn't surprising. The doors to it are badge-operated and don't have windows, so I can't even see in. When I bother the nurse at the front desk she *very* firmly tells me that visiting hours start at eight, and there's no one even at the desk outside the ICU yet.

I don't know what to do, so I drink coffee in the hospital cafeteria. It's not good coffee, but at least I won't have a headache later.

He's alive, I think. *It's been twelve hours, and he's alive, and that's good.*

I have no idea what else could happen. Internal bleeding sounds pretty bad, and shattered leg sounds pretty bad, and hell, *everything* sounds bad. I construct scenarios in my head, one after the other: he dies suddenly, still in the hospital. He's paralyzed from the neck down. From the waist down. He's in a wheelchair for the rest of his life. He's got serious brain damage and doesn't know who I am.

At 7:45, I make myself stop and go back upstairs. At 8:00 exactly, someone comes and sits down at the ICU reception desk, and I go up to her.

"Hi, I'm here to see Jackson Cody," I say.

She looks at a list.

"You family?" she asks.

I stare for a second, and I panic.

"I'm his sister," I hear myself say.

She looks down again.

"His parents didn't clear a sister," she says.

"Mom and Dad are really shaken up right now," I say. "They probably forgot. Please, just let me go see him."

She shakes her head.

"Sorry," she says.

Desperation wells up in me, and I try to tamp it down.

It's important that he's alive, I tell myself. *You seeing him is secondary.*

"Are his parents in there now?" I ask. "Can you call his room?"

"I'm not calling," she says.

"Please?"

She just looks at me.

"Look, I don't know who you are—"

The ICU doors open, and a woman with short gray hair steps through. She's fit and no-nonsense looking, with a paisley shirt tucked into high-waisted jeans. She's got blood-shot hazel eyes.

She looks at me, then looks away.

Then she looks at me again.

"Mrs. Cody?" I ask.

"Yes," she says, then frowns slightly. "Are you Mae?"

I just nod, and before I know it, she's hugging me.

"It's nice to finally meet you," she says. "I wish circumstances were different."

"Me too," I say.

She leads me back to the ICU doors.

"She's with me," Jackson's mom tells the woman.

"That your daughter?" the woman asks, a little sarcastically.

Jackson's mom looks at me.

"Sure," she says.

The ICU hall is quiet except for beeping. Mrs. Cody is a

little taller than me and walks fast, then stops suddenly outside a room.

"You haven't seen him yet," she says.

"No," I say.

"It's still touch-and-go," she says. "He looks bad, Mae. His face is all busted up, he's covered in casts, and he can't really move. Plus, he's on a heavy morphine drip, so he's not quite all there right now."

"Okay," I say.

She gives me a hard look.

"No one would blame you if you turned back," she says, her voice sinking almost to a whisper. "He's got a long hard road ahead, and if you want out, now is the time."

I stare at her. It hadn't even *occurred* to me that I might leave Jackson.

"I don't want out," I say.

She nods once, curtly.

"Good," she says. "He likes you."

Then she opens the door to his room, and I take a deep breath.

"I found a stray," Mrs. Cody says, and I walk through the door.

He's fucked up.

Jackson's got casts on both legs, bandages around his torso, a neck brace, a black eye, and a split lip. There are tubes and wires sticking out of him everywhere, both forearms and the backs of both hands.

But he's *alive*.

I just start laughing. I'm giddy with relief and joy and happiness, and his eyes slide toward me.

"Izzat Mae?" he asks. He sounds like his voice box has been through a wood chipper.

"It's me," I say.

At the side of his bed I grab his fingers and hold them in mine, because that seems like the only part that's safe to touch. I *want* to throw my arms around him, I want to kiss him. I want to hold him tight, but that's all a spectacularly bad idea right now.

His fingers curl into mine.

"Hey," he whispers.

CHAPTER TWENTY-SEVEN
JACKSON

I'M ninety-five percent confident this isn't another morphine dream, that Mae's really here. I can't see great, but I can hear her laughing and it sounds like she's trying not to cry.

She takes my fingers, which is pretty much the only part of me that isn't busted. I squeeze her hand.

"Hey," I say.

"Hey," she says, her voice not much more than a whisper. "How are you?"

I lick my lips. I can't move my head, I broke a shitload of bones, and I'm high as *fuck* right now.

"I'm fine," I say. "You know I won?"

"Of course I know you won," she says. "I got a great shot of you winning."

There was something I was going to say to her. I close my eyes and try really, really hard to remember, but my memories are scattered and fragmented.

"Lula-Mae," I start.

Landing in the sand wrong. Crash coming on. Trying to get up and nearly blacking out from the pain. Waking up in the sand, gasping for air, feeling like I was breathing through a straw, my whole body hurting more than I thought possible.

A stretcher, an ambulance, a bed. People kept telling me things but I have no idea what.

I know I had surgery, because I remember being awake and on the table and then feeling like I was falling backward into darkness and not even being afraid, just wondering what was under there.

Then I was here, and my parents were here, and I couldn't really move but I was pretty sure I was alive, though every so often I'd think I was talking to someone and their face would start to twist and morph. Always into sea creatures, for some reason, but they'd keep talking and after a few minutes I'd wake up.

"There's no brain damage?" Mae says.

I squeeze her hand.

"What?" I say.

She looks down at me.

"There you are," she says.

"I'm on drugs," I say, and she just laughs.

"You fell asleep for a few minutes in the middle of your sentence," she says.

"That isn't brain damage, that's just morphine," my dad says. "They'll taper him off it in four or five days and he'll be a little more lucid."

I remember what it was that was so important.

"Mae," I say.

"Yes?" she asks, her thumb rubbing over my knuckles.

"I didn't break my dick," I tell her. "I think."

She turns so bright red that her face is nearly purple, and the room goes dead quiet.

Then someone moves, off to my right, and my mom stands up. I'd already forgotten that my parents were there.

"We're going to go get some coffee," my mom says.

"You want anything, Mae?" my dad asks, getting up slowly. He puts his fists on his lower back and stretches.

"No, thank you," Mae says, still beet-red. "It was very nice to meet you!"

"We'll be back in a few," my mom says, and then they leave.

Mae leans over and kisses me. She's very, very gentle, and with the morphine I feel a little dizzy.

"You scared the hell out of me," she whispers.

"I'm sorry," I say.

She squeezes my fingers again, and I realize she's crying. I try to raise my arm so I can wipe her tears away, but pain shoots through me and I drop it.

Mae wipes her face with the back of her hand, and with her this close, I can finally see her face. Her eyes are puffy and red, deep circles under them. Like she's been crying hard for hours.

"It's okay," I say, and rub my fingers against hers. "It's gonna be okay."

"I'm sorry," she whispers. "I'm not even the one who's hurt."

"It's better when you're here," I say.

She kisses me again, her hair a curtain between me and the world.

I want to say *I never wanted to make you cry*, but I think I drift off to sleep again, because when I wake up, she's curled in an armchair on the other side of my bed, my other hand in hers. I squeeze it and she bends over to kiss it very, very lightly.

"My parents were here when I told you about my dick," I say.

"They were," Mae says. "That was about ten minutes after I met them for the first time. Good job."

"Help me make sure it works?" I ask, my voice sounding fuzzy even to my own ears.

Half the dreams I keep having are sex dreams, sort of. In one of them Mae's naked and walking down a hotel hallway, away from me, and I keep walking after her but she never gets to the end and I never get closer. In another one she's on the other side of a window, looking at me, and she keeps taking off her clothes, but there's always another layer underneath.

She laughs.

"Not a chance," she says. "For starters, I think you're too high to give meaningful consent."

"I definitely consent," I say.

My bed's got rails on it, and she's leaning over one.

"You've also got hairline fractures in four vertebrae and you're peeing through a catheter," she says.

"Sounds gross," I say.

"It is," Mae says.

My vision's getting a little blurry around the edges, and I think I'm starting to drift off again. Mae leans her head against the rail over my bed. I just watch her for a long moment, until everything starts to wobble.

I remember what I wanted to tell her.

"I love you," I say.

Mae's head turns into an octopus.

· · · · · ★ ★ ★ ★ · · · ·

WHEN I WAKE up this time, the sun has moved and Mae is gone, but my parents are back in the room.

"She left?" I ask. I move my fingers, just in case she's there and I can't see her.

"She was fast asleep in that chair so we made her go rest," my dad says, lowering the copy of *Guns & Ammo* he's reading. "Blame us."

"By the way, as far as the hospital is concerned, she's your sister," my mom says.

Well, I'm not doing sex stuff for a while, so I can probably act brotherly. More or less.

"I like her," my mom says. "She's nice, and she takes good pictures of you."

We watch some daytime TV. I drift in and out. Nurses feed me nutritional shakes through a straw and come in and mess with all my tubes and machines and IV drips.

At one point, I think, *I'm glad I'm so high, because this is pretty embarrassing, and also I think I might be in a lot of pain.*

Later, I wake up and Mae is sitting there, my parents on either side of her. She's got her laptop on her lap, and she's pointing at something.

"I think this one's a better angle," my mom says. "Wow, there are just so *many* of these."

"Picking ten out of a thousand is always the hard part," Mae says. "Well, one of them."

"Did you go to school for this?" my mom asks.

"I got my BFA at UT Austin," Mae says.

"Are you from Texas?" my mom says.

"I grew up about an hour from Odessa," Mae says.

I have the feeling that my mom is about to start grilling Mae about everything she's done in her entire life, and even though I can't do much, I can save her from that for another ten minutes.

"You don't have to interview her," I say.

"We were just looking at her photos of you," my mom says. "They're very good."

"Thanks," Mae says.

I hear her laptop shut and she comes over and stands by the bed again, taking my hand.

"Visiting hours are over in a couple minutes," she says. "I'll be back tomorrow, okay?"

I think we're still in Vegas. I think she has to leave, and I think maybe she was supposed to leave *today*.

"Tomorrow?" I say.

"It's the thing that happens after tonight," she says.

Mae leans over and kisses me softly.

"Wait," I say, before she straightens up, so her face is a couple inches in front of mine.

"What?" she whispers.

My dad clears his throat. Right. They're there.

"Tell you tomorrow," I say.

CHAPTER TWENTY-EIGHT

MAE

I'VE MOVED from the Wynn to a Motel 6 near the hospital, the cheapest thing I could find, and I head back there when visiting hours are over. Even though I told Jackson's parents I'd go take a nap, I actually had to move my stuff to here, and I need a little while to just lie in the bed and stare at the ceiling.

As bad as Jackson is, it's pretty much a miracle that he's alive. Somehow, when Crash ran over him, he only kicked in his ribs, puncturing his lung, and broke every bone in his right leg. If Crash had stepped on Jackson, he'd probably be dead.

He's in a bad, bad way, but he's alive.

I still haven't heard back from Erica, my editor at Sports Weekly. She's probably got bigger things to worry about, though maybe not. I called Bruce this afternoon and gave him the vague updates, and he didn't say anything about it either.

I hope it worked. I hope I'm not blacklisted from all photography forever, but right now, I don't even care. I know

I will when I wake up tomorrow, but right now, I can only feel two things.

One is glad that Jackson's alive, and that he's going to be some version of okay.

The other is tired.

I brush my teeth and fall into the bed, where I sleep for almost twelve hours.

· · * ★ ★ ★ ★ ★ · · ·

JACKSON'S still out of it. He manages not to tell me anything else about his dick in front of his parents, but he doesn't always make a lot of sense.

I split my day between holding his hand in the ICU and editing photos downstairs in the hospital cafeteria. They're due to Erica before I leave Vegas, and I just want to get this finished with.

"You missed the nurse," Jackson says the next time I head upstairs to see him. "She says I'm great."

"She said everything was going as well as could be hoped for," his mom says.

"Spoilsport," Jackson says, but he's smiling.

I stay there until he falls asleep again, and then his mom nods her head outside and I follow her.

"What did she really say?" I whisper.

She rubs her eyes.

"They're taking the chest tube from the punctured lung out tomorrow," she says. "But they need to monitor that for a few more days at least, along with the bruising to his organs, and he can't really move his neck at all right now. He's gotta have another surgery on his leg. He'll be here for another week, maybe two."

Shit.

"Okay," I say.

She puts a hand on mine.

"I want you to go back to New York," she says. Her voice is low, but firm, and my eyes widen.

I thought we were getting along.

"You need to go back," she says. "I know you have a life, and a job, and you have to pay your bills, and you're not doing any of that staying here and watching him sleep."

"I can't just leave," I say, keeping my voice low.

"That's why I'm telling you to leave," she says, her voice gentler. "Because I know you don't want to, but you need to. Go live your life, and come visit in six weeks when he's not high out of his damn mind. You can't do anything here besides make your own life harder."

It makes sense, and I know she's right. I still hate it, though.

"What happens after the two weeks?" I ask.

She sighs.

"He comes and lives with us until he recovers," she says, crossing her arms and looking into his hospital room. "And, if my prayers get answered, he doesn't go right back to riding. He's at least out for this season."

I want to ask *what then,* but I don't think she knows, either. We still don't know how long he'll be in a wheelchair, or whether he'll need crutches or a cane forever, and figuring those things out is more important than *are we gonna move somewhere and live together.*

I swallow and push my hand through my hair.

"I'll go back," I say. "You have to promise to keep me updated."

"Absolutely," she says. Then she smiles. "I like you better than Cassie, anyway. She was kind of dumb."

· · · · ★ ★ ★ ★ · · · ·

I SEND the photos in and all I hear from Erica is *Thanks, these look good.* Which is at least nicer than it has to be. Bruce calls and tells me that he talked to her, and she's pissed, but loves the pictures. He doesn't exactly say it, but I think he talked her down. I think I owe Bruce pretty big.

I read all the rodeo news and blogs and websites. Jackson's fall is huge news, and the World Championship organizers are giving press-friendly updates, but I'm nowhere to be found.

It seems like some of Jackson's luck might have rubbed off on me.

My plane leaves at an ungodly hour in the morning, so my last night in Vegas I'm curled up next to Jackson in an arm chair, his hand in mine. They're slowly scaling back the morphine, so he's stopped nodding off mid-sentence, though he's not one hundred percent lucid yet.

His black eye and split lip look better, though they're not gone. He can move his arms okay, and the tube that was sticking out of his chest is gone.

I've got a couple minutes before visiting hours end, and there's some game show on TV.

"Sorry I ruined Vegas," he says. His voice is still low and slurry, but at least he's mostly making sense now.

"We still managed to have some fun," I say. The rail on this side of his bed is lowered, so I'm sitting in the chair resting my head on the pillow next to his.

"Then I'm sorry we didn't have more," he says.

I put the fingers of my other hand on his shoulder, lightly. I can feel the muscle there through his ugly hospital gown, and he looks over at me.

His eyes haven't changed. The way he looks at me is just as wicked as ever.

"I'm gonna visit Wyoming next month," I say. "Think you can be in good enough shape for some fun then?"

"Well, now I'm inspired," he says, and grins.

Then he gasps, and I sit bolt upright.

"What's wrong?" I ask, but Jackson's just making a face.

"My dick still works," he says, grimacing.

I realize he's got an erection with a catheter in.

"Think about a kitten!" I say.

Jackson takes a deep breath, and then another. After a few moments, his face relaxes.

"Maybe it's not all bad that you're leaving," he says, his eyes still closed.

I just start laughing.

"I don't think anyone believes I'm your sister, by the way," I say.

"You're just a very touchy, devoted sister who doesn't look like the rest of her family at all," he says. "Who also does a lot of inappropriate kissing."

"Don't think about that too much, though," I tease, running a hand through his hair.

"Kittens," he says. "Thinking about kittens."

We go silent for a moment.

"I'll miss you," I say.

"Not as much as I'll miss you," he says. Then he turns his head toward me as much as he can, which is a fraction of an inch.

"Lula-Mae, am I awake?" he asks.

"I think so," I say. "Unless I'm a sea cucumber. Then you're probably having a morphine dream."

"I love you," he says. "I tried to tell you a couple times but I think I was asleep."

Suddenly my eyes are full of tears and I feel like something's wrapped itself around my throat. I swallow hard, trying to force the lump away.

"That wasn't supposed to make you cry," he whispers.

"It's not you, it's everything," I say, and even my whisper-voice is shaking. "I hate seeing you like this and I hate leaving you here like this and I was trying really hard to act okay."

"I'm gonna be fine," he says.

But what if you're not? I think, but I don't say it out loud.

A nurse steps into the room and gives us a quick glance.

"Visiting hours are over," she says, and then leaves again, and I bury my face in my hands.

"I'm sorry," I whisper.

He puts his hand over one of mine and pulls it to his mouth as I'm sniffling, doing my best not to start sobbing in front of someone who has way more reason than me to cry right now.

Then he kisses my hand and I fucking lose it. I put my head down on my arm and just sob. I feel like somehow, I've failed him completely, because he's still here and still in terrible condition and I'm just going home like nothing's wrong.

"I'm sorry," I whisper again, because I can't even find words for how bad this feels, and because I really, really didn't want to have a sobbing breakdown like this in front of him.

Jackson just holds my hand tight. After a while, I finally stop sobbing and then I'm just sniffling. Regular crying.

"I didn't want to put you through this," he whispers. "Watching you cry is the worst part of everything."

I sniffle and half-laugh, and it comes out like a weird snort.

"Only because you're still on drugs," I say. "Just wait until they pull you off the painkillers."

"Lula-Mae, I did this to myself," he murmurs. "And you've got things to do besides listen to me babble about people with fish heads while I'm half awake."

I swallow.

"You're not abandoning me," he says. "You have your own life."

I just nod, trying not to cry again.

"I should go," I whisper. "They're gonna kick me out."

I lean over again and kiss him one more time, slowly, with tongue, and I wrap both of my hands around his.

"Go," he whispers. "I'll be fine, Lula-Mae."

"I'll see you in Wyoming," I say.

I squeeze his hand one more time, and then I leave. I walk down the hospital hallway and take deep gulps of air and try to focus on the future, on what I need to do between now and my plane taking off.

I'm almost at the exit when I realize I forgot to do something, and I stop in my tracks.

Then I turn around and power-walk back toward Jackson's room. A nurse looks up, annoyed.

"Sorry, I forgot my phone," I say, smiling as brightly as I can. I probably look insane, but I don't care.

When I open the door to Jackson's room, the lights are low.

"I'm not in Wyoming yet," he says.

I take his hand and bend over his bed and kiss him again.

"I love you too," I say.

He smiles.

"You come back to tell me that?" he asks.

"Yes," I say.

"I already knew," he says.
"I wanted to say it out loud," I say.
At the door, someone clears her throat.
"Wyoming," I whisper.
Then I kiss him again and leave.

CHAPTER TWENTY-NINE

JACKSON

AFTER MAE LEAVES, the days kind of blend together. My bruises fade. I can move body parts — my arms, my left leg — without it feeling like a giant is pulling me apart limb from limb.

Mae calls me. I call her. I'm not the best conversationalist, but just hearing her voice makes me feel better, every single time.

I can tell she's worried. She's worried about me, and she's worried for herself, that she totally blew her cover when I got hurt, and now no one will ever hire her again. She tries not to say anything about it, but I hear it in her voice, and I feel terrible.

We were so close to getting away with it.

In a week, they move me out of the ICU. My hospital room fills up with flowers, from friends, from fans. ESPN sends a huge bouquet, and so do Ford and Stetson. I'm not sure why, but I think it's probably a good sign.

My doctors decide I'm in good enough shape for more surgery. I've got a hairline fracture in my right femur — my thighbone — and they can't let that go for much longer without fixing it, which involves inserting a titanium rod lengthwise through the bone. While they're in there, they want to screw my kneecap back together and probably put a plate on it for good measure.

The good news is that even though I also broke both bones in my shin, those just need to be set properly and put in a cast.

Mae calls the night before the surgery. There's street sounds behind her, and I imagine her walking from her subway stop to her house. She sent me a video once of the walk, so now I know what it looks like.

"You walking home?" I ask.

"Yeah," she says. "I got a three-day gig for an ad agency. Today I was shooting ice skaters at the Rockefeller Center. But I got good news."

"Tell me," I say.

A nurse walks in and fiddles with the machine to my left, the one that shows my blood pressure and stuff.

"The Atlantic wants to send me to Mexico for Christmas," she says. "There's this village somewhere outside Mexico City where everyone works for the whole month of December to make the whole square this elaborate, immersive nativity scene, and people flock from everywhere to see it."

I squeeze my eyes shut and think.

"I've heard of the Atlantic," I say. "That's a big deal, right?"

She laughs.

"It's a really big deal," she says, and suddenly I can hear the relief and happiness in her voice.

I didn't ruin her life. I start laughing, even though it hurts my ribs.

"I think I might have gotten your luck," she says, quietly.

"*Sports Weekly* told my agent they're never hiring me again, but I think I'm gonna be okay."

"That makes two of us, then," I say.

· · · · ★ ★ ★ ★ ★ · · · ·

THE SURGERY IS first thing in the morning. Before I go in, I get a text from Mae. It's a picture of people ice skating under a massive Christmas tree as it snows.

Mae: This is what I'm doing today while you get a metal rod put through your thigh bone.
Me: In eight hours I'll be more metal than man.
Mae: Good luck. I love you. Tell your mom to keep me updated.

When I'm on the table, the anesthesiologist puts the IV in and tells me to count backward from one hundred. This time I fight it and force myself to keep my eyes open for as long as I can, because suddenly I don't want to go under, I want to stay here. I still only make it to ninety-four.

I dream that I'm skating and it's snowing. I'm in a city I don't recognize. Probably New York, but I've never been to New York, so my subconscious gets it wrong. There's no one else there, but I can skate down streets, past shops, across a bridge and look down at a river. It's beautiful, even if it's lonely. I think about jumping into the water, but I skate on instead.

· · · · ★ ★ ★ ★ ★ · · · ·

"ANOTHER FOUR OR FIVE WEEKS, at least," my mom is saying. "After that, they might be able to put him in a walking cast instead of a wheelchair, but they don't know the exact timeline for that yet."

She's quiet for a moment. I'm staring at the ceiling. I still feel a little like it's snowing on my skin, and I'm not completely sure that this is real, either.

"The MRI is in two days," my mom says.

It is?

I wonder if I can move my fingers or the toes on my left foot. I try, but I can't tell if it's working, because I still sort of feel like I'm moving on ice skates even though I'm conscious and in this room.

"Oh, he's awake," my mom says, and holds out the phone.

I try to take it, but can't quite manage it. My mom holds the phone to my ear.

"Mae?" I say. My voice comes out a rough whisper, and I swallow.

She laughs.

"How are you feeling?" she asks.

"I'm part robot," I say.

· · * * ★ ★ ★ * * · ·

A COUPLE DAYS before I get to go home, they take the catheter out. Most of the IVs are gone. I'm still on antibiotics and blood thinners and a bunch of other things, but they finally trust me to pee on my own.

At first, a nurse has to help me get into the wheelchair. But I've made friends, sort of, with one of the male nurses on the floor, and he's nice enough to help me practice over and over until I can do it on my own.

The instant he's gone, I wheel myself into my bathroom.

Hospital rooms are pretty much public. The door's always open, and I don't think anyone has ever knocked, so the bathroom is pretty much it in terms of privacy.

It's five here, so it's eight in New York. Mae's probably off work by now.

I'm rock hard before I even maneuver the bathroom door shut and lock it. I've spent a week and a half doing my best *not* to get an erection, so it's not exactly surprising that my dick already feels like it might explode.

I wrap my fist around the base, take a picture, and send it to Mae. I try not to get my IVs in the frame.

Then I take a deep breath and hope she's not at work.

It takes about thirty seconds before my phone rings, and I grin.

"It's definitely working," she says, sounding a little breathless. "Nice wheelchair."

"See anything else that interests you?" I ask.

She laughs, and I can hear people talking in the background.

"It's like Niagara Falls over here," she murmurs.

"That bad?"

"That good. I'm not even the one who's been deprived."

I raise my eyebrows, my hand on my cock.

"No?"

"Your present's been put to good use," she says, background noise still behind her voice.

"You didn't tell me," I say.

"I'm telling you now that you're in good enough shape to do something about it," she says.

I groan into the phone.

"I pretend it's you, but it's a bad substitute," she whispers. "There's only so much a toy can do."

"What's missing?" I ask. I'm stroking myself slow, trying to last more than a minute, but it's not going well.

"From the toy?" she asks, her voice low, almost a purr. "It doesn't have a tongue. It doesn't wink at me. It's never texted me dirty pictures while I'm running errands."

I chuckle.

"Sorry," I say.

"No, you're not," she says.

I hear a door shut, and suddenly the background noise is almost gone. Mae exhales.

"If I were there I'd be on my knees with your cock in my mouth," she says, a new note of urgency in her voice. "Still sorry you called?"

My dick practically jumps in my hand, and I have to clench my jaw to control myself, the ball of fire inside me already threatening to explode.

"Where are you?" I gasp, bewildered, because I thought she was in public.

"I'm in the handicapped bathroom of a grocery store," she says. "I'm leaning against the ugly tiled wall and I've got one hand down the front of my jeans, rubbing my clit furiously, thinking about you."

"What are you thinking?" I ask.

"Besides how I want to make you come in my mouth?" she asks. "You do it to me, so it's only fair."

Jesus.

This is the dirtiest she's ever talked to me, and it went from zero to sixty in *seconds*. I've still got my fist around my cock, barely moving, because I know the moment I do, I'm going to come.

"What else?" I ask, because I can barely form coherent thoughts.

"There's a sink and a mirror in here," she says. "And I'm

thinking about you bending me over the sink and then watching in the mirror while you fuck me."

"Shit, Lula-Mae," I whisper, and my cock jerks in my hand as I come, the muscles in my body clenching. I manage to cover my dick with my hand, and I just sit there, groaning, gasping into the phone.

She's half-panting, half-laughing.

"That was easy," she says, breathlessly.

"I just imagined you were bent over that sink," I say, swallowing. "There's this noise you make when I hit exactly the right spot with my cock."

Mae gasps. My dick is limp in my hand but I keep going.

"And I'm hitting that spot over and over, as hard as I can, because I know that's what you want right now," I say.

She makes a strangled moan, like she's biting her lip.

"Keep going," she whispers. "Fuck, I wish you were here."

I can tell from her breathing that she's close, and I grin at the shower curtain.

"And when I can feel you're about to come I lean over and whisper *I fucking love being deep inside you.*"

"God, Jackson," she moans.

"Shh," I say, smiling. "Come quietly for once, Lula-Mae."

"It's pretty hard when you talk dirty to me," she says, then gasps.

"I wish I could watch you come," I say. I've got my eyes closed, imagining it, her body beneath me, writhing and shouting.

She makes another noise, almost a whimper. Then she gasps and holds her breath, and I have to imagine what she looks like, standing in a grocery store bathroom, fully clothed, coming undone. It's fucking sexy, and I love knowing how crazy I drive her. That she couldn't wait to get home to call me, that she just had phone sex almost in public because she couldn't help herself.

Mae pants into the phone, then starts laughing.

I grin.

"What?" I ask.

"It's only been a week and a half," she says. "And I'm masturbating in public bathrooms."

"That was a special test run," I say. "Thanks for helping me make sure it still works."

"I'm happy to help," she says, still laughing. "If you need to make sure your video chat still works, I can help with that too."

"When I'm out," I say. "Only a couple more days, but I don't want anyone else hearing the filthy things you say to me."

"Good," she says. "I've got a reputation as a nice girl to uphold."

She clears her throat.

"Can I call you later?" she says. "I was in the middle of getting groceries."

"Love you," I say.

"Love you too," she says.

I hang up my phone and take care of the mess.

· · · · · ★ ★ ★ ★ · · · · ·

I DO a lot of jerking off in the bathroom. Sometimes Mae's on the phone and sometimes not. The nurses probably think I have some kind of problem.

With the wheelchair, I can at least leave my room. There's a ten-year-old on my floor in a wheelchair with two broken ankles, so we start racing up and down the halls. I mostly let him win. He's already figured out how to spin in a circle while balancing on two wheels, so he shows me.

The nurses yell at us both, but especially me. Something about being a role model.

I show him my scars, from the compound fracture in my arm and the big one on my chest, and he thinks I'm super cool. He tells his mom that he's gonna get a tattoo when he's eighteen, and she glares at me.

When the Sports Weekly comes out, he knocks on the door of my room and then wheels himself right in, holding up the article inside. The big spread picture is me, Raylan, and Clay standing in front of the cattle stalls, and I've got one hand on my hat and we're all laughing. Mae's name is right beneath it.

"Is that you?" he asks, suspiciously, pointing at my face in the middle.

"Sure is," I say. "My girlfriend took it."

He couldn't care less about my girlfriend, and flips to the front. I haven't even seen the magazine yet, but it's a photo of me on Crash Junction, his back hooves in the air and his front hooves on the ground. Above my head, the clock says 8.03.

I swallow, and for a moment, I don't say anything to this kid because I'm thinking about riding Crash, the pure, sheer high of being up there and knowing I'd won. I have no idea if I'll ever get to do that again. At the very least, I won't be doing it for another year.

"That's also you," he says.

"Yep," I say.

"That's how he broke all his bones," my mom says, walking in.

The kid looks suspicious. My mom glares at me.

"She's right," I say, because she is.

I don't say, *it's also one of the greatest feelings in the world.*

"Will you sign it?" he asks.

I do. Then we race down the hallway, though I forget to let him win this time.

· · · · · ★ ★ ★ ★ ★ · · · ·

I GET THE MRI. The fractures are still there in my vertebrae, but they're healing. I hear the word "lucky" a lot. After a few more days, I get to go home. Twelve hours in the back seat of my mom's Ford Taurus isn't ideal, but when we get back to the ranch, my dad's put a wheelchair ramp up the back steps and converted the downstairs den into my bedroom.

After dinner, we sit in the living room and he brings in two bankers' boxes worth of papers. I just stare.

"You're gonna be laid up for a while," he says. "Seems like a good time to digitize the ranch accounting."

"I haven't been here four hours and you're already putting me to work," I say.

He claps me on the shoulder.

"Welcome home, son," he says, and then chuckles. "No free rides."

CHAPTER THIRTY

MAE

A COUPLE WEEKS GO BY. Jackson goes home and I go to Mexico, then to New Hampshire. I get more postcards from Wyoming and I send back ones of New York. We talk most nights. Eventually, the neck brace comes off and his face heals and from the shoulders up, at least, he looks like I remember.

I cry myself to sleep that night and I don't know why. It's part gratitude that I didn't lose him, part the awful, gnawing ache that tells me I should be there in person.

Finally, I've got the money for a plane ticket to Riverton, Wyoming, the closest airport to Sawtooth.

"I told Janice I can't do anything from the 22nd to the 1st," I say, looking at a calendar. "You got anything going on then?"

"Not a thing," he says.

"And your parents don't mind picking me up in Riverton?"

"Not at all," he says.

I exhale. It's expensive, but I don't even care. I'm just relieved to finally have a date when I'll see him again.

"I'll buy tickets tonight," I say. "Did I tell you the NYPD dredged a shipping container full of dildos out of the East River?"

Jackson laughs.

"Is that what they were looking for?" he asks.

A few minutes later, I get an email confirming my plane ticket reservation from La Guardia to Riverton, connecting through Denver. For a moment, I'm just confused, and then I figure out what happened.

"Jackson," I say, cutting him off mid-sentence. "Did you buy me a plane ticket?"

"I did," he says. "I've got eighty thousand dollars and no way to spend it, so I may as well get what I really want."

I don't say anything for a moment.

"That's you, for the record," he says.

"You didn't have to do that," I say.

"I wanted to do it," he says, and then he's quiet for a minute. "Mae, I'm still ten kinds of busted, I haven't actually showered since the morning before I rode Crash, and I'm stuck in my parents' house in the middle of nowhere. Let me do something I want to do and don't be stubborn about it."

I look out my bedroom window at the brick wall past it. I've been contacting photographers in other cities for a week now, networking. I asked Janice how bad it would be if I moved to Austin or Denver or somewhere out west, and she sighed, but she said that we could make it work.

I haven't told Jackson any of this yet, even though I tell him everything else. I don't know why I haven't, but every time I start to open my mouth, I change the subject.

"Thanks," I finally say.

· · · · · ★ ★ ★ ★ · · · ·

THE PLANE from Denver to Riverton is one of those tiny planes with only two rows of seats on either side, and it's a rough flight. Everyone but me seems totally fine, reading their books and magazines, but I've never been the most relaxed flier to begin with so I've got both armrests in my hands, knuckles white.

My impending doom is probably the only thing that can get my mind off the fact that I'm finally on my way to see Jackson for the first time in six weeks. I'm half excited and half nervous.

The part of my brain that loves to think about all the ways that something could go wrong, and it's been in full force these last couple of days. He's still in a wheelchair, and I'm afraid that I'll get there and suddenly not *want* him anymore. Never mind that I've seen him plenty and he still makes my mouth go dry with lust.

I'm afraid that when we're out in the open, when we're not sneaking around, it'll be less thrilling. I'm afraid that when we're not at a rodeo, and he's not a big star, I suddenly won't like him anymore. I'm afraid that he's boring and I never noticed, or that he's dumb and I never noticed, or that he has a giant collection of something weird, like mint-condition action figures, that he never told me about.

I don't *believe* any of these things, I just can't stop my brain from thinking about them. At least, not until I'm on a tiny plane landing at the Riverton, Wyoming airport and all I can do is hope we don't crash.

We don't. No one but me even seems to notice the rough flight, so I collect my wits, grab my carry-on, and walk across the tarmac toward the terminal. The Riverton airport isn't big enough for a jet bridge.

Outside the doors, I take a deep breath, and every stupid

anxiety and fear I've had for six weeks bubbles to the surface. I take another one and slowly, they simmer down.

I go through the doors. I follow the other passengers through a long, windowed hallway and around a corner. Then we go through another door and we're at the baggage exchange, a crowd of people milling around.

My heart's beating out of my chest as I look around for a guy in a wheelchair, but there isn't one.

Maybe he couldn't come, I think.

I skip right over the tall, dark-haired guy on crutches the first time I scan the crowd, because I'm just looking for a wheelchair.

Then I look again, and this time I see him.

He smiles at me, and I can't stop myself. I run.

I don't leap on him, even though I want to, but I wrap my arms around him and bury my face against his chest and I think I squeal. Something clatters to the floor but I ignore it as Jackson squeezes me so hard against him I can barely breathe.

I'm not nervous anymore.

After a minute he loosens his grip so he can bend down and kiss me, and I have to remind myself we're in public.

"You didn't tell me you were out of the wheelchair," I say when I finally pull away. "How long has it been?"

"Day before yesterday," he says, grinning. "I wanted to surprise you."

I just laugh. I'm pretty much giddy just to be here, with him.

Then he lets me go and turns slightly to his right.

"Mom, you remember Mae," he says.

His mother is standing about two feet away, and I didn't even notice. I feel my face flush.

"Of course I do," she says, and I *think* she's amused.

"Thank you so much for picking me up," I manage to get out.

We hug quickly and politely. The crash I heard was one of Jackson's crutches, and I pick it up for him since bending down looks like it's an ordeal.

On the ride back to their house, Jackson sits in the back seat, his right leg stretched out next to him, and I ride shotgun. His mom interrogates me very politely, with Jackson interjecting from the back seat.

I do my best to make myself sound like a polite, high-achieving, Good Texas Girl, because I want to impress Jackson's parents, and the fact that he told me about his dick in front of them almost the minute we met is always somewhere in the back of my mind.

I also want to distract her from the fact that I'm going to fuck his brains out the second I get a chance.

When we get to the ranch in Sawtooth, there's snow on the ground, though it's just a couple of inches. Jackson valiantly tries to balance his crutches and get my suitcase out of the trunk until I stop him. His mom walks toward the house, out of earshot for a second.

"If you break yourself again before I get some I will *not* forgive you," I hiss.

"I'm just trying to be a gentleman," he says, grinning.

"Gentlemen don't leave their girlfriends frustrated after not seeing them for six weeks," I whisper.

From the front door, his mom looks back. I shut the trunk of the car and follow her inside.

The ranch house is surprisingly cozy and warm, even though it's pretty big. His dad made chili and cornbread, and it smells wonderful. I take off my snowy shoes and shake out my coat, scarf, and hat.

"Here, I'll show you to your room," his mom says.

I glance at Jackson, then follow his mom up the stairs. Jackson trails us. Stairs are kind of a challenge on crutches.

"It faces west, in case you like to sleep in," she says. "There are extra blankets in the closet, and some extra pillows, too. Feel free to use the alarm clock."

I put my stuff down and nod at everything she says, but I'm really wondering what exactly her expectations are. Is this just a polite fiction, or am I really expected to sleep here and not in Jackson's room?

If she catches me in Jackson's room, is she gonna be mad?

Jackson gets upstairs as she's showing me the bathroom, the linen closet, where the towels are, and how to keep the window in the bathroom open just enough that the steam escapes.

"Okay," she finally says. "I'm going to go see how Hollis is doing in the kitchen."

She goes downstairs, and leaves Jackson and me alone in the hallway.

"What does it mean that I have my own room?" I whisper.

He glances down the stairs.

"They're kind of old-fashioned," he says.

"Do they think we're not gonna have sex?" I whisper.

"I think they kinda want to think that," he whispers back.

I narrow my eyes.

"It means I sneak up to your room and if I get caught, I say I was getting another towel," he says, grinning.

"I don't want them to hate me," I say.

He blinks at me, genuinely surprised.

"My mom's told *everyone* about how when she met you, it was eight in the morning and you were arguing with the nurse at the desk, trying to tell her you were my sister," he says. "She's given everyone in town a copy of the magazine, and the first thing out of her mouth isn't *that's Jackson*, it's *Jackson's girlfriend took that picture*."

"Then I don't want them to change their minds!" I say.

Jackson leans one crutch against the wall. Then he grabs me by the hand, pulls me closer, and puts my hand right on his cock.

He's half-hard, but in seconds he's at full-mast, and heat floods my entire body. I squeeze, and he growls quietly in my ear.

"If you think I'm gonna behave myself while you're here you've lost your goddamn mind," he whispers, his lips against my ear.

I curl my other hand around the back of his neck. Oh, my *god*, I missed this.

"And if you think I'm not sleeping in your bed, you're crazy," he says, and nips at my earlobe.

I kiss him, hard, my hand still on his cock, and he presses me against him. I open my mouth against his and he pushes his tongue against mine.

"Dinner!" calls his mom.

I pull my hand off him like it's a hot stove, and a millisecond later her face appears at the bottom of the stairs. We were obviously making out, but at least I'm not practically giving him a hand job any more.

"Sorry," she says. "Dinner's ready."

"Thank you!" I say. Her face disappears.

Jackson kisses me again, laughing.

"You're still terrible at breaking the rules," he teases.

"Shut up," I whisper, and hand him his other crutch.

· · · · · ★ ★ ★ ★ · · · ·

DINNER IS DELICIOUS, even if I'm still nervous around his parents, and it's made worse because Jackson keeps *looking* at me. With *that* look. The sex look.

Afterwards I try to help his parents clean up, but his mom shoos me out of the kitchen despite my protestations. Jackson's just standing there, laughing at me, and I make another face at him.

He kisses the top of my head.

"I think we're gonna take a walk," he calls to his parents.

I raise my eyebrows.

"It's cold out," his mom calls back.

"It's a good night for stars," he says.

Then he grins and winks down at me. We both bundle up, because it's about twenty degrees outside.

"I can't wait to hear about all the constellations you know," I tease him. "I think you should tell me about every single one."

"You can stay here if you're gonna make fun of me," he says, but he's smiling.

It's freezing, but he was right. It *is* a good night for stars, and they're stretched across the sky like they're painted on the inside of a dome. Once we're away from the house, we stand close together for a moment and look up at them.

"More than New York?" he asks.

"It reminds me of West Texas," I say. "This is one thing I miss."

"Anything else?"

"Tacos," I say.

We walk for another minute, and his trailer suddenly appears from nowhere. The dark out here is deep enough to lose yourself in.

"I was hoping I'd get to see the jizz trailer," I say.

"You won't if you keep calling it that," he says.

When we reach it, I open the door and hold it for him as he maneuvers up the steps and inside. He flips on the lights and then cranks the thermostat.

"Here we are," he says, looking around, his breath still frosting in the air. "Home sweet home."

I look around. I've seen it in pictures and on video, so it looks familiar, but it's strange to *be* here. Jackson leans against the kitchen counter, takes off his crutches and his gloves, and then pulls me against him and kisses me hard.

I get my own gloves off, slide my fingers through his hair and kiss him back. His face is a little cold but his mouth is warm and needy, and I press myself against him, that ever-present hunger yawning inside me.

After a long time he pulls back, then reaches for his crutches and I take a step back.

"Stay there for a minute," he says, and goes down a short hallway and through a door that he shuts behind himself.

I swallow. My entire insides have already turned into one warm, hollow ache, and I don't even know what he's got in the bedroom back there.

I walk to the kitchen table and look at it for a moment, then sit down. I'm pretty sure this is the view I get when we video chat, because it suddenly looks *very* familiar.

Even though I know I shouldn't, I glance up at the ceiling. There's a small, off-white spot right above the table.

Gross, I think, but I'm also laughing to myself.

Then the door to the bedroom opens, and Jackson leans against the doorframe.

"C'mere," he says.

I recognize his bedroom, too, because I've spent a lot of hours talking to Jackson while we're both curled on our sides in our beds, him in front of a window and ugly wood paneling.

Except now, both the window sills and the dresser are covered with thick white candles and the room is flickering with their glow. The blinds are open to the dark outside. There are two space heaters going full blast on the floor, and it looks like the bed has about twenty blankets on it. Somewhere, there's speakers quietly playing a song I don't recognize.

He shuts the door.

"Keeps the heat in," he says.

He touches my face with one hand and just looks at me for a long moment. It feels good just to be here where no one else is listening in or in the next room or doing dishes in my apartment. It's nearly quiet and nearly dark and we are finally, *finally* alone together.

"I missed you," he murmurs.

"I missed you too," I whisper.

Jackson kisses me again. It's soft at first, gentle and romantic, but I can't help myself. Not *now*. I wind my fingers through his hair and pull his mouth against mine. He swipes his tongue against my lips and curls his tongue into my mouth, against mine. I feel like my body is melting from the inside out, like I'm a nuclear reactor that's overheated.

We're both still wearing winter coats, but I can feel his erection against my stomach. I bite his bottom lip as he pulls back, and he groans, then grabs the front of my thick black pea coat, pulling at the buttons. He gets most of them undone, but there's more buttons on the inside and also a zipper, and he looks at it and frowns.

I laugh and take a step back as I get it off and toss it on the floor, then unwind my scarf and let that fall. I find the zipper on Jackson's heavy rancher's coat and pull it down. He's wearing a sweater beneath it but I just slide my hands under it and run my hands up his torso. The muscles aren't as thick as they were, but he's been in a wheelchair for six weeks, and I can still feel them flexing under the skin.

Jackson laughs.

"What?" I murmur.

"Your hands are cold," he says.

"So warm them up," I say, and push his shirt and sweater off over his head, and then Jackson grabs me by the hips and pushes me against the wall, the bare muscles in his arms flexing hard. I half raise my eyebrows as my back hits the wood paneling.

"What?" he growls. He leans on the dresser to step forward and then his body's against mine, his skin hot under my hands.

"I thought I might have to be gentle with you," I murmur.

He grins and puts one forearm on the wall over my head, leaning down.

"Not that gentle, Lula-Mae," he says, and kisses me hard again. I'm pinned against the wall and I grab his pants by the waistband and pull him harder against me, and he groans into my mouth. I think I can feel his erection throbbing through two layers of clothing.

Jackson pulls back just enough to get my sweater off of me, then kisses me again, his lips moving to my neck. He takes off my long-sleeved shirt and reveals a tank top, and then laughs, bending down just enough to nip at my collarbone.

"This is like a morphine dream I had," he murmurs, his lips brushing my skin, his voice sending shivers through my body.

"Was it twenty degrees outside in your dream, too?" I ask. My eyes are closed and my head's turned to one side, my arm slung around his shoulders.

"I don't know, but I dreamed that you kept taking your

clothes off, only there were always more clothes underneath," he says.

I pull my tank top off over my head and unhook my bra and before I even get it off his rough fingers are on my breasts, the pads of his thumb circling my nipples.

"Not a dream," I say, and move my hips against him. I desperately want to wrap my legs around him, for him to push me against the wall and hold me there, but I'm pretty sure the cast on his leg is gonna keep that from happening.

I settle for sliding my palm down the length of his erection, outside his jeans, and watching the hungry light in his eyes.

"For the record, I really want to pick you up and throw you on the bed," he says. His face is against mine and his voice is low and rough, enough to send tingles through my whole body. "But I've gotta settle for hobbling over."

I laugh and undo his belt and unbutton his jeans. Then I kiss him as I unzip them down the whole length of his erection until he's growling again, and he undoes my jeans and slides a hand inside, his fingers circling my clit.

I gasp and arch my back, fighting the urge to jump onto him. He kisses me harder and moves his fingers along my slit, teasing me. I moan into his mouth and he pushes one finger just barely between my lips.

"I'm never gonna get tired of how wet you are for me," he says. "Even the very first time we did this."

"That was alcohol and enthusiasm," I say. I move my hips against his hand, trying to get him to go deeper, but it's not working. "Now I'm wet because I know what comes next."

He pulls his hand out and puts his fingers in his mouth, licking them off.

"I fucking missed the way you taste," he murmurs.

"Jackson," I say, swallowing hard, "If you don't hobble to

the bed right now, I can't be held accountable for what happens next."

"What's that, Lula-Mae?" he says.

"That's I wrap my legs around you right now and we both go over, because you've still got one leg in a cast," I say. "I've only got so much self-control, Jackson, especially with you."

He kisses me, then grabs a crutch from where it's leaning against the wall and hobbles to the bed and sits. He holds his right leg awkwardly straight as he pushes his jeans down.

"Don't watch," he laughs. "There's sexier things that getting pants off over a cast."

I walk over, kneel on the floor in front of him and help pull his jeans off. Underneath he's got a cast over his lower leg and a metal brace on his knee. Higher up, by his hip, there's a thick pink scar a few inches long where he had surgery, and I run my fingers over it as I press my lips gently to his knee.

He exhales softly and put his hand on my head, stroking my hair.

"Thanks," he says, quietly. "I know all the hardware probably didn't feature in your fantasies."

"I'm actually a little disappointed," I say, pressing my lips to the top of his thigh. "All my research on having sex in wheelchairs went to waste."

I wrap my hand around the base of his cock and Jackson exhales, hard.

"What did your research say?" he asks. He's still got his hand on my head, and he's leaning back on the other one.

"Mostly to make sure you set the brakes," I say, and stroke his cock once, slowly.

Jackson groans, and the sound sends a river of heat coursing through me. I lick the head of his cock and then slide my mouth over it, and I meant to go slow but before I know it he's hit the back of my mouth and I'm sliding my lips back along the shaft and Jackson's breathing hard.

I look up at him, the tip still in my mouth, and I swirl my tongue around it.

"I fucking love watching this," he says, and I push my lips back down and listen to him moan, sucking him and swirling my tongue around the tip.

He stiffens even more in my mouth. I think my juices are starting to run down the inside of my thigh, I'm so turned on, but I ignore it and keep going.

Finally he grabs me gently but firmly by the hair and pulls me off.

"I'm gonna come if you don't stop," he gasps, and lets me go.

I stand and kiss him, pushing my tongue into his mouth and he kisses me back ravenously.

"You *like* it when I taste like your cock," I say.

"I like it when *you* taste like me," he says, and then pushes me onto the bed and pulls himself further on until he's alongside me.

Very gently, I put one leg over him, and he grabs my thigh and pulls me against him.

"I'm harder to break than you think," he growls. "You're not gonna do anything a bull didn't."

"I bet I am," I say.

Jackson chuckles, then rolls over onto his back and pulls me with him, and suddenly I'm straddling him on my hands and knees and he's grinning.

"Yeah, I never made a bull sit on my face so I could eat it out," he says.

Then he pushes me forward. I yelp but then his face is between my thighs, and I swear he's still laughing as he loops his arms around my thighs and pulls me down onto him. There's no bed frame, but I put both hands on the wood-paneled wall as he starts licking me urgently, and I moan.

He squeezes my thighs in response and doesn't stop, not for a second. I'm so worked up that I already feel like I'm close to exploding, and Jackson knows *exactly* what he's doing with his tongue.

"God, I missed you," I half-whisper, half-moan.

He flicks his tongue across my clit a little faster, and my toes curl.

"Fuck, that feels good, Jackson," I say. It's taking every-thing I've got to hold still, more or less, and not just rub myself on his face.

He keeps going, and *god* it's been a long time since he did this, and somehow it's even better than I remembered, the tight knot of white heat inside me quickly expanding and unraveling. I'm losing control fast, my breathing ragged, and he suddenly stops licking my clit and moves his tongue lower, pushing it between my lips and just barely inside me.

I gasp and it turns into a groan as his tongue moves, and then he's licking my clit again, furiously.

"Jackson," I gasp, "I'm gonna come if you don't—"

He licks harder and my words just turn into a moan. His hands tighten again, making sure I stay exactly where I am, and then the ball of white heat inside me just *explodes*.

I think I just shout as my whole body tenses and then releases, my fingers curling against the wood paneling.

"*Jesus*, Jackson," I manage to whisper. Another wave bursts through me and I hear myself moan again, panting for breath.

Jackson keeps going, even as my hands unclench. It sends jolts through my whole body, and I reach down and run a hand through his hair.

"I came, you can stop," I say, breathlessly.

He looks at me. I'm pretty sure he's laughing, and he takes one hand off my thigh.

"Do I have to?" he asks, his voice vibrating through me. He's still holding me firmly in place with his other hand.

I swallow.

"No," I say.

Suddenly he slides his fingers along my slit and then inside me, and I gasp.

"Good," he says.

He circles my clit once with his tongue, moving his fingers inside me against that perfect spot that makes my back arch.

"I've had to watch you come enough on a screen," he says.

His tongue circles my clit again, twice, his fingers stroking my inner wall.

"I think I've earned watching you come in person a couple times," Jackson growls, and then he moves his fingers and tongue together.

He starts out slow and lazy. For a minute I wonder if he's just teasing me, getting me worked up again, but then the slow, bright heat is building inside me again and I feel even more helpless against it than before.

"Make me come again, Jackson," I whisper, and his tongue moves faster and harder. He starts flicking it right across my clit and my whole body jerks, and I gasp and laugh all at once.

I swear I can feel him smile against me.

"I could sit on your face all day," I murmur.

His tongue moves faster and I groan, burying my face in my upper arm. I feel like a rubber band that's about to snap

Then he puts his lips around my clit and sucks gently.

I *shatter*, all of a sudden, and just shout *"Oh fuck!"*

My body feels like it's unraveling, like I'm totally losing control, shouting and gasping and moaning, and I'm almost certain than Jackson's just laughing but he keeps going until my whole body jerks with every lick, and then he finally lets me go.

I roll off to one side, still breathing hard, and slump with my back against the wall, my shins by Jackson's head, because I don't trust myself to move just yet.

Jackson grabs my ankle, next to his head, and grins up at me. His cock is standing straight up, thick and long, so swollen it's almost shiny. I swallow, still trying to catch my breath.

He kisses me on the leg, then puts one hand on his cock and strokes it slowly, his hips just barely moving in time with his hand. I don't know why, but watching him touch himself drives me *crazy*, every single time.

"You're gonna have to come down here," he says. "I'm an invalid."

Then he pulls my ankle and slides me halfway down the bed until I'm nearly level with him.

Invalid my ass.

He rolls over onto his side and kisses me. I can taste myself on him, almost like I've marked him as mine, and it's sexy as hell. I take his shaft in my hand, still kissing him deeply, and he pinches one nipple between his fingers, just hard enough to make me moan softly.

He chuckles and bites my shoulder.

"You're a bottomless pit," he says.

"That's not true," I say.

"You said it, not me," he murmurs, his lips against my skin as I stroke his cock with one hand. "Don't blame me, I make you come as much as I can."

He kisses my shoulder.

"A man can only do so much, Lula-Mae," he teases.

"It's just *you* I can't get enough of," I murmur.

"So you're *my* bottomless pit," he says, tracing his fingers down to my hip.

"Right," I say. "This is all your fault, Jackson."

He pushes me onto my left side and then pulls me to him. I let go of his cock and feel it press against my lower back.

"I'm not sorry," he murmurs in my ear.

I put my hand on his hip behind me, my palm over the new scar.

"I don't want you to be sorry," I say.

He moves his erection until it's right at my entrance, and I can feel myself *throbbing* again.

I twist around and put one arm behind his neck.

"I just want you inside me already," I whisper.

He enters me up to the hilt in one stroke, and I moan.

"I'll never get tired of hearing you say that," he growls in my ear. "I fucking love it when you're dirty, Lula-Mae."

I just push back against him, like I'm trying to get him as deep as I can, and he grabs my hips and pulls me back so hard I just *grunt*.

"You like it when I hit that spot?" he says in my ear. "The one that makes you make that *noise*?"

"Yes," I whisper, and rock my hips forward, sliding him out a little, and he pulls me back into him again, hard, and I make *the noise* again.

"I fucking missed that noise," he says, and he keeps going, fucking me hard and deep. "I missed how *right* everything feels when I'm inside you."

I reach behind myself, arching my back, and I grab his shoulder just because I want to hold onto him.

"I need you," I murmur. "Jackson, I need *this*, and I need *you*, and I thought I was going to lose my mind."

He pulls me back against him again, hard, and my toes curl as it feels like my whole body lights up.

"Please," I murmur.

He does it again, and again. He growls in my ear and I gasp as he hits *that* spot.

"Think you can come one more time?" he asks.

"If you keep doing that," I say.

My vision is starting to blur around the edges and I feel like a slow reaction is taking place, something slowly expanding that's going to burst soon and there's nothing I can do to stop it.

"If I keep doing that you're gonna make me come," he says.

I arch and thrust backwards, driving him deep inside again, and he groans.

"Good," I say, breathless. "It's fucking sexy when you come inside me."

He goes faster and harder, and I can feel myself tilting toward the edge.

"Don't stop," I say, nearly shouting. "God, please, don't stop."

"I'm gonna come," he growls against my ear. "Fuck, Lula-Mae, I can't help myself."

Just as he groans, I suddenly feel myself go over the edge and fall.

"Fuck, Jackson," I gasp. I dig my nails into his thigh without meaning to, and I can just hear myself whispering his name over and over again.

I come so hard I barely even realize he's pulled me against him as hard as he can, his cock throbbing. I just moan wordlessly and Jackson bites my shoulder. I feel almost knocked senseless, even as my orgasm fades and he slides his arm around me and holds me tight against his chest as I'm still panting for breath.

"I missed you," he whispers. "I know I said that but I missed you."

I turn and kiss his shoulder. There's a million uncertainties right now, about him, about us, about how the hell this is ever going to work out, but in this moment, I'm totally certain that everything will be okay.

"I missed you too," I whisper.

CHAPTER THIRTY-ONE

JACKSON

WE'RE JUST LYING THERE, in my bed in my trailer. Through the window above the bed I can see a rectangle full of stars, and I've got my face against Mae's head. I can smell her hair, and I've got one hand over her chest and I can feel her heartbeat, too.

After a minute I point at the window.

"I think those are the Pleiades," I say.

She just laughs.

"There, we stargazed," I say.

Mae wiggles and then turns around in my arms, and I roll onto my back, her head on my chest.

"Should we go back to the house and pretend like that's all we were doing?" she asks.

"Nah," I say. I run one finger up and down her spine. The bedroom is almost tropically warm because that's what happens when you run two space heaters on full blast in here, and it feels like Mae is melting into me.

"Are we just going to stay in the jizz trailer the whole time I'm here?" she teases.

"Lula-Mae, I swear to God—" I start, but she laughs

again.

I sigh.

"Is that just what it's called now?" I ask.

"Sorry," she says.

"Liar," I say. "You're not sorry at all."

We're quiet for a moment.

"They're not gonna think that we got eaten by wolves and come after us, right?" she finally asks.

"This is a don't ask, don't tell situation," I say. "They don't *ask* why we're really going on a walk in the direction of a secluded trailer after dark when it's twenty degrees outside, and I don't *tell* them that I'm crawling out of my skin to jump your bones already."

"Jump my bones?" Mae asks.

"It means—"

"I know what it *means*," she teases me. "That's how my Aunt Bertha refers to sex, too."

"Aunt Bertha sounds like a fun gal," I say.

"Depends on how much you like gin rummy."

Mae's fingers are tracing a new scar, the one where I had a tube in my chest after I punctured a lung.

Tell her, I think.

I almost don't want to end this perfect, quiet moment, but I hate not telling things to Mae. There were only thirty-six hours between getting out of the wheelchair and her seeing me and finding out, and I just about bit my tongue off.

"The Vice President of programming at ESPN called me last week," I say.

She raises her head and looks up at me.

"They're adding rodeo to their main programming lineup next year, and they're looking for a charming, good-looking, knowledgeable commentator who's currently unfit to ride," I say.

"And what did they want with you?" she teases.

"They want me to audition in Cheyenne in a couple of weeks at a pre-season exhibition," I say.

Mae grins, her blue eyes sparkling.

"Then what?" she asks.

"If they like me, I do it for the rest of the season," I say. "And if I'm charming enough, I assume Hollywood comes calling and I star in a bunch of commercials for pickup trucks."

"I'd buy a truck from you," Mae says.

"You wouldn't buy a truck from anyone," I say.

She laughs.

"You're right," she says. "I'm never gonna own a pickup truck, I hate driving those things."

"You're the least country Texas girl I've ever met," I say.

"Thank you," she says.

I swallow, and we both go quiet for a moment.

"I'd have to move if this ESPN thing goes through," I say.

"Where to?" she asks, her voice quiet.

"I'd probably need to stay out west," I say, and suddenly my heart is thumping. "But I'd need to be a lot closer to a major airport, at least. So a real city."

I look down at her, but she's looking at her hand, tapping her fingers on my chest one by one.

"But which one might be flexible," I say.

Mae rolls off of me and props herself on her elbows, not quite touching me anymore.

"I talked to my agent about moving away from New York," she says quietly.

"Is that a good idea?" I ask.

"I don't really like it there," she says. "I want to, but I don't. People keep telling me that it's the center of the photography world, but..."

She trails off and spreads her hands, staring past my head at the wall.

"Janice thought I could make it work," she says.

"Mae, I already almost tanked your career once," I say. "I'm not trying to do it again. I don't even know if I'll get this ESPN thing."

"What are you gonna do if you don't?" she asks.

"Well, I've gotta finish digitizing the books for my parents' ranch into Quicken, and that might take another five years," I say. "There's six months in nineteen seventy eight where I swear everything is written on napkins from a diner."

I pull her back against me and she puts her head back on my chest, her hand flat over my old scar.

"But after this year," she asks, slowly. "Are you going back?"

I stroke the back of her neck with my fingers.

"I'm not asking you to quit," she says. "I know you love it, and I would never ask that, Jackson, and I'm here either way, but..."

She trails off.

"I just want to know what I'm in for," she says quietly.

I've studiously avoided thinking about it. I mean, I think about it a lot, but I dance around the question, tell myself things like *not this year* and then try not to think beyond that. Even if I *can* ride again, which isn't certain, who knows if I'll be competitive.

"Right after Crash ran me over and they were taking me out, I heard you when I was on the stretcher," I say.

"You were conscious?"

"Barely," I say. "I was in and out, and all I remember hearing is you shouting *I know Jackson, fucking let me in!* And I thought, *she just told everyone about us, she's gonna get fired, and it's my fault.* And I felt terrible."

"That's oversimplifying it," she says.

"You were in most of my morphine dreams," I say. "You know how I knew I wasn't dreaming when you showed up that morning?"

"You mom called me a stray?"

"You looked like hell," I say. "Like you'd been up all night crying."

She swallows.

"Only most of it," she finally says. "No one would tell me anything for the longest time. I had no idea if you'd made it off the operating table or not, or if you were paralyzed forever, or..."

She trails off again, and I decide. All at once, I decide.

"I was really scared that I'd lost you," Mae whispers.

"I'm not going back," I say.

She looks up at me again.

"I swear to God I'm not asking you to quit," she says, her voice low.

I just laugh.

"I just broke every bone in one leg, and now there's so much metal in it that I'm barely human," I say. "I fractured four vertebrae, and it's a miracle I'm not paralyzed. My ribcage is pretty much made out of bendy straws by now because I've broken ribs hard enough to puncture lungs twice now. I can tell when it's gonna rain because my left arm tells me, both my ankles hurt when it's cold, my right shoulder freezes sometimes because I tore the cartilage once, and I've chipped five teeth."

When I say it all out loud, it's pretty compelling.

"I didn't even know about half those," Mae says.

"This way I get to go out on top," I say. "Blaze of glory and all that."

That's all true, but it's not the real reason.

The truth is, after Daffodil broke my ribcage, I started just assuming I'd die in the arena, and I realized I didn't mind. Better to burn out than fade away. Half the rodeo guys I know who make it to sixty are in bad shape, so I started figuring I just wouldn't make it that long.

Then I met Mae, and when they put me on a stretcher and loaded me into an ambulance, I realized that if I were dead I'd never see her again.

It's pretty simple, really.

"We should head back," Mae says.

"Stay here," I say. "I like pretending we're a normal couple who don't have to sneak around."

Mae laughs.

"That's your own fault for living with your parents when you're twenty-five," she says.

"I got special circumstances," I say, and kiss the top of her head. "And I only got to wake up next to you once, and you weren't at your best."

"I was such a bitch," Mae says. "I'm sorry. I'm not a morning person. I'm not."

"Stay here and I'll pretend to know more constellations," I say.

She rolls over onto her back and looks out the window.

"Okay," she says. "What's that one?"

"Orion," I say.

It's not Orion. I don't know what it is, but Mae's in my arms again and neither of us really care what the constellations are. After an hour we shut down the space heaters and get ready for bed, then crawl under the covers and curl up together. I try not to kick her with my cast.

In the morning, it's freezing, so we have sex under the blankets before we go back to the house.

· · · ★ ★ ★ ★ ★ · · ·

ESPN HIRES ME. When I tell Mae, she yelps with delight and then shouts, "I knew they would!" Later that month, she goes to Carnivale in Brazil for a week and shoots colorful samba dancers. I get my cast off while she's there and start physical therapy.

In March, I finally visit New York. We see the Statue of Liberty and the Empire State Building and a whole lot of the inside of Mae's bedroom.

In April, ESPN sends me to San Antonio for a while and she joins me there. We visit the Alamo, tire each other out in the hotel room, and afterwards, still in bed, Mae grabs her laptop and we start looking at apartments in other cities.

· · · ★ ★ ★ ★ ★ · · ·

I'M SITTING in a folding chair in front of a box, eating cereal, when my phone buzzes. It's a selfie of Mae, in front of the "Welcome to Colorful Colorado!" sign.

Me: Stop taking selfies and drive faster.
Mae: Just for that, I'm stopping for more coffee.
Me: You were stopping for more coffee anyway.
Mae: Busted.

I pace around the house. I feel like I should be cleaning and decorating and getting something ready, but there's nothing. There's a small pile of boxes in the living room, but the biggest one is the wardrobe box full of new suits for my job.

For years, everything I needed I pretty much fit into my truck, but now that it's in an actual building, it looks tiny.

I'm still staring at it when the moving truck pulls up outside. It's been almost a month since I saw Mae, and just like always, I start grinning like an idiot the second I see her.

She hops out of the cab of the truck, blond hair flying, and I wrap her in my arms before she even gets the door closed.

"I made it," she says, and she's already laughing.

"Welcome home," I say, and kiss her. She wraps both her hands around my neck and presses herself against me, her tongue licking my bottom lip, and I'm hard in no time at all. My hand's under her shirt and on the skin of her lower back and she bites my bottom lip when I pull away from her.

Already, we're *those* neighbors.

I reach out and shut the truck door.

"Want to see the inside?" I ask.

"Of course," she says.

I open the door for her and watch her face as she steps through. Mae hasn't seen the place in person yet, and it turns out that I can ride a one-ton animal for eight seconds, but choosing an apartment for the two of us to live in is nerve-wracking as all hell.

She walks through the kitchen, then the living room, checks out both bathrooms. When she comes back to where I'm standing, she looks relieved.

"You were worried?" I tease her.

"Jackson, the last place you lived was called *the jizz trailer*," she says.

"Only because you named it that," I say.

She grins and shrugs, then slides her arms around me.

"One more question," she says.

I bend down and pick her up. She yelps and throws her arms around my neck.

"Bedroom's this way," I say.

EPILOGUE

MAE

One Year Later

I WAKE up with a jolt when the car stops. It's totally dark, wherever we are, and I try to surreptitiously wipe my mouth because I think I was drooling in my sleep.

Then I look around. Behind us there are headlights winding down a road, and I look over at Jackson, who's grinning at me.

"Is this Santa Barbara?" I ask, totally confused, because I was ninety-nine percent sure Santa Barbara was a city.

"Not exactly," he says. "This is Big Sur."

I have no idea what that is.

Jackson got a surprise break from his job when a rodeo in Albuquerque was canceled, and then a job of mine got pushed back, so we decided to go on a road trip to California.

I look at the clock on the dashboard. It's 1:06 in the morning. I look at Jackson again.

"Are you kidnapping me?" I ask.

He leans over and kisses me.

"Are you ever going to get better at waking up?" he asks.

346

"Probably not," I say.

"Come on," he says.

We get out of the car, and I wrap my jacket around me. I can smell the ocean, and after a moment, I realize I can hear it, too.

Okay, so we're on the coast.

Jackson grabs a blanket and a reusable shopping bag from the trunk of my car, then walks toward me. I'm trying really hard to wake up, but riding in a car at night puts me to sleep.

"C'mon," he says. Then he kisses me and walks toward a staircase.

We head down. I was right: the ocean's right here, almost invisible in the night, and in a few minutes we're on the narrow strip of sand. The road above is totally invisible, and as my eyes adjust, I can see the rocky shoreline extending for miles in either direction, the blackness of the ocean ahead, the stars above.

I still don't know what I'm doing on a strange beach at one o'clock in the morning, but Jackson's spreading out a blanket on the sand and then we sit on it, staring out at the black water, his arms around me.

"You remember that first night in Vegas?" he asks.

"When I waited for you naked with cowboy boots and a hat?" I ask.

"Exactly," he says. "And afterward we talked about how if we got into a car right then and drove we could make it to the ocean that night?"

I look over at him. Suddenly everything clicks into place, and I know *exactly* why I'm on a beach at one in the morning, and why my boyfriend seemed oddly prepared for this excursion.

Now I'm awake and trying not to laugh from sheer delight.

"Yeah," I say, and I think I'm grinning from ear to ear. "I remember when we talked about running away together for a night."

"You could have talked me into it," he says. "If you'd said, right there, *let's go to California together,* I think I would have gone."

I run my hand lightly over his right kneecap, the busted one.

"We hadn't even seen much of each other in person, but we'd been talking nonstop, and you were all I could think about," he goes on, his voice getting quiet. "And there was this moment when we were alone, and just talking, and I thought, *this feels right, I think this is what it's supposed to feel like.*"

He puts one hand in his jacket pocket. My heart *pounds,* and Jackson looks at me.

Then he laughs.

"You figured this out already," he says.

I just grin and shrug, and he leans over and kisses me.

"The night we had sex in the bucking chute, I was afraid I loved you," he says.

He kisses me.

"And when we talked every night, and you sent me pictures of rats and postcards of trash barges, and every single time it was the highlight of my day, I thought I loved you."

He kisses me again.

"And I knew I loved you that first night in Vegas, standing in front of that window and talking about running away, and I've thought about doing this ever since," he says.

Finally, he pulls a box out of his pocket and opens it. Inside is a ring with a deep blue stone in the center.

"Marry me, Lula-Mae," he says.

Suddenly I can't talk around the lump in my throat, and I just nod and hold out my left hand.

"Yes," I manage to squeak out, and then Jackson kisses me gently. When we pull apart, he rests his forehead against mine.

"I love you too," I whisper.

He kisses me one more time, then reaches back into the bag he brought and comes out with a bottle of champagne, and I laugh.

"You thought of everything," I say as he pops the cork.

Then he looks at the bottle, looks at me, and looks in the bag.

"Not everything," he says. "I forgot glasses."

He hands me the bottle.

"Ladies first," he says.

I kiss him again and take it, still laughing. I lean against him, his arm around me, take a swig of champagne, and then hand it to Jackson. He kisses me before he takes it, drinks, and hands it back.

"You were drinking straight out of a bottle the first time I met you," he says.

"It was a less classy bottle," I say.

"Can I tell you something?" he asks.

"What?"

He takes a long drink.

"I absolutely would have done it with you," he says, grinning. "There's no question. I never could turn you down. It's a good thing the police came."

I laugh and take the bottle back. My ring clinks against the glass, and I look down at it, still sparkling in the dark.

"I found you again anyway," I say. "It worked out."

"There's no one around," he says, his voice lowering. "We could do it right now."

I look around. He's right.

I kiss Jackson hard, put one hand on his chest, grab his shirt and pull him against me.

"Are you ever gonna let me forget that?" I ask.

"Nope," he says. "I'm still gonna ask you to do it when we're eighty, Lula-Mae, and there's nothing you can do about it."

For some reason, it takes me by surprise when he puts it that way, and I swallow.

"You promise?" I ask.

"Of course," he says. "I asked you to marry me so I could get old doin' it with you."

"I did already research wheelchair sex," I say.

He kisses me again and pushes me backward until we're lying on the blanket, side by side, and I slide my hand under his jacket and shirt, his warm skin under my fingers.

"Thanks for running away with me to see the ocean," I whisper.

He kisses my forehead gently, and it's sweet and sexy and protective all at once. Right now, on this beach by the dark ocean, everything feels like it's exactly *right*.

"I'll always run away with you, Lula-Mae," he says. "You just say the word."

I just kiss him again, and then again, until I feel like our bodies are melting together.

Then we do it right there on the beach.

The End

ABOUT ROXIE

Roxie is a romance author by day, and also a romance author by night. She lives in Los Angeles with one husband, two cats, far too many books, and a truly alarming pile of used notebooks that she refuses to throw away.

Join her mailing list for release updates, free bonus scenes, and tons more!

www.roxienoir.com
roxie@roxienoir.com